# Mary Wakefield

Of the origin of the now famous 'Whiteoaks' series, the author, Mazo de la Roche, wrote in her autobiography, *Ringing The Changes*, 1957:

'*Jalna* was inspired by that part of Southern Ontario where we had built Trail Cottage. The descendants of the retired military and naval officers who had settled there, clung stoutly to British traditions. No house in particular was pictured, no family portrayed. From the very first the characters created themselves. They leaped from my imagination and from memories of my own family. The grandmother, Adeline Whiteoak, refused to remain a minor character but arrogantly, supported on either side by a son, marched to the centre of the stage.'

Mazo de la Roche died in 1961, and by the time of her death no less than twelve million volumes of the Whiteoaks novels had been sold and enjoyed throughout the world, both in English and in many other languages.

Also by
Mazo de la Roche in Pan Books

Mazo de la Roche

# Mary Wakefield

**Pan Books** London and Sydney

to **Walter Allward**
in friendship and homage

First published 1949 by Macmillan & Co Ltd
This edition first published 1957 by Pan Books Ltd,
Cavaye Place, London SW10 9PG
10th printing 1978
All rights reserved
ISBN 0 330 10133 1
Printed in Great Britain by
Richard Clay (The Chaucer Press) Ltd, Bungay, Suffolk

# CONTENTS

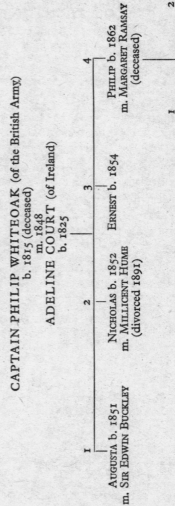

# THE WHITEOAK FAMILY

## CAPTAIN PHILIP WHITEOAK (of the British Army)
b. 1815 (deceased)
m. 1848
ADELINE COURT (of Ireland)
b. 1825

| 1 | 2 | 3 | 4 |
|---|---|---|---|
| AUGUSTA b. 1851 m. SIR EDWIN BUCKLEY | NICHOLAS b. 1852 m. MILLICENT HUME (divorced 1891) | ERNEST b. 1854 | PHILIP b. 1862 m. MARGARET RAMSAY (deceased) |

| 1 | 2 |
|---|---|
| MEG b. 1884 | RENNY b. 1886 |

# I

# THE GOVERNESS

THIS WAS like no awakening she had ever had. She was in a strange house, among strange people, in a strange land. Her few belongings she had unpacked, that lay scattered about the room, made it look all the stranger. Yet the day would come when all this would be familiar, when her belongings there would not look so alien, so pathetic; not that it was a grand room. It was just a comfortably furnished, moderately sized room with a mahogany dressing-table and washing-stand with basin and ewer ornamented with red roses, a heavy white counterpane, an engraving of the Bridge of Sighs and another of Queen Victoria and Prince Albert with their young family about them. A Virginia creeper which she had noticed last night massed over the front of the house and enveloping the porch had even extended its growth to this side and was spreading a few vigorous shoots across the window. From it the early morning sunlight took a greenish tinge.

Mary was glad she had waked early. She wanted time to lie still and collect her thoughts. Her mind appeared to her as a kaleidoscope that had been so shaken it could not regain its original pattern. The theme of that pattern had been her life in London with her brilliant but unstable father, a journalist who was always startling editors either by his good or by his bad writing. He seemed able to do nothing mediumly well. He was always startling Mary by his high spirits or his deep melancholy. Her mother had died when she was a child, so there had been no influence in her life to counteract these vicissitudes. She had come to wear rather a startled look when her eyes were not dreaming. Her eyes were grey, her fair hair so fine that it slipped from under hairpins in a disconcerting way but luckily had a natural wave in it. Her father had been proud of her beauty, so proud of it that the thought of her doing anything to earn her living had been abhorrent to him. Possibly pride in himself had had as much to do with it. Neither of them had been clearly conscious of the way he was going downhill physically till it was too late to save him. Then he was gone from her.

Now lying in this strange bed between the smooth linen

sheets Mary rolled her head on the pillow at the anguished recollection of those terrible months of early spring. His bank account had seen them through his illness, little more. Mary remembered how he had thrown money about. But at the last he had spent it on little but drink. Events, struggling to be remembered, hammered at the door of her mind but she would not let them in. Now, on this June morning, she must be self-controlled, firm in the beginning of this new life. It lay spread before her like an unknown sea, upon which she, chartless, had embarked, no past experience to help her.

She had not wanted to be a governess. If she could have thought of any other way of earning her living she would have turned to it, but there were few openings for women in the nineties. The only work she felt capable of attempting, considering her ignorance and lack of experience, was teaching the young. The fact that she had had little to do with children did not trouble her. She thought of them as innocent little pitchers which she would fill with knowledge gained from textbooks and coloured maps. She would set them to memorizing poems, lists of foreign countries, their capitals, rivers, capes, mountains, and products. The important thing had been to get the situation. Once secured she felt equal to coping with it. In truth she had to find work or starve.

She had answered a number of advertisements and indeed had obtained interviews with several of the advertisers but they all had come to nothing. She had not the sort of looks, of manner, of voice, that made people want to have her as a governess for their children. In looks she was quite lovely, very tall and slender and very fair, with a skin so delicate that it seemed never to have been roughened by cold winds or to have lost its first beauty by exposure to the heat of the sun. But it was her smile that did the most harm. It lighted her face in the most extraordinary manner and then her mouth, which had been wistful and almost melancholy, became alluring, gay, and even provocative. She looked a dangerous creature to bring into the house where there was a grown-up son or even a husband.

If only she had known, she could have subdued this smile and substituted an appropriately prim one for it, but there was no one to warn her and before each interview was over she had given herself away—damned her chances. She had not the sort of face ladies looked for in governesses, in the last decade of the nineteenth century.

Her lack of proper references had been a handicap almost as great as her too charming looks. Her only reference had been from the editor of a newspaper for which her father had sometimes written. The reference had been based on the fact that Mary had once lived in his house for a month as companion to his docile little daughter while the child's mother was ill. The editor had been very kind to Mary and when she required a reference had made much of her stay in his house, her efficiency, and her excellent way with children.

In reading over this reference Mary had not considered it as exaggerated. There was a spaciousness in her nature which made her feel capable of all that was written there. She found it no more than truth. Only after many rebuffs had her courage failed her and she had opened her newspaper and turned to the advertisements with less and less hope.

Now, with the sheet cool against her chin, she looked at the bunches of lilac on the wallpaper, held together by streamers of rose-coloured ribbon, and remembered the morning in London, less than a month ago, when she had been engaged to come to this house in Canada. Then too the air had been bright with sunshine. The sound of horses' hoofs which marked the rhythm of the life of London had seemed to have a new vitality. Drays, drawn by heavy horses, rattled over the cobbles, buses and four-wheelers and hansoms, drawn by well-fed, well-groomed horses, made the streets lively, giving an air of temperate activity and prosperity. The very breeze coming in at the open window had fresh life in it and a tremor of new hope ran through Mary's nerves as she scanned the advertisements.

Almost at once her eyes were caught and held. She read:

Wanted a capable governess to go to Canada and take complete charge of two children. Passage and all expenses paid. Only a woman of firm character need apply. Call at Brown's Hotel, asking for Mr Ernest Whiteoak.

Mary's heart began to thud violently. She let the paper fall to the floor and rose to her feet. Desire for adventure surged up through all her being. No opportunity for adventure had ever come her way. She had scarcely realized that she was capable of desiring it. She had lived enveloped in the dream world of an imaginative child, long after childhood was past. Now that its mists were swept away by the death of her father and the chill necessity of earning her own living revealed, she was, for the first time, free to become acquainted with her real self.

"To cross the ocean," she said out loud. "To be in a new country. Heavens above, what an adventure!"

She snatched up the paper and read the advertisement again. In imagination she felt the pulsing of the engine beneath the deck of the ship, saw herself wrapped in a travelling rug, in a deckchair, while a steward offered her refreshment from a laden tray. Of late she had been so parsimonious that the thought of appetizing food crept more and more often into her thoughts. She was young, and though not robust was healthy.

The second reading of the advertisement only increased her desire to obtain this situation if possible. Indeed it shone out to her as an answer to prayer. If she could not persuade this Mr Whiteoak to engage her, it might well be an end to her hopes of teaching. She would almost certainly have to take any sort of work that offered, no matter how distasteful.

So little was she acquainted with what was looked for as desirable in a governess that she set out to make herself as attractive as possible for the interview. She brought out her best shoes, the ones with the high heels and very pointed toes, and polished them. She put on a petticoat with embroidered flounces and a delicate green and white dress with elbow sleeves. Her father had forbidden her to go into mourning for him. Her wide-brimmed hat was trimmed with pink roses and their glossy green leaves. Her long gloves were of white silk and she wore a wide silver bracelet. She decided she was too pale and put a touch of rouge on lips and cheeks. The effect was good, she decided, and as she descended the stairs her step was lighter than it had been for months.

She and her father had lodged in this old-fashioned semi-detached house in Vincent Square and had made themselves very comfortable. Mary had a talent for making lodgings look homelike and there was nothing drab about these. When she reached the street she looked back at the balcony outside her apartment, remembering how she had stood alone on it, looking at the sky, on the night her father died, and she wondered what would be her feelings when next she stood there. Again her heart began to thud. She was afraid she would not be able to speak calmly and efficiently when she met Mr Ernest Whiteoak. She thought of him as with large mustachios, waxed and pointed.

She mounted to the top of a bus drawn by sleek bay horses. The streets showed fresh paint and shining brasses and there were flower sellers at the corners. If there were any wretched and ragged human beings among the crowd Mary did not see them. Her eyes were attracted by the women in elegant dresses, with frills and skirts touching the pavements, and elaborately done hair, by the men in frock coats and tall hats, by the children carrying brightly painted hoops, being led by nurses towards the Park. Yet all she saw passed in a moving haze, as she strained towards the interview that either was to mean so much to her or was to be the end of her hope of teaching.

At Brown's Hotel she was told that Mr Whiteoak was out but was expected to return shortly and was prepared to interview her in the small sitting-room. Mary walked nervously up and down the room, feeling herself too tall, as she always did when nervous and about to meet strangers. Perhaps she had better sit down, rising when Mr Whiteoak entered, and then not quite to her full height. She composed herself, arranging her skirt to advantage and folding her hands in her lap. She examined the pictures in the room, listened to the activities of the hotel, and tried to recall some lines of poetry with which to steady her nerves, but all had fled from her mind. Fear and depression took hold of her. She began to tremble so that she could see the movement in the flowers of her dress. It was the waiting. If only he would come and have it over with! She could picture him—a short stout man with an intimidating look. By the time she heard his step—for she instinctively knew it was Mr Ernest Whiteoak—she was ready to sink to the floor in apprehension.

But how different he was from the man she had expected! He was tall, slender, smooth-shaven, of very fair complexion, gentle blue eyes, and a reassuring smile. He carried his top hat in his hand, his frock coat was worn with elegance, enhanced by the flower on his lapel. He was a man approaching forty.

"I hope you have not been waiting too long," he said. "I had business that must be attended to. Am I to understand that you are——"

He hesitated, brought to a stop by Mary's charming appearance. Surely this young lady, as attractive as any he had seen in Regent Street this morning, was not an applicant for a position as governess.

"Yes," she answered, in a trembling voice, "I am desirous—I want very much—my name is Mary Wakefield."

"Ah, yes, Miss Wakefield. Won't you please be seated?" He hesitated again, then himself sat down on a small red velvet chair quite near her. His presence was reassuring. She thought, he is kindness personified.

"I suppose you understand you would be asked to go to Canada if engaged," he went on.

"Oh, yes. I—I want very much to go to Canada."

"May I ask why?"

"I want to leave England. My father died some months ago. I'm—alone. I'd like to go to a new country."

"You feel yourself capable of teaching and managing two high-spirited children of seven and nine?"

"Oh, I am sure I could. I love children."

"Good. These are very lovable children. My brother's young son and daughter. Their mother died when the boy was only two years old. He's a lively customer, I may tell you."

"I'm so glad."

Ernest Whiteoak looked at her sharply. "You are sure you are capable? What experience have you had?"

Mary produced her reference and he read it through twice.

"Certainly," he said, returning it to her, while his fair brow wrinkled in thought, "certainly you have not had much experience." Then he exclaimed, in a frankly confidential tone— "The truth is, Miss Wakefield, we are in a dilemma. My mother—the children's grandmother—had engaged a very capable, middle-aged governess for the children, one suitable in every way. Her passage was booked and she was to accompany some friends and neighbours of ours who would take her to my brother's house. My mother then went to Devon to visit my sister, her mind quite at rest. I, myself, and my elder brother are leaving for Paris in three days, so you can imagine the fix we are in."

"Yes?" Mary felt rather bewildered but forced an expression of eager intelligence into her eyes. "And where is the other governess?"

"She is suffering from broken legs."

Mary looked so shocked that he wondered if he should have said limbs. He therefore amended—"Yes—both limbs were broken. By a bus."

"Then, I suppose," faltered Mary, "that, when they mend, she will go to Canada. I mean I'm to be only temporary."

"Not at all," he reassured her. "There is considerable doubt of her limbs being really efficient again, and we all feel that she would need two perfectly good ones in this situation."

If Mary's written references were meagre, certainly her legs were admirable and she hastened to say—"Mine are."

He gave her a little startled look and then exclaimed: "Splendid."

For some reason this talk of legs had put them on a new footing. Constraint was gone. Mary's nerves relaxed and she smiled at him, showing her white even teeth.

By George, thought Ernest Whiteoak, she's beautiful! He said, in a confidential tone—"The thing is that it would be necessary for you to leave in a few days."

"As far as I am concerned," she declared, "I can leave tomorrow."

"I wish my mother were here to make the decision. It is really very difficult for me." But even as he spoke he knew that he was glad his mother was not there. He was sure she would not find this lovely creature suitable as governess to her grandchildren. But the children themselves would be charmed by her. Philip too would be delighted by her gentleness and good breeding. Then, at that moment, he made up his mind to engage her. He was naturally indolent and the thought of looking further depressed him. He began to talk to her of salary and of the dispositions of the two children, whom he described as lovable, though high-spirited and at present a little out of hand. Without his saying so, Mary knew the matter was settled. His face was bright with the lifting of a load from his mind. Ernest Whiteoak was saying:

"I'm sure you will like Jalna. That is the name of our house. My father was an officer in India and went to Canada some forty years ago, taking my mother and my sister, who was a baby then. My elder brother was born in Quebec. My father then bought a thousand acres in Ontario—mostly virgin forest —and built a house there. I was the first child born in it." He said this with pride and Mary was impressed.

"My younger brother came along eight years later. He is the father of your future pupils and, I may remark, very easy to get on with."

To be talked to so pleasantly, to be so put at her ease, was balm to Mary, after some of the interviews she had passed through. This was the atmosphere of the New World, she felt, and she yearned towards it. What was he saying?

"We have tried, Miss Wakefield, to preserve the ways of the Old World at Jalna, to keep ourselves free from the narrowness, the conceit, of the New. We have agreeable neighbours. I speak as though I lived at Jalna, but, as a matter of fact, I and my elder brother and my sister all live in England. Still, we make long visits there and I hope that, on my next one, I shall find you most happily established with the children."

No interview of a like nature could have passed off more pleasantly. If only Mr Whiteoak in Canada were half as nice as the Mr Whiteoak here she would be happier than ever she had thought possible. As she sat on the top of the bus, on her way back to Vincent Square, the air was full of happy sounds, the horses' hoofs had a gayer rhythm, there was the distant sound of a military band, and near at hand the knife-sharpener's tinkling bell. It seemed to Mary that the people in the streets wore brighter expressions and walked with lighter steps. She was, for the time being, too excited to think clearly. At one moment she was living over again the interview with Ernest Whiteoak, seeing his fair aquiline features, his reassuring smile, listening to his pleasant voice; at another her mind flew forward to that distant house where she was to live, and she saw another, somewhat younger edition of Ernest Whiteoak, with two angelic children clinging to his hands, and all about the house a great forest where moose and bear and wolf roamed at will, though never near enough the house to be frightening.

When, at last, she stood in front of the house in Vincent Square, she looked up at it with a strange feeling of unfamiliarity. It was receding from her. She was like a swan, sailing down a smooth stream, away from dangers and fears.

Now, three weeks later, she was lying in this strange bed, in this lilac-decked room. What beautiful wallpaper, she thought, and how well the picture of the Bridge of Sighs looked, hanging against it! As soon as she unpacked she would put up the framed photographs of her father and her mother on the mantelshelf. Already there, stood an oval glass case covering a wax group of flowers and fruit, three red roses, a bunch of grapes, three purple plums, three crab apples and, strewn over the sand on the bottom, some cornucopia-shaped sea shells. This ornament had caught Mary's eyes the moment she had come into the room last night. Even in her state of fatigue and excitement, even under the pale cold eyes of the housekeeper, her eyes had been held. When she had taken off her long ulster and heavy hat she had gone over to the case and had a good look into it. She had not expected to find anything so aesthetic, so enchanting, far in the heart of Canada.

Mrs Nettleship, the housekeeper, had been the only person she had met the night before. That had been a relief, for she knew she was looking very fatigued after the long train journey. She always got these violet circles beneath the eyes when she was tired, which made her look fragile. Yet, at the same time, she had a sense of being rebuffed by her reception. She had had such a clear picture of the middle-aged widower standing tall, slender, and distinguished, a shy child by either hand, saying, in a voice exactly like Mr Ernest Whiteoak's—'Here are my little motherless ones, Miss Wakefield. I give them into your keeping.' But, when the carriage had stopped at the door, and the door been opened, not in a wide welcoming gesture but in a narrow grudging way, only the thickset figure of Mrs Nettleship had been revealed. She let Mary inside and closed the door after her, as though the house were a fortress. Inside the hall one oil lamp, in a heavy brass frame, shed a calm light on the rich-coloured rugs, the straight-backed mahogany chairs, the fine staircase. A hat rack on which hung several hats, a dog's leash, and a mackintosh, had a carved fox's head inset. Mrs Nettleship wore a light blue print dress and a snow-white apron. She had frizzy sandy hair and a smile that had less geniality than most frowns. She said:

"Mr Whiteoak is not home yet and I guess, if he was, he would not want to be interviewing you at this hour." She spoke as though it were Mary's fault that the train was an hour late. She turned to the man who was beginning to introduce Mary's trunk into the hall.

"Martin," she said, "take that to the back door." Her tone intimated that Martin had better have taken Mary to the same entrance. The man, giving a glum look, withdrew.

"Are you hungry?" Mrs Nettleship asked, as though hunger would be the last straw to what she had endured from Mary.

"No, oh no, indeed, thank you," Mary answered, though she would have given much for a bowl of soup.

"That's good," said Mrs Nettleship, "for the fire's out. I s'pose you'd like to go straight up to your room."

15

"Yes, I'm—rather tired."

"You look like two sheets and a shadow," said Mrs Nettleship cryptically. "Are you always like that?"

"Heavens, no," said Mary, feeling her anger rise. "You must remember I've had a long hard journey. I was seasick most of the way across."

Mrs Nettleship looked steadily down at her feet. "I've never crossed the ocean," she said. "I believe in staying at home and earning your living in the country you was born in."

"But how would this country have got populated if everyone had stayed at home?"

"Enough came out at the first. It's time to stop."

"Well, I'm here anyway," laughed Mary. She wondered what Mrs Nettleship's position in the household was.

Mrs Nettleship enlightened her when she had conducted Mary to her room. She said, clasping her small pointed hands on her stomach—"I've kept house for Mr Whiteoak ever since his wife died, five years ago, and if anyone could have done it better, I'd like to meet them. You'll have your hands full."

"Oh, I suppose any two children are a handful."

Mrs Nettleship smiled and her eyes twinkled. "They'll do anything for *me*," she said.

Mary thought—'You're jealous. You resent my coming. Well, that's always the way. I don't suppose a governess ever went into any house where there was no mistress but only a housekeeper, that the housekeeper didn't resent it.'

Mrs Nettleship seemed to read her thoughts. Her smile widened into a grin. "As far as I'm concerned," she said, "I'm glad you've come. I can't put up with two children always running in and out of my kitchen. Of course, when the old lady comes home it's different. She's got willpower and she don't stand any nonsense from no one."

Mary could see that the housekeeper wanted to stay and talk. Her smile became wider and wider, her lips paler as she stretched them. Twice Mary yawned and repeated how tired she was. At last Mrs Nettleship left. At the door she stopped to say—"Up here on the top floor there's just you and the children. Better not make a noise and disturb them. They'll be up early. Eliza and I sleep in the basement. There's where it's cool in summer and warm in winter. You'll have to come down and see us." When she had gone her smile seemed to hang on the air like the grin of the Cheshire cat.

Mary had not expected to sleep. Everything was too new, too strange. The black, enveloping silence of the moonless night pressed through the open windows. Every room in the unknown house seemed to gather itself together, to steal in on her, to struggle to see which would first fasten itself on her mind, cling to her memory, never to be forgotten. Even though she only remained here for a month she would never be the same again. This house, this family, of whom she had met only one member, would leave their imprint on her. She drew the sheet over her head, trying to shut herself in, to protect herself from the urgency of the house. There was the room where the children slept. She wished she might have looked in on them as they lay unconscious, have studied their features, even touched them, before they were able to touch her. The confidence that had upheld her during all her preparation in London, during the voyage, suddenly deserted her. She felt alone. No matter what befell her she would have no one to comfort her, no one who cared. Like an ice-cold wave submerging her came the realization of her aloneness. She sank under it and in her exhaustion, fell asleep and did not wake till the tall old clock at the foot of the stairs was striking six.

She saw the ghost of the ship which had brought her out from England, disappearing into the ocean mists; she saw this house called Jalna, rising up like a fortification in this new country, its woods and fields all about it; she heard a cardinal uttering his fiercely joyful whistle, as though he must live every moment of this life to the utmost; she heard the bleating of sheep and then suddenly the laughter of a young boy—the boy of seven in the next room—not loud but clear and startling in its vitality. Then there were light, quick steps in the passage and something heavy bounced against her door.

She sprang up and threw open the door but there was no one there.

2

## THE CHILDREN

RENNY WHITEOAK felt brilliantly alive that morning. He came upward, out of a deep pool of sleep, like a bright-coloured fish. He wore a light blue nightshirt, his skin was milk and roses, his hair of a bright chestnut that reddened in the shaft of sunlight that fell across the bed. From the alcove where he slept he lay looking about the large room he shared with his sister, Meg. It held almost all his belongings—his shelf of books—his toy-cupboard full of toys he was outgrowing—his fishing-rod—his wind-up train that had something wrong with its mechanism and would not go—his bank, into which he reluctantly dropped small silver when ordered to, and of which his father kept the key. A large stretch of blue sky, upon which sailed a cloud shaped like a galleon, filled the window panes, excepting in one place where the topmost branch of a silver birch waved. The air was warm. Suddenly Renny kicked away the clothes and his feet shot into the air with the unpremeditated activity of a fish's tail. He kicked so high into the sunlight that only the back of his shoulders touched the bed. He did this repeatedly, deepening the hollow that had already formed in the mattress. Then he lay quite still remembering Meg's new governess who had arrived the night before and was sleeping in the next room. He thought of her only as Meg's governess. Next year he would go to boarding school as his friend, Maurice Vaughan, two years older than himself, now went. There was no day school convenient to their houses.

His mind riveted on the governess, he rolled out on to his feet and went lightly across to his sister's bed. Meg lay curled up in a plump ball, her light-brown pigtail flung across the pillow. She lay in warm feminine seclusion. Renny sat down on the side of the bed and put his face close to hers, breathing noisily. Their breaths mingled, warm and wholesome as the scent of clover in the sun.

Anger at being woken tied Meg into a round ball. Her knees drew up to her chin, the white satinlike flesh with which her forehead was padded was drawn in a frown.

"Go 'way!" She kicked at him, her body beneath the sheet convulsed.

"Meggie, listen. Your governess is here. I heard her come last night."

"She's not mine."

"She is."

"She's not. She's just as much yours."

"She'll be yours for years and years."

Up to this point Meg had kept her eyes tight shut. Now she

opened them and they were very blue. "Did you see her?" she asked.

"No. But Mrs Nettleship came up with her. I heard them talking. I'll tell you what they said." He drew his feet up on the side of the bed and clasped his knees. Meg had a glimpse of their black soles and hissed:

"Get off my bed!"

"Why?" He was astonished.

"Your horrible feet. Look at them."

He turned up the sole of his left foot and looked at it unmoved. "Oh, that."

"You're not allowed to go to bed dirty. You're not allowed to run about barefoot. If Daddy saw you . . ."

"All right, I'll go. I won't tell you."

She caught him by the tail of his nightshirt.

"Come on. Tell me what they said."

"Old Nettle said we're a handful and she couldn't put up with us running in and out of her kitchen, and she was glad the governess had come."

"My eye!" said Meg.

"The governess," Renny said, "sounded la-di-da." He had heard his father use the expression and now brought it out impressively.

"*We'*ll la-di-da her!" said Meg.

"I'll tell you what, let's dress and then fire something at her door and run."

Those were not the days of shorts and pullovers, of scant dresses and bare legs or abbreviated play-suits. Renny put on an undervest, a shirt, trousers held up by braces of which he was very proud, and a jacket, brown stockings and laced shoes. Meg, still sleepy, got into an undervest, black stockings held up by suspenders from a heavily ribbed garment called a Ferris waist, frilled white drawers, a white starched petticoat that buttoned down the back, a pleated navy-blue serge skirt, coming just below the knee, and a white duck blouse with a starched sailor collar. It was to be a hot June day.

By the time Meg was dressed there were little beads of perspiration on her nose. She dipped a corner of a towel in the ewer and scrubbed her face with it, then dried it on the other end of the towel. She hesitated before the abhorrent task of brushing her teeth. She decided against it. After all, this was a special sort of day. She would give her teeth a rest. But she would not neglect her prayers. She knelt down by the side of her bed, folded her hands and murmured:

"Oh, Lord, receive my morning prayer.
Guard me from sin and hurt and snare.
Guide me to knowledge of Thy love
And keep my thoughts on Heaven above."

Having completed her devotions Meg rose, unplaited her hair, and gave it six strokes of the brush. Her hair sprang to life, caught the sunshine, and lay thick about her shoulders in a light brown mantle. She was ready for the day. Renny was lying across the bed holding his fox-terrier in his arms. The little dog was systematically licking Renny's ear.

"Don't speak," he said. "I'm counting the licks. A hundred and eight—a hundred and nine—a hundred——"

"All right," said Meg. "You may stay here but I'm going. I want my breakfast before *she* comes down."

Renny leapt up. In one hand he held a hard rubber ball. As they passed Mary's door he threw it sharply against a panel, then, snatching Meg's hand, he dragged her at top speed down the stairs. In this second flight of stairs the steps were steep and rather narrow. It was not long since they had descended them with care, a step at a time. Now they fairly flung themselves down, then stood listening in the passage below. There was silence everywhere. The door of their father's room was shut. The other bedrooms were closed too but they were empty, with drawn blinds and beds smooth beneath white counterpanes. Meg placed her ear to the keyhole of her father's room.

"He's breathing," she whispered. "Not quite snoring."

"Let's hear." In his turn Renny listened.

Though the door was shut between, their father was as near as though he stood before them. He was the tremendous reality of their lives. His breathing was more important than other men's shouting. When their grandmother was at home she became a great figure, but when the far distant sea or Ireland or England absorbed her, she became like impressive scenery, a mountain, a cliff, that you could put out of your head, when you are distant from it. The visits of their uncles and aunt were a mixture of pleasurable excitement, for they always brought presents, and humiliation, for they were critical, telling you not to stand like this or hold your fork like that, or making you repeat what you had said, slowly and with a proper accent. Much more of this criticism came Renny's way than Meg's. His uncles would look at his father in astonishment and say— "Upon my word, Philip, this boy is becoming a little ruffian."

"He is *so* snoring," declared Renny.

"He is not. If you call that snoring you ought to hear old Nettle." (Their name for Mrs Nettleship.)

"When did you hear her?"

"Having her afternoon nap. It was like this." Meg gave a raucous imitation. This startled the fox-terrier, who set up a frantic barking. The children, followed by him, still barking, flew down the main stairway, ran down the hall and clattered down the uncarpeted stairs to the basement. At a small table Mrs Nettleship and Eliza were eating their breakfast. There was an immaculate air about them as about the room. The morning sunlight seeking every corner, lying across the scrubbed wood of the long table, shining on the polished coal range and rows of utensils, could discover no dirt or dust. The air was filled by the pleasant smell of bacon and toast. The little dog ran at once to the side of the table and sat up.

On an ordinary occasion Mrs Nettleship would have sent the children flying, but this morning she felt a mournful pity for them which she expressed by shaking her head every time she looked at them.

"Poor little things," she muttered to Eliza. "No mother and another one of them governesses."

"Dear, oh dear," mourned Eliza, surreptitiously putting a rind of bacon into the terrier's mouth.

The children stood together at the foot of the stairs.

"What is she like?" Renny demanded.

"Wait till you see her," replied Mrs Nettleship with a sneer. "Dolled up in a flagrant way, like no teacher I've ever been used to."

"What's flagrant?"

"Scandalous, that's what flagrant is."

"Oh. Was her face painted?"

"I'd not be surprised. She'd fancy clothes."

"She sounds nice," said Meg. "Better than the other two."

"Don't you be deceived. She's the designing sort. Nice to your face and tattle behind your back."

"Do you mean tell tales to Daddy?" asked Meg.

Renny went to Mrs Nettleship. He was conscious of her

weakness for him. He smiled ingratiatingly. "I want strawberry jam on my toast this morning and bacon and a fried egg.
No porridge." Her arms went round him. He saw her blue-
lipped puckered mouth reaching towards his face and bent his
wiry body backward to avoid the contact. With deliberate
fingers he tickled the back of her neck. "Come on, Nettle," he
urged. "Strawberry jam. A fried egg. *Two* fried eggs. And *no*
porridge."

She closed her eyes, succumbing. Meg looked on dispassionately. Then the housekeeper asked:

"Did you wash last night? Your feet and legs was all sandy,
you remember."

"Yes," he answered, meaning yes he remembered.

"Good boy." She looked across at Eliza, her look saying,
'See how he loves me.'

There was something in that look which made Eliza uncomfortable. She got up and began to clear the table. Mrs Nettleship had come from a town sixty miles away. No one knew
anything of her past, whether her husband were living or dead.
Before she came to Jalna she had been housekeeper for eight
years to an invalid, an old lady who had at last died. Now, for
six years, she had unflinchingly fought dirt and disorder in
Philip Whiteoak's house, and also trained Eliza to her ways. As
he often said, a man could scarcely have two better servants,
but he would add with a shrug—"They're not what you'd call
comfortable women."

"Would you like your breakfast in the kitchen?" she asked
Renny, ignoring Meg. "It'll likely be your last chance for a
long while."

For answer he drew a chair up to the table, rattling it over
the floor. Meg at once drew up a chair for herself. Mrs Nettleship said to Eliza:

"You go on with your beds. I'll look after him."

Placing his palms against the edge of the table to steady
himself, Renny tilted back his chair and watched preparations
for his breakfast with an appraising eye.

"It'll be far worse for you having that English woman here
than it will for your sister."

"I shall be going to school."

"Not for over a year!" she scoffed. "She can do a lot to you
in that time."

"I'd like to see her try."

22

There was silence while Mrs Nettleship concentrated her attention on the frying-pan. She set his plate sizzling before him.

"Ladies should be served first," said Meg.

Renny at once pushed the plate towards her. "Take this then," he said.

Mrs Nettleship angrily grasped his wrist. "None of that," she said. "I don't like being interfered with."

"If he says I can have it I can," said Meg stubbornly.

"Not in this kitchen. If you don't do what I want you'll have breakfast upstairs—with *her*."

She looked on approvingly while Renny attacked his bacon. She passed a hand over his hair. "Snakes alive, what hair! I guess you never put a brush on it this morning." She placed Meg's plate in front of her with what seemed almost calculated indifference. When she brought out the pot of strawberry jam it was set convenient to his hand.

"Now," she said, when they had finished, "I'm going to get a brush and tidy your hair, mister. Use your napkins, both of you." She disappeared into the passage which led to the maids' bedrooms.

In an instant the children were silently scrambling up the stairs. The fox-terrier, in his eagerness, nipped first one of their legs, then another, as they ascended. At the top all three cast restraint away and scampered through the hall, laughing and barking. The front door stood open. The outdoors, piercingly green in its freshness, invited them. They tore through the porch.

"I'll beat you to the gate!" shouted Renny.

3

PHILIP

An hour later Philip opened the door of his bedroom, came out, and shut it stealthily behind him. He cast one apprehensive look up the stairway to the top floor where the new governess slept. He was not shy but he dreaded the complications she would almost certainly bring into his life. He would never forget the trouble caused by Miss Turnbull, the last governess.

23

She had been the hoity-toity priggish type, disagreeable to the servants, unreasonable (to his mind) with the children, complaining to him. Sights and sounds of the farm were always shocking her. He hoped this new one would be a countrywoman. Ernest had told him singularly little of her in his letter —just that she seemed nice and quite sensible and that her references were good. Philip heaved a sigh at the thought of being obliged to have three strange women in his house but what could he do? Mrs Nettleship was certainly not capable of giving the proper care to a little girl. Well, this was the sort of thing that happened to a man when he was a widower. He'd got used to being a widower but he never ceased to miss Margaret's taking the difficult end of domestic complications. She'd had a strong nature—always thought she was right—and a temper. She'd been only twenty-five when she died; perhaps by this time she'd have toned down a bit. It was wonderful how she'd stood up to his mother's tempers, and rather terrible too. Yet his mother had known Margaret all her life—dandled her when she was a baby. He himself felt that when you'd known a person all your life you ought to understand them. But women were different.

He took his gold watch from his waistcoat pocket. He pushed out his full lips in a pout. No time to go to the stables before breakfast, as he had wanted to. He might as well face the music now, have breakfast with the children and this Miss Wakefield and get it over with. Wearing the expression of a spoilt boy he descended the stairs and looked into the diningroom. The table was set for two.

His expression changed to one of dismay. Where were the children? Surely he was not going to be forced to eat breakfast alone with that woman on her first morning! He couldn't. He wouldn't. He strode to where the bell-cord hung and pulled it. In a moment Eliza appeared.

"Breakfast, sir?" she asked.

"Eliza, where are the children?"

"They had their breakfast early and ran off, sir."

"Go and find them, please. No—I'll call them myself." He gave Eliza a pathetic look. "Eliza, where is that governess?"

"In the library. I think she's waiting for you, sir." Eliza could not help smiling at the dismay in his eyes as he heard this. "She's brought books with her and pencils and paper."

"In there!" he repeated, staring at the double doors which

24

separated the two rooms. The library, more truly a sitting-room, was particularly his own and the thought of the strange woman in possession of it was more than he would stand. She must be told to keep out of there.

He went to a side door that opened from the hall and now stood wide. He stepped out into the morning air and took a satisfying breath of it before feeling in his pocket for a dog-whistle he always carried there and which his children answered almost as well as his spaniels. It was carved from bone and had a stout silver chain to it. He blew a shrill ear-piercing blast on it, then waited. He blew another. Still there was no response. Frowning a little he drew a deep breath and emitted an even more peremptory call. Out from the orchard at the back of the house, where on the ground the petals of the apple blossoms still lay white, two little figures appeared.

"Renny!" shouted Philip. "Meggie!"

Renny hid his fishing-rod in the long orchard grass.

"I see you," shouted Philip. "Bring it along."

The two trotted towards him, Renny carrying the rod, the line dangling free, the hook nearer, at each step, to his sister's face.

"Look out what you're doing, you young idiot! Mind that hook!" Philip was at the end of his patience.

Now his children were before him, gazing up into his face. He took the rod and wound the line on the reel. The feel of it in his hand brought fishing to his mind. He thought he would go off for a few days' fishing while the governess got settled in. "There"—he stood the rod against the wall. "Now we'll go in and meet Miss Wakefield. There'll be lessons, you know."

Meg's blue eyes were large and mournful, Renny's narrowed in misery. Each slipped a hand into his. Thus fortified he felt stronger to face the ordeal. He bent and kissed each in turn. Then he noticed their hair. "Wait a jiffy," he said.

He took a small comb in a leather case from his pocket. He ran it through Renny's dense, dark red hair, exclaiming—"By George, you have a tangled mop! I must get it cut. Now, you Meg." Hers he found impossible except for tidying a bit round her face. She looked up trustfully just as his clumber spaniels did when he combed them. She and the boy were good-looking children and fairly intelligent. No one could deny that. "Come along, I guess you'll do." He led them to the door of the library and they went in.

25

Mary was standing by the window. She turned and faced them with a startled air. She felt herself growing pale from excitement. The moment was upon her—the moment of meeting her new employer and her future pupils. In a flash she was conscious of her inadequacy, her unfitness for the situation. She had never been a teacher, she didn't know anything about children. She did not even known how to live with other people. She had to brace herself against panic, and, after the first glance, against bewilderment. She had expected to see a middle-aged man, probably a few years younger than Mr Ernest Whiteoak. She thought of widowers as middle-aged, just as she thought of children as little darlings. Yet now she stood facing a young man—just past thirty—with the finest blue eyes she had ever seen, smiling at her, and two children who did not look at all like little darlings. Philip said:

"I am sorry to have kept you waiting, Miss Wakefield. I am Philip Whiteoak and these are Meg and Renny." He held out his hand, took hers, and feeling the warm clasp of his fingers she felt a lessening of her panic.

She shook hands with the children. Meg's round face was turned up to hers, with no more expression than an egg, yet somehow conveying hostility in its very lack of expression. Renny's brilliant brown eyes met hers with a wary look. He gave a rigid little smile, as though his lips felt stiff, then closed his mouth firmly. Philip asked her about her journey, then they all moved into the dining-room and took their places at table, Mary between the two children, Philip at the head of the table.

"We've had our breakfast," exclaimed Meg. "I forgot."

"Why, yes, we've had our breakfast. We don't want two breakfasts, Daddy." Renny gave a sudden small boy's explosion of treble laughter. He jumped down from his chair and ran to his father's side and threw an arm round his neck.

"I could eat a little more," said Meg. "Nettle gave me scarcely anything."

Philip looked at Mary, his eyes laughing. "I suppose," he said, "that all those English children you taught had perfect manners."

"Oh, no." What if he should ask her how many she had taught? She grew hot all over. Eliza was offering her porridge and a jug of the richest-looking milk she had ever seen. "Thank you," she said and began to force it down.

It was from Meg the dreaded question came. "How many children were you the governess of?" she asked.

"Not many. Really—just one—for any length of time."

"Was it a girl?"

"Yes."

"How long did you stay with her?"

Mary felt sure the child knew she was hedging. Her colour heightened but she turned with what dignity she could gather and said to Philip—"I hope that Mr Ernest Whiteoak did not tell you I had a lot of experience. I didn't intend to give him that impression because I haven't."

He smiled good-humouredly. "You couldn't very well. Not at your age."

"As a matter of fact," she got out, "I have only one reference."

"Only one!" exclaimed Meg, though her expression never changed.

"Sh," said Philip. "Eat your porridge."

"I don't want it. I said I could eat a little more. Not porridge."

"I think," said Mary, "that your brother must have been almost desperate when he engaged me. You see, the other one had broken her legs."

Philip nodded in sympathy for the absent governess but the children broke into derisive laughter. "Broke her legs!" shouted Renny. "Broke *both* her legs! She'd be no use after that. Did they shoot her?"

"Ha—ha—ha!" Meg threw herself back in her chair. "I never heard of such a thing! *Did* they shoot her, Miss Wakefield?"

Young barbarians, thought Mary, and felt almost afraid of them. They looked so complete in themselves, so sure of their foundation—all three of them. What lay behind the young father's good-humoured smile? She saw his handsome hands as he gave Renny a push towards his own chair, his handsome head, with the thick, rather untidy fair hair. But it was his eyes that fascinated her, not with the mysterious, lambent fire of beautiful dark eyes that had always pierced her and which she had always pictured her future husband as having, but with a benign, deep, tender blueness behind their well-cut lids. Mary stopped eating her poached egg and closed her eyes the better to think of adequate adjectives for describing Philip's.

"These children are little devils," he said. "You'll have to take it out of them."

"Why did you shut your eyes, Miss Wakefield?" asked Meg.

"The better *not* to see you," answered her father. "Now, no more questions. Don't speak till you're spoken to."

Mingled with Mary's apprehension for the task ahead of her was a strange exhilaration. Was it the warmth, the serenity of Philip's presence, in such contrast to the nervous irritability of her father's? She had lived a singularly sequestered life in the heart of London, always expected to be on hand on her father's return, never knowing when to expect him. She had it in her, though she would have denied it, to be a slave to a man. Was it the isolation with this radiant male, for surely no one, she thought, could question his radiance as he sat at the head of his table, his broad shoulders drooping a little, spreading honey on a thick piece of snow-white homemade bread?

"Our own honey," he said, as though to put her at her ease.

"Really. How lovely!"

"Are you afraid of bees? Stingin', I mean."

She noticed, for the first time, that he had a slight impediment in his speech. He could not distinctly say *th* but substituted a tentative *ve*. The truth was that Philip, as a small boy, had been too lazy to correct this impediment, though often reprimanded by his mother for it, and, as a man, was unaware of it.

"I'm afraid I am. At least, I think I should be. I don't ever remember having been near a bee."

At this Renny's treble laughter again cut the air.

"Behave yourself," said his father.

Meg, forbidden to speak, pointed to the honey, glistening in the comb, and then to her mouth. Philip winked at Mary, as though to say, See how I have them trained. That wink broke down more barriers than a month of ordinary friendliness could have done. Upper and lower lids met for an instant over the benign blueness of the orb, hiding it, then opened again and the eye looked into hers, smiling. He has no dignity, thought Mary, and he is adorable.

He helped Meg to honey, then nodding towards two oil paintings behind Mary said—"Those are my parents. My father is dead. But you'll be seeing my mother one of these days. She's a character. She's past her middle sixties but you'd never know it."

Mary screwed round in her chair to look at the portrait and Philip took the opportunity to have a better look at her. He liked the way her hair was done in a sort of French roll on the back of her head. He liked the long graceful line of neck and shoulder and thought it rather a pity that women wore those wide neck-ribbons wound twice round the neck and tied in a big bow behind. This particular ribbon was light blue with white polka dots, her shirtwaist was white and her navy-blue serge skirt just reached her instep. She looked fresh as the morning, he thought, and very young. It was a pleasant surprise, and pleasure lighted his handsome face as she turned back to him.

"What beautiful portraits," she said, "and what a joy they must be to you! My mother was quite lovely but I have only a rather faded photograph of her."

"I guess you resemble her." She felt his eyes, suddenly bold, looking her over, and blushed. She nodded.

"I am supposed to. And you are so like your father."

He pushed out his lips and wrinkled his brow. "A very poor reproduction according to my mother. You see him there in the uniform of the Hussars, though his family, which was a military one, had always been connected with the Buffs. Those two portraits were painted in London before they came to Canada. They brought them out in a sailing vessel. They built this house. I was born here and so was the brother you met in London. Nice house, don't you think so?"

"Oh, yes," she agreed enthusiastically.

"I breed horses," he said, as though to forward their acquaintance.

"How interesting!" She leaned towards him a little and Meg stared inquisitively up into her face.

"*And* cattle."

"How lovely!"

"And a few sheep. Southdown."

"I love sheep."

"I breed kids too," he went on, "horrible little kids. A perfect nuisance. I'm thinking of getting rid of them—that is, unless you can make something of them."

Again came Renny's treble laugh, this time, it seemed to Mary, with something mocking in it.

"I'm going to try very hard." She straightened her shoulders and did her best to look efficient.

"It's quite a difficult thing for a man," he said seriously, "where there is no mother." If he were looking for sympathy, there it was, in Mary's eyes.

"A fellow just has to do the best he can."

"I think you've done wonderfully well."

"Do you hear that, Renny? Miss Wakefield thinks I'm a wonderful success as a father. That means she thinks you're wonderful children." He put his arm about the little boy, then turned with fatherly pride to Mary. "I'll bet you can't produce better complexions in England."

"They look pictures of health." More and more she dreaded being left alone with the children. There was something intimidating about them. They were not at all like little pitchers waiting to be filled with knowledge from textbooks.

"I brought some books with me," she said.

"Good. And they have a supply. If there is anything you want let me know. Now I'm going about my work and you can get to yours. Renny!"

"Yes, Daddy."

"No monkey tricks. Meggie!"

"Yes, Daddy."

"Be a good girl. Help Miss Wakefield."

A moment more and Mary was alone with the two who stood regarding her appraisingly. She smiled as confidently as she could and asked—"Do we do lessons in the sitting-room?"

"Goodness, no," answered Meg. "That's where Daddy smokes." She continued to stare coolly at Mary.

The boy did not speak but stood, with a hand grasping the doorknob, swinging his body gently from side to side.

"Show me then," said Mary. She put her arm about Meg's shoulders. Heavens, the plump firmness of them! She gave the impression of stubbornness right through her clothes. She wriggled herself free of Mary's arm. Mary thought, That's the last time I put my arm about *you* without your inviting me.

Meg led the way into the hall. A door opposite the door of the dining-room stood ajar. Mary glanced through it. She gave the merest glance but both children saw her. They looked at each other and smiled in a secretive way.

"That's Granny's room," said Renny in his clear high voice. "She'll be coming soon. Everyone's afraid of her." He stared at Mary, as though to see the effect of his words.

"It was she who sent Miss Turnbull away," added Meg.

"Why?" Mary could not help asking.

"Oh, she didn't like her."

"Want to see the room?" asked Renny. As he spoke he flung open the door and stalked in, with an air of ownership. "I can do what I like in here. Come on in."

"Oh, no," objected Mary.

Meg caught her by the hand and dragged her in. "You'd better see it now," she said, "because when Granny comes home you can't."

"I always can," said Renny. "That's her bed. Like to sleep in it?"

Mary saw an ornate leather bedstead painted in a rich design of flowers and fruit, between the glowing petals and leaves of which grinning faces of monkeys appeared and heavy-winged butterflies clung, as though in sensuous rapture. Over the mattress lay a coverlet of satin embroidered in India in threads of gold and mulberry. On the mantelshelf stood the figure of a Chinese goddess, and among the English walnut furniture were pieces of inlaid ebony. The room had a semi-Oriental look distasteful to Mary, but outside the open window a great white lilac tree displayed its plumes and filled the air with its scent. Mary pictured the lovely red-lipped brown-eyed young woman of the portrait in this room, tried to visualize her as almost seventy. Perhaps she would be bent, complaining, suffering from rheumatism. She said:

"You shouldn't have forced me in here, Meg. Come, we must go to work." She took Renny's hand and was surprised by the grip of the small hard fingers. He tugged at her hand.

"Do you like it?" he insisted. "Should you like to sleep here?"

"No," she answered firmly. "Now show me the school-room."

"You don't *like* it?" he cried, his little face expressing chagrin and even anger. "Why—it's a beautiful room."

Mary hastened to say—"I didn't mean that I don't think it's a beautiful room. I only meant it's too grand for me. I like a more simple room to sleep in."

"Do you like the room you have?" Now he swung on her hand as he had before swung on the door.

"Very much. Now will you please show me the room where we are to work?"

They darted, as by a common impulse, into the hall and up the two flights of stairs. Mary heard a door slam. With dignity she followed them to the top. "Children!" she called.

Renny threw open the door of their bedroom and stood facing her. Behind him she saw a table littered with books.

"I consider," he said, "that I am too old to be taught by a woman."

"That is what your father engaged me for, so we must be pleasant about it, mustn't we?" Mary tried to keep a cheerful smile but she found the small boy intimidating.

"I consider," he continued, "that you don't know enough."

Meg threw herself on to a worn leather couch and exploded in giggles.

"I know more than you think. Come now, that's a good boy."

"I considah, I considah, I considah," he went on, in a high affected tone, his eyebrows raised superciliously.

Mary began to feel panic. What if she could do nothing with them? What if she had to confess this to Philip Whiteoak?

Suddenly Renny changed his tactics. He darted to a cupboard, opened the door, and began to rummage on a shelf. He approached her with a small glass jar in his hands.

"Want to see them?" he asked.

Meg jumped up and came to his side.

"What?" asked Mary, relieved yet suspicious.

He held the jar close to her face. She saw two revolting pinkish-brown objects.

"Meggie's tonsils!" he shouted.

"How horrid!" She drew away in disgust.

"I consider them my greatest treasures." He studied them in rapt concentration.

"Why do you keep on saying you *consider*?" Mary asked to change the subject.

His sister answered for him. "Miss Turnbull was always saying it. Don't you like it?"

"No. To me it sounds very egotistical."

He would not let her know he did not understand the adjective.

"That's why *I* like it," he said.

A step sounded on the stairs. It was familiar to the children and Mary guessed whose it was. Philip came into the room. His tranquil gaze rested for a moment on the little group before he spoke, then he said—"Well, now, that's a funny way to entertain Miss Wakefield. Are you sure she likes such things?"

The children stood motionless, except that Renny joggled the tonsils a little.

"Oh, I don't mind," said Mary.

"Put them away, Renny. No, give them to me. I'll take charge of them for a bit." The jar was transferred from his son's hands to his. "What I came up to say is, I'm going to drive to a farm ten miles along the lake shore this afternoon and if the children are good, Miss Wakefield, and I mean *very* good, the three of you may come with me—that is, if you would like the drive." His eyes questioned Mary.

"I should like it very much." Thanksgiving filled her heart. If only she could get through these first days all would be well.

"If you have any trouble of any sort, Miss Wakefield," he said, his eyes now on his children, "please let me know."

He left them and was barely to the head of the stairs when Renny, planting himself in front of Mary, drawled:

"I considah——"

"What's that you say?" called back Philip.

"Nothing, Daddy. We're just beginning work."

Philip continued his descent smiling to himself. He was not going to have that young rascal make life miserable for such a lovely girl. Each time he saw Mary he was more astonished by her looks. Whatever could have possessed Ernest to have engaged such a beauty! He wagered that if his mother or sister had interviewed her she never would have been engaged. They had been at obvious pains to choose unattractive governesses for the children. Well, they need not worry. He had no desire to marry again. He was very content as he was. He owned a fine property. His occupations could not have been more congenial. From morning to night he was doing the things he wanted to. He had a deep sense of gratitude to his father for having left Jalna to him. Neither Nicholas nor Ernest would have appreciated it half so much as he. The governor had realized that. Their tastes were of the Old World—London and Paris, with a fling now and again on the Riviera. He was all for the New. Give him Canada every time, and to him Jalna was Canada. Both his brothers had had their share of their father's money. Nicholas had spent a deal of his in extravagant living. You don't keep horses and a dashing brougham and a socially-minded wife in London for nothing. Thank goodness,

Nicholas was free of her now. Of course, divorce was a pretty disgraceful thing but it was she who'd run off and left Nicholas, not Nicholas her. The one visit she'd made to Jalna had been an irritation. She'd been so damn supercilious, and it had ended in a quarrel between her and Mamma. . . . Now, Ernest was a different sort of fellow. He was shrewd. Financial investments that were so much Greek to Philip were as child's play to old Ernie. It looked as though he might become a very rich man. Philip thought of him with respect.

Out on the smoothly gravelled drive he saw a dogcart and, just alighting from it, his father-in-law, Dr Ramsay. He was a Scotsman by birth, a man almost seventy, but still attending to a quite large and scattered country practice. He was a spare man with a bony and well-proportioned frame, a critical manner, and a vigorous belief in the absolute rightness of his own opinions. He regarded his son-in-law with a mingled affection and disapproval. He had been deeply gratified when his daughter, Margaret, an only child, had married Philip. There had been no better match in the province, in his opinion. But Philip's easygoing ways, his indolent carriage, the very slight impediment in his speech, which, in the opinion of some women, only added to his charm, were sources of irritation to Dr Ramsay. Philip was not the man his father, Captain Whiteoak, of the Queen's Own Hussars, had been.

The death of his daughter had been a great blow to the doctor. He had himself attended her in her illness and the end had been terribly unexpected. He had strained every nerve to save her. Since her death he felt, in the secret recesses of his heart, that, as his skill had failed to save her, he must do all in his power to keep her place in Philip's affections vacant. In some strange way that would reconcile his spirit to her early demise. She had been a jealous girl who could not endure that Philip should give an admiring glance to any other, though why she should have minded Dr Ramsay could not understand, for she had been as clever and handsome a girl as there was in the countryside. That neither of her children resembled her he deeply resented. He took it as a personal injury. Meg took after the Whiteoaks and the boy seemed to have gone out of the way to reproduce the physical traits of his Irish grandmother. Not that the doctor did not admire Adeline Whiteoak. She was a fine-looking woman, but, if the boy were going to resemble a grandparent, why not him?

"Good morning," Philip called out, in his full, genial tones.

"Good morning." Dr Ramsay, though he had been in Canada forty-five years, spoke with a considerable Scottish accent. "It's a beautiful day."

Philip could see him feeling about in his mind for an appropriate quotation from Robert Burns, as a man might feel in his pocket for a coin of the right size. Now he had it and smiled as he declaimed:

> "The voice of Nature loudly cries,
> And many a message from the skies,
> That something in us never dies."

"True," agreed Philip. "Very true. It's fine growing weather. We should have good crops."

The doctor took him by the coat lapel. "This country," he said, "is in for trouble, if prices continue to rise. I've been shopping this morning and what do you suppose I paid for bacon? Thirteen cents a pound! It's ridiculous. Eggs fifteen cents a dozen instead of a cent apiece! Butter twenty cents a pound! Ruin lies ahead if——"

Philip interrupted—"Now, look here, sir, why will you buy those things when you know very well that they are produced here on the farm and you're welcome to all you need."

"I didn't buy any," said the doctor. "I only priced them."

He was quite willing to accept these favours, rightly feeling that the medical attention he gave the two children fully compensated for them. To the grown-ups at Jalna he sent his bill, which was moderate.

"I don't want anything this morning, thank you. What I came in for was to see if the wee ones would like to accompany me on my rounds. 'Twould be a change for them."

The children had got past the age when to go on his rounds with their grandfather was a treat. They had ponies of their own. And also he expected too much from them in sedateness of behaviour and was given to lecturing. Philip thanked Dr Ramsay. "But they are busy at their lessons, sir. You see, the new governess arrived last night."

"Well, is that so? And what like is she?"

"Very nice."

"Very nice," repeated the doctor irritably. "That conveys nothing to me. I mean does she appear to be a woman of strong character and erudition? The last one was a fool."

35

Philip stroked the mare's neck. "I've scarcely had time to judge. I expect that my brother went into these things."

"Hm. What age is she?"

"It's so hard to tell. Youngish."

"Under forty?"

"Yes."

"I don't see eye to eye with you in bringing over an English-woman to train your children. Now, if she were Scottish it would be different."

"It's really my mother and Ernest. By the way, he's made some amazingly good investments lately."

"That's fine. For they are usually quite the revairse, aren't they?"

Philip looked after his father-in-law, sitting very upright as he rattled off in his dogcart, and wondered what he would say when he beheld Miss Wakefield. Behold was the right word for a girl so stunning as she. Yes, she was stunning. You forgot what you were saying to her, for staring at her. That is, for trying *not* to stare at her. It wasn't so much actual beauty, perhaps, as that willowy graceful form, that smile that had something melancholy in it; her mouth went down at the corners rather than up when she smiled. He wasn't sure. He must notice.

His three clumber spaniels, Sport and Spot and their half-grown puppy, Jake, came leaping about his legs. He bent and distributed caresses as equally as he could, considering that Jake was determined to get more than his share. Philip had to cuff him gently away to give the parents a chance.

"Come along, then, we'll go for a walk." He turned in the direction of the orchard where the spraying of the apple trees was going on. A fine crop promised. All the land, the woods, the fields, shone this morning, as though in beneficent mood. The very house wore its mantle of Virginia creeper with a smiling air, as though conscious of its decoration. The myriad little leaves of the silver birch trees on the lawn trembled with life. Philip had in himself a feeling of almost creative achievement, as though he were a part of the secret purpose of the universe.

# 4

# THE HOUSE BY THE LAKE

MARY HAD little trouble with the children during the rest of that morning. She gave it over to trying to make friends with them, to finding out what their studies had been and letting them show her their textbooks. Some of these had been handed down from their father and uncles, some were forty years old, dog-eared and out of date, yet for some reason it was these the children liked best. There was a tattered history of Ireland with their grandmother's name, Adeline Court, in it and her age, fourteen. The books which had belonged to Ernest were in much better condition than those which had belonged to Nicholas. Those in which Philip's name was scrawled were worst of all.

When Mary touched Meg the little girl drew away but sometimes Renny would lean against her shoulder, as though deliberately. Once he turned his eyes and looked close into hers and she wondered what lay behind their mysterious darkness. He could read and write quite well for a seven-year-old. She felt new courage to attack her work. The morning passed quickly.

The children chattered all through the one-o'clock dinner and were encouraged by their father. He felt shy of the new governess. She was so different from what he had expected. He was very conscious of her presence. Over and over he wondered, chuckling at the thought, what would be the expression on his mother's face when she saw Miss Wakefield.

When he saw how daintily she was dressed for the outing he felt he should have done something to titivate his own costume but the effort was too great. He decided to go as he was, in a rather disreputable old tweed suit and a battered straw hat. But nothing could have been more shining than the surrey and the chestnut pair harnessed to it. The horses were superbly matched. Plenty of elbow-grease had been expended on the polishing of their equipment. Their fine eyes rolled in their eagerness to be off. Mary's heart sank as she saw polished hoofs stamping the gravel. Could one pair of arms control them? Her long cloth skirt hampered her in climbing to the seat. She placed a foot on the step and Philip took her by the arm. He took her by both arms and half lifted her up. She was there, on the rear seat, and Meg scrambling up after her!

Philip took the reins from the stable boy and gave the encouraging chirrup for which the horses had been waiting. Now their hoofs made a staccato tapping on the drive and scattered gravel to the verge of the well-cared-for lawn. As they turned into the road and Mary became conscious of Philip's competence with the reins, saw with what skill he controlled the two fiery beasts, her fear subsided and she felt a kind of wild exhilaration. It was thrilling to bowl along the white road, between the spreading branches of massive oaks, her responsibility lifted from her for the moment and nothing to do but give herself up to enjoyment. How often similar equipages had passed her in London and she had looked with envy on the occupants! Now here she was, in this spacious new country, riding behind a glittering pair, her little charges docile, her employer—but no, she must not keep thinking about her employer, how well his coat sat on his broad shoulders, the way his hair grew on the back of his sunburned neck. And even while she told herself to keep her mind off him, she inwardly exclaimed—"He's like no one else! He's fascinating!"

Yet all he had done was to talk to her a little about quite ordinary things, to mount to the driver's seat behind his horses, and to display his back to her. His fascination probably lay in his difference from the men she had hitherto met. They had mostly been journalists, friends of her father's, hard-worked, often pressed for money, often disillusioned. Philip Whiteoak looked as though he had never wanted anything he had not been able to get, as though he had never worried about anything in his life. Yet sorrow had been his. He had buried the mother of his children. Probably had loved her dearly, and had lost her. Yet his blond good looks were untarnished.

Now the road led them close to the lake. The sand of the shore came close to the road. The horses curved their polished necks and looked sideways at the dancing water. What if it should frighten them and they should run away—bolt! They picked up their iron hoofs, as though in astonishment, quiverings ran through the burnished hairs of their tails. The whistle of a train on a distant crossing made them prick their ears. A white-foamed wave tumbled up the shore. The horses threw themselves into frightening speed. Trees and fields flew by on the right, the vast expanse of the lake rocked itself on the left.

Mary put out her hand and grasped the back of the seat in front of her. She could not restrain that gesture of alarm.

Philip looked over his shoulder and smiled. "Feeling frisky," he said. "Need more exercise."

"Daddy, do let me drive!" Renny put his hands on the reins.

"Oh, no—please!" Mary could not help herself. Meg turned a look of stolid scorn on her.

Round a curve a farm wagon appeared carrying a load of pigs for market. The road was narrow, the squeals of the jostling pigs were all that was needed to set the horses galloping.

"Whoa, now, whoa——" Philip put his strength on the reins. "You are a pretty pair—showing off like this for Miss Wakefield. There's no danger."

Mary realized then that she had screamed.

The horses were now subdued to a brisk trot. Philip again looked over his shoulder. "You're nervous, aren't you?" he said. "But you'll get over that."

Meg gave her another scornful look.

"I am not used to horses. I'm ashamed." Mary reddened painfully.

"Daddy," Renny said, tugging at his father's sleeve, "please let me drive."

Philip put the reins into the child's hands, at the same time giving Mary a look of reassurance. "Don't be alarmed, Miss Wakefield. Renny's a capable rascal with the reins. And I'm right here. The horses are really well-behaved."

The fright was past. Mary resigned herself to precarious enjoyment of the velocity of the muscular creatures under control of the small boy who sat, his back stiff with pride, his arms extended, his thin hands gripping the reins. Philip's arm lay along the back of the seat, she noticed the ring with a blood-stone inset on his hand, that hand which had assisted her into the carriage. Myriad leaves, as many as the waves of the lake, spread themselves in the sunshine, butterflies felt strength coming into their newly spread wings, bird-song ceased, to let the beat of hoofs be heard. The surrey rolled from temperate shade to blazing sun. Meg lolled on her seat in an abandon of wellbeing. It's glorious, thought Mary, I'm going to be happy here. Thank God I applied for this post and thank God I got it! The prayer of thanksgiving came from the depths of her being. In some mysterious way she had never been so happy before.

The ten miles were at last behind them, ten whole miles and without apparent effort on the part of the horses! Small farms were passed so quickly that Mary had no time to examine the buildings before they were out of sight. They went through a quiet village where they encountered only one other vehicle in the main street but where shopkeepers strolled to the doors to see them pass. Philip Whiteoak seemed to know everyone.

As he turned the horses through an impressive stone gateway he remarked—"This is where the Craigs live."

"Do we know them?" Renny asked, in his clear voice.

"I do. Mr Craig has been ill. He's going to sell his horses. I'm going to buy them."

"Goody!" exclaimed Meg.

The horses came to a standstill in front of a somewhat pretentious stone house, built close to the shore, the first of a row of similar houses erected by retired city people. They were evidently expected, for a man came forward and held the horses and, at the same moment, a tall, well-built woman of thirty appeared on the verandah where there were a number of jardinières holding sword-ferns and palms. Sheltered by these luxuriant plants hung a red and yellow hammock with deep fringe and it was out of it that the young woman had risen. Mary's first thought was how could she have been lying in a hammock and remained so tidy? There was an iron neatness about her belt and the 'stand-up, turn-down' collar of her shirt-waist and its tucked front was stiffly starched. She wore a fancy comb in her pale brown hair, and her wide-open light eyes were intelligent. Her wide-nostrilled nose was retroussé.

"I am Miss Craig," she said, "and I am to take you round to the sunny side of the house where my father is sitting in his wheel chair."

Philip and she shook hands, then she said—"Perhaps the children and your . . ." She hesitated.

"This is Miss Wakefield. She has just come from England to see if she can drum a little book-learning into these two. Will you mind if they stroll round while I talk to your father? That is, if you think he is well enough to see me."

"He will be delighted." Miss Craig bowed coldly, or so Mary felt as the round light eyes rested on her, but she smiled charmingly at the children. Her voice was low-pitched and pleasant. "Father does miss other men's society, even though his nurse and I do our best to amuse him."

Philip assisted Mary to alight. The children scrambled down. They attempted to follow their father but he sent them back to Mary. Miss Craig led the way and Philip followed her round the house where in a sheltered nook they found Mr Craig with a trained nurse reading aloud to him. He had suffered a paralytic stroke which had affected one side, which sagged a little. But his face was well-coloured and he looked far from ill. The nurse was stocky with little bright black eyes and a set smile. She rose and when introductions had been made she left and joined Mary where she stood admiring a large bed of geraniums and coleus. The children had already disappeared. The nurse began at once to talk to Mary with nonchalant familiarities. Mary stood withdrawn, longing to leave her.

"I think I must find the children," she said.

"Oh, you'll never find them. I saw them running after their father to the stable. This is a lovely place, don't you think?"

"Yes, indeed."

"It's pretty hard on Mr Craig to have had this sickness, so soon after he built the house, isn't it?"

"I'm sure it is."

"Miss Craig is a lovely person."

"Is she?"

"She's a devoted daughter."

"Oh."

"It's hard on her too."

"Oh, yes."

"You come from London?"

"Yes."

"Miss Craig's been there. And Paris and Rome. That's not to speak of New York and Washington."

"Really."

"Don't you think Miss Craig has a lovely figure? I call her the perfect Gibson girl."

"Do you?"

A shout was heard from Renny, and on the strength of it Mary made her escape. She hung about, hiding behind shrubs, till she heard Philip's voice. He was speaking to the man who held his horses. Mary came from behind a clump of syringas, her skirt trailing on the grass. He saw her and came to meet her.

"I'm sorry to have kept you waiting so long." He did not

41

trouble to conceal the admiration in his eyes as he discovered her with the heavy-scented blossoms massed behind her. "But the old gentleman wanted to talk. I've bought a lovely mare from him. I can't imagine what possessed him to go in for show horses. He doesn't know the first thing about them."

He spoke to Mary with an air of pleasant familiarity. How different it was from the nurse's pushing intimacy. A quiver of happiness in his returned presence passed through her. She had been feeling lonely.

"I am so glad you have bought the horse," she ventured.

He looked at her kindly. "You'll get over your fear of them, you know," he said. "And you'll enjoy the drives here. We must show you the country."

He took out his whistle and summoned the children. Soon they were flying homeward, with Mary less nervous than before, the horses unswerving in their eagerness to return to their evening feed. The shadows of trees lay across the white dust of the road. A coolness rose from the moist earth beneath them. Small birds left the eggs they were hatching to dart with sunny wings after bright-coloured insects. Mary was conscious of the moving vitality all about her. From trotting horses to insect fleeing for its life she was conscious of the vital urge that governed them.

She lost her fear of what seemed to her Philip's reckless driving. She, having no real experience of being a governess, forgot she was one, and when the horses stopped and Philip alighted and stood below her to help her alight she held out her arms to him, just as though she were a young lady visitor to Jalna, and smiled into his eyes.

"Tired?" he asked.

"Oh, no. Not at all tired."

He gave a little laugh as he set her on the ground. Mary wondered why. She would have given almost anything to know. She looked into his eyes to discover the reason but discovered only their deep blueness.

"You are tall, Miss Wakefield," he remarked. "Taller than I had thought."

"I am too tall."

"You should see my mother and my sister. They're inches taller than you."

"Then you are a tall family," she said, admiring his height.

"My brothers are taller than I. So was my father. Though

I take after him I lack his height. My mother has that against me."

The thought of anyone holding anything against him was unbelievable to Mary. She began to dislike his mother.

"I lack his distinction altogether, as you may see from his portrait."

"But then what a beautiful uniform he is wearing!"

"True. Do you know, we still have that uniform and every spring my mother takes it out and hangs it in the open air. In case of moths. I'm usually the one who helps her. It's a melancholy proceeding. But she's brave. It's hard to lose your mate."

He drew his brows together and Mary was sure he was thinking of his dead wife. Renny came to his side and he put an arm about him. "This fellow," he said, "doesn't look a bit like me, does he?"

"I can't see any resemblance." And a pity, too, she thought, for there was something forbidding in the small boy's chiselled nostrils, the hard-looking head that had an almost sculptural severity.

"He's the spit of my mother. Isn't it funny?"

Renny gave his clear high laugh. "I'm glad," he said. "I like looking like Gran."

"Why?" said Mary coldly.

"Because," he grinned, showing all his white teeth, "because everyone's afraid of her."

"But surely you don't want people to be afraid of you."

"You bet I do."

"Well, I for one aren't," cried Meg. She caught a handful of his hair, tugged it and ran off, with him after her.

"Unruly little beggars," laughed Philip.

The two were still talking when the front door opened and Mrs Nettleship looked out. She fixed a stony accusing stare on Mary.

"I beg your pardon, sir," she said, addressing Philip out of the side of her mouth, while her stare never faltered. "But I'm looking for the children. I don't know if it's still my place or not but if they're going to be tidied up before their tea it's high time it was done."

"Oh——" Mary's colour flamed. "I'll find them at once. I don't think they've gone far." She hastened after them, Mrs Nettleship's stare moving automatically in pursuit.

The horses were restively pawing the gravel. Philip lazily climbed into the seat and took the reins.

"Keep your hair on, Mrs Nettleship," he advised. "Miss Wakefield will look after the children all right." He drove off, and in a moment was hidden behind the row of spruces and hemlocks that shielded house from stables. Yet the thud of hoofs could still be heard.

"Keep my hair on, eh?" exclaimed Mrs Nettleship, addressing the hemlocks. "Keep my hair on! Yes, I'll keep it on, Mr Whiteoak. And I'll let your mother know a thing or two when she comes back! Carrying on with that fast-looking young woman before she's in the house twenty-four hours! Yes, I'll keep my hair on and keep my place too, which is more than she does."

Mrs Nettleship returned to the basement where Eliza was removing a splinter from Renny's thumb. She was suffering more than he, as he doubled up and writhed in exaggerated agony.

"Do stand still," she implored, "or I'll never get it out."

"What is it?" demanded Mrs Nettleship.

"A splinter. Such a boy as he is for doing things to himself."

Mrs Nettleship brushed her aside and took the needle.

"Here. Let me." She felt a sensuous pleasure in her power as she probed for the splinter, and in the small male body tense in her grip. Meg looked on, vaguely conscious of the difference there would have been in the attitude of the woman had the splinter been in her thumb.

"We had cherries there today, lots of them," she said, to draw attention to herself. "I don't want any tea."

The housekeeper pursed her lips and held the splinter aloft on the needle. Renny thrust his thumb into his mouth. He bunted his red head against her shoulder.

"I want *my* tea," he said.

She ran her hand caressingly through his hair. "Tell me," she said, "where did you go?"

"To Mr Craig's. We bought a horse."

"Land alive! As though there weren't enough in the stable!" She took him by the shoulders and held him in front of her. "Was Miss Wakefield nice to Daddy, eh?"

"I don't know."

"Of course you do. Did she smile at him? And laugh at everything he said and roll her eyes at him?"

"Yes," said Renny. "She did."

"She was lovely to him," said Meg.

Mrs Nettleship turned furiously to Eliza. "What did I tell you? The moment I set eyes on her I knew the sort she was. Designing. To think that they'd be so crazy as to send her into the house with a handsome young man like Mr Philip. Could you hear what your Daddy and Miss Wakefield said?"

"He told her not to be afraid," said Meg.

"*Afraid!* Afraid of *what*?"

"Of him," said Renny.

Meg uttered a squeak of delight. "That's so. He said, 'Don't be afraid of me, Miss Wakefield. I wouldn't hurt a hair of your golden head.'"

Eliza turned a shocked pink face on Mrs Nettleship. "Oh, surely not. Surely not so soon."

"Now, children, remember *all* they said and I'll make you a pan of mpale cream."

They looked at each other.

"He said he'd take her for lots more drives." Meg's lips curved in a happy smile. "And she said how lovely and he said it was no trouble at all and she said it was hard work teaching us and he said not to tire herself."

Mrs Nettleship gave a groan. "Oh, you poor little things! What else? Try to remember!"

Mary's voice came from outside. "Children! Where are you?"

"Hide," said Mrs Nettleship. "Don't answer."

They ran on tiptoe into the pantry.

Mary knelt on the grass outside one of the windows and peered down. "Have you seen them, Mrs Nettleship?"

"They were here but they've gone."

"Oh, dear, and I suppose it's their teatime."

"Someone let them fill theirselves up on cherries. They said they didn't want any tea. That's not the way to bring up children." She drowned anything further Mary said by the rattling of pans.

"I wouldn't stay in this house," she said to Eliza, "with her as mistress. I can retire any time I want to. I have money saved. As I've told you many a time the old lady I nursed left me five thousand dollars."

The children, sitting on their heels in the cool grey light of the pantry, stared in each other's eyes, noticing their own reflections mirrored there. Now the old game had begun, the game of Nettle against the governess. But it had never been like this before. Now there was something new in Nettle's anger against the outsider. They did not feel pity for Mary. They only wondered dispassionately how long she would last. Miss Cox and Miss Turnbull had lasted quite a long while. To the children the months of their reigns seemed uncounted ages. To Renny Miss Cox was a dim memory but Miss Turnbull was very clear. Though he would not have admitted it there had been something about her he had liked—a calm cool sureness of herself, a quiet inviolate sense of her own rectitude. It fascinated him.

Now, remembering her, he stood up and, looking into space, remarked—"I consider. . . ."

Meg was irritated by his introducing someone long gone from their lives, into this present exciting moment. She caught his hand and drew him towards the door. "Come on," she urged. "Let's see where she's gone."

He suffered himself to be led but preserved a melancholy dignity. His tone became la-di-da.

"I considah," he repeated, savouring each syllable, "I considah. . . ."

He passed through the kitchen looking neither to right nor to left.

5

## THE MOORINGS

Mrs Lacey, whose father-in-law had been one of the first of the group of English naval and army officers to settle in the vicinity of Jalna and whose husband had reached the rank of Admiral in the Royal Navy, sat beside the teatable in a room which seemed scarcely large enough for the impressive Victorian furniture. The sofa and principal chairs were covered in horsehair of the best quality, their frames of ornate carved walnut. Unlike the Whiteoaks, who had brought their furniture from England, the Laceys had purchased theirs from the reliable Canadian manufacturers, Messrs Jacques and Hayes. So admirably was it made that it might well last forever, but it was inclined to impart rather a sombre look to a room even though the sunshine poured in, as it was now doing. Mrs Lacey and her daughters had made a number of gay-coloured anti-macassars for the backs of chairs and the arms of the sofa and had embroidered a pale blue silk drape for the square piano. Another drape, this one of rose colour, hung from the mantel-shelf and a third, of shell pink, decorated the picture of a square-rigger in a storm at sea. One of the daughters of the house painted on china and many examples of her work decorated the room and the whatnot. The floor was covered by a green carpet with pink flowers across which the June sunlight fell, through the small windows. Perhaps there was a little too much furniture in the room but the effect was one of long establishment and wellbeing. The daughters were the third generation of Laceys who had occupied the house and that was a considerable time in this young country.

The figure of Mrs Lacey fitted in very well with the character of the room. She was short, plump, and of pleasingly fresh complexion. Her greying hair was neatly parted in the middle and crimped above her smooth forehead. She wore a black dress with innumerable shiny black buttons down the front of the bodice, a long gold chain on the end of which was a gold watch tucked inside her belt. A delicate white ruching brightened her collar and set off the pinkness of her cheeks. She always held herself upright in her chair and seldom sat down without a piece of needlework in her hand. Her expression was almost always cheerful. She was pleased with life in general. Admiral Lacey was just the sort of husband she had wanted; her daughters just the sort of daughters. Of course she would have been pleased if they had married. They had had their chances and, if they had not taken them, well, it was rather a pity but it left them at home to be company for their father. He was very fond of them and would greatly have missed them. And after all they were only in their early thirties.

Now Violet and Ethel came into the room, their hands full of trilliums, for they had been gathering them in the nearby woods.

"Look, Mamma, aren't they heavenly?" exclaimed Violet. "I've never seen such large graceful ones."

Mrs Lacey glanced at them approvingly but said—"Do put them in water and go and tidy your hair. Philip Whiteoak is coming in. Surely you didn't forget."

47

"I'm afraid we did," laughed Violet. "It isn't very exciting to have your near neighbour to tea." It would have been truly exciting to her if it had been Nicholas who was expected. Years ago she had wanted to marry the eldest Whiteoak. He was the only man she ever had wanted. But Nicholas had known her all his life. To marry her would have been tame. So he had gone off to England and married there. After some years of marriage his wife had eloped with a young Irishman and Nicholas had divorced her. Violet had not seen him since, but occasionally, in the dreamings of solitude, she thought how strange it would be if, when Nicholas returned to visit his old home, they might still come together.

Ethel held up the trilliums, admiring them.

"I have a mind to paint them," she said. "Wouldn't they look too lovely, white on a pastel-blue ground?"

"Ethel, I do wish you wouldn't use so many superlatives. Things are always too lovely or heavenly with you."

"Only flowers. One really can't use too many adjectives to describe them."

"Well, well," her mother smiled tolerantly, "call them what you like but do put them in something and come to your tea."

"Where is Father?"

"He's here, waiting as usual," growled Admiral Lacey. He came in, looking much more good-humoured than his words sounded. "I'm always waiting for one of you three women. What are those things you've got, Ethel?"

"Wood lilies—trilliums—aren't they ravishing? They seem to have gathered all the spring into their petals."

"Really," declared Mrs Lacey, "I can't do anything with that girl."

"What I object to," said her husband, "is the way those long skirts of theirs gather up dead leaves and twigs. Think of going to the woods in such a get-up!"

"What would you have us wear?" asked Ethel.

"Shorter skirts—bloomers! We men know you have legs. Why hide them?"

"You're an immoral old darling," said Ethel, kissing him.

"There is Philip at the door." The Admiral himself strode to open it.

"Now it is too late to tidy yourselves," said Mrs Lacey, in despair. She regarded her daughters as one might regard two mettlesome ponies, proud of their spirit, yet deploring their

48

unmanageableness. This occasion was a fair example of her difficulties with them.

Philip, in loose tweeds and rather sunburned, came in. Mother and daughters greeted him with dignified familiarity. When they were seated by the table and had bread and butter on their plates and tea in their cups, Mrs Lacey asked about the new governess.

"Miss Wakefield?" returned Philip happily. "Oh, she's a peach!"

The word struck the atmosphere of the room like a blow. Then a woman laughed. And the woman was Ethel.

Mrs Lacey turned in her chair to take a good look at Philip. "*A peach!*" she echoed.

"Well, what I mean is she just fills the bill. You liked her, didn't you?"

"The Admiral and I thought her quite a nice young woman."

"It was awfully kind of you to look after her on the voyage."

"It was a pleasure." The Admiral spoke rather too heartily. His wife turned her head to look at him.

He put an extra lump of sugar in his tea and stirred it stubbornly. "I quite agree with Philip," he said. "The girl is a perfect——"

Before he could utter the name of that fruit which had suddenly become obnoxious to Mrs Lacey, she drowned him out.

"Guy," she said, "if you were to die would you like to think that a daughter of yours, only a few months after your death, would deck herself in such colours as Miss Wakefield wore?"

The Admiral marked his words with his forefinger. "Her father made her promise faithfully that she would not put on black for him. I call it sensible. Who wants to see a pretty young woman trailing black garments?"

"I do, when it is seemly, and I am sure that Ethel and Violet do too  Don't you, girls?" But her daughters rather disconcertingly agreed with their father.

"Do you mean to tell me"—Mrs Lacey looked outraged—"that you would wear a spray of *yellow* poppies in a hat, with your father scarcely cold in his grave?"

"By George, this is a depressing conversation!" exclaimed the Admiral.

"If Father wished it," declared Ethel, "I should wear yellow poppies."

49

"Good girl," said her father. "It's understood, then. You are to wear yellow poppies and Violet is to wear red."

"I dislike such foolish talk." Mrs Lacey was getting annoyed. "I will go into black and the girls will go into black."

"Who for?" demanded the Admiral.

"For you."

"Well, I like that!" His colour was rising . "What makes you so sure I'm going to die first?"

"Men do," said Mrs Lacey. This was unanswerable. The Admiral looked downcast.

"My mother," said Philip, "put on widow's weeds after my father's death and is never going to take them off."

"And quite right," said Mrs Lacey, and nodded several times as though affirming that she had every intention of doing the same, though she would not hurt her husband's feelings by saying so.

"After all," Philip said reflectively, "men sometimes do outlive their wives. I'm a widower."

"Good!" exclaimed Admiral Lacey heartily, and realized almost at once that he should not have said that.

Violet interrupted tactfully—"Do tell us how the children like Miss Wakefield, Philip."

"Very much indeed. Yesterday we all drove to a Mr Craig's along the lake shore and I bought a beautiful mare. We got along famously. Between threats and bribes I persuaded the little rascals to behave."

Ethel asked—"Do tell us about these Craigs. I hear that they are very rich."

"I believe they are. And by the way, Admiral, there's another widower!"

"Splendid," exclaimed the Admiral, "and, by jingo, here comes a third!"

Dr Ramsay's spare figure could be seen passing the window. Violet ran to let him in. He entered with a diagnostic look round, as if, though no one in the room was ill, they were, at any moment, likely to be. All three of the younger ones he had brought into the world. He had seen Mrs Lacey through three accouchements. He had seen the Admiral laid low by sciatica. In humble postures all had lain on beds before him.

He declined food but accepted tea. Philip took two more slices of thin bread and butter, turned them together and proceeded to eat them with relish.

"I suppose," said Dr Ramsay to Ethel and Violet, "that you are delighted to have your parents home again." He said this with a twinkle, as though it were understood that they had been up to tricks when authority was removed.

"Oh, yes," they answered.

"It was the first time," Mrs Lacey remarked, "that we had left them alone and we did feel a little anxious."

"Not me," said her husband, "I never gave them a second thought."

"Really, Guy, you ought to be ashamed of yourself." But Mrs Lacey laughed.

"I don't know what it is to be ashamed."

"Come, come," said Dr Ramsay. "Don't tell me you are never ashamed."

"Never. Are you?"

"Many a time."

Those present looked at him incredulously. He paid no attention to their expressions but quoted:

> "God knows I'm no the thing I should be,
> Nor am I even the thing I could be."

He stirred his tea with gravity and even melancholy.

It was one thing for him to express such a sentiment. Quite another for his friends to agree. All hastened to disagree.

"Well," said Philip, "I've spent a good part of my life in feeling or trying to feel ashamed of myself. With stern parents and two older brothers and a sister I've always been hearing someone say—'Philip, you ought to be ashamed of yourself.' "

"Your father doted on you," said Mrs Lacey.

"And so does your mother," added the Admiral.

"I'm not so sure about that," he answered. "I'm often a disappointment to her. I look so much like the governor, yet I can't hold a candle to him."

"Ah, well," sighed the doctor, "there is no doubt that man reached his highest point of excellence in morals, manners, and intellect during the last two or three generations. From now on, there will be deterioration. If any of you are living fifty years from now you are likely to see a miserable world."

The two young women giggled.

Dr Ramsay turned abruptly to Philip. "I've been to your house," he said, "to have a look at the governess but she was off somewhere. I hope she's not one of the sort that is always gadding."

"It's hard to say," said Philip. "She's only been with us three days."

"Is it possible," exclaimed Mrs Lacey, "that you, the children's grandfather, haven't seen her yet?"

"I have not been invited."

"Come back with me," said Philip, "and I'll put her through her paces."

"Philip, you are disgraceful," declared Mrs Lacey. "But you must be prepared for one thing, Dr Ramsay, and that is to see her in the gayest clothes, though her father has been dead only a few months."

Philip pushed out his lips. "All her clothes aren't gay," he said. "She was dressed very simply this morning."

"I should hope she would be." Mrs Lacey spoke with a little asperity. "Teaching two children their multiplication tables is scarcely a time for fancy dress."

"Come now, Mrs Lacey, don't be hard on the girl. That's not like you."

Philip patted her knee and she took his hand with a coy look and held it a moment. She was more flirtatious than either of her daughters.

"What like is she?" asked the doctor.

"Tell him what you called her when you first came, Philip," cried Ethel. "I dare you to."

"What was that?" asked Dr Ramsay, sharply.

"Come and see for yourself, sir."

"Why have an English governess?" asked Ethel.

"Much better have a good Scotswoman," said the doctor. "That is what I have always advocated."

"Why not a Canadian?" asked Ethel.

"They don't seem to go in for governessing," answered Philip. "But I do think it would be a good idea. I think we have clung too much to Old Country ways in our neighbourhood."

Now the Admiral spoke. "The Whiteoaks, the Vaughans, the Laceys, and the others who first settled here, promised each other to preserve their British principles, culture, and——"

"Prejudices," put in Philip.

"Very well. Prejudices. Prejudice against making a fetish of material progress—against all the hurry-scurry after money that goes on in the big American cities. They wanted to lead contented peaceful lives and teach their children to fear God, honour the Queen, fight for her if necessary. In short, behave like gentlemen."

"I'm not setting myself up to criticize you, sir. I only mean that this country is growing and it's bound to grow in a new way. Why, we've got a population of several millions. We can't go on modelling ourselves on the Old Land. Now you went into the Royal Navy as a youth——"

"There was no Canadian Navy and the sea was in my blood."

"I know. But the consequence is that you're just as English as your father was. You married an Englishwoman."

"Oh, Philip, do you hold that against me?" Mrs Lacey gave him a charming smile.

"Never." He smiled back. "But this is an English household, with two English daughters."

"We were born here," said Ethel.

"I love Canada," said Violet.

Philip ignored them. "Now there's my mother. She's just as Irish as ever she was. God knows she can't help it! And my sister and two brothers live in England. When they come to Jalna they expect to see my children brought up exactly like children in England. It can't be done. I think that, as time goes on, the people of this country will probably be a good deal Americanized."

"Heaven forbid!" said Admiral Lacey.

Mrs Lacey turned to the doctor, who sat gazing at the ceiling with his arms folded.

"What are your feelings about all this, Dr Ramsay?" she asked.

Without taking his eyes from the ceiling he declaimed, in sonorous tones:

"My heart's in the Highlands, my heart is not here;
My heart's in the Highlands a-chasing the deer."

# 6

# GETTING BETTER ACQUAINTED

LEAVING Dr Ramsay in the sitting-room Philip ran upstairs to look for Mary and the children. At the foot of the second flight of stairs he stopped and listened. Then he called softly:

"Meggie!"

All was silent above. He went up and looked into the children's room. It was empty. He went to the door of Mary's room and tapped.

"Miss Wakefield!" he called low.

"Yes?" Her answer came quickly but she did not open the door.

"Look here, my father-in-law's downstairs and he's anxious to meet you. He's a stickler for convention—going into mourning and that sort of thing. I wonder if you could find a dark-coloured dress to put on. I hate to bother you but you know what the Scotch are. I think we'd better make a good impression, don't you?"

There was the tone of a conspirator in his voice that filled Mary with a delightful eagerness to do his will. She said:

"Thank you so much for telling me. If you'll just wait a moment I'll show you what I have."

Mary had lived in an unconventional atmosphere in London with her father. Now, slipping into a dressing-gown, she opened the door a little way and stood before Philip holding up a dark blue skirt in one hand and a white blouse in the other. He scarcely saw the garments. His eyes were held by the pearl-like whiteness of her arms and neck, the V-shaped bit of chest exposed.

"Splendid," he said. "Will you get into them then and come right down?"

Philip did not know and could not learn how to behave towards a governess, any more than Mary knew how to behave like one. She gave a happy little laugh.

"I'll be down before you can count ten," she promised.

He turned away and almost ran into Mrs Nettleship, her arms full of the children's clothes freshly laundered. Her expression was a strange mixture of shock and the confirmation of her worst suspicions. She elaborately moved aside for Philip to pass, though the passage was not narrow.

"I beg your pardon," she said.

"What for?" asked Philip.

"Well, I have my felt slippers on and they don't make a bit of noise. I thought I might have frightened the lady." There was a faintly derisive lingering on the word 'lady'.

"Miss Wakefield has nothing to be frightened about."

He was still frowning as he re-entered the sitting-room.

"So she's not to be found," said Dr Ramsay.

"She'll be down directly."

"Oh. You say your mother engaged her?"

"Among them they did."

"I should have prefaired a Scotswoman."

"Why didn't you say so then?"

"I have always said so."

"My mother doesn't get on with the Scotch."

"Scots," corrected Dr Ramsay.

"Scots. She doesn't get on with them."

"She gets on with me."

"She's had to, sir. You're her doctor."

"When is your mother to return?"

"Next month."

"You must miss her sorely."

"I do indeed," said Philip cheerfully.

There was a light step in the hall and Mary stood in the doorway. Not only did she wear the severely plain dark skirt but about her neck she had tied a black ribbon that finished in a bow at her nape. But severity ended there. Her golden hair curled abundantly about her sensitive face. Her lips wore their odd smile that bent downward a little, as though the capacity for pain ever lingered near. Philip introduced her to his father-in-law. When they had shaken hands and sat down, Dr Ramsay said:

"You have undertaken a great responsibility, Miss Wakefield."

"Yes, indeed." She straightened her slender shoulders as though to show her willingness.

"It is no light matter to undertake the teaching of two highly intelligent children."

"No, indeed." Mary drew her brows together to show how conscious she was of the weight of the matter.

"Have you a university degree?"

"I'm afraid I haven't but——"

"Have you considerable experience?"

"No." Colour rose to her forehead. "You see, I was engaged at the last minute. There had to be someone to take the place of the one who'd broken both legs. I understood that character was required rather than scholarship. That is—under the circumstances—and Mr Ernest Whiteoak thought—and I thought——" She turned her eyes in desperation towards Philip.

"And I think so, too," he supplemented firmly.

Dr Ramsay waved his hand and declaimed:

> "Gie me ae spark o' Nature's fire,
> That's a' the learning I desire."

Mary said, without hesitation—"From Robert Burns."

Dr Ramsay could scarcely have felt more pessimistic about Mary's attainments than he had been feeling the moment before but now a delighted smile lit his stern features.

"Amazing!" he exclaimed. "I did not think there was an Englishwoman living who could have placed that quotation."

"One of my father's best friends," returned Mary easily, "was a——"

On the side of Dr Ramsay where Philip sat the doctor was a little deaf. Philip, under his breath, said the word—"Scot."

"Scot," repeated Mary loudly.

Dr Ramsay uttered a bark of joyous laughter.

"A Scot, eh? I'd have thought the less of you if you had called him a Scotchman."

"Scot sounds so much better," said Mary. "This friend of my father's—this Scot—used often to come to our rooms in London and he would quote Burns."

"Well, well. And you like his poetry?"

"I love it."

"I'll lend you all his poems. I have them very handsomely bound. Yes, I'll lend them all to you."

Dr Ramsay fell into dreamy silence for a space. In his mind's eye he saw the room in London where Mary's father and his friends foregathered and in their midst a Scot, bearing a remarkable likeness to himself, who quoted Burns while the rest of the company hung with deference on his words.

Mary thanked him for his offer of the poems and after some

agreeable conversation, during which he promised to look in on her at lesson time and give her a little help with the children, he left. Philip and Mary were alone together. They still were standing after having seen Dr Ramsay to the door.

Philip turned his head to look at her. His eyes had a roguish light in them.

"You did well, Miss Wakefield," he said. "You did amazingly well. To think of your knowing that quotation!"

"I feel a humbug."

"Nonsense. We've got to get on with people. You can see for yourself that the old gentleman could be difficult. You've been very clever."

"And how kind it was of you to warn me about my dress."

"Well, I thought it might be safer."

She faced him, with an appeal for candour in her eyes.

"Mr Whiteoak, do you yourself find my clothes unsuitable for a governess?"

"No. Not at all. I like them."

The warmth of his tone, his approval of her clothes, thrilled her with a new sort of confidence, of pleasure in herself.

"I'm so glad, because these things I have on are my only really plain clothes. I'm afraid I'm rather given to frills and flounces."

"So am I. I love 'em."

They smiled into each other's eyes.

Philip's half-grown spaniel puppy, Jake, came from under the table. The dark red table cover was large and hung almost to the floor. Its edge now hung draped about the spaniel's shoulders as he raised his eyes pleadingly to Philip's.

For some reason it was necessary to Mary to have an outlet for her emotion. She bent down, took the puppy's head between her hands, and kissed him.

"Dear doggie," she breathed.

"You like dogs?"

"Oh, yes. I've always wanted one of my own."

"And never had one? What a shame!" He walked about the room, picked up his pipe and laid it down again. Then he said—"I think you're going to be happy here."

"I'm sure I shall." At that moment she had no doubt of it.

"I was afraid of what you might be. Prim, you know, perhaps a stickler for the proprieties. Like Miss Turnbull."

"I'm not conventional enough."

"Neither am I. So we shall get on together."

In another moment he had left her and she stood at the foot of the stairs alone. The house was very quiet. She put her hands on the newel-post and caressed the glossy bunches of grapes carved there. The doors of the drawing-room and Philip's mother's room were closed. Mary felt that there were presences behind these doors, longing to open them and come out to crowd about her and inspect her. These were the shadowy forms of Philip's mother, his brothers, his sister, attenuated by distance, but becoming more solid every day. Their steps sounded in the distance. The day would come when they would open the doors. Mary felt inexpressibly relieved that she would have this coming month in which to get used to her situation, to gain some control over the children, to enjoy—yes, to enjoy—being alone with Philip Whiteoak. She could not move from the spot where she stood without first living again the enchanting moments when they two had talked intimately together after Dr Ramsay's departure. She recalled each word he had spoken. She looked into the mirror of her mind and saw every line of his features. Did she dwell on them because he was handsome? she asked herself. No, a thousand times no. She had seen handsome men before. They were no rarity in London. Perhaps it was because his face showed such a power of enjoying his own life and the world about him. She recalled her father's face, in which bitter remembrances of the past met apprehension of the future. What a contrast to this man who seemed to be asking no questions of life but just accepting it in its fullness.

Mrs Nettleship was crossing the hall when Mary moved up the stairway. Mrs Nettleship stopped stock-still by the newel-post, as though examining it for the fingerprints of some criminal. Then she took the corner of her starched apron and began to polish it.

"It's very pretty, isn't it?" remarked Mary, pleasantly, over her shoulder.

"It ought to be. All them grapes was done by a woodcarver in Quebec."

"Dear me."

Mary, accustomed to the rare and intricate carving in the medieval architecture of London, was not impressed. Something in her tone infuriated Mrs Nettleship. It was not that she greatly admired the carving herself but she felt a growing dislike for and distrust of Mary. She straightened herself and glared up the stairway.

"What's the matter with it?" she demanded.

Mary was too astonished to reply.

At that moment Renny, running along the passage above, cast himself on the banister and came sliding down at frightening speed. The two women instinctively drew back from his untrammelled masculinity. But as he reached the bottom Mrs Nettleship caught him angrily by the shoulder.

"You're not allowed to do that!" she said vehemently. "If I tell——"

"I am allowed!" he shouted. "Grand-daddy prescribed it for me." He tore himself from her grasp and flew out through the door, giving her a daring look as he passed.

"You come back here!"

"You go to—pot!"

Mary burst out laughing. It needed no more to make Mrs Nettleship hate her.

In the weeks that followed she did all she could to hamper Mary in her attempt to control the children. To them she made fun of Mary behind her back. She encouraged them to be late for lessons, to hide when called. Once or twice Mary had a mind to tell Philip of their behaviour and of the encouragement in it they got from the housekeeper but she could not bear to cloud for one instant the brief periods they spent alone together. She strained towards these more and more. The hours of her day became divided into three distinct periods. There was the time spent in teaching the children and looking after their clothes, the meals eaten with them, at which Philip often was present, when he good-humouredly chaffed them or, with sudden promptitude, reprimanded them, and with what a quick response! Never did he embarrass her by probings into their progress but when Renny rattled off the names of all the sovereigns of England in verse or when Meg named every cape in the British Isles, scarcely taking breath because she knew that, if she stopped, she could not continue without going back to the beginning, he was delighted.

There were the times when they were alone together, perhaps discussing the children's lessons but more likely she listening while he told of the achievements of his horses, or of some advantageous sale he had made. She could not discover whether he bred horses for pleasure or profit. There seemed to be plenty of money for everything at Jalna. There were a number of men employed on the farm and in the stables, all well paid and seemingly well satisfied. Certainly Philip White-oak took life easily and, wherever he went, carried with him an atmosphere of wellbeing.

The third period of Mary's day was when in solitude she wandered through the woods. In England she had known London and the seaside. Here, for the first time in her life she stood gazing up into the dark branches of pines, remnant of the virgin forest, the ground beneath her densely carpeted by their rust-brown needles. Here was silence such as Mary had never known before, a deep resin-scented silence unbroken even by bird-song. In the woods where maple, oak, and birch throve together the birds, in their early summer rapture, sought for supremacy in song, each trilling as though he would drown out all others. But when they flew into the pinewood they were silent and rested for a while in the coolness of these sombre boughs. They did not build their nests there.

Mary would throw herself on the ground, in the deepest shadow, and stare up into their pointed pinnacles lost in un-framed thoughts, in the ecstasy of isolating herself from all living beings—save one. His presence came into the wood with her. Sometimes she tried to forget him but she could not. Almost always she consciously allowed her mind to dwell on his features, one by one. His hair that at the temples was as fair as hers, his tranquil eyes that could light like a mischievous schoolboy's, his fine mouth and chin, his strong body. How terrible it would have been, she thought, if she had never come here, never seen this place—never had the image of him as companion to her solitude.

One late afternoon he came into the wood in the flesh. She was lying on her breast, her cheek pressed on the pine needles. She heard a step and then saw him walking along the path, quite close to her. She had often pictured just such a scene; herself, in the loneliness of the wood, his coming upon her, startling them both. She had not permitted her imagination to go further but had allowed it to hover only on the verge of a scene of love. This dark wood should, she felt, be the setting for none but a profound emotion. When she was here she did not want to *feel* but just to be dreaming, on the fringe of thought. She kept very still and he passed without seeing her.

The weather turned hot, hotter than anything Mary had

ever experienced. The air was vibrant with heat. Flowers came into bloom, drooped and withered before their time. Cattle and horses stood in the shade of trees switching their tails to keep off the flies. Philip declared that it was too hot for study and the children ran wild.

"I am doing nothing," she said almost vehemently, meeting Philip in the hall, "doing nothing to earn my salary. It isn't fair to you."

"You'll find plenty to do later on." He looked curiously at the book she carried. "What are you reading?"

"Tennyson. I love his poems, don't you?"

"I confess I don't know much about them. My father-in-law is always quoting Burns. My mother Thomas Moore. My brother Ernest thinks there is no poetry worth his bothering about but Shakespeare's. Somehow Tennyson has been overlooked." He gave Mary his friendly smile. "Read me something of his, will you?"

She felt bewildered by the request, almost alarmed. "Oh, I'm not sure that I could find anything to interest you."

"Of course you could."

"I know I'd read badly."

"But why?" Now he was laughing at her.

"I should be nervous."

"Come now. Not with me. I'm the least critical person in the world. You say you're not earning your salary. Here is a way to earn it. A benighted Colonial horse dealer, sitting at your feet, yearning to hear Tennyson read."

"Where shall we sit?" Mary asked, suddenly determined to do it.

"Come with me and I'll show you the coolest spot hereabouts."

He led the way across the lawn blazing in sunlight and along a path down into a ravine which by its deep shade and the sound of the stream that ran through it to the lake gave an air of mystery to the place, so Mary thought and was instantly pleased by it. It was in truth cooler here. Philip took her hand as they descended the steep.

"Gather up your skirt," he said. "There are brambles here." His hand clasped hers firmly. She was conscious of the clasp of his hand through all her being.

On a mossy ledge he paused. The stream, green in the shadow, reflected the rushes, the boughs of evergreens. A rustic bridge crossed it and under the bridge the shadow was deepest. Philip sank down at Mary's feet with a sigh.

"What could be better than this?" he asked, looking up at her.

She sank beside him. "It's heavenly. And so still. Except for the murmuring of the river."

"It's a very little river," he said, "but I love it."

"Jalna is beautiful."

"It's a pretty good place," he agreed. "But we've talked about it before. Now I want to hear you read." He settled himself expectantly, looking up into her face, his own dappled by a narrow spear of sunlight slanting through the leaves.

She opened the book. She was conscious of the trembling of her hands and feared her voice would do the same. To gain time she showed him the portrait of Lord Tennyson in the front, as she might have shown it to Renny.

"I think it is a noble face," she said.

He agreed but he was admiring her slender white hands.

Presently she gathered herself together and began to read. It was easier than she had thought. He lay resting on his elbows, very still. There was a comfort in his presence. Perhaps her voice encouraged the birds in that dim coolness, for they began to sing quietly all about.

Philip listened, but only half-attentive to the meaning, till he heard the words:

> "No more subtle master under heaven
> Than is the maiden passion for a maid,
> Not only to keep down the base in man
> But teach high thought, and amiable words
> And courtliness, and the desire of fame,
> And love of truth, and all that makes a man."

He laid his hand on the page.

"Stop," he said, "and then read that again."

She was confused. "That . . . which?" she stammered.

"You know." He took his hand from the page and repeated the first line.

"Was I reading too fast?" she asked.

"No. I just wanted to hear it again."

"Do you like it? Shall I go on?"

"Please do."

She re-read the passage and continued, but less clearly. Her composure was shaken. Philip had picked up a small switch and was gently beating the ground with it as though to the rhythm of the poetry.

Neither saw Dr Ramsay descending the opposite slope and he did not see them till he stood on the rustic bridge. If Mary's composure had been shaken, his now suffered a tremor, as of an approaching earthquake. He could scarcely believe his eyes. Philip lying on the ground, at Miss Wakefield's feet! She dressed, not as he had heretofore seen her but in some filmy garment, with elbow sleeves! Her body curved, in a languishing attitude!

"Dear God!" muttered the doctor. "Has it come to this?"

He strode on across the bridge and mounted the path towards them with a sharp crackling of twigs. His foot dislodged a stone and it bounded down the slope and splashed into the stream. Now Philip and Mary became aware of his approach.

He was panting a little as he spoke. "I would not dream of interrupting you," he said, "especially in such a pleasant occupation, but I had brought the volume of Robert Burns's poems I promised you, Miss Wakefield. Twice before I brought them but could not find you. Ah, I see you have other poetry to engross you. Never mind. I will take it away again."

"Please don't," cried Mary. "I want them very much."

He all but threw the book into her lap.

Philip got to his feet. "Hot, isn't it?" he said.

"Yes. It is exceedingly hot driving along dusty country roads on my rounds. You are fortunate, you and Miss Wakefield, in having no duties to perform."

He strode up the path and left them.

"You'd never think he was seventy, would you?" remarked Philip, looking after him.


7

FAMILY CIRCLE COMPLETE

FOUR SUCCESSIVE Sunday mornings Mary had gone to the little country church with Philip Whiteoak and his children. As she had sat in the family pew with Renny on her right and Meg on her left and watched the people of the neighbourhood enter and take their long accustomed places she had experienced a feeling of completeness she never before had known. In London she often had stolen out quietly on a Sunday morning so as not to disturb her father and gone to service. But it had been to a church in a great city where she was surrounded by strangers. Now, in the intimacy of this small but solid building, with faces with which she was growing familiar about her, she found a deep satisfaction not so much in religion, as in a new gladness in herself.

Philip did not sit with Mary and the children but went into the vestry with Mr Pink, whose father had been rector before him, and donned a surplice. He assisted the rector by reading the Lessons. Now Mary had the opportunity to look at him unobserved, to compare him with the portrait of his father, to Captain Whiteoak's disadvantage; to compare him with all the attractive men she ever had known, to their disadvantage. Even the slight impediment in his speech only increased her pleasure in the reading, giving her, for the moment, a kind of protective maternal feeling towards him.

On the fifth Sunday the hymn, 'Eternal Father, Strong to Save', was sung, and to judge by the heartiness which Mr Pink, who had a deep bass, and the choir and the congregation threw into it, all had an earnest desire to draw the attention of the Almighty to the fact that five members of the Whiteoak family, including Sir Edwin Buckley, were en route for Jalna. On either side of Mary the children raised their clear pipes. She noticed that both pronounced peril—'peryil'. Meg knew all the words but Renny only the first verse. After singing it he was silent till the last line of each successive verse when his penetrating treble joined hers in—'For those in peryil on the sea'. Mary was thankful that there were only four verses to the hymn. If there had been one more she was sure she would have disgraced herself by giving way to laughter. For some reason her emotions, gay or sad, were near to the surface in those days. She could not understand herself, for at times she would almost uncontrollably laugh at ridiculous nothings with the children, which she knew was bad for discipline, and at other times, usually at night, she would discover that, for no reason at all, her eyes were full of tears.

As the time of arrival drew near, two women could scarcely have been more in their element than Mrs Nettleship and Eliza. From morning till night they fought with dirt and disorder in a frenzy of preparation. Mary felt that never before had she known what real cleanliness could be. Carpets were taken outdoors and beaten, rugs were shaken, walls were wiped down, windows polished till they might not have been there, so transparent were they, brass and silver glittered. The drawing-room, which had been swathed in dust-covers because Philip used only the library, now was discovered as a handsome room. Mary stood in it alone, absorbing its unknown atmosphere, the faint smell of an Indian rug, the upholstery, the cushions on the sofa where unknown heads had lain, thinking what thoughts? The china figures on the mantel, the jade monkey and the ivory elephants in the cabinet, all looked at her with an un-friendly air, as though by no possible means could they have any connection with her. There was music on the piano. The air was full of its far-off vibration. Soon the piano would come to life again but not for her, though, later on, she was supposed to give Meg music lessons. The ormolu clock had been wound and in its ardent ticking seemed anxious to make up for lost time. A bunch of roses, pressed tightly into a vase, already drooped a little as though unable to withstand the steady advance of the returning personalities.

All day the children were beside themselves from excitement. They could talk or think of nothing but the presents that would be brought to them. There was no use in trying to curb them. Mary wandered about, longing to hide herself some-where in the woods, but it was steadily raining, a sweet-smelling gentle rain following a night of electrical storms. Mary did not see Philip all day. She felt lost. She wandered about, looking in at the four bedrooms which had been pre-pared: Mrs Whiteoak's with its rich-coloured bedspread, the other three with snow-white counterpanes and huge, stiffly starched pillow shams. Even the spaniels were excited. The puppy, Jake, ran snuffling into each of the freshly prepared rooms and lifted his leg against a leg of the four-poster that was to be occupied by Sir Edwin and Lady Buckley.

The carriage was to go to the village railway station to meet the local train which connected, though not very efficiently, with the train from Montreal. Both had been late, and the evening was drawing in when the sound of horses' hoofs told of the arrival. Renny's cheeks were hot from excitement, Meg hopped ceaselessly from one foot to the other. Both wore their Sunday clothes. Mary too had put on one of her best dresses, a pale pink chambray, with a flounce on the skirt and frills in the elbow sleeves. She had taken pains with her hair, which responded in delightful puffs and little curls.

When Philip had encountered her just before leaving to drive to the station he had started back in consternation. He should have warned her not to dress up like that! By Jove, what would his mother and the Buckleys think? But—after all, she'd been engaged in England. He'd had nothing to do with it. Mary exclaimed, excitedly, quite ready to be thrown into panic:

"Is anything wrong, Mr Whiteoak?"

"No, no"—he smiled reassuringly—"I thought I saw a spider. But I was mistaken."

"On *me*?"

"Yes. But I was mistaken. I'm in quite a rush. I'm on my way to the station." But he lingered. Suddenly he regretted the coming of all these relatives—even his mother. It had been very pleasant, he and Miss Wakefield alone with the children. Her presence had been charming to return to. He had scarcely realized how charming. And he had never seen her look quite so lovely as at this moment—when he was about to lose her, he almost had thought. Well certainly things would never be the same again. Looking back over the past month he regretted lost opportunities to be alone with Mary. There had been no more reading aloud of poetry since the day when Dr Ramsay had come upon them in the ravine. That was a week ago. But —if he chose—surely he might be read to! Who was to stop him being read to, he'd like to know? He looked truculently at Mary.

"Yes?" she inquired, her whole body expressing interrogation.

"I was just thinking."

"Rather stern thoughts," she suggested. She found it so hard not to be too familiar with him.

Now he smiled. "They were about you, Miss Wakefield."

"I hope I have not given you cause to frown."

"Some day I'll tell you," he answered. "But now I must be off. Picture my family kicking their heels in the railway station. By Jove, they'll never forgive me!"

Mary, looking after him, thought—'When he says "his family", he means his *mother*. She must be an odious old lady. I'm beginning to dislike her.'

66

She drew a deep breath of nervous tension. All the rooms in the house were alive now, conscious of her, antagonistic to her. She belonged nowhere, not even in her own bedroom. The children ran past her as though they did not see her.

"Are you tidy?" she called after them. "Are your hands clean?"

They gave derisive laughs and ran on.

Jake came panting and snuffling along the passage. He ran into the room prepared for the Buckleys and again lifted his leg against the leg of the four-poster. Again no one saw him.

Mary descended the stairs and found Eliza lighting an ornate brass oil lamp in the drawing-room. Eliza was always pleasant when Mrs Nettleship was not about. Now she remarked:

"It seems early for lighting the lamp but Mrs Whiteoak does like to see things cheerful-looking when she comes home."

"No rooms could look brighter or more polished than these," said Mary. She raised her eyes to the crystal chandelier. "Every prism glitters."

Eliza was pleased. "I took each one off and cleaned it separately. Mrs Whiteoak always has a good look at it when she comes home. When she has a party we light all the candles in it. And, of course, on her birthday."

Jake lolloped down the stairs and looked into the drawing-room. He raised himself on his hind legs and stood against Mary. Mrs Nettleship came from the basement. She gave Mary and Jake looks of equal disapproval.

"I won't have that dog about my clean rooms," she declared and clapped her hands vindictively at the spaniel.

He uttered a yelp of horror, flinging himself past Mary and almost knocking her down. He rushed through the open front door, still yelping. Outside he spied his decorous parents and flung himself at them for protection. First he tried to push himself inside his sire's body, then, failing that, his mother's. Mrs Nettleship slammed the door after him.

Nearly an hour dragged itself by. Again and again Mary took her watch from where it was tucked inside her belt and looked at its laggard face. Her own face burned. Now the lamps were needed, for it was almost dark.

Horses' hoofs clattered on the drive.

Mary fled upstairs to her own room.

There she stood in the open doorway listening. The hall seemed full of people. Surely those few could not make all that

67

noise. Above the talking came every now and again the sound of a laugh, almost masculine in its vitality, yet with a feminine gaiety. Later she heard luggage being carried up the stairs. She heard voices in the bedrooms below. She heard a man's deep voice call—"Come here for a minute, Ernest." Then the voice of the Mr Whiteoak she had met in London replied—"All right, Nicholas. I'll be there when I've put on a fresh collar."

Mary resolutely closed her own door. She made up her mind to stay where she was till sent for. She would read, and yes—she would smoke a cigarette! Mary's own father had introduced her to this decadent habit, and it had grown on her to such an extent that, in times of stress, she not infrequently sought its comfort. In ordinary times one a day sufficed her. She had brought several packets with her.

Now she sat down, with both windows open, so there might be a current of air to carry away the smoke. She put a cigarette between her lips and lighted it, taking care to throw the match as far as possible into the shrubbery. She inhaled gently. She took up the copy of *Lady Audley's Secret* which had kept her awake for hours the night before, and began to read. Either the house was quieter now or she had succeeded in isolating herself. She started when a peremptory rap came on the door. The cigarette had been finished long ago but she dashed a little good scent on her hair and collar to allay any lingering odour of tobacco.

"Miss Wakefield!" called Renny.

She opened the door.

"You're wanted downstairs. My grandmother wants to see you. And what do you suppose they brought me? A train that winds up and runs right across the room! And a music-box for Meggie! Come and see!"

He caught her by the hand, with a warmth he had never before shown, and dragged her through the door.

"You smell!" he exlaimed.

"Of what?" she demanded, startled.

"It's nice," he said, and tugged at her again.

He was still holding her hand when they entered the drawing-room. That close grasp gave her strength. Anxiously she looked about her, seeking the figure of Mrs Whiteoak.

But there was no need to seek. Her vigorous presence caught and held the eye, though all those in the room, save one, were

68

strongly individual, and even he, Sir Edwin, was far from insignificant, if only because of his contrast to the others. Mary had expected to see an old woman, but, at sixty-eight, Adeline Whiteoak might have passed for fifty, had it not been for the clothes, which were of a massive cut, and the fact that she wore a lace cap with ribbons on her head. The cap was wired to give it body. It also added to her look of imperiousness. There was little of grey in her hair which still retained a hint of russet. Her handsomely cut, aquiline features, her expressive brown eyes, her fine teeth, brought an admiring shine into Mary's own eyes. Above all, she was smiling and Mary smiled in return.

"How do you do, Miss Wakefield?" She held out her hand and Mary's hand was enfolded in it. Renny still gripped the fingers of the other.

"Come," he persisted, "come and see my train."

It seemed to Mary that at least a dozen voices ordered him to be quiet.

"I hope you are getting on well," said Mrs Whiteoak. "I hope you are able to put some knowledge into the children's heads."

"I'm trying hard." Mary's voice was scarcely audible.

"I think I must be getting deaf." Mrs Whiteoak cupped her ear in her palm. "I can't hear you."

"I'm getting on nicely, thank you." Now her voice came clearly and, she felt, a little too loud.

Meg spoke up. "We haven't had lessons lately. It's too hot."

Her grandmother's bright glance discovered her. "There are other things besides lessons," she said.

"What other things?" asked Renny.

"Behaving yourself. Does Miss Wakefield make you behave?"

He gave a peal of laughter.

"Is there a party or something?" demanded Mrs Whiteoak, looking Mary over.

Her dress! She should not have put on that gay dress! She felt ready to sink through the floor.

Ernest Whiteoak now came forward. His expression was faintly apologetic, though whether to his mother or to her, Mary could not guess. But he shook hands kindly.

"It seems quite long while," he said, "since I interviewed you, on behalf of my mother."

"And saw Miss Wakefield through your mother's eyes, I'll be bound," added Mrs Whiteoak. She turned to Mary. "How old are you, my dear?"

"Twenty-four."

"H'm. That quite tallies with my son's description of you. He said you were—youngish, that your hair had not gone grey and that you had your own teeth. Well—so have I and I'm sixty-eight."

Mary was too confused to be certain whom Mrs Whiteoak was making fun of. She stood looking down at the older woman, fascinated.

Renny had run off and joined Meg with their toys in the sitting-room.

"Now I had better introduce you all round," said Mrs Whiteoak. "Nicholas, Augusta, Edwin—Miss Wakefield. Miss Wakefield—Mr Whiteoak, Sir Edwin and Lady Buckley."

The tall dark gentleman with the moustache, who was standing by a window talking to Philip, smiled pleasantly and bowed. Sir Edwin and Lady Buckley inclined their heads without smiling.

"Where are the children?" demanded Mrs Whiteoak.

"They've taken their toys to the library," answered Philip.

Mrs Whiteoak gave an imperious wave of the hand towards Mary. "You'd better join 'em," she said. "They'll be up to mischief." Mary noticed the hand, long and supple. She saw the flash of rubies and diamonds on it.

With a little bow Mary withdrew. Scarcely was she in the hall when she heard Mrs Whiteoak say:

"Somebody please shut that door."

It was closed and the six people left in the drawing-room exchanged looks of untrammelled intimacy. Nicholas was the first to speak.

"A lovely creature," he said. "A very lovely creature." He turned to his brother Ernest. "Upon my word, Ernie, you've a very pretty taste in women."

"She looked quite different in London," replied Ernest hastily.

"Doubtless the climate here has rejuvenated her," said Sir Edwin, who was small and neat and mouse-coloured.

"Are we to take that remark seriously, Edwin?" asked his wife, who was tall, with a massive curled fringe about her forehead and a plum-coloured dress. She spoke in a rich contralto voice.

"I offer it as the only possible explanation," he replied. "Ernest himself says she looks different."

"If she looked as she does now, Ernest must have been demented," declared Lady Buckley.

"What's the matter with her looks?" demanded Philip.

"Everything," returned his sister. "She looks and dresses like an actress."

It went against the grain of Adeline Whiteoak to agree with her daughter, so she ignored this remark and asked of Ernest:

"How was she different in London?"

"Well, Mamma, it's hard to say. But there was an impalpable difference."

"I do not engage governesses on impalpable grounds."

"We never should have trusted Ernest," said Lady Buckley. "He is too easily carried away by a little charm."

Ernest replied tartly—"I am the only one of us who has not been carried away into matrimony."

Sir Edwin giggled. "My charm was too much for Augusta, eh, Augusta?"

His wife looked at him as though she failed to discover a remnant of charm in him. She said:

"A girl like that is no companion for the children."

"What do you want me to do?" exclaimed Philip hotly. "Turn her out because she's pretty and wears pretty clothes? Well—I refuse. You sent her to me. She's a damned sight nicer than the other two were." He went on more calmly— "Wait till you're acquainted with her before you condemn her. I'm sure you'll like her."

"Philip is right," agreed Ernest. "Let us be patient and calm."

This remark had no calming effect on his mother. She sprang up and swept the length of the room. "By the Lord," she exclaimed, "you have a way of bringing out the worst in people, Ernest."

"Not in me," said Augusta. "For I know that Ernest's intentions are good."

Mrs Whiteoak came back up the room. She was smiling. "We certainly must give the young woman a chance, as Philip says. On my part I intend to be very civil to her," she said.

"The thought of being uncivil to anyone," came in Augusta's contralto tones, "never enters my head."

"We'll all be nice to her," said Sir Edwin gaily, "and see what happens."

"She'll be extremely grateful." Philip smiled at him. He was about to add—'And so shall I,' but thought better of it.

Nicholas gave a yawn. "I'm off to my room to unpack," he said. "Come along, Philip." He put his arm affectionately through his brother's. They moved towards the door.

The Buckleys rose and followed them. Augusta asked: "Is there anything I can do to help you, Mamma?"

"No, thanks. Mrs Nettleship will help me."

Ernest had no mind to be left alone with his mother.

"Anything I can do?" he asked cheerily, when the others had gone.

She shook her head.

"It's so nice to be home again," he said.

"It may be, for you. It is well to be so irresponsible."

"But—nothing has happened, Mamma."

"Something will. Did you see the look on Philip's face when he spoke of that girl?"

"No."

"Then you are very unobservant. He is attracted by her. He may even be attached to her."

Ernest gnawed his thumb, not knowing what to say. There came a tap on the door. Before opening it he turned to his mother and said: "Everything seems in very good order at Jalna, doesn't it?"

"Good enough. Good enough," she muttered. Then, with a look of complete exasperation, she added:

"Oh, Ernest, what a fool you were to engage that flibber-tigibbet girl!"

Ernest could not deny it. He was thankful when a second light knock sounded on the door. He opened it.

Mrs Nettleship stood there, her little pointed hands folded on her stomach. Ernest slipped past her and went up the stairs. She said—"Excuse me, ma'am, but is there anything I can do to help you?" She closed the door behind her.

"Yes. You can unpack for me but not till morning, except for my dressing-case."

"I have that already unpacked."

"Then there's nothing. Wait—you may pour me another

glass of sherry." She had seated herself on a sofa and was half reclining on its cushions, her long lithe body displayed to advantage, despite its cumbersome clothes.

With short silent steps Mrs Nettleship crossed the room and gently took the decanter from the silver tray. "I thought you'd be tired and would like a little sherry," she said.

"A good thought. Just half a glass this time."

Mrs Nettleship brought the sherry to her.

Adeline Whiteoak put the glass to her lips and looked keenly over its rim at the housekeeper.

"How have things been going—of late?" she asked.

"Do you mean in the last five weeks, Mrs Whiteoak?"

"Yes. Exactly that."

Mrs Nettleship was bowlegged. Even through her skirt and two petticoats it was discernible. Now she planted her feet firmly on the carpet.

"The last five weeks," she said, "have been terrible hard to bear. If it wasn't for you, Mrs Whiteoak, I wouldn't have stood it. It was affecting my health."

"Just what do you mean?" Adeline Whiteoak spoke above a sharply indrawn breath.

"It's that governess. It breaks my heart to look at those dear little children and think what she's set out to do."

"What has she set out to do?"

"Oh, Mrs Whiteoak, don't ask me to say it out loud! I just couldn't. But I lie awake at nights thinking what this house would be like with her at the head of it. Of course I wouldn't stay, but wherever I was I'd be thinking of the poor little children." She gave a deep sigh.

Adeline spoke calmly. "Tell me—what has Miss Wakefield done to make you feel like this?"

Mrs Nettleship drew a step closer and the pupils of her pale eyes were fixed in a gimlet gaze. Now the words poured out of her.

"Oh, Mrs Whiteoak, it began as soon as she came under this roof. I saw that she was sly. She wasn't dressed in a proper way but always as though she was going somewhere. She'd perfume on her. She'd worse than perfume on her, ma'am, she had *paint* on her!"

"Paint! Where? On her cheeks?"

"On her lips. I noticed they was redder sometimes than they was at other times. Then—I *saw*."

"Ha! What else?"

Mrs Nettleship came very close and lowered her voice till it was almost a whisper.

"On the third day," she said, and paused.

"Yes? Go on."

"On the third day, I was carrying the children's laundry up to their rooms. I had slippers on and I didn't make any noise. On the *top* floor, at Miss Wakefield's door, was Mr Whiteoak. The door was open and she was standing in it with a *loose* wrapper on." The peculiar stress which Mrs Nettleship laid on the word *loose* implied the most immoral intentions possible on the part of the wrapper. She watched Adeline Whiteoak's face closely and was satisfied with the effect of her disclosures.

"What did they do when you appeared?"

"Miss Wakefield was just plain flustered. She didn't know what way to look. But Mr Whiteoak spoke real sharp to me."

"What did he say?"

"I apologized and said I hoped I hadn't scared the young lady, and he said *she'd* nothing to be scared of."

"Hm. And what then?"

"Dr Ramsay came in—he'd been twice before to see her but couldn't find her—and after a while she dressed and came downstairs. After he'd left I was passing through the hall, and she and Mr Whiteoak was still in the library. Jake was there too and I thought I'd better see if he wanted out. We've never had a puppy that was so much trouble. Well—I didn't go into the room, Mrs Whiteoak. I didn't go in. I know my place better. Especially after the way Mr Whiteoak had spoke to me, outside her bedroom door. I just scurried down to the basement as fast as my poor legs would carry me."

"What, in God's name, did you scurry for?"

"Why, to keep out of Mr Whiteoak's way!"

"Woman alive—can't you speak out plain?"

Mrs Nettleship's voice became suddenly harsh. "I'd heard a *kiss*. A soft little kiss. And then Mr Whiteoak gave a pleased laugh."

"Perhaps she kissed Jake!" Adeline exclaimed grimly.

"Ha, ha, that's a good one, Mrs Whiteoak. But I don't see that young lady kissing a *dog*. Not with a handsome young man about."

Adeline set down the empty sherry glass. "Is there anything more to tell?" she asked, almost casually.

"Just this." The housekeeper put her hand in the pocket of her apron and took out a small packet wrapped in tissue paper. She unfolded the paper and disclosed several cigarette-ends. She held them out for inspection. "I found *these* amongst the shrubs underneath *her* window. She *smokes*, Mrs Whiteoak."

Adeline blew out her breath. "Well, well," she said. "Quite a forward young woman."

"*Forward!* Forward's no name for her behaviour. Twice this week she's gone through the house *singing*. Just as though she was mistress here!"

Adeline rose. If Mrs Nettleship expected an explosion from her she was disappointed. She appeared more calm than she had been earlier in the recital. But, when she was in her own room with the door shut behind her, she was seething with mingled anger and consternation. She stood with her back against the door, her palms pressed against the panels, only by a great effort restraining herself from going straight to Philip, demanding an explanation from him. But wisdom, experience of life, told her that it would be far, far better to wait, to discover for herself how far the affair had gone.

As for Ernest, she would gladly have taken him by the shoulders and shaken him. To think that he would deliberately throw such a temptation in his brother's way. "If I had the ninny here," she said aloud, and struck one clenched hand into the palm of the other. She did not finish the sentence, for at that moment the Indian gong that summoned the family to meals sounded in the hall.

8

## NO EMPTY ROOM

MARY CROSSED the hall and went to the door of the sitting-room, which stood open. She felt confused by the meeting with the various and highly individualistic members of the family. They seemed to raise a wall between her and Philip. She pictured him, as though from a long way off. With the sound of voices all about her, she was isolated, alone. The air was oppressive. Another storm was brewing.

In the sitting-room the children were playing with their new toys. Renny was kneeling on the floor, winding up his train. Meg stood by the table where her music-box was tinkling out 'Children of Vienna'.

"Listen," exclaimed Meg. "Isn't that a pretty tune?"

"Charming," agreed Mary. "What beautiful presents!"

"We have battledore and shuttlecock, too," cried Renny, "and I have a lot of lead soldiers and Meggie a workbasket, with a thimble, and two books each!" He sprang to his feet and began to show off the treasures. His small being was vibrant with vitality and enthusiasm. Meg did not know what it was to experience such joy as he did, but she egged herself on to a simulation of it, not wanting to be outdone by him in the eyes of the grown-ups.

Mary examined all the presents but her mind was not there. She was thinking—'What is going on behind the closed door of the drawing-room? What are they saying about me? For some reason they are not pleased with me.' She longed for a word, a glance from Philip to give her confidence.

It was with difficulty that she persuaded the children to carry their presents up to their room. But at last this was accomplished. Still she could not persuade them to go to bed. They must first go downstairs to say goodnight to their elders. It was not a question of allowing them to go. They swept past her and scampered down the stairs.

Mary stood by the windows looking out. The air was full of moisture and a threatening heaviness. Sheet lightning flashed almost constantly behind the trees that rose beyond the ravine, the ravine where she had sat reading to Philip Whiteoak. She felt cut off from any such pleasant intercourse with him now. From now onward all those people below would stand between. She was alone in this house full of people. Her head throbbed and she pressed her temples. That word *alone*! The close-knit family below had no room for her. And why should they? One day she would disappear, leaving no impression behind her— no more than had Miss Cox or Miss Turnbull. No impression on Philip Whiteoak? Oh, surely, surely he would hold a faint remembrance of her in his breast. She could endure the thought of his forgetting her, because she did not really believe in it, but the thought of his remembering her brought tears stinging her eyes. She heard the children coming up the stairs, putting down their feet hard to make sure that all the household heard what they were doing.

They had come from the dining-room where supper was in progress. Each had been given a taste of whatever they fancied. They were hilarious.

It was long before Mary closed her own door behind her. By that time the storm was drawing nearer. These electrical storms were a source of fear to her. Never before had she experienced any storms equal to them in ferocity. When they came at night they were so much the worse, with the darkness as a background to their sinister brightness. She wished the children had asked her to stay with them for company but she knew they did not want her. Yet Meg dreaded the roar of thunder. Why did Meg not want her companionship? Mrs Nettleship was to blame for that, Mary felt sure. If only she would let the children alone. But it was easy to guess her influence on them.

At last the storm passed down the lake. Not even a distant rumble could be heard. Its passing was complete, leaving a great stillness behind. It passed like the dream of a battle and Mary, tired out, fell asleep. She slept dreamlessly in the hot night for an hour or more, and then the storm came back. It swept majestically up the lake, retracing its course, gathering itself together as for a display of pomp and terror. As yet no rain fell, though the trembling of the leaves might well have been mistaken for rain. They trembled against each other with a pattering sound.

Mary sprang up at the first crash. She was dazed and for a moment could not collect her thoughts. She crouched with thudding heart waiting for the next clap. Simultaneously with it the room sprang to life in a pinkish glare, picking out every smallest detail, giving a transparent vivid beauty to the fruit and shells beneath the glass. The thunder crashed above the very roof. Mary cried out in terror but her cry was no more than the squeak of a mole in its burrow.

She must go and see if the children were all right! The air in the room was stifling. Her hair clung damply to her temples. She drew on her dressing-gown and hastened to the next room. A strong draught greeted her in the doorway. She heard Meg crying, and flew to her side.

"I'm here, dear," she said, putting her arms about the child.

Meg clung to her. "Shut the window!" she sobbed.

"Oh, what a fool I am!" Mary cried and flew to shut the window. As she did so, another flash of lightning fairly blinded her and a crash of thunder shook the universe.

Meg screamed and Mary almost staggered to her, sitting on the side of the bed, gripping her in her arms.

"Light the lamp," sobbed Meg.

With trembling hands Mary struck a match and lighted the oil lamp. It had a white china shade with pink roses on it and once, in a state of temper, Meg had scratched off one of the roses with her nail.

Now the light calmed her. She looked up at Mary out of tear-blurred eyes. "Don't go," she said, then, as a fresh crash thundered, she cried—"I want Daddy to come!"

"Won't I do?"

"No. Tell Daddy to come. I'm frightened."

"Daddy's here," said a voice from the doorway.

Philip, dressed in shirt and trousers, came into the room.

"It's a snorter, isn't it?" he said pleasantly, almost as though in praise of the storm.

"Come here! Come here," cried Meg, "and sit on my bed!"

He sat down and she scrambled on to his knee, clasping him tightly about the neck.

"Have you shut Renny's window?" he asked of Mary. Then exclaimed—"Why—you are frightened too! Aren't you a silly pair!"

With his tranquil presence in the room Mary's fear had already subsided. Her heart beat less heavily. But she was humiliated that she had forgotten Renny's window. With an exclamation of dismay she ran to the alcove where he slept. It was brilliant in a blaze of lightning. The window stood open. In the wild draught Mary's thin dressing-gown bellied like a sail. With her golden hair loose about her shoulders she looked like an angel in some old painting.

Renny was standing naked in front of the window looking out at the storm. The lofty peal of thunder that now rever-berated among the clouds did not make him flinch. He stood motionless, the rain, which was now falling fast, blowing over his naked white body. Then darkness came again and out of it Mary spoke.

"Renny! You *are* naughty! Don't you know how dangerous it is to stand in a draught in a storm?"

She groped her way, feeling the carpet wet beneath her bare feet, to the window and drew it down. As she closed the window at which he stood his small wet hands gripped hers and tried to restrain her.

"I want it open," he said, "I like it."

Simultaneously came a fiery flash and a terrific explosion. Mary uttered a moan of terror.

"You're afraid!" he laughed. "But I love it! I love it! I wish it would keep up all night." He began to dance and prance, his slim body illuminated by a steady flickering.

Fear made Mary strong. She snatched up his nightshirt from the floor, captured him, and thrust him into it. She took him by the hand and dragged him into the room. But when he saw his father there, he ran from her and threw himself against Philip. He caught up Philip's hand and rubbed his cheek on it.

"Daddy!" he cried. "I'm so glad you've come. I want you always to come."

Philip, between them, laughed up at Mary. He hugged them to him. There were sounds in the rooms below. People were talking. She hesitated, wondering if she should go back to her own room.

"The storm is lessening," Philip said. "It will soon be over."

The children chattered. They asked for drinks of water.

An odd tremulous domestic atmosphere was created. Was Philip conscious of it? But it was impossible to read his thoughts. Perhaps she was making no more impression on him than Miss Cox and Miss Turnbull had. Suddenly he said:

"Well, my family are back."

This was so obvious that it seemed no comment was necessary.

"Quite a lot of 'em," he said.

"Yes. The house seems quite full."

"They're like that."

"They're very—distinguished-looking."

"Especially my mother. Don't you be afraid of her. She's peppery but she's really kind-hearted."

"I'm afraid I haven't a strong character."

"Not strong! But I think you have. It took strength of character to come out here, so far from home."

"I had no home."

"Miss Wakefield," he said seriously, "I want you to tell me something——"

She interrupted him by a glance at the children. She could not speak of herself, of her feelings, not with Meg's inquisitive eyes on her, the possibility that what was said would be repeated in the kitchen.

Philip looked puzzled, then understanding.

Lady Buckley's voice came from below. "Philip! Are you with the children?"

He went to the door and called back. "Yes. I'm up here with them."

"Are the children all right?"

"Quite all right. I'm coming down in a jiffy. The storm is over."

He took Renny back to bed. Mary tucked up Meg where she lay very still, looking up at her with a cool considering gaze. Mary could see that she did not want to be kissed. She said:

"Please, Miss Wakefield, leave the lamp burning."

"But it will soon be daylight."

"I want the lamp, please."

"You won't touch it?"

"No. I promise."

Mary lowered the lamp and left the room. There was quiet. Myriad drops were falling from the leaves like a slow sweet rain.

Philip came into the passage, closing the door of the children's room. Mary said hurriedly:

"I'm sorry. I must have seemed abrupt. But . . . the children. . . . Not that it mattered. But—you were going to ask me something?"

"Yes. Are you happy at Jalna? Do you"—he looked straight into her eyes—"like us? I mean the children and me."

She could not answer. She could find neither words nor voice to utter words.

He persisted. "You do like the children, don't you?"

Her voice shook as she answered—"Yes. Oh, yes, I like them very much."

"Well, that's the important thing. But I feel this about you. You're too sensitive. By Jove, if things went wrong, you'd take it very hard. I hate to think how hard you'd take it."

She exclaimed, almost harshly—"You asked me if I liked the children and I said I did. And you asked me if I liked you and —I do. How can I help? You're so——"

"That's splendid," he interrupted. "Now you go straight to

bed. You're overwrought by the storm. You'll feel a wreck tomorrow if you don't get some sleep." He touched her arm in a comforting gesture and went down the stairs.

Mary could hear voices below. He had left so suddenly she wondered if he had thought his sister was waiting for him at the bottom of the stairway. She went into her own room and closed the door.

It was not quite dark. A moist grey twilight showed behind the trees. There was a steady drip from the leaves. Mary put her hands on the foot of the bed to steady herself. She said, as though speaking aloud to someone on the bed—'But I don't *like* him. I *love* him . . . I love him.' She repeated the words over and over and felt calmer. She repeated his name.

Then she remembered how he had cut her short. Had he seen that she was about to give herself away—say something foolish? She had a moment's wild desire to run down the stairs and beat on the panel of his door and call out a denial. She thought of all the other people, from all the other rooms, coming forth in amazement and scorn. Most clearly she pictured Philip's mother, mounting from her richly-coloured lair like a tigress to protect her son.

And he cares nothing for me, Mary thought, no more than he cared for Miss Cox or Miss Turnbull!

She was shivering. She crept into bed and drew the covers over her head but she did not sleep again.

In the morning she put on her dark blue skirt and white shirtwaist. She looked pale and wan. After breakfast she gathered the children into their room and shut the door. Meg was weary too and lolled across her copybook. Renny insisted on standing with his arm about Mary's neck while she taught him his multiplication table. By no other means could she persuade him to be still.

9

## NEXT MORNING

ADELINE WHITEOAK had slept well and she felt singularly refreshed. The storm had cleared the air, leaving the countryside fresh washed, with all its outlines sharp, as though etched.

The shout of a man driving a team in a distant field could be distinctly heard in her bedroom.

The thought crossed her mind as she was dressing that it was a pity women's clothes were so cumbersome. It would be grand, she thought, to have on no more than shirt and trousers, like that fellow in the field. She grinned when she pictured what she would look like in them. Still, she would look better than most women. Thank goodness, she had never got broad across the beam or thick through the breast. With something of complacency she put herself into her long, whaleboned stays, each metal fastening snapping sharply into place. She put on a black cashmere dress. She put on a heavy gold chain and locket. As she held the locket in her hand she raised it to her lips and pressed a kiss on it. This she did every morning because of the lock of hair inside.

The dining-room was empty, for she had slept late, and this rather pleased her. She liked having the first meal of the day in solitude, with only the pleasant, familiar sounds of home about her. On this morning, after an absence of months, they were particularly pleasing. Among the vines outside the window young birds were twittering as their parents fed them. A turkey gobbler let forth his boastful shout. A man was raking the gravel of the drive. Adeline smiled as she drew the large linen napkin from its silver ring and tucked one corner of it under her chin. She was not going to risk a drop of milk on the front of her dress. The porridge was delicious, cracked wheat, and cooked till it was almost transparent. As for the milk! She had not tasted any to equal it while she was away. After the porridge she had a dish of ripe raspberries, smothered in cream, two thick slices of toast well buttered, and three cups of strong tea. As she ate her eyes roved about the room, taking in first one object and then another, savouring their familiarity and how well they were cared for. Once her eyes rested on the two portraits, but not for long. They were too lifelike—herself and her Philip in their prime. She could look at the portrait of herself with a little appreciative smile, thinking—ha, I was like that! A handsome girl! But the two of them together, he in his fine uniform, she in her yellow satin ball dress, brought memories too poignant to be borne. How they had loved! The paltry loves of most people were, in her opinion, scarcely to be considered. The love, for instance, of Nicholas and his wife, and young Philip and his. Not that she had never looked at another man. She wasn't the sort of woman to fasten her feminine egotism on to one object, to stifle the loved one's spirit by her unremitting concentration. Adeline's nature was too lavish for that. But she had had only one great love.

Now Eliza came into the room to see if she wished for anything.

"Not another pot of tea, ma'am, or a little more toast?"

"Not a sup or bite more, Eliza. You'll have me fat, if you keep on feeding me like this. Where's everybody?"

"The gentlemen have gone over to the stables, ma'am. Lady Buckley is in her room. And the children are with Miss Wakefield."

"H'm . . . I miss Boney. Do you think Miss Pink knows I'm home?"

"Word was sent to her. I believe he's been keeping very well."

"I'm glad of that. Poor old bird. He'll be thankful to see me."

Eliza agreed, though she felt no warmth of affection for the parrot. Then she exclaimed:

"I hear wheels now. Mebbe that would be Miss Pink."

She hastened into the hall and then turned back to say:

"Yes, ma'am, it is Miss Pink and she has the bird."

"Show her into the library and tell her I shall be there directly."

Adeline energetically wiped her lips, rose, decided that she would like one more raspberry, took one from the dish and popped it into her mouth. She went through the hall, where the door stood open. She could see the Pinks' fat pony and the trap. She entered the library with a welcoming smile already on her lips.

Lily Pink was standing in the middle of the room holding a parrot's cage in her hand. It was she who had undertaken the care of the bird in Adeline's absence. She was twenty but had the innocent expression of a sweet little girl of twelve. Her light brown hair was drawn back from her face into a tight bun at the back of her neck. She wore a pink dress with leg-o'-mutton sleeves. Her grandfather had been the first rector of the little church built by Captain Whiteoak, forty years before. Her father, also a clergyman, had been a missionary in China, where his children had been born. Ten years ago he had returned to take charge of the parish that had been his father's.

"Lily, my dear child!" exclaimed Adeline, kissing her. "I am so glad to see you. *And* Boney! Has he been well?"

"Perfectly well, Mrs Whiteoak. All the time."

"I'm so grateful. I couldn't have been satisfied to leave him so long, with no one more tender-hearted than Mrs Nettleship. Then there were the children. I was afraid they'd let him out. I can't trust young Renny."

She bent her long supple body above the cage and the parrot, with a scream of joy, hopped into the doorway, climbed up the side of the cage, and from the top flew to her shoulder. She turned her face to his. He pressed his beak against her nose, uttering low chuckling sounds, while his bright-plumaged body vibrated with his love for her.

"Has he talked much?" she asked.

"Very little, Mrs Whiteoak. Except in anger. He's missed you dreadfully."

"He talked in anger, eh? What did he say?"

Lily blushed. "Oh, I don't know what he said." She could not tell that her father had ordered her to cover the bird's cage in his outburst of colourful language.

Boney was the successor to the parrot Adeline had brought from India. At his death, fifteen years ago, Adeline had been so distressed that Captain Whiteoak had not rested till he had found another, similar in plumage, to comfort her. Between them they had taught him the first Boney's vocabulary, in which he became so proficient that in time the two birds were merged into one in the minds of the family.

Adeline moved her head gently up and down while the parrot rocked his body in sensuous enjoyment. He hated everyone but her.

Now he spoke. "*Dilkhoosa . . . Dilkhoosa,*" he murmured caressingly. "*Nur mahal . . . Mera lal.*"

"Is he swearing?" asked Lily.

"Swearing? Not a bit of it. He's making love. Oh, they know how to make love in the East, Lily. Pearl of the hareem. That's what he called me, Lily."

Lily Pink had a sense of shock that a woman of Adeline's age, the mother of middle-aged sons, a grandmother, should take such obvious pleasure in these unsuitable endearments. She felt that older people should not have love words addressed to them, even by a parrot. She herself never expected to be the object of masculine endearments. For three years she had

84

cherished a hopeless love for Philip Whiteoak which she expressed by falling into almost complete silence in his presence and avoiding his eyes.

Now, from the side door, he entered the hall.

"Hullo, Mamma," he exclaimed. "Up already?"

"Already! The morning's half gone. And this is the first time you've sought your mother!"

"Not at all. I've been in here twice before. Good morning, Lily. So you've brought Boney back."

Lily bowed and silently moved her lips. Philip kissed his mother and chucked the parrot under the beak. Boney snapped at his finger, then once again concentrated his attention on Adeline.

"It's glorious weather," said Philip. "The air is marvellously cleared. What are you going to do?"

Adeline concealed by a forced smile the sombre look she turned on him. The air is not cleared, my fine fellow, she thought, and the first thing I am going to do is to find out what you've been up to. She said:

"I think I shall go to see the Laceys. Lily can drop me at their door. Will you do that, my dear?"

"Oh, I'd love to, Mrs Whiteoak."

"Good. I'll get my hat. But just let me give you this." She took from her pocket a small box and out of it a pretty leather belt with a silk-lined purse attached. She fastened it about Lily's waist.

Philip looked on approvingly. "There's a waist you could span," he said.

"She'd never let you try, would you, Lily?"

Lily thanked Adeline for the present, while keeping her eyes resolutely turned from Philip. She was in a state of panic at the thought of being left alone with him. She followed Adeline into the drawing-room and helped to hang the parrot's cage on its stand. It took considerable coaxing to persuade him to enter the cage, and when Adeline, after many endearments, left him he shouted Hindoo curses after her in his disappointment.

"I shall soon be back, my darling," she cried, and hurried to her room to put on her hat.

Philip stood smiling at Lily, stranded alone with him.

"Like that thing my mother brought you?" he asked.

"It's lovely," she said, but quite inaudibly.

He fingered the purse, opened it, and peeped into it.

"Nothing in it," he said. "Not a penny."

She managed to get out—"Nor ever will be. I never have any money." Her cheeks flamed as she said it.

"Never mind, Lily. You will. One day some millionaire will come along——"

Adeline appeared, wearing a wide-brimmed straw hat. Philip went with them to the pony trap, assisted them to climb to the seat, patted the pony, gave him a mouthful of grass. They jogged down the drive, the pony munching while green saliva dribbled from his lip. His hoofs splashed in and out of puddles, his small hard flanks glittered in the sunshine. Adeline thought how contented she would be, if only Philip had behaved himself. She remarked:

"I suppose you've met the children's governess."

Away from Philip, Lily could talk. "Yes. I met her at Mrs Lacey's and Mother has had her to tea with the children. Twice I've met her on the road. Do you think she's pretty, Mrs Whiteoak? All the gentlemen are raving over her."

"Your *father*?"

"Oh, yes."

"Admiral Lacey?"

"Most of all."

"Dr Ramsay?"

"No. I haven't heard him."

The situation seemed worse than Adeline had imagined.

"Make the pony move faster, Lily," she said. "Give him a tap with the whip."

Lily took the bent whip, though reluctantly, from its holder and administered a tap on his right flank. He looked over his shoulder at her.

"Give him another," said Adeline.

Lily gave him one on his left flank. He stopped.

"Come, come," Adeline urged him. "Get up with you!"

He looked over his shoulder at her.

"Here—give me the whip."

Lily surrendered it and Adeline gave him a sharp cut.

He walked down into the ditch, all but spilling them out.

"He always does that if he's touched with the whip," said Lily.

"Why didn't you tell me? Will he come up again if we pull him?"

"No. We shall just have to wait here till a man arrives."

"I could do it myself," said Adeline, "but I should get burrs in my skirt. Oh, you rascal!" She struck the pony's flank again. He looked round at her out of his large, remote eyes and made as though to lie down in the ditch. Both women clambered hastily out of the trap, and at the same time Dr Ramsey appeared on the road driving his big mare. He greeted Adeline with warmth.

When he saw their predicament he alighted from his buggy and, with a masterful air, led the pony back to the road, the pony coming eagerly, as though this were just what he wanted.

"What do you suppose was wrong with him," asked Adeline, "that he should go into the ditch?"

"He has been going into the ditch ever since I've known him," said Dr Ramsey, "and I've known him twenty-five years."

"Which way are you going, Doctor?" she asked. "If it is in the direction of The Moorings, I think I'll go with you."

"That is just where I am going, for I am taking a bottle of liniment for the Admiral's back."

"Is it bad then?"

"Just a touch of lumbago. Do come with me, Mrs Whiteoak. I'd like a chat with you."

Adeline said goodbye to Lily and mounted to the seat beside the doctor. He flicked the mare who set off at a good pace, the pony, on his short legs, doing his best to overtake her.

"Well," said the doctor, looking with canny admiration into Adeline's lively eyes, "you look none the worse for your journey."

"I'm all the better for it. There's nothing like a change from the worries and responsibilities of one's own home."

"True. Very true. And Lady Buckley, is she quite well?"

Adeline disliked her daughter's title, for she resented being in a position socially inferior to her, but Dr Ramsay never missed an opportunity of using it, though he had called her Augusta to the day of her marriage.

"Augusta is well enough."

"And Sir Edwin?"

"If he's ailing he hasn't remarked it."

"And Nicholas and Ernest?"

"Fit as fiddles. Ernest is by way of becoming a rich man. He's got a wonderful knowledge of investments."

"Ha. He'd better be cautious. If I had money to invest, I'd

87

put it into property. . . . And how did ye find everything at Jalna?"

Adeline looked straight between the mare's ears. "I found a pretty kettle of fish there."

"You did?"

"Come," she exclaimed, "don't tell me that you've heard nothing."

"Nothing but praise for the young woman. Excepting from Mrs Lacey. She seems to be quite a charmer."

"Well, my housekeeper has a tale to tell of her. She saw her *en déshabillé* at her bedroom door talking to Philip, before she'd been in the house a week. She heard them kiss in the library."

Dr Ramsay drew up the mare at the gate of The Moorings and gently flicked the flies from her flanks. Lily Pink and the pony passed, he hastening home to his oats, she waving and smiling.

Now the doctor turned a sombre look on Adeline, and spoke in a deliberate tone, his Scottish accent strongly marked.

"I said I had *heard* nothing but now I shall tell you what I *saw*."

Adeline sat planted firmly, a hand on either knee.

"At the first I had trouble in finding the young person. Twice I went to Jalna but she was out. On the second occasion Eliza told me that she had been seen walking in the direction of the wood. I followed her: for, as the children's grandfather, I felt I had a responsibility. I walked a long way and then I came to that wee clearing in the midst of the wood. There is nice smooth grass there and what do you suppose I saw?"

"Goodness knows."

"I saw Miss Wakefield, with her shoes and stockings off, running about on the grass. She was holding her skirt up to her knees. It was a feckless sight and a wanton one. I came away."

"You did well," said Adeline, with a mischievous look.

"Then one day I found her in and I had a short talk with her. I must say that my suspicions were allayed, for she showed an intelligence I had not expected. During our conversation I happened to mention the poet Burns, and she expressed a keen desire to read some of his poetry. I promised to lend her a volume. About a week ago I brought it. I had made a professional call on the Vaughans, and I left the buggy there and walked to Jalna through the ravine, where it was fairly cool. The day had been almost unbearably hot. I was crossing the bridge when I espied them."

Adeline turned her head and looked into his face.

"Yes?" she breathed.

"They were reclining, Mrs Whiteoak, in attitudes of complete abandon. She was reading aloud to him. A love poem by Lord Tennyson. I heard some of the words. I strode up to where they were. I gave her the book, with what disapproval I could put into my demeanour, and left them. I have not seen them since."

"Well," said Adeline, drawing a deep breath, "it's bad enough but I've heard of worse things."

"Doubtless no one has seen the worst, Mrs Whiteoak. When I think of that girl as successor to my daughter, my spirit draws back in dismay."

"Men don't always marry the women they make love to," said Adeline, testily. "Now let us go and see what Mrs Lacey has to tell us."

They found Mrs Lacey and her daughters sitting in rustic chairs beneath an old apple tree. Mrs Lacey was sewing and Violet and Ethel were shelling peas. All three jumped up to embrace Adeline and ask her questions about her journey. Ethel galloped to the verandah to fetch a rockingchair for Adeline. Dr Ramsay intercepted her and forcibly took it from her.

"What a harum-scarum that girl is!" exclaimed Mrs Lacey.

Ethel tossed her curled fringe out of her eyes, reseated herself, and scooped the contents of a pea-pod into her mouth. Her mother gave an expressive look at Adeline.

"I'll wager," said the doctor, "that you haven't sat in one of those all the while you were away."

"I have not. And very soothing they are." She seated herself and rocked as hard as she could, considering that the rockers rested on grass.

"The ground is still dry," said Dr Ramsay. "It's so hard from drought that the rain ran right off it." He lingered a little and then reluctantly went indoors to see his patient.

A silence fell.

Then Mrs Lacey asked—"Are you pleased with the new importation?"

"You mean Miss Wakefield?"

"Of course. She's the most exciting thing that's happened here in many a day."

"She's very good to look at. A little too smartly dressed, perhaps."

Mrs Lacey nodded with solemnity. "If that were all! But, Mrs Whiteoak, the girl *paints her lips.* Mrs Pink discovered it first. Ethel and Violet can't deny it, even though they are on her side. Indeed they seem quite fascinated by her."

"Oh, no, Mother," denied Ethel, "it is simply that she is an oddity. Someone so different."

"She's good fun when you get her alone," Ethel went on. "I mean away from Mrs Pink and Mother." She laughed daringly.

"Really, Ethel, you are incorrigible. Now that you two have the peas shelled, you had better take them to Cook. Mrs Whiteoak and I want a little private conversation."

"Very well, Mother," said Ethel, "but don't be too hard on Miss Wakefield."

When her daughters were gone Mrs Lacey exclaimed— "Really, those girls are incorrigible."

"They are sweet creatures."

Mrs Lacey tried to conceal her pride in them. "I'm glad you think so. But they do so easily get carried away."

Adeline ceased rocking and stretched out her long legs in a manner which Mrs Lacey found very unladylike.

Adeline remarked—"I am a woman of the world. I say if a girl in London wants to paint, to smoke, to be fast, let her. But I do not want her at Jalna tempting my youngest son. I don't want any new mistress there. You know what a time I had with Philip's first wife. We didn't get on well, you remember."

Mrs Lacey did indeed remember.

"Do you say," she asked, "that this girl *smokes?*"

"Yes. Mrs Nettleship found cigarette-ends on the ground beneath her window."

"It's unbelievable!"

"It's true. I saw them."

"Mrs Nettleship had saved them to show you?"

"She had. Now, if Philip must marry, let him marry a woman of means. Someone who will be an asset. I will not endure him marrying this fibbertigibbet girl."

"You haven't spoken to him?"

"No, no, not yet. In truth he may have no notion of marrying her. But it's plainly to be seen she's setting her cap at him. *Poetry!* Reading Lord Tennyson's poetry, if you please."

Mrs Lacey's eyes were shining. "Talk of Lord Tennyson's poetry! The things that young woman reads! My girls took her into our orchard and sat there under the trees. They came out *different*. They've never been quite the same since. But I believe in keeping their confidence and I encouraged them to talk. They told me that Miss Wakefield has read *all* of Rhoda Broughton's books, and not only that, she's read all of Ouida's. Did you ever read her *horrible* novel, *Friendship*? I'm ashamed to say I have, and it's the *height* of immorality. She has copies of the *Yellow Book*, with quite crazy illustrations by Aubrey Beardsley, and a magazine with an article by Oscar Wilde, called 'The Decay of *Lying*'. I think that is significant, don't you, Mrs Whiteoak? She raves about the little restaurants in Soho, where she says 'the *atmosphere is colourful*'. Really, my husband almost exploded when I repeated the expression to him. Men who write for newspapers took her. She met actors and actresses several times. She says she longs to see the life of Paris and Vienna. Well, we all know the immorality of those cities. The three girls spent the whole afternoon under the apple trees talking of things like that."

Adeline grinned. "No wonder Violet and Ethel have never been the same since," she said.


10

THE MEETING WITH MISS CRAIG

MARY WONDERED if she would be required to go to church, now that the children's grandmother and aunt were at home to superintend their behaviour. She had not seen Philip alone since the arrival of the family two days before. Now she sought him out to ask him. If she were not required to go she would spend the morning in the pinewoods by herself.

She saw him standing on the lawn outside the door that led from the hall at the top of the basement stairs. He stood there with his pipe in his mouth, wearing such an expression of tranquil goodwill that she wondered if ever he were ruffled.

She shrank from disturbing him. For some reason she had a feeling of constraint towards him.

However, as she hesitated in the doorway he saw her and took his pipe from his mouth.

"Good morning, Miss Wakefield," he said. "I hope you have recovered from the effects of the storm. You were frightened, weren't you?"

"A little. Nothing to speak of. You see, I'm not used to them."

"But you will be. You'll get used to everything."

"Oh, I have. That is, practically everything. What I wanted to ask is if I should go with the children to church, as usual, this morning."

"Don't you want to go?"

She looked him straight in the eyes. "Mr Whiteoak, that is not the question. I *must* find out just what is expected of me."

He smiled amiably. "To enjoy yourself, of course."

"Then," she returned firmly, "it would be quite all right if I were to wear my oldest clothes, take the dogs, and go tramping through the woods."

"So that's what you'd prefer?"

"Yes."

He shook his head. "That wouldn't do at all. My mother wouldn't like it. You'll have to go to church, I'm afraid."

"Thank you. That is all I want to know."

Instantly she felt that she had spoken curtly. But how was she to speak to him? She never seemed to know.

"There's a lovely cool breeze," he remarked.

She had noticed the breeze but only because of the way it lifted the thick fair lock on top of his head. His spaniels rose from where they had been stretched in the sun and came to him, touching his legs with their noses.

"They know it's Sunday," he said ruefully.

"Yes. Sunday seems more Sunday here than anywhere I have ever been. It's restful. I like it."

"And you don't too much mind going to church?"

"Of course not. I love the little church. Now I must find the children and get them ready."

She left him, her spirit suddenly elated. Whatever is the matter with me? she thoughs. I'm not in the same mood for two minutes together. . . . Then she remembered all she had been through just a few months before and thought it no wonder if she were a little odd.

She put Renny into his white man-o'-war suit and helped Meggie with her hair ribbon. They chattered all the while.

"Gran has twelve pairs of silk stockings."

"Uncle Nick has a stop-watch."

"You are not to call him Uncle *Nick*. It's rude."

"I don't care. I'll say Uncle *Ernie*, too."

"It's rude, isn't it, Miss Wakefield?"

"Miss Wakefield doesn't care," he declared.

"Aunt Augusta says our manners get worse and that it's your fault, Miss Wakefield. It is true, isn't it?"

"Miss Wakefield, do you get paid for teaching us?"

She answered, while brushing his hair vigorously—"I certainly do."

Renny's dark eyes opened wide with shock.

"*Paid!*" he repeated. "With *real* money?"

"Certainly. Did you think I came all the way across the ocean to teach you, just out of love for you?"

"Yes, I did." He looked at her, seeing her in a new light. "And were Miss Cox and Miss Turnbull paid money, too?"

"Of course."

He turned up his face to have his scarf adjusted, with a subdued look. It was shocking to him to discover that people were *paid*, actually paid, to do what should be only a pleasure.

From an old but well-polished carriage and a roomy phaeton nine people stepped decorously, descended nimbly, were assisted, or lifted down, according to their sex and age, in front of the church. They were an impressive array to have come from one house. Mary was astonished to see Philip in a Prince Albert coat and top hat. As though in protest he wore the hat slightly to one side. Under pretext of speaking to Renny he whispered to Mary:

"Isn't it ridiculous dressing up like this to go to church in the country? But my mother will have it."

Mary had never before seen him looking well-groomed: now, in this splendid array, he drew her unashamed admiration. All she could say was:

"I don't blame her."

"Do you say that because of the conventions or because I look so beautiful?"

"You all do." And her eyes rested on Nicholas, Ernest, and Sir Edwin, similarly attired.

As they mounted the steps the sonorous ringing of the bell made speech impossible. Adeline, wearing her widow's bonnet with the long veil falling about her shoulders, was a familiar figure to all who attended the church. When she was away they missed her. Now it was good to see her back again. As for her she drew a deep breath and hesitated mid way up the steep steps, not because of the exertion of climbing, but because she felt, as always when returning after an absence, the nearness of her husband, by whose side she had watched this church being built, stone upon stone, and whose bones now lay in its graveyard. The bell ceased its ringing.

"My Philip," she murmured, and let out the deep breath between her lips with a whistling sound.

"Did you speak?" asked Sir Edwin at her side.

"No, no. Just grunted."

"It is quite a climb in warm weather."

"Not to me. The heat feels good—after England."

They were in the vestibule now. Philip had left them to go to the vestry. Renny saw the bell-rope dangling and, before he could stop himself, he sprang up, caught it, and began to swing on it. As he hung there Nicholas administered a sounding whack on his seat, lifted him down, placed one hand over his mouth to stifle a possible outcry, then took him by the hand and led him up the aisle.

"That boy," said Augusta, in a whisper to her husband, "will come to a bad end."

"Most boys do," he returned amiably.

With an offended air, she swept into her seat.

Mary sat with the two children in a pew in front of that occupied by Adeline, her two sons, her daughter, and her son-in-law. She felt that five pairs of eyes observed her every movement. She felt so conscious of this observation that she trembled as she found the places in their prayer-books for the children.

The volume added to the singing by the newcomers was tremendous. They had good voices. They knew the hymns by heart. They let themselves go. From the first Sunday in the church Mary had noticed the weakness of the choir. Now she saw it submerged, rendered helpless. Its members sang away, opening and shutting their mouths unheard. The service seemed unconscionably long. Mary kept her face turned from where Philip sat, waiting to read the Lessons. When at last he mounted the lectern she let herself look at him. To her his head, the shape of his shoulders beneath the folds of his surplice, were more moving than the words he read.

His brothers exchanged a look. They had forgotten how badly Philip read.

Renny dropped the ten-cent piece that was his contribution and it rolled far into the aisle. Mary did not know whether she should allow him to get it. But he was uneasy till she did. Then, in a grasshopper jump, he retrieved it and threw a triumphant look at his grandmother behind him. She leant towards him, the smell of her heavy crêpe veil enveloping him. "Be a good boy," she whispered, "or it will be the worse for you." The scent of the crêpe came to him.

He grasped the coin and stared at his Uncle Nicholas helping to take up the collection. When Nicholas held the alms dish in front of him he planted his offering in the middle of it with a flourish.

"He is completely out of hand," observed Augusta to Ernest, who nodded agreement.

Nicholas and Chalk, the blacksmith, a fine-looking young man, stood shoulder to shoulder at the chancel steps and presented the alms dishes to Mr Pink, whose complexion was but inadequately described by his name. The best that could be said of his sermons was that they were brief; the worst that they never were to the point. He always appeared about to make some profound observation but always it eluded him or possibly, as Nicholas said, was never there.

At last the congregation trooped down the aisle. Renny managed to get next little Maurice Vaughan, two years his senior and a schoolboy on his holidays from Upper Canada College.

In the porch Adeline was surrounded by friends to welcome her home. She stood like a queen with courtiers encircling her, a pleased smile curving her full lips. Mr Vaughan brought a newcomer to her.

"This," he said, "is Miss Craig, who lives quite a long way off and drives the ten miles to come to our church."

"Now I call that a compliment," said Adeline, taking her hand and looking her over approvingly. "Tell me why you come so far to our insignificant little church."

"Your son told me about it and how you and Captain White-oak had built it in the wilds. I came first because I was curious, and several times since because I like it so much."

"You are newcomers in this part then?"

"Yes. My father built a house on the lake shore. Unfortunately he has had a stroke and goes nowhere."

"Well, well, that's sad."

She turned to greet a neighbouring farmer and his wife.

"This is our wedding anniversary, Mrs Whiteoak," the man said. "Forty years married."

"Six children and eighteen grandchildren," added his wife.

"Good for you! Well, you're lucky to have your man still with you."

"Oh, Mrs Whiteoak, I remember the Captain and you dancing at our wedding. What a grand-looking gentleman he was!"

"He was that. I must go now and see his grave."

She led the way into the churchyard, her family, now joined by Philip, following her. Mary also followed but at a little distance. She saw them gather about a plot marked by a massive granite plinth and enclosed by a wrought-iron fence. There were two graves in the enclosure, that of Captain Philip Whiteoak, the other of the younger Philip's young wife, Margaret. A small marble cross bore her name.

Adeline's tall black-robed figure halted by the grave of her husband, the summer breeze spreading her veil. Augusta bent her head. The four men removed their hats.

There came into Augusta's mind the image of her father carrying her on his shoulder when she was a little girl in pantalettes, and she smiled tenderly at the recollection of that tiny girl. "Dear Papa," she murmured in her deep voice.

Sir Edwin remembered how he always had felt especially insignificant when standing beside that stalwart military figure, how Captain Whiteoak had stared at him out of his prominent blue eyes, as though in wonder at his being there at all. 'Yet,' thought Sir Edwin, 'he could be very agreeable, very agreeable indeed—when he chose.'

Into the mind of Nicholas there suddenly flashed the remembrance of an especially severe tanning his father had given him. He'd had a good many, but he could recall the smart of that particular one to this day, though he'd forgotten what it was for. Yet how generous the hand that had administered the

tanning had been in giving money! And that hand now . . .
Nicholas felt a contraction of the heart as he, for an instant,
pictured that hand now. How many bones were there said to
be in a hand? Twenty-eight? Twenty-eight small bones—dry
—perhaps disjointed—in that box, beneath the summer grass!
Instead of the large handsome hand he remembered.

An officer and a gentleman, if ever there was one, thought
Ernest, gazing down at the grave. And how well he could tell
a story! Particularly a story of his life in India. But he had not
been intellectual. Sometimes Ernest wondered from whom he
himself had inherited his intellect. Not from his mother. For
though she was highly intelligent it was in an intuitive feminine
way. . . . That look on her face hurt him. He wished they
might leave the grave.

Dear old governor! thought Philip, and resolutely kept from
his mind any sad reflections. He turned his eyes to where Mary
stood, her wide-brimmed straw hat shadowing her face.

Adeline's heart cried out—'My darling, oh my darling!'
For one blind instant she felt that she would throw herself
on the grave, pressing it to her breast, as she had pressed
him when he lay dying—he who only an hour before had
left the house, sound and well! But she held herself together.
She put up her hand and arranged the widow's veil on her
shoulder. She led the way from the grave with an unfaltering
step.

Renny was left alone with the granite plinth. For a long
while he had wanted to climb it. Now suddenly he felt strong
enough. He hopped over the iron railing, put his arms about
the monument, placed a foot on the lowest projection, hung on
like a limpet, though the foothold was precarious. With his
utmost effort he gained the highest ledge and clung there. He
took off his sailor cap and placed it on the very pinnacle of the
monument. He laughed with the joy of achievement. He
could not stop himself. He shouted:

"Hurrah!"

The family turned, transfixed by the sight.

Philip strode towards his son. "I'll warm his seat for this,"
he exclaimed.

But Adeline held him back. "No, no," she said. "Let the
boy be. He means no harm. Indeed he makes a pretty picture
there. I like it."

At the one o'clock dinner she was in great good humour.

Whatever Mrs Nettleship's faults might be she was an excellent cook. To some people the meal might have seemed a little too substantial for such a warm day, not so to Adeline. She relished every mouthful. Her neighbours, the Vaughans, had joined the family and she enjoyed their company, particularly as Robert Vaughan had, as a youth, been in love with her, though she was already married, and had never quite got over it.

After dinner they repaired to the shuttered coolness of the drawing-room and there Adeline asked of Mrs Vaughan:

"What about these people, the Craigs? The young woman is quite comely. She's a good shape, too."

Mrs Vaughan did not consider a young woman's shape a proper subject for discussion in mixed company. She repeated:

"Yes, she is quite comely. She is very nice, too. I feel sorry for her because she is cut off from the pleasures suitable to her age. There they are, in that big house, quite unable to entertain their friends, and only a trained nurse for company."

"Miss Craig is quite an heiress," added her husband. "One of you three chaps should make up to her."

Adeline's eyes sparkled. "What a good idea! Nicholas is the man for it. That wife of his was an extravagant one to keep and to get rid of her cost quite a lot. He's the man to marry Miss Craig."

It had been painful to the Vaughans to hear Nicholas's divorce mentioned. The suggestion that he should marry again was acutely embarrassing. How often in their long friendship with Adeline Whiteoak she had embarrassed them by her remarks! Both of them flushed but Nicholas remained imperturbable. He said:

"Once bitten, twice shy. I'll never marry again."

"What about Philip?" asked Sir Edwin.

"Philip has enough on his hands," said Adeline tersely.

"It's to be Ernest then," said Nicholas. "He has a new suit that he's irresistible in."

Ernest tried not to look conceited. "What nonsense you talk, Nick. As for me, if I ever marry it will be for love. I am thankful to say that money is no longer any consideration with me."

"Yes," agreed Adeline complacently, "my son, Ernest, is

98

quite a financier. There is nothing he doesn't understand about investments. You had better get his advice, Robert, and double your capital."

Adeline herself, though possessed of a respectable fortune of a hundred thousand dollars, invested in the most conservative manner, was quite satisfied with the low interest she received. She lived at Jalna without expense to herself, save in personal matters. She never referred to the fact that she had means of her own. Indeed she would sometimes speak of herself as a poor widow, dependent on her son Philip.

Philip, his father's favourite son, had had the house and land bequeathed to him and enough money to live on without extravagance. A considerable part of his income was derived from the fertile farm lands of Jalna. In money matters he was generous to the point of extravagance. Dealings in money confused him. He spoke of himself as a farmer and horse breeder.

His older brothers had inherited, in addition to what their father had given them, quite substantial amounts from their father's sister in England. Nicholas, unknown to any save Ernest, had lost a good deal of money in the previous year, in Portuguese, Greek, and Mexican bonds. Nicholas, who from his mother had inherited a love for the foreign and picturesque, was drawn to these investments. He was thankful that he had kept these losses to himself, for he could imagine what Adeline's caustic remarks would be, had she known of them.

Ernest too had had losses. Grand Trunk Railway shares had fallen. British Rails had suffered a fall. But these losses were as nothing compared to his gains. Standing with one hand in the breast of his coat, he talked fluently of his investments and of how his capital was doubled. It was a delightful sensation to him to boast a little.

Mr Vaughan was greatly impressed. He was of a cautious nature but his ambition for his young son who had come to him late in life was unbounded. He wanted him to be a noble man, to exert great influence for good in the country. Surely the possession of wealth would aid him in his great future, for undoubtedly his future would be great. He was such a serious and altogether remarkable child, a contrast to that harum-scarum little Renny.

Robert Vaughan said firmly—"I shall be glad of your advice, Ernest. Certainly Sunday is no day for the discussion of money matters, but if you are free tomorrow morning I should like to come over and have a talk with you."

"Ernest will put you on the right track," encouraged Sir Edwin.

"He's a perfect wizard," said his sister admiringly.

Ernest almost simpered. It was so wonderful to feel oneself a successful man of affairs.

"I'll do what I can," he said.

Philip was pulling burrs from his dog's tail and hiding them under the chair where he sat.

"The land is good enough for me," he said. "I'd rather invest in wheat and oats and apples."

Ernest looked down at him tolerantly. "I think you're very wise, Philip, to stick to what you understand."

"I get rattled when I bother about money."

His mother craned her neck to look at him. "Whatever are you doing?" she asked.

"Nothing. Just sitting here. Twiddling my thumbs." He winked at Augusta, who could not forbear a smile in return even though she saw the burrs beneath his chair.

## II

## THE PARTY

"I WANT a dinner party," said Adeline, "and a dance afterwards. I like my friends to know I'm home."

"Everybody knows you're home, old dear," returned Philip. "And don't you think you'd better wait till the weather cools off? People would melt, dancing in this heat."

"I have danced in hotter weather, with tight stays on me and an enormous bustle. I don't see what makes you so lazy, Philip. Neither your father nor I had a lazy bone in our bodies."

Philip lighted his pipe and concealed the burnt match beneath the chair he was seated on. He said—"Neither you nor my father ever did what I call an honest day's work that I ever saw——"

His mother interrupted him in outraged tones. "Not work! Your father and I not work! You should have seen him when this place was being built. He'd heave up a timber, with two men at the other end! He had the strength of two."

"Yes. I've heard about that. But it took only a short while. Not a whole day."

"He had to conserve his strength. A man needed to conserve what strength he had in those days."

"As for me, I have my oats to get in before the weather changes. I pitch in and help my men, you know."

"And a pretty beet-red colour you've got yourself!"

"It makes me feel nice and safe. No girl would run after a beet-red widower."

Adeline laughed scornfully. "Look in your mirror and you'll see how your looks are spoilt. That sunburnt face makes your hair brighter, your eyes bluer, your teeth whiter."

"How dreadful," said Philip. "I sound like a picture on a cigar-box."

"You're a handsome man and very like your father."

Adeline did not often acknowledge his likeness and Philip was duly flattered. He grunted appreciatively.

"You were his favourite child."

"H'm."

"He had great hopes of you. And so have I."

"What sort of hopes, Mamma?"

She was put to it to say what were these hopes. Philip was just past thirty and had never shown ambition.

He insisted—"What are those hopes, Mamma?"

She took his brown, strong hand in her long supple hand and squeezed it. "That you'll never make a fool of yourself—in any way. That's a good deal to hope for any man, isn't it?"

"Too much."

"Ah, Philip, you're my white-headed boy. 'Twould break my heart if you were to throw yourself away in a foolish marriage with some silly girl."

"Your heart is made of tougher stuff than that, Mamma."

"You talk of my never having worked. Just think. I bore three sons in the wilds of Canada and brought up my four children, with just what help I could get."

He gave his engaging smile. "How well you talk, Mamma! If you go on like that you'll have me crying."

His pipe had gone out. Again he lighted it.

Adeline exclaimed—"I saw what you did with that burnt

match! I see the two of them under your chair. Pick them up this moment, Philip, and put them in a proper place."

Renny ran into the room. Philip drew the little boy to him and put the burnt matches in the pocket of his blouse. "Something nice for you," he said. "Bury them and fireweed will come up."

"It won't, will it, Granny?" He climbed into her lap and clasped her neck. "Sing me something," he begged. "Like you used to."

She hugged him close. "I can't sing."

"You can so."

She had, as a matter of fact, a quite good voice but little idea of tune. She sang:

> "There was an old woman had three sons,
> Jerry and James and John;
> Jerry was hung, James was drowned,
> John was lost, and never was found;
> And there was an end of her three sons,
> Jerry and James and John!"

Renny lay, lolling on her lap, savouring her song. His bare brown legs lay relaxed on hers, his heels gently kicking her shins. She looked across his head at Philip.

"This boy," she said, "is the apple of my eye."

"He certainly looks like you, Mamma."

"Oh, he showed his good sense!" She kissed him rapturously on the mouth. Boney, in his cage, cried out in jealousy.

"I wish," said Renny, "that I had a little brother."

"And what would you do with him?"

"I'd teach him to ride. I'd take care of him."

"No, no. One small boy in the house is quite enough."

Sir Edwin Buckley looked in at the door. On seeing him Renny leaped from Adeline's lap. "Uncle Edwin," he cried, "you promised to help me with my train. It won't run."

Sir Edwin looked at him disapprovingly. "A little restraint, please, if I am to help you with it."

The little boy galloped from the room and back again carrying the train. Sir Edwin tweaked up his trousers at the knees, knelt gingerly, and bent his side-whiskered face above the toy. Philip and Adeline leant forward fascinated.

Augusta, coming into the room, remarked—"Edwin's bent towards mechanical things always amazes me."

"You forget, my dear," said Sir Edwin, "that my grandfather was a scientist."

"And got a baronetcy for discovering something about bugs!" laughed Adeline. "It's always struck me as funny."

"It was an extremely important discovery," said Sir Edwin with dignity, "and has saved thousands of lives."

"If we go on saving lives to the extent we now are," she returned, "the world will be overcrowded in the next fifty years."

Sir Edwin did not hear her. His gaze was riveted on the little locomotive.

"Mamma wants to give a party," Philip remarked to his sister.

"I think it is highly appropriate," agreed Augusta.

"You don't think the weather too warm?"

"In Canada," said Augusta, "the weather is always too warm or too cold."

"People will get very hot dancing."

"If the liquid refreshment is good, they will not mind. And iced claret-cup will help."

In an aside to Philip, Adeline remarked—"I never get anything better than cooking sherry in her house."

Presently the little locomotive was repaired and toddled across the floor. Renny clapped his hands in delight.

Nicholas and Ernest agreed with their mother that a party would be delightful. Invitations to a dinner for sixteen people were sent out and three times as many were invited to a dance afterwards. Everywhere in the house there was a bustle of preparation.

Mary was in a state of uncertainty as to whether or not she was expected to be present. Her mind was soon relieved by Adeline's saying, with a smile—"You must wear your best bib and tucker on Friday night, Miss Wakefield."

She has a beautiful, a gay smile, thought Mary, why is it that I fear her? She answered:

"Thank you. It is very kind of you."

"You dance, I suppose?"

"Oh, yes."

"So do I. Does that surprise you?"

Mary felt that Mrs Whiteoak was rather old for dancing, but, on the other hand, nothing she might do could surprise her.

"I'm sure you dance very well," she said.

Adeline grinned. "Oh, I can still move my legs to the music."

From now on Mary could think of nothing but the party. It was madness, she knew, to beautify herself for Philip's sake. She scarcely saw him nowadays, except at mealtimes, when she sat isolated between the two children, who were now not allowed to talk at table. They sat speechless, drinking in the animated talk of their elders which to Meggie was more interesting than food. What a contrast these meals were, Mary often thought, to the first one she had had at Jalna.

Mary brought out her one evening dress. It was turquoise blue, a thin material and cut low. It looked sadly wrinkled, yet Mary shrank from taking it to the basement to press. She waited till Mrs Nettleship was away for the day, then took it down, hoping she would meet no one on the way. Eliza was agreeable. She admired the dress. Neither Miss Cox nor Miss Turnbull had had anything approaching it. When parties were given they had kept to their room. When the dress was pressed it satisfied even Mary's scrutiny. She felt that she could look her best in it.

She did not realize that her looks had been enhanced by the outdoor life, the sunshine, at Jalna. Her neck had rounded, the lovely pallor of her cheeks was tinged by colour. She only knew that she felt stronger, and could walk over quite rough ground without fatigue.

The weather turned cool on the night of the party. A fresh breeze from the west sprang up. Adeline felt justified in her choice of the day and again and again drew attention to her perspicacity. She was dressed for the dinner quite an hour before the time appointed, but she did not mind. She was out to the porch, into the dining-room to inspect the table, to the drawing-room to inspect the floor, to the kitchen to give final directions there. Mrs Nettleship was in a state of chill and hollow-voiced disapproval. She detested all forms of entertaining. Though she curried favour with Adeline, she disliked her, as she disliked all women. She liked men, almost she loved them, but took a sadistic pleasure in making things uncomfortable for them.

Rugs and carpets had been taken up and floors waxed. Doors and windows stood open to the evening air. The air coming in at the windows was heavy with the scent of nicotiana, its starry flowers already white against the August dusk. The days were beginning to shorten.

Mary, from her window, could see the guests arriving for dinner. She had not been invited to share this part of the entertainment. The guests were old friends of the family and she would, she told herself, have felt *de trop*. She was glad to sit quietly upstairs waiting for the dance. She had had a time of it to persuade the children to go to bed. She wondered if there were any other children with such high spirits. Even though she was much stronger she found them tiring.

As she sat, with an elbow on the window-sill and her cheek resting on her hand, she pictured Philip sitting at the head of his table, being charming to his guests. She wondered if, during the whole day, he had given one thought to her. She wondered if he had given a thought to his brief married life, and regretted the young wife who should have been at his side to-night. Mary had a moment's poignant pity for Margaret. The children had shown Mary their mother's photograph in an album with a heavy silver clasp. They had shown it, hard-hearted little creatures that they were, without a trace of pity or regret for the stern-faced young woman, holding a spray of lilies in her hand.

Now Mary heard them pattering about in the passage. She went out to them, drawing her brow into a frown of authority. How she wished they had gone properly to sleep! But any frown she could produce was quickly obliterated by their looks of astonished admiration.

"Oo! Miss Wakefield," from Meg, "don't you look beautiful!"

"She's a princess," cried Renny, and threw his arms about her.

"Renny," said Mary, "you're squashing my dress!" She tried vainly to restrain him.

Meg pulled him off and then said firmly—"Turn round and let's see you properly."

Mary showed off her dress for their pleasure.

"Whirl round," commanded Meg, "till we see what you'll look like when you dance."

Up and down the passage Mary whirled, her full skirt billowing about her like sea waves.

"I hear wheels on the drive!" shouted Renny. "People are coming to the dance!"

The children flew to look out of the window. She would have a time of it to get them to bed. 'Let them stay up,' she thought, 'it won't hurt them just this once.'

In her own room she took a dark red rose from a tumbler of water, wiped its stem, and fastened it in her hair, just at the nape, where the curling coil was. But she could not make up her mind to go down the stairs. Twice she hung over the banisters listening to the first sweet music of the two violins and the harp, and fled back up the stairs again. Oh, if only she had someone to go down with! But she was alone—always alone.

Then Eliza appeared. "I've been sent to ask you if you'd care to come down to the dancing," she said.

Philip had sent for her! She was sure Philip had sent for her. "Who sent you!" she asked.

"Mrs Whiteoak."

"I'll come right down."

Why had Mrs Whiteoak troubled to send for her, she wondered. The truth was that Adeline would not risk Philip's looking on Mary as a poor down-trodden governess. He might forget her himself but his mother must not.

Adeline's fine arched eyebrows flew up when she saw Mary enter the room. Beauty! And beauty far from unadorned. The number of flounces! The sweep of shoulder and milk-white breast exposed! There was not another such low-cut dress in the room. Adeline's eyes sought for her daughter. It would be worth her own shock to witness the far greater shock on Augusta's face. There she was! And looking full at Mary Wakefield. Adeline could not control a chuckle of delight as she beheld the change which came over that long sallow countenance. It changed from an expression of urbane hospitality to one of positive outrage—even unbelief in her own senses. Then dancing couples came between them. Augusta's face was lost.

Adeline made her way to Mary's side.

"Well, my dear," she said, "you look very pretty and gay."

"Thank you, Mrs Whiteoak," Mary answered, colouring.

"But you must not stand here unattended. A set of the lancers is just being formed. That is the one dance our dear Mr Pink knows. I'm sure he'd be delighted to dance it with you." She caught Mr Pink, who was just passing, by the arm.

"Here's a lovely partner, all set to dance the lancers with you."

Mr Pink had dined well. He had strong ideas on feminine modesty in dress. He would not have allowed his own daughter to wear a low-cut gown. But if Adeline hoped that he would be too replete to enjoy springing about or too outraged by Mary's décolléte to desire her as a partner she was to be disappointed. Mr Pink bowed with alacrity and curved a plump elbow for Mary's hand. He looked like a happy cherub in a clerical collar.

The violins and the harp sang. The room was full of people, for when Adeline set out to give a party she remembered more and more people whom she liked to entertain. Unlike the parties of the present day which are given exclusively for people of the same generation, when different generations bore each other to the point of misery, this party was composed of many ages. Lily Pink was not the youngest, or Adeline the oldest. All romped merrily together through the lancers.

If Mr Pink looked like a cherub, he danced like an angel. He was light as a feather. Probably during the whole course of their married life Mrs Pink had never disapproved of him so thoroughly as during this set of lancers, when she saw him buoyantly marching with the other gentlemen, only to meet Miss Wakefield at the end of the march and whirl her off into a waltz; when she saw him acting as pivot with the other gentlemen, while Mary, with the other ladies, flew on the outer edge. It was the expression on his face that Mrs Pink most disliked. Positively, she thought, he looks like a cave man. She wondered fearfully if, during his long years of work among the heathen, he might not have picked up some heathen ways.

When the lancers were over he thanked Mary and wiped his perspiring face.

"Quite warm, isn't it?" he remarked. "But you look cool as a cucumber."

"I never get too warm dancing," she said, "and the music is divine."

"You can always depend on Mrs Whiteoak to have good musicians."

"It makes such a difference in one's pleasure."

"Yes. Good music, and a partner who dances as you do, Miss Wakefield."

"You dance well too, Mr Pink."

"Well, I don't get a great deal of practice. This is the only house where I have the opportunity."

"What a pity!" Mary's tone of voice was so sincere that for a moment Mr Pink wondered if he had not made a mistake in going into the ministry, with its manifold restrictions.

"Ah, here comes the Admiral!" said Mr Pink. "And they are playing a schottische. Lucky man."

Admiral Lacey bowed, asked Miss Wakefield for the honour of the dance, and led her off. Now it was his turn to be unpopular with his wife. She liked to see him enjoy himself. No wife took more pleasure in her husband's pleasure. But his jauntiness on this occasion, the way he did the 'one, two, three and a kick', was past belief. No couple in the room could compare to them. In fact, the other couples, one by one, dropped out and left the floor to them. Mrs Lacey looked about for her daughters. She hated to have them see their father so disporting himself. But that madcap Ethel had gone out into the garden with her partner, and Violet seemed to have eyes for no one but Nicholas Whiteoak. Really Mrs Lacey had cause for concern. There was her elderly husband dancing like a sailor on the lower deck, with a young woman only partially clothed, and there was one daughter out in the darkness with dear knows whom, and the other daughter brazenly flirting with a divorced man. Mrs Lacey admired Nicholas, his air of a man of the world. At one time she would have been delighted by a marriage between him and Violet. But that was when his name had been untarnished by divorce. Now, a thousand times no!

As for Mary, at this period in the evening it mattered little to her who was her partner, provided he could dance. To dance—yes, to dance—that was her one desire. To feel free as air, light as music, to cast off all that bound her, to remember nothing.

Now Mrs Whiteoak was coming towards her followed by a most presentable young man. Mary marvelled that Mrs Whiteoak should trouble her head about her, find partners for her.

"Miss Wakefield," she said, "this is Mr Clive Busby and he's eager to dance with you." She added, as the young man bowed, "Mr Busby's family were already settled here when we arrived. Now he lives in the West."

In the rush of the polka it was possible to converse only in breathless gasps but the young man begged for the waltz that followed and, as they circled round and round, for he seemed not to consider reversing, he pictured for her the wonderful life on his ranch. Mary listened enthralled; her eyes, on a level with his, made him want to tell her all the story of his young life. He asked her if she would go for a drive with him the following day. He could borrow a horse and buggy from the Vaughans where he was visiting.

Adeline looked on, a smile curving her lips. She was pleased by the success of her manœuvre. Mary was the very type to captivate a young fellow with a ranch who needed a good sturdy, thickset, down-to-earth wife, with no nonsense about her. If only she could get Mary away from Jalna, without trouble from Philip, how happy she would be! The thought of Philip's taking a second wife was intolerable.

Now young Busby and Mary were disappearing through a french window into the garden. The scent of the nicotianas enveloped them. He had told her that, to his mind, Mary was the most beautiful name for a girl.

"I suppose you," she said, "were named for General Clive."

"I was. And my father was named for General Brock."

"General Brock?" she asked, mystified.

"General Isaac Brock, you know. The Battle of Queenston Heights, where we defeated the Americans."

Her puzzled expression showed that she had not heard of the occasion. Young Busby was shocked. He stood silent inhaling the scent of the flowers.

"Of course," she hastened to say, "I've heard of the Battle of the Plains of Abraham."

That did not mollify him.

"I thought everyone," he said, "had heard of the Battle of Queenston Heights."

"I am terribly ignorant, I'm afraid."

"And you a teacher!"

"But I want to learn about Canada."

"The place to learn is the West," he declared. "These old Provinces are worn out."

"Do tell me more about your ranch."

He was happy again. They strolled across the dewy lawn and Mary got her feet wet without ever noticing. Clive Busby talked interestingly. She felt so free.

But, after a time, she began to be restless. She forgot to listen to the young man's descriptions of life on the prairies.

She longed to go indoors, to discover if Philip Whiteoak would ask her to dance. So far this evening they had no more than touched hands in the Grand Chain. There had been no more than a smiling interchange of glances.

When, at last, her partner reluctantly led her back to the drawing-room, the first couple she saw were Philip Whiteoak and Muriel Craig. They were dancing the gavotte, and Mary had a swift pang of jealousy when Clive Busby exclaimed:

"What a stunning couple! Do you know who the young lady is? By Jove, she can dance."

They stood just inside the door watching the dancers. From the summer darkness without, above the sound of the music, came the melancholy cry of a whippoorwill. Mary stood, leaning on Clive Busby's arm, half stifled by that pang, even to the pain of which she felt she had no right, since Philip had not noticed her that evening. She was nothing to him. All his thoughts were fastened on Miss Craig. And no wonder. Mary was forced to admit she was well turned out, and had to acknowledge to herself that she was not without beauty. She was less tall than Mary, her neck and her face were shorter. Her neck was round, white and strong, her shoulders, rising above the cream-coloured brocaded taffeta of her dress, were boneless. Her thick light brown hair was piled on her head and high in it shone a pearl and a diamond sunburst. Her lips were parted, so Mary thought in her jealousy, as though she were breathless in the admiration that shone up at Philip out of her round light eyes.

"Shall we dance?" asked Clive Busby.

"No, thank you. I'm a little tired."

"Come now"—he looked his unbelief—"not really?"

"Yes. Just a little. Anyhow this dance is over."

"Of course, there'll be other fellows you'll want to dance with. I can't expect to monopolize you."

"It's very kind of you to ask me."

"Dear me, how formal we are! Are all English girls so formal?"

"I'm not really."

"I wish I knew what is in your mind."

"You might be surprised."

"I'll bet I'd not be half as surprised as you would be if you knew what's in mine."

"Whatever are the musicians playing?"

"Don't you know? That's a Highland fling. I believe that Mrs Whiteoak and Dr Ramsay are going to dance it."

Adeline and the doctor were indeed taking the floor, he wearing an expression of almost mournful gravity, her face lit by a hilarious grin.

"This," he announced, "is a Scottish reel and I taught it to Mrs Whiteoak in her youth."

"Nonsense," she declared, "it's an Irish jig and I taught it you."

Whichever it was they were at it, their bodies galvanized by Gaelic energy, their feet flying. The doctor's expression never changed, indeed one might have said his life depended on the accuracy with which he executed the steps. Only once more did he open his lips and then it was to utter the brief shout so in keeping with the dance. It seemed a pity that he was not wearing the kilt.

Adeline had opened the evening, partnered by her eldest son. They had been a striking couple. Since then she had danced several times but there was something of wildness and reckless-ness in this dance that best suited her nature. She held up her violet *moiré* skirt that was trimmed with heavy gold passe-menterie, showing her slim feet and ankles, in black silk stockings and low-heeled black satin slippers with silver buckles.

Augusta looked on at this performance in mingled wonder and pain. She wondered at her mother's ability so to skip about. She could not have done it. She thought the dance barbarous and was pained by Adeline's obvious delight in it. She had a feeling that Dr Ramsay had always been in love with Adeline and this made her uncomfortable.

Nicholas and Ernest regarded the exhibition with amuse-ment and gratification. They were proud of Adeline. At the height of the reel Philip took his nose in his hand and emitted an amazingly good imitation of the bagpipes.

It put new life into the dancers, who were beginning to pant a little, but his three spaniels, who were outside the french win-dows waiting for him, recognized his voice, even though so distorted, and thinking he was in dire predicament rushed in to save him.

The music stopped.

Philip caught Sport and Spot by their collars and dragged them out but Jake ran here and there yelping in a panic till captured by Mary. He lolled blissfully against her shoulder and she followed Philip on to the lawn.

His face lighted with surprise as he saw her.

"Good girl!" he exclaimed, and gently took the puppy from her.

Mary stood looking at him, her spirit crying out in her distress—'Good girl! And you have never once asked me to dance and never will!'

Adeline appeared in the doorway, followed by Clive Busby. She was well pleased with her son for his attentions to Miss Craig. She was almost pleased with Mary.

"Those dogs of yours behave disgracefully, Philip," she said. "Do shut the door on them and then bring Miss Craig in to supper. All our guests are starving. And here is Clive Busby eager to take in Miss Wakefield." She stood with her hand on the doorknob, smiling at Mary as she passed. Then she said, in an undertone to Philip:

"That's quite a case. Young Busby is plainly smitten. What a capital match it would be for that girl!"

"Yes," he agreed absently, and wondered what Mary could possibly see in Clive Busby.

"Now, Philip, don't keep Miss Craig waiting, while you play with your dogs." She ordered him about, with feminine pleasure, as though he were a big boy, and he obeyed, half sulkily.

Muriel Craig tucked a firm white hand under his arm. She gathered up her skirts in the other. She said:

"This is the happiest evening I've had in a long while. You can't imagine how dull life has become for me, since my father's illness."

"I'm glad you've enjoyed the dancing."

"I think our steps suit, don't you?"

"Indeed I do." His eyes followed the musicians, who were leaving to go to the basement for refreshment.

Muriel Craig continued—"I do hope you will come often to see Father. He's taken a great fancy to you. He gets so bored by the society of his nurse and bored a tiny bit by me too, I'm afraid."

"I'm going to see him tomorrow," said Philip.

"In the morning?"

"Yes."

"Will you stay to lunch?"

"I'd like to. Thanks very much."

The dining-room was full of people gathered about the table where wax candles in the tall candelabra cast their radiance on white and red roses and gilded the sheen of the damask cloth. There were hot chicken pasties, and cold tongue, and devilled eggs, and sliced peaches in thick cream, and brandied peaches and ice cream, made with much exertion, in a churnlike freezer, by Eliza. There were coffee and claret cup and coconut layer cakes and almond-meal macaroons and brandy snaps. In short, Adeline had ordered the supper.

She enjoyed having her friends, young and old, about her after an absence. She enjoyed the good food, eating it with gusto, in the knowledge that no digestive complications would follow. She was pleased with her sons. Nicholas, well rid of that wife of his, looked happy and handsome. He was laying himself out to make their guests happy. Who wouldn't be pleased with a son like Ernest?—making money, hand over fist, with no more exertion than the notifying of his intentions to brokers. As for Philip, he seemed to have forgotten all about the governess and was listening to seemingly entertaining talk by Miss Craig.

Muriel Craig had chosen a corner where Philip's back would be towards the room, and Mary Wakefield. She talked rather breathlessly, never allowing his attention to waver. She really was, he thought, a quick and amusing woman. She not only talked of her travels, she had been about quite a bit and could scarcely bear to hear about a place she had not visited, or a book she had not read. Philip was an excellent companion for her because he was by nature receptive and had neither travelled nor read widely. His pleasant laugh punctuated her anecdotes. She said she adored ice cream and he saw to it that she had several helpings.

As they were returning to the drawing-room, from where came the sound of the musicians tuning their instruments, she said: "I think you are so fortunate in your children's governess. She strikes me as a most good-natured creature."

"Yes. She's very nice," he answered, a little coldly.

"It means so much to have a good kind creature about them."

"It does indeed." He looked about him for the good kind creature but she was not to be seen.

"I can't possibly dance after all that supper," said Muriel

Craig. "Could we go out for a stroll? There's such heavenly moonlight."

Adeline came into the hall. "How sensible you are!" she exclaimed. "That's just what I should like to do, but the night air gives me a buzzing in my left ear. Infirmities of age coming on me, you know." She showed her fine teeth in a smile that quickly sobered as she saw Mary standing alone on the porch.

"Ah, there you are, Miss Wakefield," she said. "I have been looking for you. Here is a young man who is dying for a waltz with you. Mr Robertson"—she turned to the young man whom she had only that moment espied—"this is Miss Wakefield, who waltzes like a dream."

Mr Robertson was pale, with hair parted in the middle, and a very high collar which had gone very limp from the heat. He vaguely offered his arm to Mary, and began vaguely to waltz round and round with her. Apparently he never had heard of reversing.

Mary felt slightly dizzy. A surge of almost intolerable disappointment made her limbs heavy. She wished she were up-stairs, alone in her bedroom. She had a mind to make an excuse to go to see if the children were safely tucked up. She had a sudden feeling of love for the children. With them she might find ease from the anguish of jealousy. But Mr Robertson, though vague-looking, was firm. He held her closely, turning round and round.

And, after him, returned Clive Busby to make sure she had not forgotten her promise to drive with him.

The time dragged on. It was past midnight. It was two o'clock. The guests were leaving. Horses, scarcely able to endure the waiting to return to their own stables, pawed the gravel drive. Carriage lamps flashed. There were shouts of "Whoa!"

Lily Pink was spending the night at Jalna. Her mother was delicate and could not endure late hours, so Lily was to remain. Like Mary she had an ache in her heart. Not that she had expected Philip would ask her to dance and, even if he had, she was sure she would have danced her worst. But she could not comfort herself. The ache persisted. She stood smilingly with the family in the drawing-room that now looked very large and bare, while they congratulated themselves that the party had gone so well.

"And did you enjoy yourself, my dear?" Augusta asked her kindly.

"Oh yes, Lady Buckley. It was lovely."

"You looked very nice dancing. I always like dotted Swiss muslin on a young girl."

"Mother and I made the dress ourselves."

"Your mother is an excellent needlewoman and I'm glad you take after her. I have always enjoyed sewing."

"I've always hated it," said Adeline.

Ernest observed gallantly—"My very best dance of the evening was with Lily."

"She treated me with scorn," said Philip. "Never once looked in my direction."

"But there were those who did," put in Sir Edwin. "No one could fail to notice the die-away looks Miss Craig gave you."

Nicholas remarked—"That young woman is a strange mixture of rigidity and voluptuousness. From the waist down she dances like a boarding-school miss, and from the waist up like Salome."

"This is scarcely proper conversation in front of a young girl," said Augusta.

"Oh, I don't mind." Lily blushed prettily. "And after all, Salome is Biblical."

Philip went to the dining-room, where all signs of supper had been cleared away, save for the remains of the tongue on a platter on the sideboard. He cut three slices from the tongue and, with these on his palm, went to the back of the hall where, in a small room, his three spaniels had retired to their respective mats. He fed a slice of tongue to each. The parent dogs took their share gently and a little reproachfully, as though this were poor compensation for the evening they had spent, but Jake wolfed his, trying to swallow Philip's hand with it. He patted all three.

"Good dogs. Now lie down. Go to mats."

Jake tried to take possession of each of his parents' mats in turn but when driven off by them curled himself up on his own, with only an upturned roguish eye to show that he lived.

As Philip returned through the hall, he reflected with content that the party was over, his crops, which were above the average in quality, were almost completely garnered, his horses promised well. In a day or two he would go on the fishing trip he had been looking forward to. Before long there would be the duck shooting. Would he ever get Jake properly trained for a gun dog? He doubted it. Jake was a bit of a fool. His best friend couldn't deny that.

When he was passing his mother's door she called to him.

"Come in, Philip, and tell me goodnight."

He found her still dressed but with her hair hanging about her shoulders. Her parrot, sitting on her wrist, gazed into her face with a possessive air. He chuckled in pleasure over her return to him.

"He won't let me undress," she said. "He's for billing and cooing the whole night through."

"No wonder. He appreciates how alluring you look with your hair down. I hope you're not too tired."

"Well, I am rather tired. But I've given my party and I'm satisfied."

Adeline was pleased with her youngest-born tonight. Holding Boney at arm's length, so that he should not bite him, with her other arm she clasped Philip to her bosom and planted a warm kiss on his mouth.

"You darling boy," she breathed.

"Dear old girl."

"Not one of the others means to me what you do."

"Not one of them feels as I do about you."

They swayed lovingly together till Boney began to walk up her arm with murder in his eye. Then she gently pushed Philip away. "The bird is jealous. You'd better go."

"Goodnight, Mamma."

"Goodnight, my dear."

He closed the door behind him.

He discovered the drawing-room empty, with the exception of Lily. When the older ones had gone upstairs she had lingered, she did not know why. Quite a time ago Mary had disappeared up the stairs. She had not said whether or no she would come back. Lily looked at her own reflection in the mirror above the mantelpiece. It was a very old mirror and gave back her reflection in a wavering way, like an image mirrored in water. But she thought she had never looked so pretty. She wished that the Swiss muslin dress might have been low cut. Then Philip might have danced with her. She knew her arms and shoulders were lovely, for her own mother had told her so.

Philip stood looking into the room.

"Everybody but us gone to bed, Lily?"

"All but Miss Wakefield. I don't know about her."

They stood looking at each other, silent. Then he came into the room and lighted a cigarette. Eliza looked in at the door.

"Shall we lay down the rugs tonight, sir?" she asked.

"No. Get to your beds. You must be tired."

"Thank you, sir, but I'm not really tired."

Again they were alone. Lily was speechless but she could hear the thumping of her heart. The scent of the nicotiana came in, almost unbearably sweet. Chaotic thoughts choked Lily's mind. Oh, if only she could speak! Oh, if her heart did not beat so fast and hard!

She heard Mary coming down the stairs. What relief! And what disappointment!

Philip stood, looking Mary over as she came into the room. He said—"Well, Miss Wakefield, Lily and I had given you up. We thought we were the last of the party."

"I went up to see if the children were all right."

"At this hour! What did you expect them to be doing?"

"It was hard for them to settle down."

She thought his smile was sceptical, that he knew she had gone up to tidy her hair and put fresh powder on her face. She wished she had not come down again.

"Did you enjoy the party?" he asked, a slight constraint in his voice.

Her back was to Lily. She framed the word *no* with her lips.

Lily asked quite loudly—"What did you say, Miss Wakefield?"

"I said nothing."

"Lily," said Philip. "Play something."

"Me? Why should I play?" She could force herself to speak now that a third person was there. "My playing would sound dreadful after the real musicians."

"Nonsense. I thought they sounded rather tinny. Didn't you, Miss Wakefield?"

"I liked their playing."

Lily asked—"Should I disturb the others—your mother?"

"They're not in bed yet. Play, Lily." He closed the door.

Lily spread her skirt on the piano stool. She bent her head over the keys, thinking what she should play. She who was aching to dance with Philip herself must play for his dancing with another. She felt a sob rising in her throat and drowned it in the opening chords of a Strauss waltz. Not only would she play but she would play her best.

There was an old moon and it now could be seen through one of the french windows.

Philip said, "We don't need the light." He took an extinguisher from the mantel and began to put out the lights of the chandelier. The lights from the many candles illumined his face. Scores of crystal prisms reflected their flames in all colours of the rainbow. The candles were extinguished like stars and, as the chandelier swayed, a faint, tinkling music came from the prisms. Philip put his arm about Mary's waist. They moved slowly into the waltz. Moonlight now flooded the room.

One thing besides sewing Lily could do well—play dance music. But never before had she played like this, when she could scarcely see the keys for tears. But she did not need to see the keys. The music flowed from her heart through her fingers. The two on the floor moved as one body. No other dancers that night had been like these, Lily thought. Their grace, their delight in the rhythmic movement, their long gliding steps that seemed to take them beyond the room, out into the moonlight, filled her with bitter joy. She sought for comparisons. 'They are like two birds flying together—they are like two waves dancing together—they are like two flowers blowing on the one stalk.' She could not be flowery enough to please herself—to torture herself.

"Good," said Philip, at the end. "Splendid, Lily."

Mary still leant against his shoulder, without a thought in her head. Her mind was as smooth as a beach that a summer storm has swept.

"Like another?" he asked, after a little.

"Yes."

"Another waltz. Play us another waltz, Lily."

Lily turned the knife in her breast and played better than ever. She put all her longing into the slow beat of the waltz.

They danced to the far dim end of the room and there Mary felt Philip's lips touch her hair, his arm tighten on her waist. She willed the rest of the world to stay away, to give her this moment, but the sound of the piano had flooded the house, for, at the last, Lily had played with passion. The door opened and Adeline stood there in her dressing-gown.

Dancers and music stopped.

They looked at her speechless.

"I had a glimpse of you before you stopped," she said. "I've never seen prettier dancing. Why didn't you dance like that when all the people were here? They'd have loved it."

Philip moved from Mary's side to his mother's.

"No need to be nasty," he said in a low tone.

But she answered loudly:

"Be quiet till I've had my say!"

He looked at her silently, his face hardening. The light from the lamp in the hall poured in through the wide doorway.

"Miss Wakefield," said Adeline, "I think you have missed your vocation. You should not have been a teacher but a professional dancer. You're too good at it for a private drawing-room and I'm glad you had the sense to restrain yourself till my guests were gone, for they're a conventional lot and I am afraid they would have been scandalized to see such abandon. I'm not conventional but your dancing opened my eyes to what a young woman will do when she lets herself go."

"You flatly contradict yourself," said Philip. "You say you never saw prettier dancing, and why didn't we do it when all the people were here and they'd have loved it. The next instant you say you're glad we restrained ourselves and that they'd have been horrified."

"You know what I mean!" shouted Adeline.

"I'm sorry," Mary got out. She turned and fled from the room.

Lily Pink was weeping over the keyboard. Adeline said to her more quietly:

"Go to bed, my dear. It's nearly morning."

Lily rose, her face distorted like a child's from crying.

"There's nothing for you to cry about, Lily," said Philip, as she passed him. He put out his hand to give her a comforting pat but she shrank away as though he were about to strike her and cried out—"No!"

"Well, I'll be damned," said Philip, looking after her.

"You may well be," said Adeline gloomily.

"What have I done?"

"You've done enough to make me want to take a stick to your back. If your father had come in on this scene he'd have raised the roof with the rage that was in him."

In the doorway Augusta, Nicholas, and Ernest now appeared. Augusta wore a long dark red wrapper but her brothers were in nightshirts, over which they had pulled trousers.

Nicholas's thick dark hair stood up in magnificent confusion, but Ernest's fine fair hair was still sleek.

"Whatever is up?" demanded Nicholas.

"We were dancing," answered Philip.

"*We?*" echoed Augusta's deep tones.

"Yes," he returned with a brazen look at her. "Mary Wakefield and me."

He was purposely ungrammatical and it made what he said the more brazen.

"Tell them," said Adeline, "just how you were dancing."

He was still imperturbable. "Well," he said, "I hadn't danced with the poor girl all the evening. We had the room to ourselves."

"Yes," said Adeline, "they had the room to themselves. He put out the candles but there was moonlight. Plenty of light for me to see the shameless performance."

"Who was playing the piano?" asked Nicholas.

"Who but Lily Pink!"

"I didn't think she had it in her."

"Edwin remarked to me," said Augusta, "with the bed-clothes over his head—for he was trying to go to sleep—that the music sounded to him positively *vicious.*"

A smile flickered across Adeline's face, then faded.

"It was that," she said, "and I guess her poor parents would have hidden their heads in shame, if they had heard it and seen what I saw. The children's governess swooping up and down the room, draped over Philip's arm like a courtesan! Ah, she's no better than she should be."

"I won't hear a word against her," said Philip.

"You'll hear whatever I have to say," declared Adeline, her eyes blazing.

He was standing quite near her but in his anger he shouted as though she were deaf:

"I repeat that I won't!"

"Don't you dare shout at me, sir!"

"Then don't you say such things of Miss Wakefield."

"I say she's a wanton!"

"Then you lie."

Adeline sprang on Philip and caught him by the shoulders to shake him, but he took her wrists in his hands and held her. Boney, who had not yet got over his joy in the return of his mistress, paid no heed whatever to this disturbance but continued to snuggle himself beneath her chin and to utter caressing words in his foreign lingo. Mother and son, locked together, glared into each other's eyes.

Nicholas rumbled—"That's no way to speak to Mamma. I can't allow it."

"I'm sorry," muttered Philip. "But she drove me to it." He still gripped Adeline's wrists.

"Free me, sir!" she demanded, her face only a few inches from his.

"What will you do, if I do let you go?" he asked half laughing.

"You'll see," she hissed, like the villainess in a play.

Ernest came and gently withdrew Philip's hands.

"This is bad for you, Mamma," he said. "You should be in your bed." She shook him off.

"I want," she said, folding her arms and facing Philip, "to be assured that that"—she hesitated over what she should call Mary, then went on—"wanton young person shall leave the house tomorrow."

"I can't do it," returned Philip calmly. "In the first place, she's done nothing wrong. In the second place I've engaged her for a year."

"You are not bound if she misbehaves herself."

"She hasn't."

Nicholas put in—"I shouldn't go into that again, if I were you. Let's talk over the affair tomorrow."

"There is no talking over this quietly," said Adeline. "She is to go."

"No, Mamma." Philip spoke with pointed calm. "I cannot and will not dismiss her."

Adeline demanded fiercely—"How often have you been up to her bedroom?"

Augusta uttered a contralto groan, as she saw peaceful retirement receding.

"Not once," Philip answered with great distinctness.

Adeline laughed. "Come now, come now, tell the truth. How many times?"

"That sort of pastime may have been the custom in your dear father's house—not in mine."

"Philip"—Adeline spoke with passion—"why will you always be saying that Jalna is yours? Everyone knows it already."

"It's very irritating," said Nicholas.

"And after all," put in Augusta, "Nicholas is the eldest son."

"All I said was that in *my* house that sort of thing is not done."

"And you insult my poor father's memory," cried Adeline, "and he is in his grave!"

"Many a time I hear you say worse of him."

She could not deny this. She struck one clenched hand into the palm of the other. "If *your* father," she said, "who we all agree *was* a man of good character, even though *my* poor father —God rest his soul—was not——"

Ernest interrupted—"Mamma, why must you talk in that Irish peasant way when you are upset? It sounds so affected."

"It makes what I say more impressive," she returned. "And God knows it's myself who needs to be impressive, with my youngest son blackening my father's memory and flaunting his——"

"Better not use that word, Mamma," said Philip. "Because it only makes me more determined not to be overriden in this affair."

"What I am trying to say, only I can't get a word in edge-ways, is that if Philip's father were here he would send that girl off tomorrow morning."

"I wish," put in Augusta, "that I might have seen the dance."

"Yes," agreed Ernest, "if only we had come down a little sooner!"

"I wish you had," said Philip. "You could have seen nothing wrong."

Adeline grinned. "No. Because you had taken care to put out the light. *Why* had you put out the light?"

"Because I liked the idea of dancing in the moonlight."

"I am sorry to see," said Adeline, "that you, a young father—widower of as noble a young woman as ever drew breath——"

Philip's eyes were prominent with astonishment.

"You are late in discovering it, Mamma."

"Mamma"—Ernest thoughtfully bit his thumb—"just what did you mean when you said that Miss Wakefield was draped across Philip's arm? I think a great deal depends on that."

"I'll show you," Adeline answered with gusto. "Step back and I'll show you. Put your arm round my waist, Philip . . . You might play me a waltz, Nicholas."

Before Philip could stop himself he put an arm about her waist. He held her rigidly a moment, then drew himself decisively away. He strode to the door and from there he said, with an angry tremor in his voice:

"I tell you all that you are wasting your time and had better be in your beds, for nothing you can say will make me dismiss Mary Wakefield and that's flat."

They heard him going up the stairs.

Adeline's face fell. Then she brightened. "Ernest, you put your arm about me and we'll show them."

"I can't, Mamma. It would be quite different."

"The point is," said Nicholas, through a yawn, "that Philip is in one of his mulish moods. Nothing we can say will change him."

"He is adamant," said Augusta. "But he cannot go on being adamant, if he feels disapproval of his behaviour from every side, combined with complete restraint and perfect politeness."

"Augusta is quite right," said Ernest. "Also I am positive that Philip has only a passing regard for this girl. He was lonely and she was thrown in his path."

"By you," added Adeline grimly.

Ernest grew pink but went on—"Tonight I noticed that by the end of the party he had a little—a very little—too much to drink. That, combined with the moonlight, the music——"

"Good God," interrupted his mother, "he's thirty! He's been married once. If he can't withstand a little feeble moonlight and a waltz played by Lily Pink . . ."

"Certainly," said Nicholas, "she put her whole soul into her playing."

"Then," declared his sister, "there is something terribly wrong with Lily's soul."

Nicholas laughed. "I'm going to bed," he said. "Let me take you to your room, Mamma."

"No," she said, with sad dignity. "I'll go alone. The time has come for me to learn that I'm a poor widow whose children will not stretch a helping hand to her."

She kissed each in turn and, only slightly drooping, left the room. The parrot had lowered his breast to her shoulder, puffed himself, and closed his eyes.

Nicholas winked at the other two. "A very fine exit," he said.

When they reached the passage door above there was silence throughout the house, except for a bubbling cosy snore from Sir Edwin.

# 12

## MEETINGS ON THE ROAD

THE MAJESTY of the garnered harvest was at Jalna. Day after day heavy wagons had borne their rich loads to the barn. There never had been a better year for crops, except for the corn which Adeline would call maize. It had grown to a great height but had been battered down by a heavy storm. Nevertheless it had half raised itself again and was saved. The boughs of the apple trees were weighted by sound fruit, the Duchess, the Astrachan, the Baldwin, the Northern Spy, the pippin, the snow apple—best of all. Down where the stream passed near the stables grew a wild apple tree whose little sweet apples tasted like pears and were valued most by Meg and Renny. They hid in this tree, eating its fruit; it was always in their pockets; they stored it under their pillows for bedtime refreshment. It was responsible for lack of appetite, for hives, sometimes for pains in their insides. But nobody suspected the apple tree.

The sun, having ripened the grain and coloured the fruit, now turned his wayward strength to painting great splashes of gold and purple in the ditches and the edge of the woods where goldenrod and Michaelmas daisies drew what moisture they could find through their tough stalks. Even the mushrooms did not escape his colouring, for here and there there appeared red ones and others that were mauve. To Adeline these were toad-stools and poison and so she trained the children. They discovered the pale Indian pipes which alone never saw the sun, picked them, carried them a little way, then threw them down and trampled them.

Philip's cows and sheep and pigs had done well, but they were of small account compared to his horses. He had got a name for himself as a breeder of the best Clydesdales in the country. Yet he was not happy, and no prosperity on the land could overcome the discomfort of his life in the house. One could not be at outs with Adeline and forget it. Her atmosphere advanced before her as an outrider—hung on her skirts like a train. If she were displeased, her displeasure was unforgettable, to herself and to its object. Now she was displeased with Philip and her displeasure was dark indeed. She was mystified because, though Philip had so bluntly refused to let Mary Wakefield be dismissed, he had so far as she could discover never seen her alone since the night of the dance. And how she had watched him and how she had watched Mary! 'Upon my word,' she would say to herself, 'I shall be worn out with all the watching, yet it is my duty and do it I must.' Mary was not difficult to watch, for of late she had spent most of her free time in her own room, but Philip was here, there, and everywhere. She would send Ernest or Nicholas on some pretext to look for him. They well knew what was in her mind but humoured her, Nicholas cynically—feeling sure that Philip was carrying on his affair with Mary in his own indolent but persistent fashion—Ernest anxious to prevent any alliance that would cause trouble in the family. In truth he gave only a small part of his mind to the matter, for he had anxieties of his own, of which he would speak to no one but bore them in secret.

He, Nicholas, and the Buckleys were shortly returning to England. Adeline would be alone with Philip and the children. By that time, she was confident, she would have Mary on the way to departure also. She had almost entirely ignored Mary since the night of the dance, but when she did speak to her it was with a kind of fierce graciousness, as though in the twinkling of an eye she might bite her head off. As for Mary, the mere sight of Adeline walking towards her was enough to make her heart pound. She avoided all the family but the children. The days passed in a sort of dream. Something, she felt, was bound to happen. She could not go on like this. The pageantry of autumn began to unroll, as though in the last act of a play, in which she, the heroine, did not know her lines, did not even know whether the play were melodrama or farce. She was conscious that she was inadequate to hold her own among these other players whose roles so well suited them.

Passing the drawing-room she would have a glimpse of the two older brothers, Lady Buckley, and Adeline playing a game of whist. It would be after tea and the evening growing cool but not yet dark enough for lamplight. The sun, very low, would send its light flickering through moving branches. It was not always easy to distinguish an eight-spot from a ten-spot. Augusta would be holding her hand high, on a level with her eyes, to catch the light; Ernest trying not to see what cards she held, yet somehow glimpsing them. Nicholas would be wearing the eyeglasses which he had just lately taken to for reading and card playing, and from which depended a black ribbon. But Adeline, with a humorous twist of her mouth, would be scrutinizing the faces of the other players, as if from them, rather than from her own hand, she would be guided in her next play.

Sometimes Mary would have a brief picture of Sir Edwin playing at backgammon with his mother-in-law. His even-featured face, between his neat side-whiskers, was as impassive as an egg. When he spoke it was in a clipped monotone, but Adeline's voice came out hard and clear.

"Deuce!" would come softly from Sir Edwin's lips.

"Trey!" would be rapped out from Adeline's strongly moulded ones.

"Doublets!"

"Quatre!" And Boney, on her shoulder, would repeat the word.

If they heard Mary pass, they gave no sign.

All appeared to have forgotten the scene on the night of the party. All appeared to be hardly aware of Mary's existence. Her dance with Philip began to seem like a dream. Yet in solitude she enacted it over again, lived it as though it were all that was real in her life—the return down the stairs, with hair and face freshened—she scarcely knew why, but—there was the hope! It had been an unacknowledged hope, without foundation, for he had not come to her once that night. Then—how the hope had been justified! It had blazed into bloom, almost stifling her with its power. Unbelievably she had found herself in Philip's arms, his powerful body moving so lightly beside hers, his arms bounding her world. Nothing else had mattered but the sweep of their embraced bodies in the long room, lighted only by moonlight, the throb of the waltz, the scent of the nicotiana coming in at the window. There was her world, her life, she had thought. Nothing could ever be the same again. That must go on—encircling her.

But things were the same again—now painfully the same. The routine of her days, the long wakeful nights, moved on, with no one to notice her changed looks, her heavy eyes. Even her hair seemed changed and did not want to curl but hung in limp locks.

She was sure that Philip avoided her—that is, when she was alone. If the children were with her he would appear as his former self, chaffing Renny, stroking Meg's hair, asking questions, to which he scarcely seemed to expect an answer, about their progress. Sometimes Mary, with an almost fierce determination, would persuade his eyes to meet hers. When they did for an instant, it was as if they were alone together, with the beat of the waltz on the air, instead of the voices of the children; her heart would palpitate, she would look away from him speechless. If only, she thought, her position had not been so ambiguous—if only she had felt sure of her ground in any quarter. But, even with the children, even with Mrs Nettleship and Eliza, she felt uncertain. Sometimes the children were friendly, even clinging, but again they would whisper together and eye her as an outsider. Then, she thought, Mrs Nettleship had been at work.

Once Renny suddenly kissed her right on the mouth, then rubbed the back of his hand over his own lips and examined it.

Mary was startled, then angered. She exclaimed—"If that's the way you feel about my kisses, don't kiss me again."

"I wasn't rubbing away your kiss," he said, "I was just finding out if the paint comes off."

Mary flushed scarlet, but she said calmly—"You are a very silly little boy."

"You do paint your lips though, don't you?" Meg's clear eyes had a tormenting gleam.

"But why?" demanded Renny. "If you're going to paint them why don't you paint them green or blue or something different?"

"It's to make her prettier, stupid," said Meg. "Nettle says so."

One day she found Renny with an old clay pipe he had found, between his teeth, and took it away from him.

He looked at her haughtily. "Well, if you smoke I guess I can smoke too," he said.

Mary was aghast. Was there anything the two didn't know about her? She remarked, as though casually:

"Mrs Nettleship again, I suppose."

They looked at each other and laughed.

"Supposing we'd smelled it on you?" said Meg.

Renny drew his finely marked brows into a frown of disapproval.

"Miss Turnbull," he said, "never painted or smoked."

"Do you, Miss Wakefield?" asked Meg directly.

"That is not your affair. Now let us get on with our geography."

"I considah it my affair," said Renny, and intoned unctuously—"I considah . . . I considah . . ." till Mary had to threaten to take him to his elders.

Nicholas, strangely enough, Mary began to look on as almost an ally. Out of his deep-set dark eyes he would occasionally give her a glance, half mocking, half sympathetic, as though he understood the difficulties of her position and was, at any rate, not against her. He would stand no nonsense from Renny and once when he was struggling and shouting against being taken upstairs by Mary, Nicholas had appeared, promptly laid him across his knees, and administered several salutary smacks on his behind.

Since the night of the party Mary had met Lily Pink only once. Both had been alone and they had met face to face on the public road near the church. Lily had given Mary the impression that, if she could have run away, she would. 'Upon my word,' Mary thought, 'I might almost call it that "fateful night".'

She went towards Lily smiling. It was late afternoon and their shadows lay long across the road.

"It's two weeks and more since we met," Mary said, after greeting her.

"Yes, time flies," observed Lily, like a grandmother. She carried a sheaf of gladioli.

"What lovely gladioli!" exclaimed Mary.

"They are for the church."

"Are you going there now?"

"Yes. To practise on the organ."

"You play so well. I shall never forget how you played for our dancing."

Lily's face quivered at the mention of that night which should, she thought, be buried in oblivion forever.

"You played," Mary insisted, "as though you composed the piece that very moment, for that very waltz. It was wonderful."

"I'm glad you enjoyed it." Lily spoke with puritanical rigidity, as though the very thought of enjoyment were base.

"And we danced rather well, didn't we?"

"I never noticed."

Mary was crestfallen. They drew apart.

A farmer's wagon with a load of hay came down the road, the great feet of the horses treading softly in the dust. The girls separated to let it pass between them. Mary drew a deep breath of the scented load. The gladioli caught a wisp and held it draped across their bloom.

"Well, goodbye," said Lily, and then she gave Mary a look, almost of panic. "He's coming!" she breathed, and the gladioli trembled on her arm.

Philip looked singularly carefree to them, as he approached, as though their existence or the existence of any other woman meant nothing to him. He looked complete, bright and untarnished in his masculinity.

"I must hurry. I'm late," said Lily, but she lingered.

"Hullo!" he called out. "What are you two gossiping about?"

Lily looked at him in silent panic. Mary smiled and said— "We have only one subject for gossip."

"I'll wager I know what that is," he said. "Me."

Lily gazed at him in wonder. What *would* he say next!

"We were talking of Miss Pink's playing." Mary looked straight into his eyes.

He returned cheerfully—"Lily's a wonder. She looks so cool and remote. Yet who can tell what's in her? A bit of the devil, I sometimes think, eh, Lily?"

She turned and left them, almost running along the road, the gladioli bobbing on her arm.

"Now I've upset her. I shouldn't have said that."

Philip stared after the retreating figure.

"Was she always so shy?"

"Ever since I've known her and I've known her all her life. But she's getting worse. I'm inclined to think she dislikes me."

For an instant Mary felt like telling him the truth. 'Dislikes you! Why, she loves you madly.' But she said:

"I think it would do her good to get away for a bit. She's far too sensitive."

"Yes. It doesn't do. I'm afraid you are inclined to be like that too."

"But in a quite different way."

"You know, Miss Wakefield"—he cut a thistle with a switch he was carrying—"I've been intending to tell you how sorry I am my mother spoke to you as she did on the night of the dance. But she's like that. She'll come down on you like a thousand of bricks and then forget all about it."

Mary's lips felt stiff as she answered—"But she hasn't forgotten. I'm sure she dislikes me. So does Lady Buckley. It's horrible to be disliked."

"No, no, they don't dislike you."

"I think I ought to go."

"The children and I—why, we'd be disconsolate."

That cut her, to hear him speak of his feelings and the children's as comparable. It meant just one thing. He had been dallying with her. There had been nothing of real feeling in him. Now he was shielding himself behind his children. She hardened herself to say:

"Of course, if I'm giving satisfaction. . . ."

"Satisfaction!" he repeated warmly. "Your being here has meant so much more than that. You've been so"—he hesitated, then found a word he could use—"so congenial to me. I want you to feel that you're needed."

"Thank you," she said stiffly.

"And you won't talk of leaving?"

A cloud of dust showed the approach of Dr Ramsay in his buggy. He drew in his mare and saluted the two on the road with a grim smile.

"The drought continues," he said. "I doubt if we shall have good crops next year."

"The rain will come," said Philip easily.

"Out West the land is famished for water."

"I must say I enjoy this weather," said Philip.

"Naturally. You have the temperament to enjoy the passing pleasure, with no concern for the future. It's a good way to be, eh, Miss Wakefield?" Without waiting for an answer he demanded abruptly:

"Can I give either of you a lift? I have room for only one."

"Thank you, but I am going the other way. And I need the exercise. Good morning." Mary began to walk quickly along the road.

Philip looked pensively after her, then climbed into the buggy beside his father-in-law.

"A nice geerl," observed Dr Ramsay. "It's a pity she's so delicate."

"Is she delicate? I hadn't noticed."

"You don't think she looks strong, do you?"

"Well, perhaps not exactly *strong*, but healthy, I think."

"I wish I could agree with you. She has a weak heart. I could tell that by the way she breathed. She should not take these long walks. Also, I fear her lungs may not be good. Poor geerl. She is lucky to have a nice quiet home with you."

They were meeting another buggy. It was driven by Clive Busby, whose visit to the Vaughans was long extended. For some reason which he did not analyse Philip always encountered him with a feeling of distaste. Now he craned round the side of the buggy top to look after him. The young Westerner had given too confident a grin. His necktie had too gay a stripe. Was he going to settle down on the Vaughans for the autumn? Certainly they must be tired of him. He saw the buggy stop, Clive Busby alight and assist Mary to the seat. Dr Ramsay was amiably talking. The mare jogged peacefully on.

"What luck," Clive Busby was saying, "to overtake you. As a matter of fact I knew you were walking because I've been to Jalna with the sailboat I made for Renny and the children told me you had come this way."

"You are so kind to the children. You do so many nice things for them."

He turned to look at her. He was breathing rather quickly. "I think you know why," he said. "It isn't for the children's sake."

He had one of the nicest faces she had ever seen, she thought. He was a man whom, young as he was, people were always confiding in, telling their troubles to, confident of his sympathy. In the weeks since the dance he had managed to spend a good deal of time with her. She had been conscious of his drawing nearer and nearer to her with every meeting. There was something deadly in it, like the growth of a quickly growing tree in front of a little house, protective, but shutting off the outer world, the light, freedom. All the while she liked him better, felt more and more confidence in him, found him easy to understand. The Whiteoaks she never would understand, she thought. They were always making new combinations, expanding impressively, taking in all that was around them, then contracting into an impenetrable knot. Sometimes she wished she were a thousand miles from them, a thousand miles from the one she loved. Well—she might well go a thousand miles—two thousand—how far was it to the prairies?

Clive Busby was saying—"You know, I can just see you out in the West, with the wind blowing your hair and the length and breadth of the land about you. I'd be afraid to tell you how often I've pictured you there."

It was coming! She almost put out her hands to hold it off. She said:

"I'm afraid I'm not the sort pioneers are made of."

"But you are!" he exclaimed eagerly. "You are. You have no idea how many of your sort go out to the West and like it. It's a grand life. Nothing would induce them to come back to the East. Oh, Miss Wakefield—do you mind if I call you Mary?"

"I'd like it."

"And will you call me Clive?"

"I always think of you as Clive."

He turned his alarming blue eyes on her. They made her glad that his hands were occupied with the reins. "Do you really? Well, that shows you like me, doesn't it?"

"Oh, yes. I feel as though I'd known you for years."

"And yet we've gone on Mistering and Missing each other! Me *Missing* you! There's a pun for you. A pretty bad one, I admit. But I can't afford to miss you. You're the only girl in the world for me. I hadn't intended to say this today. I had it all fixed up to propose to you by the light of the new moon and here I am doing it out on the road in a buggy!"

Suddenly her mouth went perfectly dry. Her lips were stiff as she got out—"It's as good a place as any, but——"

He took the reins in one hand and laid the other on her two clasped hands, pressing them together, as though they represented himself and herself and he was uniting them in marriage.

"Mary"—he lingered on her name—"don't say no. We were made for each other. I tell you, if you search the world over, you won't find another man who loves you as I do."

She looked down at his strong hand, with the tan of the prairies on it. She felt the comfort, yes, the comfort of his presence. She pictured herself thousands of miles away from this place where nobody cared for her, secure in the shelter of Clive Busby's love. She, who had no one in all the world, would have him. She would no longer be alone, wondering what this one thought, wondering what that one thought, surrounded by undercurrents, stifled by people, yet alone. She would be in a house with a man whose presence was comfort and security, and, beyond the house, the clear flat land, stretching to the radiant horizon.

"But Clive," she began.

"Say it again," he interrupted. "It's wonderful to hear you say my name. Say it again. . . . Mary."

She was not getting on with her rejection of him. Before she realized it she would be accepting him. He looked so eager it went to her heart. "Clive," she repeated, and it was borne in on her how happy she could make him. What better could she do with her life than to make him happy?

"Yes"—he prompted—"you're saying yes, aren't you, Mary?"

"Give me time. I can't answer today."

"How long? Tomorrow?"

"No. A week."

His face fell. "A week? It seems very long—still, if you want a week, Mary dear—I'll wait a week. God knows I'd wait a year, if I thought you'd say yes at the end of it. . . . Mary—there's no one else, is there?"

"No one else wants to marry me."

"Thank goodness for that. I thought I had to compete with some rich fellow. Someone—like Philip Whiteoak."

"Oh, no."

"Mary, I believe you'll say yes—in a week. May I see you every day, in the meantime?"

"No, not once."

"Not once?" He looked despairing.

"No. . . . Please, Clive."

"Very well. I'll try to bear it but it will almost kill me." With a grim look he took his hands from hers, gripped the reins, and flapped them on the horse's back. The horse broke into an ambling pretence of going faster. The sun came out hotter, the goldenrod blazed in the ditches.

Lily was walking up the aisle of the church, the gladioli resting on her arm. Strangely the church looked even smaller when it was empty. The stained-glass windows seemed very near her. Their sumptuous colours were reflected in the flowers she carried. She walked gracefully, as though a long train fell from her shoulders and trailed behind her. She walked with dignity, as though every eye in a crowded church were on her.

When she reached the steps of the chancel she halted there a pace, with closed eyes. The figure of Philip Whiteoak, in a Prince Albert coat, with a white carnation in the buttonhole, had been waiting for her. Now they moved closer, till they stood side by side. Her father, in cassock and surplice, was about to begin the wedding ceremony.

So Lily stood, going through the service, word by word, inaudibly making the responses, in her imagination hearing Philip's voice repeat the words assigned to him. Was he placing the ring on her finger? What was she doing? Perhaps this pretence was wicked! She opened her eyes. The emptiness, the silence of the church were frightening. What would her mother think if she knew what play-acting she was up to? Surely she was a wicked girl. Surely she had, as Philip Whiteoak said, a bit of the devil in her. A bit of devil . . . devil. . . . She could not help laughing as the word echoed through her mind. She actually shook with silent laughter and the gladioli trembled.

Then she pulled herself together. She went to the vestry and got the two brass vases for the flowers. She went outdoors to the pump and filled them with water. She raised her innocent face to the sky and thought how blue it was. She looked down at the stream below the churchyard and saw how it reflected the blue of the sky. The vases were ice-cold in her hands.

She carried the flowers to the chancel and placed them reverently on the altar. She backed away a few steps and stood admiring them. . . . Then she went and sat down before the organ. Her hands were cold and wet from being under the pump. She rubbed the palms on her skirt.

In another moment the music of Mendelssohn's Wedding March filled the church.

# 13

# REVERSES

IN THESE weeks the mind of Ernest Whiteoak had been greatly disturbed but until now he had been able to keep his anxiety to himself. He had lost money in Crystal Palace A shares. He had lost money in Breweries. He had lost money in Cotton. He had been fooled by a broker into buying shares on margin. More and more good money had been thrown away to retain his shares. He was indeed playing with capital that was not his. He was gambling on market changes and only had to put up a small proportion of the sum at stake. This had given his somewhat credulous nature a false feeling of power, and a pleasant exhilaration in the exercise of that power. He was even less fitted to gamble on the stock market than was Nicholas, but his earlier successes had made him bold.

Now he bitterly regretted leaving England. His communications with his broker had of necessity been made by cable. He was positive that, if he had been on the spot, he could have managed his affairs efficiently.

The latest messages he had received had made him incapable of clear thought. His mind was too confused by his losses to be able to do more than reiterate—'If only I had been there!'

He had been so sure that, not only was he going to augment his fortune, as indeed for a time he had, but that he would double it. Now, with a sinking heart, he sought out his brother Nicholas.

Nicholas was sunning himself on the rustic seat, beneath a stately silver birch that grew in the centre of the lawn. Between his feet sat Jake, gazing up into his face with ecstasy, as Nicholas fondled his ears and gently tickled the back of his neck.

Ernest came swiftly across the grass and stood in front of his brother.

Nicholas looked up. Then he saw the expression on Ernest's face and asked—"Anything wrong?"

Ernest gave a groan of affirmation, then sat down on the bench beside him.

"Wrong! It could scarcely be worse. New Gaston Mining stock has fallen from $3\frac{1}{8}$ to $\frac{1}{2}$."

"Ha! What can you do about it?"

"Nothing. South-Eastern Railways has declined."

Nicholas turned his large eyes sympathetically on his brother.

"Hard luck," he muttered.

"If only I'd been in England I'd have got out of it in time."

"I wonder. I didn't, you know."

"Nick, you haven't the flair for speculation that I have. Oh, if only I had been there!" He sprang to his feet and began pacing up and down.

"There is one thing certain," said Nicholas. "We shall have to draw in our horns when we go back to London."

"Nick, when I have sifted the dregs of this catastrophe, I think I shall find myself a poor man."

"Surely it isn't as bad as that."

"Nick, I shall have to spend more time at Jalna."

"Yes. There's always Jalna."

"Oh, if only I were in England now!"

"You couldn't have done anything, old man."

"Curse that broker."

"Only a few weeks ago you seemed quite pleased with him—and yourself."

"I was. I thought I was going to more than make up for my earlier losses."

"I told you more than once that you depended too much on him."

"No one could have depended more on a broker than you did on yours."

"I don't pretend to be knowing about investments."

"Neither do I. I don't *pretend*, but I am very cognizant of what goes on in the market. My broker told me it was quite remarkable—I mean my grasp of it all. Oh, I wish I were in London!"

"Why not go?"

"It's too late, I tell you. Unless, of course, I had more capital. I wonder if Mamma——"

"Never. She'd never lend you a penny."

"She might if I promised to double it for her."

"You're more optimistic than I am."

"Perhaps Philip. . . ."

"You can try him but I doubt it."

"There he is now. He's been fishing. It's a propitious moment."

Philip, seeing them, turned in their direction. He had on a disreputable old jacket, a pair of baggy duck trousers, and he needed a haircut. For once, the immaculate Ernest did not notice these details of his brother's costume.

"Hullo, Philip," he greeted him genially. "Had any luck?"

Philip held up his fishing basket, in which lay eight gleaming trout.

"Oh, very nice. Quite a change from last time when you didn't get even a bite."

"Enjoyed it just the same," said Philip, laconically.

"Still, it was not like having a nice little catch like this."

"N-no. But I enjoyed it. A lovely morning, that was."

"Autumn is coming."

"Yes. Look at this birch tree. I like its little yellow leaves. They're the first to turn."

Nicholas leant forward to look at the fish. "Good ones," he said. "I shall have one for my breakfast."

"Sit down, Philip," said Ernest. "I want to tell you something."

They made room for him on the rustic seat. He sat down and lighted his pipe. Jake, with an apologetic leer at Nicholas, moved from between his knees to between Philip's. Philip looked inquiringly and a little defensively at Ernest.

Ernest came straight to the point. "I've had bad news," he said. "Stocks I've been holding on to have fallen. I'm going to lose quite a lot of money, I'm afraid."

"What a surprise," said Philip. "I thought you were getting rich."

"So I was! And so I should yet, if I had more capital. I'll explain the whole matter."

He embarked on a long explanation of the state of his affairs, and if at times he grew a little confused, it did not really matter.

"It's all Greek to me," said Philip. "What do you want me to do?"

Ernest's self-esteem was returning. "If you could make me a loan," he said, "it would save the day."

"How?"

"Well, these stocks are bound to revive. I could hang on till they do."

"I never like the idea of gambling in stocks." Philip opened

137

Jake's mouth and looked with concentrated interest at his teeth.

"You can't call this gambling, Philip. These investments are sound. There'll be little risk. Don't you agree, Nicholas?"

"I won't commit myself."

"Well, as my broker has often remarked, I have a remarkable flair——"

"What's all this?" asked a strong voice. The three rose and discovered Adeline close behind them. She placed her hands on the back of the seat and looked quizzically from face to face.

How much had she overheard, Ernest wondered. But, whether it were much or little, she was bound to find out all. He could not keep anything away from her and he knew it.

"Come and sit down, old girl," said Nicholas. He went to her and put his arm about her. He led her to a seat, gently smacking her on the hip with the flat of his hand.

A harsh note came into her voice as she spoke.

"You've lent Ernest money before this, Philip," she said. "Don't you do it again. I won't have it."

"Then," exclaimed Ernest hotly, "you would have me lose my investment, for lack of a little more capital!"

"I had rather you lost it than to cripple Jalna. If Philip were anyone else, I'd say go ahead."

"Perhaps then you yourself would be willing," said Ernest eagerly.

"I am a poor woman," she returned, looking gloomily at her shoes. "I have little enough to live on."

"Poor old girl," said Nicholas.

"Then," said Philip, wanting to hear her confirm her opposition, "you advise me not to go into this?"

"I don't advise. I say I won't have it."

Nicholas winked at Philip.

Adeline laid her hand on Ernest's knee, who had sat down beside her. "Come," she said. "Take this loss like a man. I heard all your explanation and I'm sure this is a bad case. Be thankful you have something left and don't throw good money after bad. I hope Robert Vaughan has not invested in these things."

"I'm afraid he has," answered Ernest. "But by no means disastrously."

Adeline groaned, then exclaimed vivaciously, "I'll tell you

what—you, Ernest, must marry Muriel Craig! She will inherit a considerable fortune. You needn't worry any longer."

"Miss Craig cares nothing for me," said Ernest, crossly. "It's Philip she is after."

"Then you should make her care for you," said Adeline. "What is your feeling towards her?"

Ernest put the tips of his fingers together and said judiciously—"A kind of tepid admiration."

"You couldn't have a better beginning, with your temperament. You will warm to her as time goes on."

"I repeat it is Philip she wants."

"Well, here she comes like Paris with the golden apple and here are the three of you waiting. Let her make her choice."

From the thick evergreens that fringed the drive Muriel Craig's trap emerged, drawn by a pretty chestnut cob. She sat very straight, holding the reins high, the small elegant whip in one hand. She looked self-conscious, rather than confident. The three brothers went quickly towards her. Adeline, looking after them, thought—"If she chooses by distinction, it's Nicholas—if by elegance, it's Ernest—if she prefers an untidy rapscallion, as she probably does, it's Philip."

She greeted Muriel Craig warmly, giving at the same time an appraising look at her, out of narrowed dark eyes.

"How fresh you look, my dear, and what a pretty striped shirtwaist!"

"I'm glad you like it. My father thinks the stripe rather loud."

"Not a bit of it. If anyone can wear that stripe you can. What do you say, Ernest?"

"I say she can wear it," he returned, tepidly.

"Mr Ernest does not sound very enthusiastic," said Muriel Craig. "I'm afraid he also considers it too loud." She turned to Philip. "What do you think, Mr Philip?"

"I always like stripes. Like 'em loud, too."

Nicholas thought—"The girl is positively languishing for Philip. Ernest has no chance whatever."

The children ran out of the house shouting, their lessons over, free for the rest of the day. They began to pull handfuls of grass for Miss Craig's cob.

"Oh, the sweet children!" she exclaimed. "I must go to see them." She sprang up and swept across the grass. A straight line might have been drawn from her chin to her instep.

"Children!" she called. "I have brought you candy!"

From the seat of the trap she took a small box of butter-scotch. They were delighted. Meg thrust a square of it into her mouth, and mumbled her thanks.

"You should have passed it round first, you greedy girl," said Renny.

Her cheek distended, her teeth glued together, Meg, holding the box in front of her, proffered it to her elders.

Philip made as though to join Miss Craig.

Adeline gave him the dark look she had for him nowadays.

"Don't go," she said. "Leave that to Ernest."

Ernest rose. He refused butterscotch but Adeline took a piece with eagerness. "A very small box," she commented in an undertone to Nicholas. "I hope the girl isn't mean."

Philip watched Ernest's progress with amusement.

"An ardent suitor, what!" he remarked.

"That fellow," said Nicholas, "will never reach the point of proposing to any girl."

"Ernest has plenty of character," said his mother. "Give him time."

Ernest had reached Miss Craig's side. He smiled pleasantly and said—"How is your father, Miss Craig?"

"Improving every day. He is beginning to walk again. He has a most efficient nurse who seldom leaves his side."

"How very satisfactory."

"Yes. But she really is a detestable woman."

"How annoying."

"But I hear that all nurses become overbearing."

"I shouldn't wonder." After a silence he asked:

"Would you care to see our dahlias? They're very fine."

She hesitated. "I'm afraid I should be going. My father. . . ."

"The dahlias really are especially good."

Her eyes wandered to the group on the lawn.

Ernest thought—'I was never meant for this. A fortune-hunter. It's humiliating.' Then the remembrance of Mr Craig's wealth stood out as promising deliverance from his financial worries, and she was a personable girl—an attractive girl. He wondered at his own coldness.

Mary came out to the porch where its drapery of Virginia creeper was just beginning to redden. Soon the frosts would set it flaming and turn the dahlias black.

"Ernest is taking Miss Craig to see the dahlias," observed Nicholas. "That looks promising."

"There's Miss Wakefield!" cried Renny. "May I take her a piece of butterscotch?"

"Not just one piece," said Adeline. "Offer her the box. Then ask her if she will be kind enough to go to the rectory and ask Mrs Pink for the recipe she promised me. You children had better go with her. Come first and kiss me."

He clambered on her knee, hugged and kissed her.

Philip rose. He extracted a piece of butterscotch from between Jake's jaws, which was causing him acute misery, and threw it into the shrubbery. Jake at once set out on an intensive search for it.

"Don't go, Philip," said Adeline, more kindly than she had spoken to him since the night of the party. "I've scarcely set eyes on you today."

"I'll be back before long, Mamma," he said, stubbornly. "Nick will be with you."

He went towards the porch.

"Look at the shape of his trousers!" exclaimed Adeline. "The set of his jacket! I can't imagine what any girl sees in him. Think of your father's back—the way he wore his clothes! The contrast is terrible. I wonder Philip can be my husband's son."

"Don't worry about him, Mamma. All the girls are after him."

"Ah, if only I could get that governess out of the house! And do it I will, by hook or by crook."

Philip stood looking up at Mary.

"Did you get my mother's message, Miss Wakefield?" he asked. For the first time he noticed how she'd gone off in her looks.

"Yes. I'm setting out now."

"We want to go too," immediately came from Renny.

"I don't think he should," Mary said. "He runs so much on the way and gets hot and it makes his hives itch."

"I'll stay with him," volunteered Meg.

"Good girl," said her father.

She clung to one hand, Renny tugged at the other. Between them they made a wall, always between her and Philip, thought Mary, and believed he wished it so.

"Are you quite well?" he asked, thinking of what Dr Ramsay had said of Mary's health.

"Perfectly, thank you." Did he think she was slack in her duties?

"You look a little pale to me. Perhaps you are losing your English complexion."

Meg began to laugh. She put an arm about Renny's neck and whispered in his ear—"She forgot her paint."

"I felt the heat," Mary said, "but this weather is lovely."

Ernest and Muriel Craig came round the house.

"What heavenly dahlias!" she cried. "I've never seen their equal. Mr Whiteoak has promised me some bulbs." She greeted Mary with that air of condescension which made her long to escape from Miss Craig's presence or be rude to her.

"How well your charges look!" she exclaimed. "Really they are a credit to you."

"We look well," said Renny, whose grin showed a front tooth missing, "because we paint."

"Oh, you rascal!" Miss Craig threw both arms enthusiastically about the little boy. "The things you say! I tremble for what *you'll* be when you're a man."

She spoke as though she had suffered a good deal at the hands of dashing men, yet not entirely without pleasure.

"He'll be a rip, I fear," said Ernest.

Still holding the child to her, Miss Craig said to Philip: "I have a message from my father for you. He is *so* anxious to see you—about something, I'm not quite sure what it is. Your mere presence helps him. He wondered if you could drive back with me. Then, this evening, one of our men is coming in this direction and would bring you home. For my part I'd be grateful for a lesson in driving this cob. I know I'm a silly little thing but I'm terrified of him."

Renny had never before heard a woman call herself a silly little thing. Neither his grandmother nor his aunt was in the habit of so describing herself. Mary posed as an encyclopaedia of knowledge and a Gibraltar of firmness. Yet there was something that did not ring quite true in Miss Craig's words. He and Mary exchanged a look that on his side might almost have been called sardonic.

Philip agreed with alacrity. He had noticed Miss Craig's self-conscious and inefficient manner of handling the reins.

"But first I must tidy myself," he said.

"Please don't. We know you have been fishing. If coming with me forced you to change, I should never forgive myself. *We* think he looks very nice as he is, don't we, children?"

The children chorused yes.

Philip, however, went into the house to make himself respectable. Mary at once set off on her errand, for she would not remain a moment longer than necessary in Miss Craig's company. Ernest and Muriel Craig watched her figure disappear along the drive. He felt deeply rebuffed by Miss Craig's open lack of interest in him and in the dahlias. For once in his life he made no attempt to be agreeable to a visitor but stood silent and abstracted. Muriel Craig was silent too. Her round light eyes took in every detail of Mary's dress and seemed to probe beneath the dress into the very body that pulsed beneath.

But, as Philip's returning steps were heard in the hall, her eyes turned to where the children were romping on the lawn with the spaniels, and she exclaimed:

"How I love those two children!"

Ernest made no reply but Philip gave her a gratified look. "I'm glad to hear it," he said. "Sometimes they're pretty bad, you know."

She refused to believe any such thing. Ernest held the cob steady while Philip assisted her to mount to the seat. A well-shod foot, a pretty ankle, and a rustling taffeta petticoat were, for an intriguing moment, visible. Ernest said goodbye coolly, and, lighting a cigarette, paced a number of times up and down before the house. His naturally sanguine nature took heart. After all, he was not ruined. He still had enough to live on, and live quite well too, provided he spent part of each year at Jalna. He always enjoyed being there. Philip was a good-humoured and generous host. In truth, Adeline and her three older children scarcely looked on Philip as a host but rather as the youngest son who had by good fortune been chosen by his father as inheritor of the estate and whose duty it was to make them welcome at all times. As for Philip, there was nothing he liked better than to have them there with him.

Now Ernest made his way back to the garden seat and dropped down on it with a sigh. Nicholas gave him a dubious look. He hoped Ernest was not going to remain in the dumps over his losses.

Adeline remarked—"Did ye notice how well the cob moved down the drive? He knew he had a good man at the reins."

"That young woman," said Nicholas, "handled them as if they were hot pokers."

Adeline turned to Ernest. "Did you make any headway with her?" she asked.

"Not a bit," he replied testily. "And to tell the truth I don't want to. She is not at all my sort. I have no wish to be married."

"It seems a pity," said Adeline, "never to put out a hand to capture all that money. These losses of yours, Ernest, show how easy it is to lose it. Now here is a fortune, at our very door, and I have two attractive sons——"

"What's the matter with Philip?" asked Nicholas.

"I don't want another woman at Jalna."

"Mamma," said Ernest, "it is inevitable that Philip will marry again. It's plain that Miss Craig wants him. Take my advice and don't do anything to discourage him. If you do you may get a daughter-in-law you'll like much less. You might even get Miss Wakefield, who hasn't a shilling to her name."

Adeline turned to him sharply. "Have you seen anything suspicious since the dance?"

"N-no. But propinquity often leads to regard."

"Ernest, you did a bad day's work when you engaged that designing creature. I might have known better than to trust you to show any sense where a female is concerned."

"You might indeed," he returned tranquilly. "I don't know the first thing about the average woman. You are the only woman I pretend to understand, but then you make yourself so clear."

"Certainly," put in Nicholas, "Miss Craig makes her intention clear. She is tooth and claw after Philip and, in my opinion, he wants to be hooked."

"Speaking of being hooked," said Ernest, "here are his fish. He's gone off without a second thought for them. I think I had better carry them down to the kitchen." He picked up the basket from where it stood on the rustic table. He hesitated a moment and then said—"I have an investment in mind which I am positive will recoup the losses I have had—not only cancel them but make me a great deal more. The things is that I shall be on the spot to watch the fluctuations of the stocks. If I had been there this summer things would be very different with me now." He went to the house gently swinging the basket of fish in his hand.

144

"D'ye think he may do what he says?" Adeline asked, her eyes following Ernest.

"I shouldn't be surprised. He has a decided flair for speculation, but don't you ever be persuaded, Mamma, to invest anything on his advice."

"Trust me to hang on to what I have!" she exclaimed. "It's little enough, God knows, but 'twill keep me in my old age."

She watched Nicholas light a fresh cigarette and put out her shapely hand for one. However, she surreptitiously took the light he gave her and looked almost fearfully towards the house as she inhaled.

"That hussy, Mary Wakefield, smokes," she said. "I wouldn't have Nettle see me do it, not for anything."

The trap bowled brightly along the tree-lined road, the cob moving in accord with the pleasant pressure he felt on the reins. Philip and Murial Craig made a handsome pair, she very upright, her sailor hat tilted forward, he wearing a checked coat and yellow gloves. He twiddled the whip, admiring the scarlet ribbon bow on its handle.

"I can't tell you," she said, "how nice it is just to sit here with my hands in my lap, and watch someone else drive—particularly when they handle the reins as you do."

"This cob," he said, "is gentle enough, but he needs more exercise. I'm afraid you're a bit nervous, Miss Craig."

"I am—I am! And I'm so ashamed. I don't think I should be half so nervous on horseback. It's the thought of this high trap overturning that makes me tremble. My father promises to buy me a saddle horse if I'll learn to ride it. But who will teach me? There are so few who ride excepting your family."

"I'll gladly teach you."

She clapped her hands. "Oh, how lovely that will be! Are you sure it won't bore you?"

"Come now, Miss Craig, can you imagine my being bored in your company?"

"I wish I couldn't," she said humbly, "but I'm afraid I can imagine anything. I'm far too imaginative."

Philip looked into her round, matter-of-fact eyes and doubted it. A couple of generations ago, he decided, she would have been pretending to swoon.

"Oh," she cried, "there is Miss Wakefield on the road ahead

of us! Do you think we could squeeze her into the seat with us? She walks as though she were so tired."

"It would be a close fit," he returned, his eyes searchingly on Mary's back. "Besides, she's going only as far as the Pinks'. Do you really think she seems tired?"

"Perhaps it's just her shoes. I always feel that shoes should be chosen for the wear they're to have. What I mean is, on rough country roads it's better to have brogues like I wear."

They had overtaken Mary. Philip drew in the horse. She looked up at them defensively. Miss Craig leaned towards her with a solicitous air.

"We think you look *so* tired, Miss Wakefield. We'd love to give you a lift but there's scarcely room for three on the seat. So I'm going to propose that Mr Whiteoak shall drive you to the Pinks' while I trudge manfully along the road in my big brogues. Your shoes are so dainty, they're better suited to city pavements, aren't they?"

"Thank you. I'm not at all tired."

"Oh, yes, you are! You can't fool us. We know, by the way you walk. Do let me out, Mr Whiteoak."

"If anyone is to get out it will be me." He put the reins into Miss Craig's hands. Their hands touched and she gave him a small, intimate smile, as though they spoke in a language no one else could understand.

Mary included him in the icy look she gave Miss Craig.

"I want to walk," she said. "My shoes may be all wrong but they feel quite comfortable to me. Good morning." She turned away.

"Now we've offended you!" cried Miss Craig. "Please, please, don't be offended, Miss Wakefield! It breaks my heart if I think I've offended anyone. You mustn't misunderstand me. I think your shoes are quite the prettiest I've ever seen. I only meant—I'd love to walk and let Mr Whiteoak drive you to the Pinks'."

Mary gave her a look of speechless anger and literally strode down the road. Little whorls of dust circled about her skirts.

Miss Craig returned the reins to Philip. She drooped, almost on his shoulder, and he saw that her eyes were swimming in tears.

"Why," he exclaimed, in astonishment, "surely you're not crying!"

"Oh, I'm such a silly," she sobbed.

"You are indeed." His eyes were puzzled and kind. "I don't know what it all was about."

"She hates me and I can't bear to be hated."

"Now that's sheer nonsense."

"You saw the look on her face."

He could not deny that he had.

"But you mustn't cry," he said, and patted her hand.

His sympathy was more than she could bear. Now her head was indeed on his shoulder, her sailor hat tilted precariously over one ear. He flapped the reins on the cob's back and they jogged past Mary in this position.

Philip had never been more uncomfortable. With Miss Craig's head so unexpectedly on his shoulder—'just as though I were a hired man—taking my girl for a buggy ride,' he thought—with Mary's eyes boring a hole in his back, he thought yearningly of the tranquil hours he had spent with his fishing-rod.

He shifted his shoulder a little and she sat upright and straightened her hat. Her face was flushed and smiling now. He had never seen her look so pretty. She was leaning forward to smile at a figure that was just emerging from the shadow of a clump of cedars.

"Did you see?" she laughed. "Young Mr Busby? He's waiting for Miss Wakefield. No wonder she was annoyed with me for offering her a lift. She didn't want to miss him."

"He's probably not waiting for her."

"Oh, certainly he is. I felt something in the air. And now I'm *so* glad because I know she wasn't really angry at me but only at my interference with her plans. I'm *so* glad, because I think she's a dear thing, and always *so* unhappy looking." Her voice took on a new intimacy. "Just glance over your shoulder and see this meeting. It will be fun to see them get together, in spite of our efforts to divide them."

"Indeed I shall do nothing of the sort." He flicked the cob with the whip, and stared sulkily between its ears. After a moment he asked—"Well, did they meet?"

"You *know* I'm peeping! But I just can't help myself. It's so fascinating to get a glimpse of a romantic love affair at close quarters. The rich young rancher and the poor governess! Now—they *have* met! And what a meeting! Did I say her feet were tired? I take it all back. She fairly ran to him and he's taken both her hands. Oh, it's divine! Why *will* you drive so fast, Mr Whiteoak? Don't you think it's good for me to see two happy people?"

Mary had watched the passing of the trap, the attitudes of its occupants, with astonishment. She was so astonished to see Muriel Craig's head against Philip's shoulder, her sailor hat pushed rakishly to one side, that, for a moment, she felt no other emotion.

"Good heavens!" she said out loud. "Is that the way things are with them! He'll be kissing her next—out on the open road!" Her voice shook and was strangled in her throat by a surge of jealousy. She could only say—"Oh, Philip, how could you! Philip. . . ." The beloved name became a knife to stab her breast. Jealousy made her feet uncertain. She scarcely could keep to the road. She had a mind to throw herself into the dusty ditch, to tear at the nettles and thistles with her bare hands. She had not imagined jealousy could be so devastating as this. Her feelings on the night of the dance when he had ignored her were as nothing compared to the vehemence of what she now suffered.

What could have passed between them to make that stiff-starched creature droop to his shoulder like a flower in the heat of the sun? And her hat! Mary's sensitive lip curled at the thought of Muriel Craig's hat. The fool—the stupid creature —and *he*, the flirt—the heartless flirt—treating her, alone in a strange country—so terribly alone—with calculated cruelty!

Her eyes, though they were wide open, were unaware of Clive Busby coming towards her. She would have passed him, oblivious of him, but he hastened to meet her with his hands outstretched. He took hers into them and his grasp was sharp on her fingers. She looked into his face, scarcely seeing him.

"Why," he exclaimed, "why, Mary, your hands are ice cold! And out in the sun—on a day like this!"

Over his shoulder she saw the trap disappear round a bend in the road.

"I have been sitting most of the day teaching," she said. "My circulation is poor. But I'm quite all right." She gently withdrew her hands and walked on.

He fell into step at her side.

"Are you sure you're all right?" he persisted. "You're very pale."

"I'm perfectly well."

"Mary, you didn't turn pale because you saw me coming?"

"I didn't see you."

"You know what day it is?"

"No. What day?"

"Mary . . . you're tormenting me!"

Then she remembered.

"The week is up," she said. "I remember now."

His voice trembled in his hurt. "Does it mean so little to you then? Oh, Mary. . . ." She saw the rich colour flood his face.

She spoke in a breathless staccato way. "I've been thinking so much—my mind is confused. I'd forgotten the exact day. But you mustn't be fond of me, Clive. You mustn't."

"As though I can help it. You might as well say to Niagara, 'Restrain yourself.' Mary, I've lived years in this past week and all of them with you—out on the prairies. All of them with you."

She turned her eyes away from him. "Haven't you thought of the reverse?"

"No! I wouldn't let myself. I made up my mind to have this week of hope—even if—no, I never let myself think of—I couldn't." He was not able to speak coherently but tried with his appealing eyes to draw her eyes back to him.

Is all this so important, she thought, does it matter what I do—whether I marry him or not? Does it matter what becomes of me? But I do mind being alone. It is comforting to have him walking along the road beside me—to know if I put out my hand I can touch him. When she spoke her mouth felt dry and her lips stiff. The poison of jealousy had run through her, like fire in prairie grass.

"Clive," she said, "you wouldn't want to marry a woman who——"

"Loves someone else!" he broke in, his voice suddenly harsh. "That's what you're trying to say. I know you love someone else and I think I know who it is. Mary, is it Philip Whiteoak you love? Are you trying to tell me you love Philip Whiteoak?"

She looked at him aghast, as though a stranger had stopped her on the road and talked to her of the secrets of her heart. What colour she had ebbed from her face. She walked faster, the fresh breeze blowing the thin stuff of her dress against her taut body.

"You have no right," she said. "If I did love him it would be my secret, but I don't love him. I hate him."

"So that's it," he said slowly. His legs seemed to grow heavy beneath him and he fell behind her. "That's what the trouble is."

She stopped now and waited for him. He looked young and pathetic. She felt a maternal pity for him.

"Clive," she said, her eyes clear and candid, "I wish it had been you. I'd have loved to love you."

"The point is," he answered fiercely, "that it satisfies you better to hate him than to love me."

"You have no idea how unhappy I am."

His hands touched hers for an instant.

"I wish I could do something about it," he said. "But I can't do anything, can I? This is the funniest rejection I've ever heard of a fellow getting. To be told that the girl he adores would love to love him. Gosh, it makes a fellow's head swim!"

"It's true."

"But my case is hopeless, eh?"

"You wouldn't want a wife who didn't love you."

"You've said that before!"

"Clive, I'd rather make you happy than anyone I know."

"Rather than *him*! Come, now, Mary."

"*He's* happy," she returned bitterly. "Happy as a man need be."

"Now I look at it this way. Philip Whiteoak is rich. He's generous and kind, so they say. But I say he thinks only of himself. He'll never trouble to understand any woman. He'll just go on in his happy-go-lucky way, not noticing if his wife's happy or not. Now this may be a mean thing to say but I've been told that he didn't make his first wife very happy."

She turned to him passionately. "Why should you explain Mr Whiteoak to me? He's nothing to me. Nothing. If I said I hated him I spoke foolishly. I take these violent dislikes. The truth is I dislike the whole family. So much indeed that I feel I must leave and find a new post. There's something in that house I can't endure."

"Mary, is all this true?"

"Yes."

"And you're really going to leave Jalna?"

"Yes."

"Then come to me, Mary darling. I'll love you so dearly you won't be able to help loving me back. Do say yes."

Looking into his face she felt that she could learn to love him. Her feeling for him was almost love. Surely a deeper kindness was in her than many a woman brought to her marriage. He would take her to a new free life, far from this place, from these people whom she never wanted to set eyes on again. Oh, she was so lonely! Loneliness cried out in her. And here was a man who loved her truly and unselfishly. She might go through life and never meet such another. His love, his nearness, overpowered her. She could not speak but she stretched out her hand to clasp his.

## 14

## CONGRATULATIONS

SHE SLEPT more peacefully than she had for many nights. She gave herself up to sleep as a wave-tossed boat sinks into the soft sand of the shore. Her sleep was deep and she dreamed her favourite dreams, the childish dreams that she did not want to be woken from. There was the one in which she was back in school and had won all the best prizes and the other students and visitors looked at her in astonishment and admiration because she never did win prizes, being always too much confused by the examination papers. Then there was the one in which she, at will, rose from a crowded street and floated above the heads of the people, who stopped whatever they were doing, to gaze up at her. Sometimes she would perch on a gable and wave down at them, sometimes hide behind a chimney-pot. Always she ended on the dome of St Paul's Cathedral, while traffic, buses, carts, drays, carriages, horses of all sorts, flower sellers, porters, beggars, gentlemen in top hats, stood spellbound. Yet, all through her dreams was the suspicion people were laughing at her.

Not through all the night did she dream of Philip Whiteoak or Clive Busby or even dream that she was quite grown up.

Very early she was woken by the clangour of the turkey gobbler's voice on the lawn beneath her window. Never before had he brought his family there at such an hour. Now he put forth all the power in his breast to rouse the world, to defy it for the sake of those in his train.

Mary got up, wrapped a blanket about her, and went to the window. She wanted to look out on this new day, with this new feeling in her heart, and discover what it was like. She saw the turkey cock, his head on one side, staring at the east where the light was clearest above the treetops. But all colours were quiet excepting the wattles of the cock, which were bright red. He shook his head and tossed them, eyeing his seven wives, his many sons and daughters. The air was so cool and fresh it felt like frost. The sun now began to appear above the blackness of the trees. The vast sky filled with light. It was a mackerel sky and like the scales of a fish the countless small clouds took on brightness. The bed of geraniums rivalled the turkey cock's wattles.

Now he dropped his burnished wings with a metallic sound and moved slowly in a circle. The tassel-like appendage above his beak, his wattles, grew fiery red. The tips of his wings scored the dew-grey grass. He eyed the circle about him with potential fury. His eldest son shook his plumage, half dropped his wings but drew them up again. The hen turkeys uttered little wavering cries.

Mary drank in the pure air, scented with pine. She huddled the blanket about her, feeling herself safe inside it, as the kernel of a nut inside the shell. She lived only in the upper part of her mind, keeping one chamber of it locked away. In that chamber was the figure of Philip Whiteoak. The walls would narrow on it, day by day, till at last it was obliterated.

The sunlight, with a little warmth in it, now fell full on her face and her hair. It gave her strength, as sunlight always did. She began to make her plans for the day. She would seek out Mrs Whiteoak and tell her she wished to leave. She knew how gladly that news would be received. She would beg to be allowed to leave as soon as possible. Clive would come and tell Philip how eager he was for an early marriage. He could not remain much longer in the East. He wanted to take Mary back with him as his wife.

She thought of the flat sweep of the prairies, the wooden house, with the stiff new furniture, the piano, a few small shrubs growing in the shelter of the house, the unfenced waving grain, the half wild horses, the thriving cattle, all so young and full of hope. Clive himself, with his shoulders always between her and the roughness of life, his kind hands. Perhaps she would have his children. But she drew away from the thought of that. It was too great a leap forward. The chasm that separated this day from those to follow was enough. She lay, almost indolently, across the sill preparing herself. . . . When the children's lessons are over I will go straight to Mrs Whiteoak and say I hope she will not find it an inconvenience if I leave. I will ask her if she can possibly let me go quite soon. I will stand looking straight into her eyes and talk coolly to her. If she asks me my reason I will say I am engaged to be married. I will let that sink in for a moment before I say anything further . . . then I'll say it's to Clive Busby. She'll be pleased, and God knows I'm sorry to please her. . . . And *he*, what will he think? Let him think what he likes! It is nothing to me.

The turkey cock had led his family down into the ravine, and from there his *gobble-gobble* came, vibrant with his own importance. What treasures were down there, in the cool shadow, waiting to be ravaged by vigorous beaks? The stream could be heard faintly murmuring its way through the ravine, weakened by drought. There was farewell in its murmur. She had loved it. And she had loved the little bridge that spanned it, and the trees that shouldered each other down to the brink of the stream.

Now it was goodbye to them all.

She rose, folded the blanket, and began to dress. Deliberately she kept her face set and cold, like a marble wall she erected against the people in this house. All but the children. She felt a sudden pity for them. What an unsympathetic stepmother Muriel Craig would be! The children were nicer than usual this morning. They were quieter, as though they felt something different about her, and Meg looked at her with a critical air, as though she wore a new garment.

Mary made the lessons as easy as possible for them, and put them in a good humour, giving them a feeling of proficiency. They sat up straight, beaming at their books and at her.

"How nice you are this morning," observed Renny, his eyes on her face, as though he would wrench her niceness from her and examine it.

"I thought I always was nice."

He gave his high treble laugh. "Not you. You're often as nasty—as nasty as I am."

"Which is saying a good deal."

"What does that mean?"

"Well, you can be pretty nasty."

He raised his eyebrows and looked down his nose, as he had seen Miss Turnbull do. "I considah," he said, "that I do it only for your good."

On a sudden impulse Mary put an arm about him and hugged him. How responsive he was! His wiry little body was galvanized into an answering embrace. Meg looked on disapprovingly. She said:

"Nettle thinks it's silly for a boy to hug his governess."

There it is, thought Mary, antagonism on every side! How glad I shall be to leave! She rose, went to the window, and looked at the sky, as though for freedom. The room became unreal to her. She felt herself already on her way.

The children were clamouring to be off to their ponies. She dismissed them and went slowly down the stairs.

The character of the sunlight had changed in these last days. Now it gilded all it touched with the ruddy tinge of autumn. The light from the stained-glass window in the hall lay in rich-coloured patches. As Mary reached the last steps a green light was cast on her face and for a moment she looked like a drowned woman. She stood listening, her hand on the carved grapes of the newel-post. In front of her stood the hat-rack, with one of Philip's hats on it, a soft, rather battered hat that, more than once, had been romped with by Jake. She turned her eyes from it.

From the sitting-room came the sound of a pen moving scratchily over paper. She went to the door and saw Adeline Whiteoak seated at the writing-desk. Unobserved Mary looked in on her.

She had never been more impressed by her air of distinction. She had always thought that the lace cap, wired to a peak on the forehead, added to it, but now the cap had been left off and the shape of the head disclosed, and the way the hair grew. Her shoulders were beautiful, so were her hands, Mary thought. A frown bent her brows as her sharp pen dug and sputtered on the notepaper. She looked up and saw Mary.

"Miss Wakefield," she said, "have you such a thing as a new pen-nib? If I don't remember to put mine away each time I have written a letter, one of my sons comes along, uses it, and leaves it wrecked."

"Yes, I have one. I'll get it for you right away."

"No. Not now. This letter is finished and a pretty sight it is. But this afternoon I'd be greatly obliged for a new nib."

"Mine are stubs, I'm afraid."

"I can use any sort. This is one Nettle gave me and I must say it reflects her temper."

Mary stepped inside the room. "Mrs Whiteoak, may I speak privately to you?"

"Yes. Of course. Come in and shut the door." Her brown eyes were narrowed by curiosity, her lips firm, as though she expected trouble.

"I want to tell you," Mary said slowly, "that I should like to leave."

"To leave? Why?"

"Because——" Mary's colour rose and she ended quickly, "because I'm going to be married."

"To be married! Ha——"

"I am wondering if it might be possible for me to leave rather soon. Of course, I don't wish to inconvenience you or Mr Whiteoak, but if I could——"

"May I ask whom you are going to marry, Miss Wakefield?"

"Mr Busby."

Adeline's face relaxed into a look of profound relief. It seemed too good to be true. The scheme she had so spontaneously adumbrated on the night of the dance now was presented to her clearly defined, complete. She raised her eyes, shining with good will, to Mary's flushed face.

"Miss Wakefield," she said, "I am really pleased because I don't know another young couple who I think are so well matched. Clive Busby is manly, strong, ambitious, and has an affectionate nature. I've known his father and his grandfather before him. All fine men. You need have no fear. On your side you will give him the comeliness, the taste, his nature craves for. My dear, you have shown your good sense. I congratulate you—and Clive too. I will write to my friend Isaac Busby and congratulate him on his future daughter-in-law."

She rose and took Mary's hand for a moment. They looked into each other's eyes. Then Mary asked:

"What about the length of the notice I should give? I believe the usual time is three months, but——"

Adeline snapped her fingers. "The usual time doesn't count in this house. I want to help you all I can. I shall be frank and tell you it's even more for the sake of my old friend's son than for you. I know he wants to get back to his ranch. He must get back. And I'll see to it that he can take his bride with him."

"Yes?" Mary was trembling with eagerness. She could not be off too soon to please her. To go far from this house, to make a new life for herself, to tear the thought of Philip White-oak from her heart.

"How soon then?" she asked.

"As soon as you like." She sat down, slapped the flat of her hand on the letter she had been writing and showed her still fine teeth in a smile. "By a curious coincidence this letter is to an aunt of Clive's. She's always begging me to go and pay her a little visit. I've told her I'll go the day after tomorrow. I'll be able to take the good news. While I am away, which will be less than a week, you can make your preparations. When I return we'll have the wedding. Is that too soon?"

"I—well, I suppose I can do it."

"You'll not want a trousseau, going to the prairies, will you?"

"Oh, no."

"You'll not want a large wedding, I take it."

"Heavens, no."

"You shall be married from this house. My son, Mr Nicholas Whiteoak, will be pleased to give you away. We must invite the Vaughans, the Laceys, the Pinks, just the near neighbours. I want you to let me buy you a good warm musk-rat coat. It is the thing for the prairies. Not that it's terribly cold there but it's sharp. Very exhilarating. I've always wanted to go there myself. When my husband and I came out to this country, I think we might have gone straight to the West, but my dear father was against it."

Mary was bewildered. All she could say was, "Oh, thank you. You're very kind."

"Not at all. It's little enough I'm doing for you. I have only one favour to ask. Keep this secret till my return. If the children get wind of it you'll never be able to control them again. If my daughter, Lady Buckley, is told, she'll interfere with all our plans. She'll insist on your giving the usual three months' notice. Much better keep it to ourselves. Tell Clive that, will you?"

Mary eagerly assented. The children's curiosity, Lady Buckley's interference, were evils to be avoided. To leave Jalna unnoticed, to go as she had come, that was what she wanted.

When Adeline was alone she sat motionless for a time, her lips parted in a pleased smile. She took up the letter she had written and read it with a judicial air. Then, frowning at the scratchiness of the pen, she added a postscript. "Abigail dear, I find I can arrange the little visit with you after all, so Philip and I will arrive sometime late tomorrow."

She carried the letter to the stables where Philip was examining the strained tendons in the leg of a favourite horse. He straightened himself and smiled at her.

"How's the leg?" she asked.

"Coming along well."

"Splendid." He knew he was back in her favour by the way she returned his smile.

The mare turned her eyes on him and nibbled his sleeve.

"She's a sweet creature," said Adeline.

"She is, and I love her."

"Do you love your mother enough to come on a little visit with her? I've been promising to go to see Abigail Rutherford —that was Abigail Busby—for many a long day and at last I've made up my mind to do it. Her place isn't above thirty miles from here but hard to get at by train. Will you drive me there, Philip?"

"Gladly, but I can't stay."

Adeline drew a deep sigh. "Ah, well, I'll not go then. I'd planned this little jaunt, just by ourselves, because what with my being away in Ireland and your being so busy, I seem to have seen very little of you. But 'tis of no account to anyone but myself. I'll just tear up this letter and write another declining the invitation."

"No, no. You mustn't do that, Mamma. I'll drive you there and go back for you, at the end of your visit."

"What! Drive a hundred and twenty miles for the sake of a little visit? Let's say no more about it. I'll go by train, though there'll be two hours' wait at some godforsaken junction. But I don't mind. Yes, I'll go by train, even if it does bring on the pain in my back."

"But I thought that pain was quite gone, Mamma."

"Ah, it comes and it goes."

"Do you think the long drive may be bad for it?"

"No. It's the jolting of the train that plays the mischief."

"Then I'll drive you there and stay with you," he exclaimed warmly, though not altogether without thought of self. He would not at all mind going away for a week. He found himself being drawn inexorably into spending more and more time with Muriel Craig. Now there were the riding lessons he had promised her. There were the urgent invitations from her father. Everywhere he went he seemed inevitably to meet her. It was as though there were a plot to throw them together. He liked her, he admired her, but, since the moment when she had allowed her head to droop to his shoulder, there had been qualifications to his regard. She was too easy. His wife had been a woman of reserve. She had never given herself away and, though she had not always been easy to get on with and her caresses had been sparingly given, when they had been given they were worth the waiting for. It seemed strange that one of so much character should have left two children who bore no resemblance to her, either in face or in nature. Yet he could imagine a gentle girl like Mary having a son the image of her. Why had the thought of Mary come into his head, he wondered. He saw little of her nowadays and, when he did see her, he was conscious of a change in her. What was it? A coldness? A shrinking?

His mother's lips were on his. His forehead tied itself into a knot, as he tried to think of two things at once and could think of nothing. Adeline was saying:

"You'll be glad you came. Why, it's years since you visited there with me. Do you remember?"

They went through the orchard, arm in arm. Adeline ate a red harvest apple while they made their plans, which horses he would drive, the route they would follow, what presents she should take her friends. This was the way she liked it to be—an excursion undertaken with gusto, carried through with leisure and ceremony.

At the time appointed she and Philip set out behind a well-groomed pair of bays, with the rest of the family watching the departure with admiration, for Adeline, to show off, had taken the reins herself and handled the restive pair with ease, if a little flauntingly. The long weeds of her widow's bonnet were lifted above her shoulders by the breeze and added a note at once sombre and elegant to her appearance.

Raising her eyes for an instant, as the equipage moved along the gravel sweep, she had a glimpse of Mary's face at an upper window and smiled benignly.

# 15

# DISCLOSURES

THE DAYS of that week moved in autumn splendour at Jalna. An early frost had set the Virginia creeper and the soft maples blazing into red. The yellowing leaves of the silver birches began to fall. The sky was of such a blueness as made people say that Italy could do no better. The farm horses lounged in the meadows, as though a life of leisure was what they were made for, and all their great muscles were but show. Birds were not yet leaving for the south but here and there they held mysterious meetings, while some twittering leader told them of his fears. Jake suddenly grew larger and assumed a sagacious air but it was a spurious sagacity, for underneath he retained his callow ways. He spent most of his time watching for Philip's return, and ran yelping at the sight of Mrs Nettleship. When she came out to shake her duster he hid among the shrubs, but when she had gone he returned to wait for Philip.

Mary and Clive had long talks. Nobody could help noticing that he came every day to Jalna and that Mary made less and less pretence of restraining the children. Mary lived in a kind of dream. All about her was so unreal. But her resolve to marry Clive Busby and go far away from Jalna was real. Each night this resolve kept her to her bed like an anchor, without which she would have sprung up and walked the floor, unable to sleep or rest. She was thankful that Philip was not beneath the same roof with her. She wished she might leave without seeing him again. That would scarcely be possible, but, when they did meet, their interchange would be cool and business-like. He would pay her what salary was due her. She would apologize for leaving without the usual notice. He would be genial and congratulate her on her coming marriage. She would smile happily and say how much she was looking forward to living on the prairies.

Then she would leave.

The thought of a wedding at Jalna was not to be borne. Clive was to take her to his brother's house, a hundred miles away, and they would be quietly married from there. He had confided in this brother and also in Mr Pink, who was helping him to get a special licence. It was all quite simple. All she had to do was to steel herself for the break; after that she would look back across a momentous chasm to the life she now lived. Day by day it would grow dimmer. Philip's face would become blurred in her memory, his voice forgotten. So she soothed her aching spirit with lies.

There was no one she could talk to with truth.

One day she found Jake sitting in a patch of sunlight near the entrance gate. With an inexpressible melancholy look his spaniel's eyes, with their drooping underlids, were fixed on the road. When he saw her a momentary pleasure agitated his tail, then he returned to his waiting.

She ran to him and put her hand on his curling topknot. "Dear little Jake," she said, "how you love him! Far, far better than Sport and Spot do."

He received the caress with sad dignity but kept his eyes on the road.

"Never mind," she said. "He will be back tomorrow."

There was something in her voice that made Jake very sorry for himself. He whimpered, and at the same time wagged his tail, as though to reassure her. "I'm afraid you're going to take life very hard," she said. "And it's bad for you, Jake. You must try to be tranquil like your father and mother, and like your master. You may be sure he's not thinking about us."

In the branches of the evergreens pigeons were shuffling and cooing. They preened their greenish-blue plumage as though it were spring and not fall and the time for lovemaking past. The sky was a clear virginal blue, reflected in shining pools on the road, for it had rained the night before. Mary saw Clive swinging down the road, taking strides as though in them he must expend his happy energy. 'I must go and meet him,' she thought, 'and I don't know how to do it. Jake, you must come and help me.' She took him by the collar and drew him to his feet. Together they went through the gate.

"We're coming to meet you," she cried, and tried to make her walk swinging and free, as Clive's was.

He caught her hand and held it, then looking about to make sure they were not seen, kissed her on the cheek. He bent and patted the spaniel.

"I must get you a dog," he said, "for your very own. I have two sheep-dogs but they follow me about all day on the ranch. What breed will you choose?"

"A pug," she answered without hesitating.

"A pug!" he exclaimed. "A snuffling little pug, with a cork-screw tail. Oh, surely not, Mary."

"Yes. I love them."

"Then a pug you shall have. I well remember the first one I ever saw. I was on a visit to the Vaughans with my parents. Captain and Mrs Whiteoak were coming to tea. I was a small boy. It was the time when enormous bustles were worn. I saw them coming in at the gate and walking up the drive. Jove, they were a striking couple! He was the sort of man who had the look of wearing a uniform even when he was in tweeds. What you'd call a dashing officer. But she was the one who really cut a figure. She'd on a kind of dolman and a wide skirt. She'd a broad-brimmed straw hat and she'd trimmed it with bright-coloured pansies, fresh from the garden, and her eyes looked large and dark, under the brim, and her teeth very white. Well, the hat was odd enough but what staggered me was a pug dog sitting on her bustle. Sitting on it as large as life, and twice as spectacular. When he got tired of walking, she said, she just lifted him on to her bustle and there he rode like a prince."

"I shall make myself a bustle," laughed Mary, "and teach my pug to sit on it."

She talked of dogs and horses, asking Clive questions about the ranch. He never tired of describing it or picturing the time when they would be there as man and wife. He often referred to Adeline's part in bringing them together. "I love her for it," he said. "Not that anything could have kept us apart."

The next day he had business in the town and would not be able to see her till evening.

"Mrs Whiteoak comes home tomorrow," she said, "and her son."

"I'm glad of that, for then we'll not need to keep our engagement secret any longer. I've nearly let the cat out of the bag a dozen times. Now I can write and tell my relations, who must think I'm crazy staying away from the ranch so long."

Mary felt tired that night, as though she were living under a strain, instead of happily preparing for her marriage. No calm and settled thought of her marriage with Clive could make her sleep or quiet the tension of her nerves. At first the hours went by with painful consciousness of every restless minute. She threw her pillows to the floor and tossed on the flatness of the sheet. Then, by degrees, she could keep her body still but it was with the stillness of a cage against which a bird beat himself. She lay straight and stark, her wide-open eyes watching for the dawn. When at last it came she fell asleep and woke without realizing that she had slept. The children were laughing and running from room to room with the fox-terrier.

It was mid-afternoon when the sound of horses' hoofs warned her that Adeline and Philip had returned.

He took his mother's hands and she alighted with a buoyant step but an inward apprehension of what effect the news of the engagement might have on himself. However, the apprehension was not enough to dull the pleasure of homecoming. A week in the badly run establishment of her friend had been quite enough, even though the eyes of that friend had been filled with admiration for all she said and did and Philip had been able to buy two Jersey cows at a great bargain. Even if he were not pleased by the near departure of Mary Wakefield, what could he do about it? Nothing. The girl was promised to young Busby. Mr Pink had promised to help them get a special licence. Tomorrow she would invite the neighbourhood to a tea-party and announce the impending marriage, almost as though Mary were a daughter of the house. She herself would give her a silk dress to be married in—dark blue would suit her and be useful later for special occasions in her prairie home—dark blue, with a lace bertha, and a blue taffeta petticoat to match. She would buy the muskrat coat for her and, yes, she would choose some nice bit of jewellery—a small locket and chain perhaps—from among her own belongings. There was linen to be thought of. She would give Mary three tablecloths, twelve napkins, six sheets, and a pair of fine white blankets. Let the Busby family toe the mark and give silver. These pleasurable arrangements gave her plenty to think of on the long drive. Philip too seemed to have plenty to think of.

"Tired?" he asked her.

"Not in the least. It's been a very nice visit. Don't you think so?"

"First rate. Hullo, here's Jake!"

The young spaniel suddenly turned, crept, with lowered belly, to touch Philip's hand. The beloved scent of that hand filled him with frantic joy. He tore round and round, his ears flapping, uttering cries of welcome. He fell over himself, rolled in complete disorganization, righted himself, and sat down at Philip's feet gazing up at him.

"There's a grand greeting," said Adeline, bending to pat him. "And here come the family."

The voices of the Whiteoaks were so strong that Sir Edwin's milder tones were unheard but he smiled pleasantly and kissed his mother-in-law on the cheek. Boney, the parrot, flew to meet her and now even the Whiteoaks could scarcely make themselves heard.

"Where are the children?" shouted Philip.

"On a picnic with their governess," returned Augusta's contralto tones.

"We are having tea early, Mamma," said Ernest, "you must be starving," and putting his arm about her and drawing her close he whispered in her ear—"I have had good news from England. Certain of my stocks are rising. I'm going to make a lot of money out of them."

"Splendid! You'll need to go over and look after them."

"I shall indeed."

"Ernest, I am delighted."

"I knew you would be."

Eliza, immaculate and rosy-cheeked, announced that tea was ready in the dining-room. It was more substantial than usual and they seated themselves about the table with an air of pleasant anticipation. No detail of the visit was too slight to be related and to be heard with interest. The family were all the more happy in being together because so soon were they to be divided by the return of the Buckleys and Nicholas and Ernest to England. Ernest was so exhilarated by the good news from his broker that he laughed easily, ate and drank more, and drew everyone's attention to how well Adeline was looking. He remarked:

"You have a special sort of air, Mamma, as though you were the bearer of good news."

These words seemed to push Adeline towards the divulging of the engagement. And, after all, what better time could she choose? Mary and the children were out of the way. If Philip were going to be annoyed, let him be annoyed now and get it over with. She put her cup to her lips, drank the last of her tea, and clasped her hands on her stomach.

"I have good news," she said. "Very good news."

They looked at her attentively.

"I consider it very good news and I'm sure you will. It's

always good to hear that a girl who is alone in the world has made a good match for herself."

"Whom on earth are you talking about, Mamma?" demanded Nicholas.

Adeline looked straight into his eyes, avoiding Philip's.

"I'm talking about Miss Wakefield. She's a very nice girl, though rather silly, and I've felt from the first that she needed a nice forthright young man, with prospects, to look after her."

"Is it Clive Busby?" asked Augusta.

"Yes."

"She couldn't do better," exclaimed Nicholas. "A very decent fellow."

"He has been here every day since you left," said Augusta. "I confess I began to feel anxious."

"No need for anxiety. It's all settled. They're to marry immediately."

"This explains a great deal," said Ernest. "She has been avoiding us all this week."

"She strikes me as a very artful young person," put in Sir Edwin.

Adeline laughed. "Oh, she knows how to look after herself. I saw from the first that she was setting her cap for Clive Busby. I saw that he hadn't a chance. But I'm glad. Very glad. She'll make him a good wife."

Adeline now let her eyes meet Philip's.

He was staring at her, his blue eyes prominent, as his father's were when something had roused him. It gave her a little shock but she kept the smile on her face.

"How long have you known this?" he demanded.

"I had it from Abigail, just before I left."

"Had Busby written to her?"

"Yes."

"Then she's a terrible liar, for the last word she said to me was, 'Tell Clive to write to me. I've only had one letter from him since he came from the West.'"

"Aye, that was the one."

"But she told me that was written when he first came."

"Ah, Abigail's a great muddlehead."

"When do you say this letter came?"

"She was vague about it."

"Why didn't you mention it before now?"

"Clive asked to have it kept secret till I was back at Jalna."

"Why?"

"Well, I guess Miss Wakefield thought the young ones would be out of hand if they knew she was leaving."

Philip fixed his eyes on the silver muffin dish and kept them there while the colour mounted steadily to his forehead. He was silent.

Augusta said—"For my part I shall be glad to see her go. I think she was extremely unsuitable as a governess."

Sir Edwin added—"She never convinced me that she had any ability to teach."

"Poor young Clive," said Nicholas. "What a wife for the prairie! I see her in five years, with three or four delicate children hanging on to her trailing skirt."

Ernest smiled at the picture and said—"One thing is certain. *I* will not choose the next governess."

Adeline stared down the table at her youngest born, with a half-teasing smile. "Have you nothing to say about the suitability of the match?" she asked, her own temper reaching out towards his.

"Just this," he answered and picking up the muffin dish he dashed it to the floor.

Augusta almost dropped the cup of tea she was raising to her lips. Half the contents were spilt. Sir Edwin blinked rapidly.

Adeline struck the table with the flat of her hand.

"I won't have such tantrums! Philip, how dare you?"

He rose and went to the door. There he turned and said:

"It's all a plot to get her out of my way. I can see it now. And you're all in it." Without waiting to hear anything more he flung through the hall and out of the house.

Eliza came running up the basement stairs.

"Did something fall, ma'am?" she asked of Adeline. "Was I wanted to pick up?"

"Yes. Mr Philip upset the muffin dish. You'd better gather them up."

Eliza bent her back and collected the fragments.

"Shall I bring fresh ones?" she asked.

All declined to have more.

When they were alone again Ernest remarked—"It's quite singular how Philip can fly off when you least expect it."

"I expected it," said Adeline.

"I saw his forehead turn pink," said Augusta. "That's always a sign of temper in him."

"My grandfather"—Sir Edwin spoke in a consciously pacific tone—"not the one who was given a baronetcy but the one——"

"Who manufactured stockings in Birmingham," put in Adeline eagerly. "I always like the sound of him best. Tell us about him."

Sir Edwin continued—"Always hiccuped when he was angry. You'd hear a hiccup and you'd know what was coming."

"What if he'd hiccup by chance, when he wasn't angry?" asked Adeline.

"He never did. He was always angry when he hiccuped."

"It goes to show," said Ernest, "how anger works on the digestive organs."

"Impossible." Adeline helped herself to another piece of cake. "I've never heard of such a thing."

"The point is," said Nicholas, "that Philip is greatly upset by this news. It may mean trouble."

"Philip can do nothing," returned Adeline. "It's all settled. I intend to give the girl a nice wedding, a fur coat, and some table and bed linen."

"The girl for Philip to marry," declared Augusta, "is Miss Craig."

"I'd hate to marry her," put in Sir Edwin.

"That," said Augusta, "is a contingency which need not be considered."

Adeline rose. "I don't want a second wife of Philip's at Jalna," she said, "but, if there must be one, let her be a woman of character and not a flibbertigibbet like this Mary Wakefield."

She led the way into the drawing-room and Ernest closed the door behind them. "Now," he said, dropping into a comfortable chair beside her, "tell us all about it, Mamma, right from the beginning. I feel that you've been very clever in managing the affair and steering Philip clear of . . ." He hesitated.

Augusta finished for him. "A very wretched entanglement."

Philip strode along the path toward the stables, scarcely seeing where he was going. All other feelings were for the moment submerged in his angry astonishment. He had been the centre of a plot, moved about like a pawn, knowing nothing of what was going on. He had been frustrated, while that fathead, Busby, had wormed himself into Mary Wakefield's affections, got engaged to her. All the family had been in the plot against him. He could see that now. All had been afraid that he would fall in love with Mary—ever since the night of the dance. But they were mistaken. He wasn't in love with her. He simply did not want to lose her. The children needed her. He had a mental picture of himself as a pathetic young widower, with two motherless children.

He could not think clearly. As a scutter of horse's hoofs sounded behind him he moved aside. A groom, riding the mare he had bought from Mr Craig, overtook him. The man turned in the saddle and looked back.

"She's doing fine, sir," he called out proudly.

"Good." He ran his eye over the mare's silken flanks, glittering in the sunlight, but she looked a long way off, remote.

He wheeled and turned into the path leading to the apple orchard. There he could be alone and think. He passed the old pear tree that stood by itself outside the orchard. The pears were enormous. But there were wasps eating them. One of those that had fallen had three wasps digging into the same hole, as though their lives depended on it. Philip kicked it and it flew off in fragments, the wasps circling back to the tree.

The orchard was quiet, the heavy fruit waiting for the final ripening. Clumps of Michaelmas daisies rose above the coarse orchard grass and above them hovered small white butterflies. Philip halted and, resting his hand against a thick branch, stood staring at the ground. He forced himself to think more calmly, to try to discover what his real feelings were. He was not in the habit of analysing them but of following his impulses. His fury on hearing of Mary's engagement still tingled through his veins. He was glad he had thrown the silver dish to the floor. He felt violence moving inside him. 'Upon my soul,' he thought, 'if it were fifty years ago, I should be ready to fight a duel with Busby!'

But then, he thought, what had Busby done? Merely got engaged to a pretty girl who was thrown in his way. . . . But Busby'd been so underhanded about it. . . . The sly dog! He'd never seen Mary and Busby together, except on the night of the dance. Yes—there was that time on the road when Muriel Craig saw her run to meet him! And again the day when she had been loitering with Lily Pink, obviously waiting for Busby. Oh, there'd been times enough! His mother was right, Mary had been setting her cap for Busby from the start.

And why not? She'd a right to get married if she . . . But he didn't want her to get married. He wanted her at Jalna. He needed her. He'd had a pretty uncomfortable time with those two who preceded her. Always getting in his way, looking self-righteous or injured or making complaints. Mary was so lovely. . . . She'd behaved badly. . . . She'd hurt him. She'd hurt him deeply. . . . Why, he didn't think of her as a gover-ness, someone he employed. He thought of her as a friend. He loved her! That was the truth. He loved her.

And she'd chosen that stolid, matter-of-fact fellow, Busby— turned him, Philip Whiteoak, down! She'd never given him a chance. He liked to take his time about things. Things as im-portant as marriage. Why, he'd known Margaret for twenty years before he proposed to her. To be sure they had been only a few months old when they first met, but it went to show that he didn't like being hurried. . . . And the damnable plot against him! His mother persuading him to go on a visit with her, so that he would be out of the way. He'd wager that she and Clive's aunt had chuckled over how well they had managed the affair—the scheme—the confounded plot!

The blood mounted to his head. He pressed a thumb and middle finger against his throbbing temples. A chipmunk ran through the tree against which he leaned, and was transfixed into stark immobility within a yard of his hand. Every single reddish hair stood up. Its bright eyes stared in astonishment. It clasped its body in its little forelegs, as though to keep from flying to pieces. Philip made reassuring noises between his teeth. Moments passed, then the chipmunk, with a flurry of its tail, leaped into another tree and was gone.

'I'll go and find the girl,' Philip thought, 'and see what she has to say for herself.' He moved steadily on through the orchard, in the direction of the woods. If Mary had taken the children on a picnic that was where they would be.

Mary, just emerging from the pinewood with Meg and Renny, saw him leave the orchard and cut across a stubble field in their direction.

"Children," she said, "there is your father. Wouldn't you like to run and meet him while I carry the hamper home through the orchard?"

They did not hear the end of the sentence. Renny pushed the handle of the hamper into her hand, overtook Meg, and flew across the stubble. They shouted their welcome.

Mary almost ran towards the orchard and, once in its shelter, turned to see what direction Philip and the children had taken. She saw them still standing close together, the children's faces turned up to his. She waited, gripping the handle of the hamper, moving her toes inside her thin shoes, conscious of the soft sandy loam of the orchard path. She saw the little group separate then and the children run towards the house. Philip stood motionless, watching, till they reached the lawn. Then he strode straight towards the orchard.

But she would not meet him there. She could not endure to meet him without the protection of the children. Not once, if she could help it, would she meet him alone, before she left Jalna. Yet she would prepare herself for such an encounter, be ready to look into his eyes with coolness. She would accept his congratulations, or whatever he had to say to her, with composure—but not now. Now the thought of meeting him alone was intolerable.

Yet he was crossing the field at such a slant that he was bound to meet her just as she came out of the orchard. If she remained among the trees, all he had to do was to follow the path, for it was clear that his intention was to meet her now and alone. That was why he had sent his children on to the house. For a moment she stood rooted in perplexity. Had she not better nerve herself to the meeting, have it over with? She had a glimpse of him entering the orchard, the last of the sunlight brightening his hair to gold.

That glimpse of him was enough. This was a spot where she could not meet him. It was too beautiful in the sunset, with the trees bending beneath their load of burnished apples and an oriole singing his farewell song from the very branch where hung his empty nest. Mary ran swiftly away from the path and among the trees till, at the far side of the orchard, she came to the shed where barrels and crates were stored to be convenient for the packing. She entered it and stood in a dim corner draped with cobwebs. A broken toy of Renny's lay on the floor. She felt safe from Philip here. She pressed her hand on her side to quiet the beating of her heart.

The oriole indolently let fall his notes as though he felt the silence of autumn creeping close to him. The chipmunk ran chattering across the roof of the shed, then peered in at Mary through a crack. She heard Philip's step turning in that direction. The chipmunk had given her hiding place away. Now, as he scrabbled about, he sent a sifting of dust down through the crack. Mary waited for the step to pass. It did not and Philip now stood in the doorway.

At first he could not see her, then her form separated itself from the gloom. He saw her white hands and face.

"Why did you hide from me?" he asked.

"Hide? I—just came in here."

"You hid from me and I will tell you why. You were ashamed because you'd treated me so badly."

Mary's eyes dilated. She was frightened by the very solidity of his accusing presence. After a silence, in which she collected her strength for defence, she said:

"I don't think I have treated you badly—unless you mean——"

"Well—what?"

"Not giving you proper notice?"

"You know that is not what I mean."

"Then you mean about my engagement?"

"Yes."

"It amounts to the same thing, doesn't it? It amounts to my leaving the children without a——"

He interrupted—"Why will you go on talking to me as an employer?"

She answered, with a new note in her voice—"I don't know how you want me to talk to you, Mr Whiteoak. I never have known."

"*Mr Whiteoak!*" He shot out his name with scorn.

"Surely you don't expect me to call you by your Christian name!"

"I expected you," he returned fiercely, "to treat me as a friend. I behaved in a friendly way to you, didn't I?"

"Yes."

"Do you call it treating me like a friend to let me go off with my mother—all unsuspecting that you were carrying on a courtship with Clive Busby—and were, in fact, engaged to him —you were engaged to him before I left, weren't you!"

"Yes."

"You kept it all secret. Then, at the moment I return, my mother tells me what everyone but myself has known all the while. Why did you hide it from me?"

Mary came from behind the barrels that smelt sweetly of new wood. There was a look of challenge in her eyes.

"I didn't think it mattered to you," she said.

"Not matter to me! Not after the way we waltzed together! Do you forget that, Mary?"

It was the first time he had called her Mary. It was the first time he had spoken of the dance which she looked back on as the most precious moment of her life. She put both hands on the barrel behind her and leaned against it as though for support.

"I shall never forget it." He could barely hear the words.

"And yet," he went on, the flush deepening on his face, "you've engaged yourself to another man. I don't understand you."

"And I don't understand you." Her voice had come back to her. It was almost harsh. "You never noticed me on the night of the dance—not till everyone but Lily was gone. Then you remembered that I had been there. You looked about and saw me and thought—Poor thing, I really should give her the pleasure of a dance with me! We waltzed and our steps suited. We danced too well. Your mother didn't like it. I think she was right. A man who cares nothing for a girl shouldn't dance with her like that."

"But I did care!" he cried.

"For that one waltz," she answered, almost as though she forced coldness on herself, "you cared. But since then you've hardly given me a thought."

"I have given you a thousand thoughts. But I'm not one of those men who can't let a woman they're attracted to alone. I looked on you as rather remote—detached."

In a shaken voice she asked—"After that waltz? I thought I let myself go shamelessly."

"Mary—did you love me that night?"

"No, for I didn't think. I hadn't a thought in my head."

"You were just carried away by the pleasure of it. So was I. Let's look at it like that. Let's think calmly of our relations. They were friendly from the start, weren't they?"

"Yes."

"There was even something special in them."

"Yes."

"Then Clive appeared on the scene." Philip came closer to her and gently took one of her wrists in his hand. "Tell me, did Clive come between us from the start? Was it love—almost at first sight? It must have been, because he hasn't been here very long."

She drew her hand away and the wrist he had held tingled as though a brier had bound it.

"How can I tell?" she asked, and then she broke out—"Clive couldn't come between us—because—you weren't there!"

"I wasn't there—in your affections—you mean."

"Yes. . . . Clive loved me. He wanted to marry me."

"And you love him?"

"Yes."

"And you never felt anything approaching love—for me?"

"How can you be so cruel, Mr Whiteoak! You have no right——"

"It's you who are cruel, Mary." He spoke with a childlike appeal—deliberately putting it in his voice and his eyes, she thought, and steadied herself to answer:

"If you loved me you kept your love well hidden. There have been weeks when you have scarcely looked in my direction."

"I was happy just to feel that you were under the same roof. I thought you . . ."

"Tell the truth," she interrupted wildly. "You did not give me a second thought. You were satisfied with your fishing—the life you lead—and no wonder. I don't think I've ever known a man more happily placed. You've everything."

"I have an indolent nature. I'm willing to let things take their course."

"Then let them take their course. You know what it is."

"Good Lord God," he shouted, "am I to lose you without raising my hand to prevent it?"

"It's too late."

He could see the beat of her heart, in her throat.

"That means," he said, more quietly, "that you did—perhaps still do—love me."

She looked into his eyes, without speaking.

"Can you love two men, Mary?"

"Yes," she breathed.

"It's impossible! Or it's not the same sort of love. I think you feel affection, kindness, towards Clive. I think you love me. . . . But you don't feel kindness towards me, Mary."

"What kind of love do you feel for me," she cried, "when a few scornful remarks from your mother were enough to make you shun me for weeks?"

172

"I think you shunned me too. I think we both were a little shy. We'd felt an emotion we weren't prepared for."

"Perhaps." She hesitated and then brought out what had so rankled in her mind. "I've wondered what emotion you felt when you drove Miss Craig home, with her head on your shoulder."

He was so disconcerted that he was for a moment comical, then he made a grimace.

"Discomfort," he said. "Acute discomfort. Nothing more. I swear I said nothing that should have made her feel sentimental and by the time we were round the bend in the road she was sitting up properly. Muriel has never had any real attraction for me, but all the while you've been at Jalna, Mary, my love for you has been taking a greater hold on me. You have heard of entertaining an angel unawares. I've done that with my love for you."

"Oh, I wish you wouldn't say such things." She shook her head from side to side as though looking at some object that moved her to pity. And she repeated—"It's too late."

"Now I'm conscious," he continued, as though she had not spoken, "all through me, of how much I love you."

She stepped swiftly past him into the orchard. Then, facing him, said:

"I can't treat Clive like this. I can't listen to such words from another man. Do you think I have no loyalty in me?"

"Then you're going to marry him?"

"Yes."

He followed her and put his arm about her.

"I won't let you."

"Nothing can stop me. I've promised."

"You don't love him."

"I love him dearly."

"Not as you do me." Both his arms were about her and he held her close to him. The enchantment she had felt in his touch on the night of the dance now flowed through her, intensified to the point of ecstasy. The oriole, his plumage gilded by the sun's last rays, may have felt so, as he poured out his song.

Philip bent his face to hers, whispering—"My dearest, sweetest Mary. . . . My darling one. . . . I won't let you go. . . . You can't make me. . . . Kiss me, Mary."

She returned his kisses.

"There'll be a moon tonight, Mary," he said. "We'll go out in the moonlight together."

"No." She put her hands on his chest and would have pushed him from her but he would not let her go.

For an enchanted moment they were as still as though turned to stone. Then Philip was roused by clumping steps on the orchard path. He released her and they saw a farm labourer, Noah Binns, drawing near, his dinner pail swinging in his hand, his pleased grin showing black and broken teeth, though he was still young.

Noah Binns's pig's eyes were fixed on them in curiosity but, to show that his mind was occupied by other affairs, he remarked:

"Bugs is breedin'."

"Bugs! What bugs?" asked Philip.

"Tater bugs. Where there was one, there's ten."

He clumped on.

Mary and Philip stood looking after him. Their moment was broken. They didn't know what to say. Then Mary gave a little laugh. "What a strange creature! Every time I meet him he says something about bugs or worms or rot or decay." She laughed nervously.

"He enjoys thinking of life like that. . . . He saw us, Mary."

"Does that mean he'll tell?"

"Of course. But it doesn't matter."

"It matters terribly to me, as I'm going to be married so soon. People will talk. But I needn't mind. I'm going far away."

"Mary, are you being deliberately cruel?"

"I'm trying to put this afternoon behind me."

"You can't! No more than I can. It would be there between you and Clive, if you were to marry him. . . . But you can't *marry* him. . . . It wouldn't be fair to him, Mary, loving me as you do."

She had turned her face away from him but now she looked into his eyes. "What has just passed," she said, "was a little moment of our lives."

"It has made everything different," he said. "I knew I loved you, but—now I know you love me."

"You loved me!" she cried. "Then why in God's name didn't you say so?"

"I was a fool. . . . I was willing to drift along."

"Now it's too late."

"Mary"—he took her hand and drew her back into the shed where the air was heavy with the smell of apples. "Let's talk this over. It's not too late. No one can keep us apart."

She suffered herself to be led. Her eyes were wide and shining with tears. They were tears of pity for him and for herself. Each one was the haven the other had sought. What was either but a fragile being whose life might, at any moment, be engulfed? She raised her face to his and put her arms about his neck.

And though at the moment there was no strength in her, power from her passed through him like a flame. He felt capable of sweeping her up in his arms, away from the very face of the earth. He kissed her hands, the little hollow of her throat, her lips.

"Now let me go," she said, and he did not restrain her.

She followed the orchard path, crossed the field where the old pear tree stood, whose fruit now shone like gold. The windows of the house shone too, flaming in the sunset. But, as she drew near it, the sun sank behind the pinewood and the house stood in chill twilight. She met no one in the passages. The sound of Nicholas's playing on the piano came from the drawing-room. Mary went straight to her own room.

## 16

## THE STORM

NOAH BINNS plodded on. His boots had so many times been wet through and dried in the oven that they no longer seemed to be made of leather but of some rough and corrugated wood. Their toes turned stiffly upward, their laces dangled as he clumped over the road. Every now and again he gave out a *whew* of relish.

He saw Lily Pink coming towards him along the quiet road. She carried a bottle of blackberry cordial, a present from her mother to Adeline Whiteoak. She smiled gently at Noah Binns and inquired about his mother's rheumatism.

"It's no better, thank you, and it'll get worse, as I keep a-tellin' her."

"But that's not a cheerful way to talk to her. My father says you should always comfort a sick person."

"That's your father's business, Miss, to comfort the sick and bury the dead. He's paid for it. I'm not."

Lily looked at him blankly, unable to find anything to say.

"Would you be going in the direction of Jalna?" he asked.

"Yes." She answered coldly. What business was it of his?

"Then, Miss, I advise you to keep away from the apple-packin' shed."

"Why?"

Noah shook his dinner pail up and down, listening to the rattle of the tin cup inside, as though the sound afforded him sensuous pleasure. Then he answered—"There's lovemakin' goin' on by the shed."

Lily drew back from him in horror.

"What—why——" she stammered.

He grinned at her discomposure. "Don't mind—don't mind—it's all over I guess. I guess you'd be safe goin' that way now."

She stood fascinated.

Noah went on—"I guess the boss has a right to make love to the governess, or whatever they call her, if he wants to, but she's been traipsin' through these woods steady with that there Mr Busby, hasn't she?"

"I don't know," answered Lily, fiercely. She left him and hurried in the direction of Jalna but took the path outside the orchard.

Noah Binns looked after her reflectively. "Dang it all," he said to himself, "what's she fussed up about? I've got a right to say what I saw, haven't I? If she'd seen the bugs I have, she might get fussed up. *Ten* where there was one!"

Lily stood in the porch waiting. She had not allowed herself to think, after she had left Noah Binns, for fear she would not have the courage to go on. Now she stood clutching the bottle of blackberry cordial as pink-cheeked Eliza opened the door.

"Mother sent this," she said. "Please give it to Mrs White-oak."

"Is that Lily Pink?" called Adeline's voice from inside.

"Yes, Mrs Whiteoak." Eliza drew back and Lily stepped into the hall.

"Come into my room. I want to see you."

Lily went down the hall to Adeline's room. The door was open and she was seated before her dressing-table. She had on a wide, flounced cambric petticoat, with rows of lace insertion, and a many-gored low-cut corset cover. So, all in white, with her hair down and shoulders bare, she had a festive air about her. Boney was perched on the head of the bed. When he saw Lily he opened his beak and screamed, yet with a jocular air:

"*Shaitan! Shaitan ka batka! Shaitan ka butcha!*"

"Shall I come in?" asked Lily. "Will he mind?"

"No. He'll not mind. Come right in. My, what a good colour you've got! I like to see a young girl with a bright complexion. One doesn't often see it in this country. Ireland's the place for that. Look at our little Renny. He's peaches and cream. But what will he be in twenty years? Weather-beaten. What's that you have in the bottle?"

"Blackberry cordial. Mother sent it. It's good to have when winter comes and there are coughs about."

Adeline was delighted. She took off the white napkin that wrapped the bottle, held the bottle to the light to admire the colour of the cordial, uncorked it, and savoured a sip.

She smacked her lips. "Ha, that's good. There's nothing better for the throat. Thank your mother a thousand times. . . . And now I have something for you."

From a drawer of her dressing-table she produced a small blue velvet box and from it a gold thimble.

"Now give me your hand." She took Lily's right hand and placed the thimble on its middle finger. "It was given me by my godmother when I was just your age."

"But Mrs Whiteoak, you shouldn't part with it!"

"Ah, I've never been one to sew much. I used to do embroidery when I was young. But now my bit of mending is all I do trouble about and a silver thimble is good enough for that."

Lily's face glowed. She threw both arms about Adeline's neck and hugged her. She murmured incoherent thanks. Then suddenly she broke down and clung to her, shaken by sobs.

"Well, well, well, now—whatever is the matter with you, Lily?"

She clasped the girl close, her bare arms enfolding her, her body giving off a pleasant scent of Windsor soap, her starched petticoat crackling.

"I don't know." But she went on sobbing.

Adeline patted her back. "Tut, tut, now, that's enough. You're not into any sort of trouble at home, are you?"

"Oh, no."

"Lily. . . . It's no love affair, is it?"

"No!" she cried hoarsely.

"Then, in God's name, what is it?"

"It's. . . . It's that governess. Mary Wakefield."

Adeline held her closer. "Whisper to me. What is it she's done?"

"She's bad! That's what she is! Bad."

"What do you know, my dear? Come, we'll just sit here quietly on my bed and you'll tell me."

Lily stumbled to the bed and sat down leaning heavily against Adeline.

Out of her distorted mouth she sobbed—"I wish I hadn't said anything."

"Ah, but 'twas right that you should. It will do you good to clear your mind of what's troubling you. Besides, Miss Wakefield lives in my house and teaches my two innocent grandchildren. It's my right to know what she's up to."

Lily sat up and wiped her eyes with the hand on which the gold thimble still shone.

"It's a shame," she said, "that I should go on like this just after having such a lovely present given me." Through blurred eyes she examined the thimble.

"Come, come"—Adeline was growing impatient—"what's all this about, Lily?"

"Mrs Whiteoak, *she's* engaged to Clive Busby, isn't she?"

Adeline's brows shot up. "Well—and who told you that?"

"Oh, I know it's a secret. But Clive told Violet Lacey. He made her promise not to breathe a word of it but he was so happy he couldn't help telling her."

"And she told you?"

"Yes, and I promised not to tell and I haven't except to you and I guess you know already."

"I do. Now, what has she done?"

"I don't know. . . . I really don't. . . . But as I was coming here just now I met Noah Binns and he told me, with a *hateful* smile, not to come past the shed where they keep the barrels and crates at the far end of the orchard and naturally I asked why and he said—oh, I can't repeat it!"

"Now, Lily, don't be silly. Go on."

"He said not to come past that place because there was *love-making* going on there. He said it was Mr Whiteoak and Mary Wakefield. I don't know what he meant, do you?" Lily's eyes were avidly bright as they looked into Adeline's.

Adeline smiled. "Noah Binns's sort have nasty minds. You mustn't listen to them, Lily. As for my son—he knows of the engagement and he's as pleased as I am. He was probably making arrangements with her about the children. Is that all Noah said?"

"He said she'd been *traipsing* through the woods with Clive and now she was in the orchard making love to Mr Whiteoak. It was the way he said it. He *leered*."

"Ah, well, he's a nasty fellow and I think I'll have a word with him. Now you run along, my dear. . . ." She talked to Lily of other things.

When the door had shut behind her, Adeline stood motionless for a space, a very different person from the comforting, kindly woman who had kissed the girl goodbye. Her brows were drawn in a black frown, her lips compressed.

'So . . . that's what she's like,' she thought. 'A bitch—a wanton! Just what I thought that night I caught her dancing like a *fille de joie* with my Philip. She's got the two of them on strings—young fools that they are! And she'd had me on a string—old fool that I am!' Then she said aloud, but softly— "What's to be done?"

Her anger at the thought that Mary had deceived her burned even more hotly than the thought of her playing with the two men. She wondered how she could face her calmly at the supper table. Yet—perhaps that silly girl, Lily, had worked herself up over nothing. Yet why had Noah Binns warned Lily not to go through the orchard? Why had he leered? Adeline had never seen so much as a half-smile on his face. And he seemed a decent fellow. Mr Pink thought well of him. If only it had been she who had met him instead of Lily!

Mary did not appear at the supper table. She had complained of a headache, Eliza said.

Emotion made Adeline hungry. Never had cold lamb, thick slices of dark red tomatoes with plenty of vinegar and sugar on them, tasted better. All the while she was seething inside. Her daughter and her two elder sons were conscious of this and expected an explosion at any moment. But none came. She finished the meal as she had begun it, in affable description of her visit with Abigail Rutherford. It gave opportunity for her power of mimicry and lively wit.

It was a wonder she could be lively with Philip facing her from the other end of the table in sombre silence. After supper she played backgammon with Sir Edwin. At the usual time she said goodnight to her family, with the exception of Philip, who had taken the dogs for a walk, and retired to her room. Philip had sent a message to Mary by Meg saying he wished to see her. The child had returned with word that Mary was not well and was lying down and would it be all right if she saw him in the morning. "And she really does look ill, Daddy," Meg had said, feeling something in the air. Philip had muttered, "Very well, Meggie. Tell Miss Wakefield I'll see her the first thing in the morning." He felt baffled. For a moment he had a mind to go to her, but, with family and children about, how could they two have privacy? He would have to wait till morning. But it was now that he wanted her with him. Now, out in the moonlight, he'd make her forget the very existence of Clive Busby.

He could not bear to be near the house or even in his own woods. He turned through the gate to the road that led to the lake. The moon was just past its first quarter but capable of throwing distinct black shadows on the silent road. In all of the two miles he met no vehicle, but, in a field, two horses came and looked at him over the fence. The three spaniels and the fox-terrier trotted continuously on and off the road, in and out of ditches, snuffed at the openings into burrows, flattened themselves to get under fences into fields, where they ran about with noses to the ground, but always reappeared. There was no need to whistle to them. They would not lose him. They were too joyous in his return.

He passed through a lane, followed a path winding among scrubby cedars and alders, and was on the beach. The lake spread cold and tranquil, reflecting the moon. The shingle crunched beneath his feet, and then came the sand at the water's edge. Wavelets, rimmed with silver, spent themselves soundlessly on the beach. The dogs came to the water's edge and drank as though in great thirst, letting their forepaws get wet. The fox-terrier shivered but he would not stop drinking till the spaniels did.

Philip thought of the countless times he had come to this spot, of how the countryside round about was as familiar to him as the face of one of his family. His brothers had gone away, his sister too, but this was where he wanted to be. This was his life. In this place he had grown up, married, begotten his children, lived his short married life and now loved. . . . If only Mary were with him by the lake! He would pour out all his new-found love on her—not in words, but he would make her feel it, in the very touch of his hand, in the beat of his heart, in his breast against hers. The air moved cool on his forehead. He raised his face to it and walked along the lake's rim. If only she were here! No matter how many years they might have together he always would regret this night—the night when they should have walked together by the lake, the night when they should have watched the moon sink into the gleaming water, have walked, with fingers interlocked, along the beach. Was she really ill? Yes, he believed so, otherwise she could not have denied him this night. But a night's rest would make her well and tomorrow he would settle everything—with his mother—with Clive. His mother—he smiled wryly when he thought of her. He did not feel as angry at her as he had, but he would show her who was master at Jalna.

Adeline remained in her room reading till she heard Philip put the dogs to bed and mount the stairs. Then she went into the hall and stood there, her fingers resting lovingly on the carved grapes of the newel post, till she heard his windows opened for the night. Then she went up the stairs and stood in the passage till the pencil of light under his door was gone. She stood very still now, close to his door, listening intently. She heard his steady regular breathing. She went up the stairs to the top floor.

Very lightly she tapped on Mary's door. There was a light inside.

Mary's voice came from close to the panel. "Yes? Who is there?"

Adeline thought—'She's expecting Philip.' She said—"May I speak to you for a moment, Miss Wakefield?"

The door was instantly opened and Mary stood there, white-faced, defensive, scarcely seeming to breathe.

"Thank you." Adeline came into the room and closed the door behind her.

They stood, tall women, eye to eye, in long white night-dresses, up to the throat, down to the wrist, Adeline's elaborately tucked. About her shoulders she had a brilliantly coloured Oriental shawl. Her hair, which she had been brushing, hung loose about her neck and down her back. She was a superb and deliberately picturesque figure.

Mary's hair hung in a single plait, she was barefoot.

"Yes, Mrs Whiteoak?" She found herself trembling like a leaf, already intimidated.

"I want to know," Adeline said, "what you mean by playing fast and loose with young Busby."

"I'm not playing fast and loose with him. I mean to marry him."

Adeline laughed. "You mean to marry him and yet you were in the arms of my son this very afternoon. Kissing him. Now I have the right to know what this means."

"It doesn't—I wasn't——"

"Don't be a fool," interrupted Adeline harshly. "You were seen by one of the men—everyone knows it by now. Why— within half an hour the tale was carried to me. I've suspected from the first that you were no better than you should be. But —carrying on with two men at the same time—one, the son of my friend—one, my own son! Good God, do you imagine you can pull the wool over everybody's eyes? What *are* you trying to do? That's what I want to know."

Mary backed away from her. Her brain would not act. It was in a whirl. She could find no words in which to explain.

"Do you imagine Clive Busby will marry you after this?"

"I don't know," Mary answered, in a strangled voice.

"Perhaps you think Philip will marry you! Not he. He's had enough of marriage. Are you his mistress?"

The question was shot at her like a blow.

"Are you his mistress?" repeated Adeline. "Come—how often has he been up to your room?"

Mary put her hand to her throat. She wanted to scream. She was alone! She had no weapons. The figures of Clive and Philip loomed like enormous shadows in the room, Clive looking at her with hate, Philip . . .

"He has been up to your room, at night, hasn't he?" —

"Will you let me alone!" cried Mary.

"I want an answer. *Are you Philip's mistress?*"

Mary's fear, her hysteria, turned to rage.

"Yes," she answered, in rage, "I am."

Adeline's jaw dropped. She had not expected any such confession. For a moment she was too astounded to speak. She looked at Mary as though seeing her for the first time.

Mary's trembling ceased. She stood exhilarated, like an actress taking a triumphant curtain call.

"And do you expect," Adeline asked quietly, "to marry Clive after this?"

"I will not tell you anything more. What I am going to do is my own affair." She still looked exhilarated, triumphant.

She swept, her nightdress flowing, past Adeline, to the door and threw it open.

"Will you please go, Mrs Whiteoak?" she said.

"I will not leave you till we've talked this thing out." Adeline melodramatically folded her arms.

"Go! I tell you!" Mary shouted. Her restraint was ebbing. She would have the household awake, Adeline thought.

"Very well," she said, "I will go, but let me tell you this—so far you have called the tune, tomorrow you will pay the piper." In the doorway she turned and added—"It was a bad day for Jalna when a hardened adventuress like you came on the scene, but—there will be a reckoning tomorrow."

Mary shut the door behind Adeline with a bang that sounded loudly through the silent house. Adeline expected the family would be disturbed, that Ernest, at least, being the most highly strung, would appear from his room. But Ernest was far away in London, dreaming of speculations, the dazzling success of which outstripped anything he had formerly achieved.

Adeline slowly descended the stairs. The house was very dark. She was glad when she reached her own room where the nightlight threw Boney's sleeping shadow on the wall. But her coming woke him. He flew straight to her shoulder, rumpling himself in pleasure, and, in his foreign lingo, called her Pearl of the hareem. She sat down by the table on which was a photograph of her husband in a velvet frame, and with an elbow on the table and her chin in her palm she sat, lost in thought, for a long time. Never had she been more mistaken in anyone than in Mary Wakefield—Mary, with that die-away look, those large appealing eyes, to have behaved like this! To have faced her with a look that was almost intimidating—to have ordered her from the room! A smile of ironic admiration bent Adeline's lips.

"It was little sleep I had last night," was her greeting to Augusta next morning.

"I'm sorry for that, Mamma. You generally sleep so well."

"I don't complain, but many a wakeful night I've had, worrying over my children. You and Edwin did well, Augusta, whether intentionally or from lack of ability, not to have any."

"Is it anything special, Mamma? Will you care to tell me?"

"It is enough to scandalize the countryside. Are the children with Mary Wakefield?"

"Yes, I suppose so."

"As soon as I've had a little food to stay me, I want to see Philip."

"Alone, Mamma?"

"No. I want you all to be there. Tell Philip to be waiting in the library."

The children were not with Mary. They had woken at the usual time, been the first to have breakfast, a meal which Mary almost invariably shared with them. Now, this morning, being free of restraint, they had wild spirits; Renny, although the smaller, able to run faster, leading the way, Meg panting close behind, her light brown mane flying. They were off to the pigsty to see a new family of piglets, pink and clean, squirming beside the protective bulk of their mother.

Philip discovered them there, long past lesson time, and sent them back to the house. Up the two flights of stairs they ran, and, on tiptoe, went into their room. Mary was not there. The door of her bedroom was shut.

"Her headache's worse," giggled Meg. "She's going to stay in bed."

"Hurrah!"

"We shall have the day off."

"Hurrah!"

"Let's sneak out of the house, down into the ravine, over the bridge, through the woods, pretending we're Indians."

"Hurrah!"

"We'll go to the Vaughans'. Mrs Vaughan bought six baskets of peaches yesterday, I heard her say."

"They're putting a ring in a boar's nose! Hodge told me. Let's run. We may be in time."

They were gone and no one saw them go.

When Adeline had had her third cup of tea she rose and sailed majestically towards the sitting-room. She seated herself in a high-backed chair, the light from the window full in her face. She could see the wild clouds of the equinox already gathering to obscure the sun. One cloud sent down a scatter of glittering raindrops and then moved away.

Nicholas came into the room with his tolerant look of a man of the world that said nothing that might happen could surprise or upset him.

"Good morning, Mamma," he said, kissing the top of her head, "you slept late this morning."

"I did and no wonder, for I lay awake half the night worrying about the goings-on in this house."

Nicholas blew out his cheeks. "Well, Gussie told me something was troubling you. Let's hope it isn't serious."

"Should I be lying awake if it weren't serious?"

"Of course not. Will you tell me what the trouble is?"

"Wait till we all are here. Where are the others? Why don't they come?"

"They're coming."

Augusta, Sir Edwin, and Ernest now entered the room. Augusta seated herself on the sofa. Ernest, after he had greeted his mother, seated himself by her side. Sir Edwin stood hesitating.

"Perhaps," he said, "I had better not intrude."

"It will be no intrusion," returned his mother-in-law. "I want you."

"I am sure," said Augusta, "that, if advice on any delicate matter is needed, yours will be most valuable."

"This matter," Adeline said decisively, "is not delicate."

"Has this matter to do with Philip?" asked Ernest.

"It has."

"And Miss Wakefield?"

"Yes."

"Dear me."

Augusta put in—"Perhaps, after all, Edwin had better go."

Adeline gave her sudden mordant grin. "It's never too late to learn," she said.

"How true that is," exclaimed Ernest. "Only a few years ago I knew practically nothing of the stock market. Now I have, you might say, its intricacies at my fingertips." He placed the tips of his delicate fingers together and smiled complacently.

His family looked at him with respect.

185

"*Where* is Philip?" demanded Adeline. "Ernest, do go and find him."

"I hope he is in a better temper than he was last night," said Nicholas.

Philip's voice came from the hall. "Anybody calling me?"

"I think you had my message," answered Adeline.

He stood in the doorway. He said—"What's all this about?" He looked his usual good-tempered self.

"Sit down, sit down, my dear," said his mother. "We want a few explanations from you."

Sir Edwin flushed. "Not I. Really not I, Philip."

Philip gave a short laugh. He sat down just inside the door.

"Well, after all," thought Sir Edwin, "it's his house. He has a right to do as he likes in it."

Jake came in and sat between Philip's feet.

Adeline clutched her chin in her hand as a man might clutch his beard. She regarded Philip in silence for a space and then asked—"Tell me, Philip, have you considered Miss Wakefield to be a young woman of a character you were willing to entrust your children to?"

The good-humour left his face. He frowned.

"I certainly have."

"Shut the door, Philip."

He put out his hand and shut the door.

"Yet," she went on, "that girl has got herself engaged to Clive Busby, who is as fine a young fellow as I know, and, while preparing for her marriage to him, allowed you to make love to her."

"I've scarcely spoken to her in these weeks. There's been nothing between us."

"No? What about your meeting in the orchard last evening?"

"Did Noah Binns tell you that?"

"No. He told Lily Pink and she told me."

"Little fool!"

"You don't deny that there was a passionate love scene between you?"

"Noah Binns! Passion! You make me laugh. I thought his mind rose no higher than bugs and blight."

Adeline fastened on the last word. "Blight! That's what she's been. A blight on this place. She is to marry Clive Busby next week. Yet she clasps you in her arms and——"

"Come now," he interrupted, "don't tell me that Noah went into details! Or perhaps it was Lily?"

Adeline raised her voice, her eyes blazed into his.

"Don't try to be funny over this, Philip. I won't have it. And I don't need Noah Binns to tell me what that woman is to you."

"What do you mean?"

"I mean that she is your mistress."

"That's a lie!" he shouted.

Adeline sprang to her feet. "Do you dare tell me I lie?"

He answered more quietly—"It's malicious gossip, whoever is responsible for it. Mary is as virtuous as any girl living."

"I repeat," said Adeline, "that she is your mistress." She held up her hand, in a peremptory gesture. "She told me so herself."

A shock of consternation went through the room. Ernest rose and took a step forward, as though he would put himself between his mother and Philip, who had turned startlingly pale. Nicholas tugged at his moustache, to hide the sardonic smile that hardened his lips. Augusta's sallow face flushed deeply. Sir Edwin nibbled at some inaudible words. He took out his watch and looked at the time. Time for a row, he nibbled inaudibly, time for a row.

"Mother," said Philip, his voice trembling, "can you look me in the face and tell me that?"

"I can. I went up to her room last night——"

"Why didn't you come to me?"

"I wanted to give her a chance to defend herself."

"When was this? Where was I?"

"In bed. As I say I went up to her room——"

"Poor little thing!" exclaimed Philip.

"Don't worry about her. She can look after herself. She's an adventuress with a past behind her. Now—don't interrupt. . . . I asked her, quite simply, what she meant by preparing to marry young Busby and at the same time carrying on a love affair with you. She had nothing to say for herself. Then I asked her, plump and plain, if she was your mistress. She wouldn't answer—then I said 'He's been up to your room at night, hasn't he?' And she said yes."

"She didn't understand you," cried Philip.

Adeline's flexible lips curled in scorn. "Not understand *me*!

187

Do I not generally make myself clear? She understood me well enough. I repeated, 'Are you his mistress?' Oh, she understood! You might as well try to paint a blackamoor white as to make her out virtuous."

"She could not have understood you," he repeated doggedly.

"Bring her down! I'd like to hear her deny it."

"I will, by God!"

He flung open the door and leaped up the stairs, two steps at a time. Jake, thinking this was some new game, ran after him joyously barking. They could be heard ascending the second flight of stairs. Then nothing more could be heard.

"I should like," observed Sir Edwin, "to know what they are saying up there."

"You are much better not knowing," said his wife.

"It was I," said Ernest, "who brought this trouble on us, and I'm very sorry about it. I never was more deceived in my life. The next time a governess is engaged, somebody else can choose her."

"What astounds me," said Nicholas, "is that she'd be so brazen. Tell the truth, Mamma, weren't you surprised?"

"I was indeed."

"What do you say she'll do now?"

"Sh—Philip's coming!"

All faces turned expectantly towards the door.

Philip was alone. Augusta and Ernest looked relieved; Adeline, Nicholas, and Sir Edwin disappointed.

"She's not there," said Philip quickly. "She's gone!"

"She's out with the children," suggested Ernest.

"She's gone, I tell you! Her trunk is packed. Her portmanteau gone. The bed hasn't been slept in."

"Eliza had made the bed," said Augusta.

"No. She was up there and I asked her. She said the room was just as it is now when she went into it." He turned to Adeline. "You have driven Mary away. God only knows what you have shocked her into doing." His eyes were tragic. In his excitement he had run his hand through his hair. Standing erect it added to his distraught appearance.

Adeline laughed derisively. "Me shock her! Ah, my dear, she's not so easily shocked. She can look out for herself. But— brazen as she is, she could not face us this morning after what she told me last night."

"I tell you she didn't know what she was saying!"

"Have sense, Philip," Nicholas put in tersely. "Mary Wakefield is no ignorant schoolgirl."

"Indeed," added Sir Edwin, "she seems to be a woman of strong character."

"I was taught," said Augusta, "to look on such a character as frail."

"Now then, Philip," Adeline spoke with an air of finality, "it's time to put this nonsense out of your head. I have no doubt that you are not the first with Mary Wakefield. Nor will you be the last. . . ."

"I will not hear another word against her," he shouted. "And if you won't believe her, perhaps you'll believe me. I have never been to bed with her. I swear it—though I despise myself for going to the trouble of denying what anyone who knows Mary . . ." He could not go on. He stood, with hands clenched, glaring at them.

"But surely," said Ernest, "no girl would knowingly damage her own character."

"She did know," declared Adeline. "She knew exactly what I said and what she said."

"Then she is deranged," said Philip.

"Perhaps her derangement is just love for you," suggested Nicholas, "and disappointment because she isn't getting you."

"She *is* getting me! Make no mistake about that. I'm going now to find her and I'm going to marry her."

"You fool," cried Adeline. "You would marry a girl who will have no rag of reputation left after this!"

In the hall Renny began to sing, in his penetrating treble voice, the new song he had just learned from a stableman.

"Ta ra ra boom de-ay—
Ta ra ra boom de-ay——"

Adeline called him and he appeared, red-cheeked, red-haired, brown-eyed, brown jacketed, as in autumn colouring. He had forgotten he had run away that morning but now he remembered and stood rigid.

"Have you seen your governess this morning?" asked Adeline.

"No, Granny. She's sick."

"How do you know?"

"She didn't come out of her room."

"And you haven't heard anything about her?"

"No. I haven't."

"Very well. Run along now."

His brow cleared. He relaxed and ran out singing:

> "Ta ra ra boom de-ay—
> Ta ra ra boom de-ay——"

## 17

## ESCAPE

WITH HER ear to the panel of the door Mary could hear that Adeline was descending the stairs. She listened for a moment, even after all was silent. Then she came back and stood facing her reflection in the mirror. It was as though she looked at a stranger. A different Mary was looking out at her, a Mary with dilated nostrils and bold, defiant eyes. A stranger. She laughed at her own reflection in triumph. I had the best of Mrs Whiteoak, she thought, she was dumbfounded, she didn't know what to say. I had the best of her.

She began to pace up and down the room, unable to think clearly, except for that one thought—I had the best of her. She came up here to humiliate me, to accuse me, but—I took the wind out of her sails. She thought she'd frighten me but I was equal to her! Those eyes of hers that seem to blaze into yours —but she found mine could blaze back. Never in my life had I such a moment. It was like something on the stage, only they'd never dare put such a scene on the stage—a girl declaring she was loose, when she was—just the reverse! It would upset all ideas of morality. It would be shameful. People would say what a horrible play. And no wonder! I am a horrible woman. . . . Yet I don't mind. . . . I don't care. . . . All that matters to me is that I got the best of her. I did not allow myself to be intimidated. Every single bit of her has been intimidating to me—the way her eyes are set in her head, the way she uses her hands. There's been something fatal in her for me. But tonight she must have felt stunned. . . . She must be wondering at this minute what on earth to do. She must be wondering what I am going to do. That girl, she'll think, can never marry Clive now! What if she intends to marry my Philip?

Philip. His name was like a cold hand laid on her heart. Her exalted brain halted in its imaginings. Her taut nerves slackened. Suddenly her legs felt weak and she sat down on the bed. She stared blankly in front of her. She did not know how long a time passed, but she began to be very cold. Her mouth felt unbearably dry yet she could not bring herself to the point of getting a drink. She sat like one doomed, while his name rang like a bell through the empty chambers of her mind.

After a while a few scalding tears filled her eyes. She wiped them away on the frilled cuff of her nightdress. But they freed her from the weakness, the lethargy, that had overtaken her. She looked about the room noticing the strange shadows thrown by the lamplight. She noticed the worn spot in the carpet in front of the dressing-table. She noticed the wax flowers and fruit under glass on the mantelshelf. She looked down and saw her bare feet, side by side, close together, on the mat by the bed. They looked very white, and somehow pathetic. They will carry me, she thought, far away from this house, as they brought me to it. . . . For now the knowledge that she was going away came clearly to her. In the morning Mrs Whiteoak would tell Philip what she had said. Never again could she look him in the face after the preposterous lie she had told.

Now she went to the washstand and filled a glass from the water bottle. The coldness of the water showed how the nights were becoming cold. She drank it down thirstily. Then she took the folded 'comforter' from the foot of the bed, wrapped it round her and sat down, this time drawing her feet up. She clasped them in her hands. It was hard to know which were colder, hands or feet, but they comforted each other.

She must think what to do.

Now she could think. The exhilaration of her encounter with Adeline was gone, the exhaustion which followed it was gone. She could think clearly with a part of her mind. In its recesses there still was a dark turmoil of emotion.

Should she go to Clive, tell him everything? Would she be able to convince him that what she had said to Adeline was a lie? And if she could, would he be willing to marry a girl to whom such a lie would occur? But she did not want to marry Clive! She would die rather than tell Clive what she had done. She would die rather than marry him when she loved Philip with her whole being. Now that Philip had touched the torch of her love for him into full flame she wondered that she ever had contemplated marrying Clive. . . . Yet, if Clive would be disgusted if he knew what she had said in her anger, what would be Philip's contempt! Philip who had told her he loved her, had kissed her in the orchard, had begged her to walk with him in the moonlight. They would not understand, and how could they when she herself did not understand? Even sitting on her bed, wrapped in the comforter, with the chill dawn greying the window, the thought of that moment when she had taken the wind out of Adeline's sails made her pulses thrill in renewed exhilaration. How those dark eyes whose fire she had found so hard to face had stared in blank astonishment! How that mouth, with the strong lines about it, had dropped open! At the recollection Mary laughed, even though she knew that in that moment she had ruined her life.

She thought of the words people used in speaking of a girl who had been seduced. 'He ruined her.' Well—it could be said of her that she ruined herself. Mary's laugh was fixed in an ironic smile which made her pale face oddly older.

One thing was certain—she must leave Jalna. The thought of meeting Philip, the thought of facing the family, was not to be borne. So acute was the stab of this thought that she sprang up and began to put on her clothes. She did not know where she might go. There would be time to make plans when she was safely outside the gate. Standing in her petticoat she poured water from the ewer into the basin. She had always liked this basin with its big red roses shining under the clear water. The water came from a cistern and was soft, as though just fallen from the clouds. She dashed it on her face, pressed it to her burning eyes. The large linen towel smelt of the outdoors.

She packed her trunk, strapped it, packed things for immediate use in her portmanteau, then put on her hat and coat. She was now breathless with haste. The sun was touching the tree-tops. At any moment the servants would be astir, the dogs barking to see her set out. She must not be seen.

She took a last look round to make sure she had forgotten nothing. This room, so stamped by her emotions, could it ever be the same again? Surely, in far-off years, someone lying in that bed would be conscious of the shadow of Mary Wakefield.

Carrying her portmanteau she crept down the stairs.

Outside Philip's door she hesitated, her heart seeming to

halt its beat while she willed a last message through the panel. . . . I love you, Philip, and never shall love any man but you. Goodbye, my dearest love.

She stole down the stairs.

The front door stood wide-open and the incomparable sweetness of the September morning poured into the hall. She was not the first member of the household to be about! She heard Mrs Nettleship's harsh voice in the kitchen below singing a hymn. "Pull for the shore, sailor, pull for the shore," she sang in quavering appeal. Jake's acute ear discovered Mary's soft step in the hall. He scratched at the door of the dogs' room and whined. In panic she hastened through the door and down the steps. She did not look back till she was safe behind the heavy branches of the evergreens that made the driveway a tunnel of greenness. Then between the branches she looked back at the house. Bluish-grey smoke curled straight up from two of its five chimneys. Where the sun struck warmest on the roof the pigeons had gathered, bowing to each other, making rich confidential noises in their throats, their iridescent breasts gleaming. Now that many leaves of the Virginia creeper had fallen the pinkish red of the brick was shown. The house, now forty years old, was like a comfortable fresh-complexioned matron in early middle age. It looked serene, complacent, confident of the beneficence of the future.

She turned away and trudged down the drive. Strangely enough her thoughts were not fixed on Philip but on Adeline. Since their interview of the night before, Adeline's image was so imprinted on her consciousness that she wondered if ever again it could be erased. If I were a sculptor, she thought, I could do a head of her from memory. Her nostrils, her eyelids, her lips, are clearer to me than my own. The worst of hating her is that something in me has always been drawn to her. But what matter, for I shall never see her again. Or pass through this gate again, or see *his* face again.

The portmanteau was heavier than she had expected. It kept thudding against her leg as she walked. She shifted it from hand to hand. The distance to the railway station was little more than a mile, however. She knew there was an early morning train to Montreal. She would take that train and, in Montreal, find some employment, no matter what, and through it save enough to return to England. She might get the passage paid in return for caring for an invalid or children. The one clear purpose in her mind was to go far away from this place. I would starve, she thought, rather than meet any of them again.

She heard the sound of a horse's hoofs on the road and stepped aside to let it pass. As it drew close she saw that the man in the buggy was Dr Ramsay. He drew in his horse and stared down at her in surprise.

"Good morning, Miss Wakefield," he said. "This is a surprise, meeting you abroad so airly. And your portmanteau too! Are you off for a holiday?"

"Yes," she returned, "I'm catching the train."

"And they let you come afoot! And carrying that heavy load! Come, I'll take you to the station." He began to tie the reins to the dashboard. "Just a wee minute and I'll have you and your baggage in the buggy."

"No—no, thank you. The rest of the walk is nothing. I'd—I'd rather walk. I like it."

Dr Ramsay had heard too many women tell too many lies to be taken in by this.

"What's wrong, Miss Wakefield?" he asked, his shrewd, good-looking face alight with curiosity. "This is no ordinary holiday you are on, I'm sure of that."

Whatever she said he would go to Jalna and repeat, she was sure of that. She said:

"If you must know, Dr Ramsay, I'm giving up my situation. I'm returning to England."

"Well, this is a surprise. I think I know a certain young man who will be heartbroken."

"No one will be heartbroken, Dr Ramsay." For an instant a terrible temptation to burst into tears assailed her. To cry out, through her tears—'No one but me! No one but me!' But she controlled herself and looked straight into his eyes. "I'd much rather walk," she said. "Goodbye." She stretched out her hand to shake his.

His hand caught hers in a strong bony grip, a grip to give confidence. Mary felt that, if once he got her into the buggy, he would have the truth out of her.

She made her pale lips smile. "Goodbye," she repeated. "And please give my love to the children."

"I'd insist," he said, "but I'm on an urgent call to a lying-in case. Goodbye, Miss Wakefield, and good luck to you."

Nothing but the urgency of his call dragged him away from

Mary and his desire to drive straight to Jalna and find out what all this was about. With set lips he turned towards duty. He gave his old horse a touch with the whip and it ambled on.

Mary passed the two shops and the few houses of the tiny village. The road into it was guarded by two rows of the noblest oaks and pines in the province. Mary looked up into their massive branches and remembered Mrs Whiteoak's possessive pride in them. 'One would think she owned the earth the way she looks and acts.'

There were the railway tracks to be crossed, the harsh cinders gritting beneath her feet, the high platform to be mounted. She was beginning to be in a panic for fear she would miss the train. The stationmaster looked out of the wicket through steel-rimmed spectacles. Mary asked for a ticket to Montreal.

"Was you goin' today?"

"Yes. On this morning's train. Is it late?"

"Late! It's gone. Ten minutes ago. Didn't you hear it whistle?"

"Oh—no, I didn't hear the whistle."

It must have passed through while she was talking to Dr Ramsay. She was filled with dismay. She sat down on a seat in the waiting-room, the portmanteau at her feet. For a time she could not decide what to do. If only she had let the doctor drive her to the station, she would now be miles and miles away. I always seem to do the wrong thing, she thought. If there were nineteen right ways and one wrong, I should choose the wrong. From behind the wicket came the steady ticking of the telegraph.

She went out of the station, closing the door softly so that she might not be heard, recrossed the tracks and set out towards the lake-shore road. She remembered that it was only about seven miles to Stead, the next village. She would go there, where there was a good hotel, take a room, and leave on the next train for Montreal. She would almost certainly be offered a lift on the way. But the road was unusually quiet. A great load of hay passed her, a wagon from which two timid calves looked out on her, a buggy whose seat was crowded by a fat married couple, and a man in a gig training a trotter for the Fall Fair trotting races. The speed of this vehicle almost took Mary's breath away, it seemed dangerous on the open road.

Lake gulls drifted above the fields and back over the lake.

It was grey-green, roughening because a strong wind was rising. It blew the clouds in great battalions, bright and billowing against the blue, till one covered the sun and turned them to threatening purple. Mary was little more than a mile on her way when a shower came slanting down as though it chose her for its special object. Even the thick hemlock branches beneath which she took shelter were not enough to keep her from getting wet. She looked disconsolately out at the road, stretching long before her. Already she felt tired out. Blisters were forming on her palms. The coil of her hair began to loosen, a hairpin slid under her collar down her back. The damp earthy smell of the woods came out to meet the smell of the lake.

The shower passed. Once again Mary set out. She had got a pair of gloves from the portmanteau and now the carrying of it was less painful. But it grew heavier and heavier as she plodded on. Her long cloth skirt, wet from the rain, dragged at her knees. Now the sun was out again, the gulls leant in the wind or dropped to ride with assurance on the rowdy green waves.

Surely, surely, Stead was not far off. Mary stopped at a farmhouse by the road to ask how far. Still another mile, she was told, and the farmer's wife asked her if she would come in and have a cup of tea. A pan of buns had just been taken from the oven. The kitchen was hot and the air heavy with the delicious smell of the baking. Mary was glad to sit down by the table and drink a cup of tea and eat a bun, so hot that the butter melted on it. She realized she was faint for food. She had eaten nothing since the picnic with the children. The farmer's wife seemed glad of her company. Her own mother had come from England. She told her mother's name and the name of the village she had come from.

Mary had expected to feel refreshed, stronger to face the rest of the walk, but food and drink had made her sleepy. She felt as though the pith had gone out of her. She stumbled as she walked, with not a thought in her head, save to keep walking. Mechanically she stepped aside to let a wagon pass. She had not the wit now to hail the driver and ask him for a lift. The wagon rumbled on, the blond manes of the farm horses tossing in the wind. The driver was an old man, humped up on the seat. Old brute, thought Mary, he might have seen that I was ready to drop. Tears filled her eyes and ran down her cheeks. She did not trouble to wipe them away. Her mind was again a blank.

She did not see the shining trap and well-groomed horse coming towards her down a side road till it was quite near. Then she wiped her face with her handkerchief and prepared to appeal to the driver. There was no need. The horse was drawn up sharply by Mary's side. She looked up into Muriel Craig's round face, with its cool stare fixed on her.

"Why, Miss Wakefield," cried Muriel Craig. "To think of meeting you, of all people, trudging along the road so far from home."

Mary smiled coldly. "I am walking to Stead," she said.

"Then you must let me give you a lift. I go right past there."

Mary would have been glad of a lift from the devil himself. She heaved her portmanteau into the trap and clambered in after it. "Thank you," she murmured.

In a moment the trap was bowling swiftly over the road to the rhythmic cadence of hoofs. Mary sank back into the comfortable seat and gave herself up to her relief.

"I'm glad," said Muriel Craig, handling the reins with conscious elegance, "to see you with sensible shoes. You simply have to come to it in this country."

"I brought these with me from England."

"Did you really? Oh, I can tell that now when I look at them. English shoes are the very best." She smiled at Mary in a way she never had before. Her smile seemed to embrace Mary in its friendliness.

"You must let me out when we come to Stead," said Mary. "I can easily walk to the railway station."

"What train are you taking?"

"The next one to Montreal."

"Then you're leaving Jalna?"

"Yes."

"Just a holiday?"

"No. Permanently. I'm returning to England."

Muriel Craig drew in the horse to a walk. She sat silent. Mary glanced sideways at the retroussé profile, uptilted beneath the down-tilted sailor hat.

Then Muriel Craig spoke. "I guess you've had words with someone at Jalna. I suspect it's Mrs Whiteoak. I hear she's very difficult to get on with."

Mary snatched at this interpretation of her leaving. "Yes, yes, she's very difficult."

"I believe she was so overbearing with the other governesses that they could not endure it."

"I daresay."

"Have you any position in view?"

"Not exactly. I think you'd better let me out here. I don't want to take you out of your way."

"Now, look here. I have something to propose. I do hope you'll be interested."

Mary began to understand what people found to like in Muriel Craig. Now that she had dropped her patronizing airs she appeared candid, pleasant, full of dependable common sense.

"This is what I have to propose. I have a friend in New York. Very well off—really rich. She has three tiny children. She would be perfectly delighted to get someone like you to teach them. She must have someone reliable. Then, any time you felt like returning to England, there you would be, right at a seaport. You'd have twice the salary you'd get in Montreal. Now, my dear, you're not going to be so silly as to refuse. You couldn't be. This is a heaven-sent opportunity. I'm going to take you straight home with me and you're going to stay there while I write to my friend." She put a hand over Mary's and clasped it with comforting warmth. "This friend has been *so* good to me and I'm dying to do her a good turn. As for you— you'd love her and her sweet little children too."

Mary was so exhausted by lack of sleep, by the long walk, carrying the portmanteau, that a friendly hand held out to her was irresistible. She felt a rush of contrition for her misjudgment of Miss Craig. Her lips trembled as she answered:

"It seems to be the perfect position for me and it's so kind of you to offer to take me in, but I think I should stay at a hotel."

"Hotel! The very idea. As though I could tolerate such a thing. No—you're coming straight home with me. There is that big house, with just my father and me in it and a poor little thing like you talking of going to a hotel." She brought the whip down sharply on the horse's flank, clicked her tongue at him, and now they were speeding along the road at a pace that was almost alarming. It was as though Muriel Craig were afraid Mary might change her mind.

Mary was surprised to find Mr Craig walking across the lawn leaning on his nurse's arm. He was the sturdiest-looking invalid imaginable and a summer's tan added to his look of health. He greeted Mary hospitably.

"You are very welcome, Miss Wakefield. Make yourself quite at home. . . . I don't understand about your being here. Have you left the Whiteoaks?"

His daughter answered for her. "Miss Wakefield is going back to England, Father."

His particular illness had made him slow to understand. The nurse kept looking at him with a quizzical look, as though of perpetual encouragement.

"Well, well," he said, "however it is, you look very tired, young lady. You should go and lie down. Get my nurse to make you an eggnog. She's famous at eggnogs."

At the earliest possible moment Muriel Craig led Mary upstairs and installed her in a large bedroom. She carried up the portmanteau herself as though it were nothing. She remained for some time giving Mary more alluring descriptions of her friend's house, her children, her good-heartedness.

"Now," she said at last, "you must have a good rest while I go and write to my friend. How thankful I am I found you, you poor little thing! You looked such a picture of distress, trailing along the road, lugging that heavy portmanteau."

Impulsively she came and threw her arms about Mary and kissed her.

'Poor little thing indeed!' thought Mary. 'I'm taller than she. But what vitality! She's like a steamroller.'

Mary herself longed for nothing but to throw herself down on the bed and let oblivion enfold her. But what a bed! It was covered by a heavy white counterpane, the ponderous pillows shielded by stiffly starched pillow shams with fluted frills. Mary gingerly lifted one off and stood not knowing what to do with it. And how should she ever arrange the bed to look as it looked now? Oh, for that eggnog which Mr Craig had advised! Her stomach was touching her backbone. For an idiotic moment she pictured herself as eating the pillow sham in her famine.

She was trembling from fatigue and hunger. She replaced the pillow sham and taking the folded satin quilt from the bed laid it on the floor. She opened a window, for the room was airless, and threw herself on the floor, her head pillowed on the quilt. She had thought to fall instantly asleep but a painful throbbing swept through her nerves. She opened her eyes to their widest, a future black as night spread like a desert before them. Alone. Alone. She could not sleep. She was too tired for sleep. Never could she sleep again. The satin quilt, smelling of camphor, suffocated her. She flung it away and lay flat on the carpet. Large greenish medallions on a maroon ground swarmed about her. Like hideous hungry monsters crawling towards her. She pressed her hands to her eyes, shutting them out. That was better. A fresh cool wind made the curtains billow. It blew across her, bringing with it the moist earthy smell of autumn. Mary lat quiet now and presently she dropped into a deep dreamless sleep.

## 18
## THE SEARCH

RENNY'S VOICE came down to them from the top floor, clear and high, like someone blowing with all his might on a flute. Nicholas observed:

"What an inane song!"

"I heard Hodge singing it," said Ernest.

"I often have wondered," mused Sir Edwin, "why the repetition of meaningless words is fascinating."

"Yes," agreed Ernest, "in the songs of Shakespeare's time it was the same. With a hey nonny nonny, you know."

These remarks were like little waves rippling about two glowering rocks. Adeline and Philip, their eyes on each other, said nothing.

Then Nicholas went to Philip and threw an arm about his shoulders. "Come now, old man," he said, "take this affair sensibly. You'll be glad later on. I'm sure you will."

"I suppose you mean that I should sit twiddling my thumbs while the victim of this plot—the girl I love——"

"I know of no plot."

"There was a plot. Mamma knows there was a plot."

Adeline demanded—"Was it part of a plot that you should follow the girl into the orchard—when you knew she was to marry another man next week—and make love to her?"

200

"That had nothing to do with the plot."

"It has set all the neighbourhood talking."

"What do I care for the neighbours? All I care about is to find Mary."

"Philip, you didn't trouble your head about Mary till you heard she was going to marry Clive."

"She was here in the house—by my side. I loved her."

Augusta put in—"I beg of you to think this over coolly, Philip."

He turned away, then said over his shoulder—"All your talk is wasted, I can tell you that."

The sound of wheels came from outside. Ernest, nearest the window, exclaimed—"It's young Busby! Looking grim."

Philip strode onto the porch. Clive Busby was alighting from the buggy, tying the horse to the ring in the nose of the iron horse's head by the steps. His face was extraordinarily pale and set.

The rest of the family followed Philip to the hall, with the exception of Sir Edwin, who looked out between the curtains, while nervously fondling his side-whiskers.

Clive came up the steps like the bearer of bad news.

"Good morning," he said, in a controlled voice. "May I see Miss Wakefield?"

"She's not here," answered Adeline, her eyes holding his. "I had a talk with her which she didn't like and she's left. I think you should follow her, Clive. The girl's impulsive and rather foolish but she'll be all right."

"Not here!" he repeated, dazed. "Where is she?"

"No one knows. We've just not discovered it."

"My God," he said wildly, "she may have done something terrible."

"Scarcely. She carried her portmanteau with her."

The sound of another vehicle was heard and Dr Ramsay, the accouchement dealt with, urging his old mare, appeared. He greeted the group without surprise.

"A blustery day," he said. "That was quite a shower we had."

"Have you seen Miss Wakefield, by any chance?" asked Philip.

"Miss Wakefield? Ah, yes. She and I had a little chat airly this morning. She was on her way to catch the Montreal train, as I suppose you know."

"Montreal!" echoed Philip. "She took the train to Montreal! Did she tell you where she was going to stay?"

"No. She was not very communicative but she evidently had her plans well laid."

Clive Busby turned to Philip. "Can I see you alone?" he asked.

"Yes. Come along."

Adeline exclaimed—"I think I'll come too."

"Thanks," said Philip. "We'd sooner be alone."

He led the way into the tunnel of pines and hemlocks that marched from gate to house. There, with the greenish light on their faces, Philip's deeply flushed, Clive's greyish-white beneath the tan, they measured each other, as though for a duel. Then Philip said:

"This engagement of yours, Busby, must come to an end. Mary loves me. She made a mistake. I'm sorry."

"I will not give her up till she asks me to, with her own lips. She has been perfectly happy in our engagement. We've planned everything together. The mistake is on your side."

"Tell me, why did you come over here?"

"Because of some gossip I'd heard."

"Noah Binns?"

"God, do you think I'd listen to him?"

"Lily Pink?"

"No. Mrs Pink. She came to Vaughanlands this morning."

Philip gave an exclamation of anger, then his brows cleared.

"It's as well that this should be settled between us now. . . . I suppose Mrs Pink said I'd been seen kissing Mary in the orchard."

"Yes."

"It's true."

"You can't make me believe Mary doesn't love me. When I find her she'll explain."

Philip broke off a twig of hemlock and examined it. With his eyes still fixed on it he said:

"I wonder if she will tell you what she told my mother."

"What?"

"She told my mother that she was my mistress."

Clive's lips had had colour in them. Now they went greyish-white like his face.

"You lie!" he shot out.

"No. She did say that to my mother. But it's not true.

202

There has never been anything more passionate between Mary and me than what Mrs Pink repeated. I swear that, Clive."

"I don't want to hear you swear anything," Clive exclaimed miserably. "It makes me sick that we should stand here discussing her in such a way. Mary, of all girls! She'd die of shame if she knew."

"The fact remains," said Philip, "that she said that to my mother last night. You can't be more astounded than I am to hear it."

"I won't believe she said any such thing. Your mother imagined it."

"My mother is not in the habit of imagining things of that nature."

"You have treated me badly. You knew Mary and I were engaged."

"Not till I came home yesterday."

"Then you went straight to her and tried to push me out!"

"Yes. Because I intend to marry her."

"Mary will never jilt me. She's too honourable."

"Would you marry a girl who loves another man?"

"I will not discuss her!" interrupted Clive. "I'll find her and she will tell me the truth."

"That's all I ask. I'll come with you."

They turned, side by side, and came out on the gravel sweep before the house. Clive untied the horse and got into the buggy. His eyes met Philip's with a look of mingled hurt and hate. He said:

"I'm going to Montreal by the next train."

"So am I. But there's not another till tomorrow morning."

"It's a long while to wait."

Without another word Clive drove away and down the road. I shall never, he thought, enter those gates again.

Instead of turning the horse towards Vaughanlands he drove to the railway station. Better make sure that Mary really had gone by the train.

The stationmaster did not hurry to appear at the wicket. Clive forced himself to ask coolly:

"Can you tell me whether Miss Wakefield went on the train to Montreal this morning?"

"H'm. She was the young lady up at Jalna?"

"Yes."

The stationmaster grinned. "She missed the train. It's

funny, in a country place like this, folks could miss a train with nothing else to do but catch it. But she missed it all right."

"Did you notice what way she went afterwards?"

"Well, she sat a while and then she went out very quiet and took the road to Stead. I reckon she planned to spend the night at the hotel and take the morning train to the city and change there for Montreal. You see, this here's only a local line. Or she might take this evening's train to the city and stay there for the night. Whatever she does she's got to change trains in the city."

"Oh. I didn't know. Thanks very much."

She had missed the train! If he drove straight to Stead he might be able to find her there in the hotel. He got into the buggy and set out along the lake-shore road. Colour had returned to his face but his head felt as though an iron band encircled it. A feeling of terrible urgency made him drive the horse at a gallop along the road. He would not be able to rest till he had come face to face with Mary, had wrung the meaning of all this bewilderment from her.

He inquired for her at the hotel in Stead. He went to a smaller, very poor hotel and inquired there. He went to the railway station. She had not been in any of these places. He came to the conclusion that Mary had a friend in Stead with whom she was staying. There was nothing to do but wait till the evening train.

He drove back to Vaughanlands and put the horse in its stall. The tightness in his head had developed into a raging headache. He lay on a sofa and kind Mrs Vaughan made him tea and rubbed camphor on his head. She tried to lead him on to talk of his trouble, but, when she saw the misery in his eyes when she tentatively touched on the subject, she fell silent, putting all her sympathy into the stroking of his forehead. If she knew all, he thought, what would she think? His spirit writhed at the remembrance of what Philip had told him.

Somehow the rest of the day passed and again he drove to the railway station at Stead. She was not there. He had told the Vaughans that possibly he might be away for the night. He was thankful he would be able to spend it alone. He had several drinks in the bar of the hotel, then went to bed. He slept better than he had expected, a deep, almost dreamless sleep.

Next morning, in a heavy downpour of rain, he walked to the railway station. Mary was not among the sleepy passengers waiting for the train. Neither had she appeared when it drew out. He went back to the hotel and forced down some breakfast. He tried to think what he should do next. He could not go to every house in Stead and ask for her, yet he was sure she must be there. When the rain had eased he walked doggedly through the streets of the village, looking up at the houses, hoping to see her face at a window.

At last he decided to drive back to the Vaughans'. It was possible that there he might hear news of Mary. He heard nothing, but Robert Vaughan casually remarked that Philip Whiteoak had gone to Montreal. Clive smiled grimly to think of that wild-goose chase. He went out and wandered through the dark woods where Mary and he had walked hand in hand, planning the future which now looked as gloomy to him as these dripping trees shedding their summer's pride.

In late afternoon he drove again to Stead and searched for her at the station. Again he spent the night in the hotel and repeated the vain search on the following morning. He began to be in a panic. Mary had drowned herself! She had gone out of her mind and drowned herself in the lake. As he drove homeward he looked in growing apprehension at the tumbling green waves. To him, a Westerner, the lake was an ocean. The gulls hovered above something in the water. Clive's heart froze with fear. Then he saw that it was a log. He stopped at several houses and asked if anyone there had seen Mary. The woman who had given her tea and a bun was one of these. She looked with curiosity at Clive and enlarged on Mary's look of weariness and how she herself had felt worried about her.

The horse needed no encouragement to hasten back to his stable.

Mrs Vaughan met Clive with a letter in her hand.

"Miss Craig's man brought this, Clive," she said, so anxious to help him with looks of sympathy, longing to put her arms about him and comfort him, as though he were her own son.

Clive tore open the letter and read:

DEAR MR BUSBY

Mary Wakefield is staying with me. I think it would be a good thing if you were to come and see her. She doesn't know I am writing this but I am sure she is still very attached to you. If you come let it be today and please ask for me.

Sincerely,
MURIEL CRAIG

# 19

# AT THE CRAIGS'

MARY HEARD the light but decisive tap on the door twice before she could drag herself from the well of sleep into which she had sunk. At first she could not remember where she was. Why was she lying on the floor? Had she fainted and fallen there? The knock came again and a voice.

"Miss Wakefield! Mary! May I come in?"

Mary staggered to her feet. She was aching in every muscle. "Just a moment," she called. She threw the comforter on to the bed and opened the door. Her eyes, glazed by exhaustion and heavy sleep, could scarcely focus on the figure in the doorway, so trim, so alert.

"What a draught!" exclaimed Muriel Craig. "It's a wonder you weren't blown out of bed. But—you didn't lie down! Goodness! I was sure you'd lie down and have a sleep."

"I sat in that nice big chair," said Mary, "with the comforter wrapped round me. I slept like a log."

"Really." The word somehow expressed disapproval. "You look completely washed-out and chilled. Let me feel your hand. Why, it's icy. And you must be starved, too. I kept lunch back as long as I could to give you a chance to rest but now my father's clamouring for it. You can't imagine what my life is. Between his demands and his nurse's I'm driven almost crazy."

She had seated herself to wait for Mary, who would have given a good deal to tidy herself in privacy. Her hands shook as she opened her portmanteau and took out her brush and comb.

"What nice hair you have," Muriel Craig said, as Mary's silky hair flew before the brush. "And fine too, though not so fine as mine. Mine is a perfect nuisance it's so fine. These peculiarities are a nuisance, aren't they? It's the same with my instep. It's so high I have a terrible time getting shoes to fit me. After this I think I shall have them made to order."

"What a nuisance," said Mary.

"Of course, some people admire them. But I don't." She put forward her perfectly shod foot and studied it with great concentration. "Another trying thing is my tiny waist. Have you noticed it? I never can get my skirt-bands to fit properly. Dressmakers are so stupid. . . . I had not heard that Mrs Whiteoak was home from her visit till I met you. Did she have a nice time?"

"I think so."

"I like the simple way you do your hair. It suits you . . . I suppose her son came with her?"

"Oh, yes."

"Should you like to go to the bathroom and wash your hands?"

She led the way and waited in the passage for Mary who felt a little refreshed after bathing her face in warm water. They descended the stairs together. Mr Craig was already seated at table with his nurse and excused himself from rising.

"You'll have to pardon my bad manners," he said.

"Oh, Mr Craig," exclaimed his nurse, "your manners are beautiful."

"Nurse says my manners are beautiful," he remarked to Mary. "Some people are easily pleased, aren't they?" He wanted to talk all through the meal about his illness and the wonderful care he had had. He was confused as to which hand should hold his knife and which his fork, till the nurse put him right with her air of whimsical encouragement. Her beady eyes sparkled at all his little jokes, but his daughter's pale gaze seemed to try to ignore him.

Mary felt more unreal than ever she had felt in all her life. Her brain was numbed and she was grateful for Mr Craig's little jokes, for them she could understand and smile at. He could not say enough in praise of Dr Ramsay and his treatment of him.

"There's a fine man," he said, in his slow, rather thick voice. "There's a grand man. And he's got a grand son-in-law, too. Mr Philip Whiteoak. Do you know him?"

"Miss Wakefield has been governess to Mr Whiteoak's children, Father," his daughter cut in impatiently. "Surely you knew that."

"Forgot," he muttered.

"Naughty forgetful man!" cooed the nurse, patting his hand.

"I can tell you someone who admired *him*," Mr Craig said. "My daughter. That girl there. But she won't get him. He's not going to take a second wife, Dr Ramsay tells me. He's devoted to the memory of his first wife."

Muriel Craig's face had grown an angry red, but she was silent.

"And that's right too, isn't it, Miss Wakefield? I'm sure you don't approve of second marriages. Neither do I. I had a wonderful wife. What you'd call a perfect helpmate. But . . . she wasn't sympathetic. I'd never have come through this sickness without sympathy."

"You're very much better, aren't you?" said Mary.

"Better! Why, I'm coming on like a house on fire."

He made a wide gesture that overturned his glass of milk. The nurse quickly began to mop it up with her table napkin.

"Naughty boy!" she chuckled.

He caught a string of her apron in his hand. "Tied to her apron strings—that's what I am!" he declared dramatically, addressing the ceiling.

The first pumpkin pie of the season was on the table and a large dish of purple grapes. Muriel Craig was too angry to touch either. As soon as Mary and she could escape she led Mary to the verandah. They sat down side by side in the hammock.

"My father talks like an old fool," Muriel said vehemently. "He's always trying to be funny and he certainly doesn't succeed, except in the eyes of that imbecile nurse. Don't you dislike her?"

Mary could say with truth that she did not see much to like in her.

"It's so nice to have you here," said Muriel, putting an arm about her and gently swaying the hammock. "I have very few real friends."

After a silence in which Mary desperately tried to think of something worth saying, Muriel remarked:

"You have such a nice skin it seems a pity you put powder on it. My mother always said to me—'Muriel, you have a flawless complexion. Don't ever powder your face,' and I never have. Would you like me better with powder?"

"I admire you as you are."

"It's a good thing someone admires me."

"I think everyone I know admires you."

"Do you think Philip Whiteoak does?" Her large clear eyes looked straight in Mary's.

Mary laughed. "He would scarcely confide that to me."

"He might. Doesn't he ever confide in you?"

"I was at Jalna to look after his children—not as his confidant."

"But you liked him, didn't you?"

"Oh, yes. He is very kind."

"Very kind! Dear me." Her arm tightened about Mary. "I think you might confide in me. I think you might tell me what the trouble was and why you left Jalna so suddenly."

"Mrs Whiteoak and I had words."

"Heavens! I'll wager you came off badly. I'd be afraid of her. *Do* tell me about it."

Mary's colour rose. "I really can't."

"Was it just you two alone?"

"Yes."

"And *he* didn't know about it?"

"No."

Muriel put forward her foot and sat in concentrated admiration of her instep before she said, in a thoughtful tone:

"I know someone who is badly smitten on you. But of course everyone knows that."

Mary looked inquiring.

"Clive Busby. Someone—I forget who it was—told me you were engaged. But you'd never be running off like this, if you were engaged to him. But you could be, if you wanted to. I'm sure of that. One day I met him at a garden party—it was given by some of the officers of the Queen's Own Rifles—and when I told him how much I admired you his eyes positively *shone*. Oh, he's terribly smitten! Don't tell me he has proposed."

"I'm not telling you anything," Mary said coldly. "I'm not at all a communicative person. I hope you don't mind."

"But I *do* mind! I want us to swing here together in the hammock and pour out our feelings. I've written the letter to my friend in New York and it's posted."

"Thank you. That is kind." Mary put her hand to her eyes. Muriel Craig's head, enormously magnified, was floating before them. "I'm ashamed to say it, but—I must go and lie down again. I feel a little dizzy. It's very silly of me."

Muriel sprang up. "Rest is what you need and rest you shall have. And right in bed, too."

In her abundant energy she all but dragged Mary up the stairs. She prepared the bed for her while Mary changed into a dressing-gown, Muriel talking all the while, but now of her difficulties with her father and his nurse. She covered Mary with the satin comforter, patted her shoulder, and told her to sleep till she was rested through and through.

I wonder if ever that day will come, thought Mary. She welcomed the comfort and solitude of the bed, as a fish welcomes water. She covered her head and submerged herself in sleep. But she had no real rest in her sleep, for wherever her dreams carried her, Adeline Whiteoak was there to drive her away.

Fortunately she woke up before she was called, so that she was able to dress in peace. She saw by the looking-glass that she was less pale and that the blue circles beneath her eyes had almost disappeared. This gave her confidence.

After the evening meal Mr Craig proposed a game of euchre. He had not played a game of cards since before his illness. Miss Wakefield's visit was doing him good. So a card table was placed in the chilly drawing-room and the four sat themselves about it, Mr Craig and his nurse playing as partners. The light from the incandescent-gas fixture that hung from the ceiling cast intense shadows on their faces. Muriel looked very discontented, her father very pleased with himself and his twinklingly solicitous nurse. It was hard for him to remember what was trumps or to decide what card to play. Time and again the nurse sprang up and ran round to help him. Mary noticed how, when she bent over his shoulder, her cheek seemed always to touch his head. Muriel noticed nothing but sat pouting at her cards like a sulky schoolgirl. Mary had a momentary vision of the Whiteoaks playing at cards or backgammon, the vivid laughing faces, the hilarity when Adeline was the winner and Boney joined his shouts to her triumph.

Mr Craig was not satisfied till three games of euchre had been played. Then, leaning heavily on his nurse's arm, he stumped off, after a kindly goodnight to Mary and his thanks for putting up with an old man's stupidity. Muriel and he exchanged a casual nod, a muttered something before they parted. With a pang Mary remembered the warm embrace her father had given her when they said goodnight, the smell of his tobacco and the way his moustache tickled her cheek. She remembered the audible kisses of the Whiteoaks.

To Muriel's disappointment Mary said she must go to her room and write a letter. Fortunately she had brought her little leather writing folio with her. All her writing things were in her room, she said. Might she go there to write her letter?

"Oh, what a different evening from the one I'd planned!" cried Muriel. "I thought we'd talk and talk till midnight."

"I'm sorry," was all Mary could say, "but I really must do this letter tonight."

At last she escaped.

In her room she sat down by the marble-topped table. It was ice-cold beneath her bare arm.

'My dear Clive'—she wrote and then stared out into the darkness. . . . Again she made the attempt.

MY DEAR CLIVE,

To me the writing of this letter is a great grief. It is to tell you that I cannot marry you—to tell you—oh, that I could find the gentlest words in the language—that I do not love you deeply enough for marriage. I reproach myself for not having discovered this before. Dearest Clive, I am not good enough for you. I will always remember your goodness and kindness. I don't ask you to forget me but I do beg of you to forgive me, and to try to think of me without bitterness.                    MARY

She read the letter. It was not all that she would have liked to say to Clive but it must do. She could find no other words. She addressed the letter, sealed and stamped it. She would not let herself think of Clive's face when he had read it.

And now that other letter, the letter to Philip. Surely she had the right to send him a message of farewell . . . just a line to say she loved him and would never love any other but him. Here, in this dim room, with the cavernous, dripping night beyond the window, she might free her spirit, pour out to him on paper what would never pass her lips. She took a sheet of notepaper and wrote:

MY DEAR, MY ONLY LOVE—

Then her hand refused to move. A terrible cramp came into it. Though she set her teeth and tried to force it, her hand would not move. She gripped her wrist in her left hand to control it, but, when she put pen to paper, she could only scrawl his name. She was powerless to write.

She buried her face in her arms and broke into wild crying. Hoarse sobs shook her. She did not care if people in the house heard her and came running. She cared for nothing but to let the sobs tear her to pieces. But no one heard her and, at last, she was quiet. She got up, undressed, knelt by the high bed in her long white nightdress and said her prayers. She made no mention in them of her unhappiness, sent up no petition, but the accustomed words comforted her.

The next morning she asked Muriel Craig where she could post a letter. She had it ready in her hand.

"Give it to me," said Muriel. "The man's just going in for the mail and he'll take it. What a morning! Pouring with rain!" She caught up the letter and hurried off.

In the passage she stood thinking, after she had read the address. Then she went softly up to Mary's room and looked about. She saw the writing case and opened it. Nothing but notepaper and two English postcards inside. She looked in the waste paper basket and discovered some torn bits of paper. She pounced on these and tiptoed with them to her room. Guilt was written all over her but no one saw her.

She pieced together the bits of paper and read what Mary had written—'My dear, my only love,' and his name, 'Philip'. The paper was blistered and the writing blurred by tears.

What did it mean?

It meant possibly that Mary was breaking off what relations there were between herself and Clive and was reaching out to-wards Philip. What else could it mean? But Mary would not get her clutches on Philip—not if she could prevent it.

Her face was flushed with excitement as she finished her note to Clive. She flew downstairs with it to the reluctant man, waiting in his rubber cape to go out into the rain.

"Take this," she said, "to Mr Vaughan's and leave it for Mr Busby. When you bring back the mail from the post office bring it straight to me."

For the seventh time Clive Busby was driving along the road by the lake, in search of Mary. To him it had become the most hateful stretch of road in the world. Every bend of it, every tree, every stone, every patch of thistles, he felt he knew like the palm of his hand. The horse knew it too and hated it. He showed his resentment by jerking his head and splashing through puddles so clumsily that drops of muddy water flew over the dashboard.

At last I shall know the truth, Clive thought. At last the truth . . . from her own lips. His weary mind had reached the point where what he craved most was to know where he stood, to sweep away the web that entangled him.

When he reached the Craigs' he tied his horse and strode to

the door. A maid left him in the hall where he took off his mackintosh, folded it neatly across a chair, and passed his hand over his hair. But the heavy thudding of his heart told a story less cool. He heard voices in the next room. Then the door of the room opened and Muriel Craig came into the hall. She said smiling:

"Mary's in there. She doesn't know it's you. Katie just said 'a gentleman'."

As Clive went into the room she closed the door after him, but she remained near it.

He was alone with Mary.

The first thought of each was shock at the appearance of the other. Her eyes were reddened, her features blurred. He looked ten years older.

Then panic seized her at being alone with him and she exclaimed—"Didn't you get my letter?"

"*Your* letter? No."

"Of course, you couldn't. I forgot. It was only posted this morning."

"Did you ask me to come, in the letter?"

"No. I asked you not to come."

"Mary"—he had been standing just inside the door, now he came closer to her—"for God's sake tell me what happened!"

"Clive—I beg you—don't make me talk of it. Go back and read my letter—try to believe that it breaks my heart to treat you like this." She pressed her hand to her trembling mouth.

"No letter will do. I must have it from your own lips."

"Then . . . if you must . . . I don't love you well enough to marry you. I mean I don't love you in that way. Oh, surely you understand."

"I'm trying to but it's hard. Only a few days ago you and I were happy together. You held my hand and we laughed, as we walked through the woods. Why—you even chose the sort of little dog you wanted me to buy you." His voice broke.

"I know. I know. I must seem a horrible person to you—and no wonder."

"What happened? Something happened after Philip White-oak came home."

"Yes."

"In the orchard?"

"Yes."

"He told you not to marry me? You do what he says?"

"I needed no telling!" she broke out. "I love him. I've always loved him. I think you guessed that. But I stifled it—my love for him—I choked it down. I turned to you—thinking I could make you happy—perhaps be happy myself—but then he came back and he told me that he loved me——"

"Are you going to marry Philip?"

"No! I'm not going to marry anyone."

"Why aren't you going to marry him? You love him 'in that way', apparently. Why did you run away from him, Mary?"

He came nearer, as though to take her hand, but she put her two hands behind her back.

"I ran away," she answered, looking steadily in his eyes, "because I did not want to see him again or anyone I had known in that place."

Clive looked sombrely at the floor, then, with the heavy colour rising in his face, he asked, in a low voice:

"Mary—did you say anything to Mrs Whiteoak that you have regretted since?"

"Did *he* tell you that?" she demanded hoarsely.

"Yes. But he said it wasn't so."

She stared at him speechless.

"Mary—tell me—for God's sake, tell me the truth."

Like a trapped bird beating itself against bars her mind beat itself against his questioning. If she told him she had spoken the truth, he would loathe her. If she told him she had lied, what would be his scorn.

"*Will* you let me be! *Will* you leave me! I regret nothing I've said or done. All I want is to be let alone—never to see any of you again!"

Clive flinched as though she had struck him.

He drew back, his eyes mournfully fixed on her distorted face. With the hand on the doorknob he said:

"Goodbye, Mary," and was gone.

Late that afternoon he went to Jalna to tell Adeline Whiteoak goodbye. He would have gone off without seeing her, thinking he would write to her after he reached home, but Mrs Vaughan insisted that he must say goodbye in person. Adeline Whiteoak was an old friend of his family, had been very kind to him. He must not treat her without ceremony.

The rain had stopped. There was a flashing, wild brightness through the clouds. The wet-winged turkeys, trailing through the ravine, stopped, each in its attitude of that instant, to watch him cross the bridge. The stream, rejuvenated by the rains, tripped gleaming past the water weeds and cress that edged it.

As Clive reached the top of the opposite side of the ravine the house rose before him, its mantle of vines newly washed by rain, its windows reflecting the sun. He looked up at the windows of Mary's room and a fresh pang and a new, painful wonder struck his heart. What thoughts, what acts, had that room sheltered? What mysterious impulse had driven her to become a different Mary from the one he loved?

Adeline met him at the door. She had seen him coming. She stepped out into the porch and shut the door behind her.

"Well, Clive?" she said, her eyebrows arched, and gave him her hand. "Why, your hand is cold! My dear boy, young people's hands shouldn't be cold."

"I guess it's because my heart's cold, Mrs Whiteoak. I don't want to talk about my affairs. I—I can't talk about them. It would kill me and that's the truth." He gripped her hand so that he hurt her. "I've come to say goodbye. And—I want to thank you for all your kindness."

"Now, don't despair. Sit right down and tell me everything. You'll feel the better for it."

He wrenched his hands away. "I'm sorry—but—I can't. Goodbye."

There was nothing to do but to let him go.

At Vaughanlands he found out that Philip Whiteoak was at the Windsor Hotel in Montreal. From the railway station, on his way to the West, Clive sent this telegram to Philip:

MARY WAKEFIELD IS STAYING WITH THE CRAIGS. C.B.

## 20

## BY THE LAKE

ONLY ONE passenger alighted from the morning train and that was Philip Whiteoak. He left his travelling bag at the station to be called for and set off up the road on foot. He walked as though there were no time to spare, yet he was not unconscious of the clear crisp beauty of the autumn morning, the harebell blue of the sky, the shining little clouds, puffed up to importance by the lively wind, the coloured leaves that skipped nimbly over puddles on the road. All this suited his mood, which was one of pleasurable impatience, not unmixed with apprehension.

Jake was waiting for him at the gate. For the moment he had forgotten Philip and was tentatively pawing a brown and black caterpillar. When he heard the step he looked round, with one paw still resting on the caterpillar. For an instant his astonishment and delight made him powerless, then he was galvanized into movement, rushed at Philip with cries that seemed rather of pain than pleasure and threw himself against Philip's legs.

"Hullo, Jake." He snatched up the half-grown dog and held him aloft. "Glad to see me, eh? But look at the muck you've put on me, you rascal!"

They went up the drive together, Jake doing his best to run between Philip's legs or fall over himself directly in Philip's path. They met Ernest in the hall.

Ernest, anxious to be on friendly terms again with Philip, asked, in a warmly solicitous tone:

"Any word of Miss Wakefield?"

"She's not in Montreal," Philip answered tersely.

"Well—that long journey for nothing then."

"Yes."

"It is certainly mysterious."

"I know where she is."

"Yes? Do you mind telling me where?"

"With the Craigs."

"Really. You amaze me. I thought those two girls were rather antagonistic."

"So did I. But—you never know with women. Where is Mamma?"

"At Vaughanlands."

"Ha!" Philip gave a short explosion of laughter, then he asked—"What about Busby?"

"He left for the West yesterday."

"Did you see him?"

"No. But he came to say goodbye to Mamma. Philip, you know I am the last one to interfere in your affairs but I do feel —I earnestly feel——"

"Meaning you feel like Ernest," laughed Philip. "All right,

old man, go ahead and feel like Ernest. He's a pretty good egg." He ran up the stairs, leaving his brother half angry, half pleased, a state often induced in his family by Philip.

Soon he reappeared, his clothes changed to riding things.

"Going out again so soon?" said Ernest.

"Yes."

"To the Craigs', I suppose."

"You're right."

"You know, Philip, I hate to interfere, but I do——" He tried to stop himself but before he could he had said—"I do *earnestly*——"

"Good," said Philip, going through the porch, with Jake at his heels. "Keep it up. Go on feeling like Ernest. But it's not going to change me."

Presently Jake was shut in the stable with his parents, and Philip, on his chestnut mare, trotted briskly through the gate and along the road by the lake. His relief at finding out where Mary was made him almost happy. His concern, his consternation, at her disappearance, the two days of miserable searching of hotels and steamship offices in Montreal, the search at the pier when a ship for England was to sail, lay behind him. His sanguine nature strained forward to the meeting with Mary. The message from Clive had allayed his fear that she was deranged. Clive never would have sent him the message, Mary never would have been at the Craigs', if anything of that sort were wrong. It was clear that Clive had discovered her and that she had broken off their engagement. Philip's heart went out to Clive in gratitude for his telegram.

Muriel opened the door to him. She had seen his horse cantering down the road, so she was prepared to meet him with a happy smile.

"Good morning, Mr Whiteoak." Her eyes said that the morning was good indeed when he appeared at her door.

"Good morning." He hesitated, considering just how he should make his request.

"Did you want to see Father? I'm afraid he isn't up yet. But he soon will be. Do come in."

"Thank you." He came into the hall.

"Miss Craig," he said, "I really came to see Mary Wakefield. I am told she is staying with you."

"She was. But she's left. She's gone to New York to take a position there."

"Are you sure?"

She laughed. "You're teasing me, Mr Whiteoak."

"I think it is you who are teasing me."

"I don't know what you mean." She flushed pink.

"I mean that, when I rode up the drive, I saw the two of you at a window. You were looking out, your heads close together."

"You're mistaken."

"Oh, no, I'm not."

Her breast rose and fell in her agitated breathing. She said, almost in a whisper:

"Mary doesn't want to see you. She told me to say she'd gone to New York."

For a moment he stared unbelieving, then remembered that Mary had run away from his house.

"She must see me. Go and tell her she must see me. I won't leave till she does."

"I am Mary's friend. I must help her. All she wants is to go far away and forget the unhappy time she's had."

"If you are Mary's friend you will beg her to see me if it's only for five minutes. . . . Or take me to her. Will you do that?" His eyes implored her.

"I'll ask her, but—I'm afraid she won't."

"Tell her what I say—that I won't go till she has spoken to me."

In a strangled voice Muriel said—"You love her, don't you?"

"With all my heart."

She turned and hurried from the room.

On the stairway she flung herself against the banisters and began to cry. After a little she pulled herself together and went slowly up to Mary's room. Mary was standing by the window watching to see Philip go.

"Has he gone?" she asked.

"No. He refuses to go till he's seen you."

"Oh, Muriel—I don't know how I can meet him."

"I wish it were me! Oh, how I wish it were me he wanted! It does seem hard, when I've loved him from the first time I met him——" She leant against the door crying.

"I'm so sorry, Muriel."

"Why won't you meet him?"

"I can't tell you."

"I have the right to know, after all I've gone through and loving him as I do."

"I can't tell you."

"Well, you can tell me this: Are you simply playing with him—to inflame his passion?"

Mary gave an hysterical laugh. "Good heavens, no! I have only one thought and that is to avoid him." Her panic increased. To meet Philip's eyes, with the brand of that monstrous lie on her forehead, would kill her. She might be dooming herself to a life of loneliness, but face him she could not.

A tap came on the door and the nurse handed Muriel a telegram.

"Oh, Miss Craig, I do hope it's not bad news," she said, her eyes twinkling into the room.

"It's nothing to worry about," said Muriel coldly. She waited for the nurse to go, then said:

"Do you think she could see I'd been crying?"

"Oh, no. Is the telegram from New York?"

Muriel tore it open and read—"POSITION SATISFACTORILY FILLED AT PRESENT THANKS FOR SUGGESTION WRITING."

"Oh, how disappointing!" gasped Muriel. "Now there is nowhere for you to go. Whatever shall you do?"

"I must just find a new post."

"You may stay here with me till you do."

"And run the risk of meeting *him*?"

"But where shall you stay? A young girl like you cannot stop at a hotel by herself."

"I will go to Montreal, as I intended to at the first."

"But have you enough money for your return passage?"

"I will work for it."

"But it is not easy to find your sort of work. Supposing you can't get work?"

Mary walked up and down the room wringing her hands. Muriel asked—"Does Mr Whiteoak owe you money?"

"Yes. But I shall never ask for it."

"I'll do that for you. I'll go straight down and ask him."

"No. I couldn't endure that." She stopped in her walking, and looked with melancholy reserve at Muriel. "No. I have changed my mind about seeing him. There is nothing else to do. . . . I will see him—but, oh, how can I?"

"Shall I go with you?"

"No, no, I must do it alone. . . . But not indoors."

"It's perfectly private in the parlour and I'll wait just outside."

Mary had her suspicions of Muriel waiting 'just outside'. She was determined that, if meet Philip she must, no word of what passed between them should be overheard.

She said—"We have kept him waiting so long that I think it will be best for you to say I'd gone out into the grounds—that you'd searched for me—but I shouldn't ask you to lie for me."

"Oh, I don't mind," cried Muriel. "And I think you do quite right to see him and put him out of his misery." She flew to the looking-glass and began to put her hair in order, while asking:

"Where shall I say he can find you?"

"By the lake. Give me a few moments' start."

Mary left the room and went softly down the back stairs.

Muriel returned to Philip.

"I'm afraid you'll think I've been gone quite a while," she said.

"It does seem rather long."

"As a matter of fact she's gone out."

"I see. She went out to avoid me."

"I guess she did. She's very nervous. Do you think you could send her a message by me? It might be better."

"Not possibly. Please tell me which way she went."

"Before I tell you I want to remind you, just once, of that wonderful drive we had—that day we saw Mary running so joyfully to meet Clive Busby."

"I saw nothing."

"I'm afraid I behaved very foolishly that day. A girl never should show her feelings the way I did."

Philip felt extreme discomfort. He made sounds to express that he thought her behaviour had been perfect.

"No, no," she denied. "I should have controlled myself. But, oh, it's so hard for me to conceal my feelings! You will forgive me, won't you?" She came and laid her hands on his arm. For a moment of apprehension he expected her head to fall once more to his shoulder.

He patted her back with what repressive force he dared and said—"There is nothing to forgive and I do thank you for your kindness to Mary. Now, I must be off to find her."

He left the house and crossed the closely mown lawn behind

it. Beds of cannas edged by silver-leafed geraniums stood up primly, denying the nearness of the tumultuous lake, stirred to green breakers by a gale of the night before. But the wind was now no more than a breeze, the great waves were sunny and fell in lacy foam. Mary was standing on a breakwater, her dress whipped close about her, a strand of her hair, like blond sea-weed, blowing free.

Philip stood a space, drinking in the beauty of the picture she made, as he drank in the sharp autumn air, before he called her name.

She had been facing the lake, now she turned and her eyes met his. A long while seemed to have passed since last their eyes had met. She drew on all her courage for the ordeal, but the effect she gave was almost one of challenge. He came to the lake's edge.

"Mary," he said, having still to raise his voice above the noise of the waves, "what is your idea in going out there? Is it to throw yourself into the lake if I attempt to lay hands on you?"

"No—oh, no."

"Then do come back, unless you want to talk to me out there. In that case——"

Before she could answer he was by her side.

She had thought never to see him again. Now his nearness almost overpowered her. His nearness and the noise of the waves confused her. "I can't talk to you," she said. "Not here."

"Then we'll go to that seat and sit down and you'll tell me everything."

She let him lead her to the rustic seat but she would not sit down. She supported herself against its rough bark-covered back. A red-berried shrub rose behind the seat.

"At least we can't be seen here," he said. "I shouldn't put it past that woman to spy on us."

Mary stood silent, her eyes on her white ringless hands that clung to the seat.

"Now tell me, for God's sake," he demanded, "why you ran away."

"You know why. You must know."

"I suppose because of my mother—her going up to your room. What did she say to you?"

"Does it matter what she said to me?" Mary cried wildly.

221

"Nothing matters except what I said to her. If you care for me—if you ever cared for me—don't make me talk about it. It's cruel."

"Mary," he said gently, "I beg of you not to be so foolish. . . . Surely you can speak to me of anything. If you love me you won't shrink from speaking of this. You do love me, don't you?"

"I—don't know."

"You don't know! Why—you astonish me. Do you forget our meeting in the orchard?"

"I did love you then."

"And now—you don't know!"

"My brain is confused. It won't act."

Now he scanned her face in sharp anxiety. "You are tired out," he said. "If you would cast yourself on me—tell me everything—then you would not be confused. You would be well again. I can see that you are not well." He laid his hand on her hands that were clasped on the back of the seat. "Come, my darling."

The word *darling* from his lips! To be called his darling! Tears suddenly fell from her eyes and splashed on his hand.

"I thought you would utterly despise me," she said.

"How could I despise you! I'm simply trying, with all my might, to find out why you told my mother you were my mistress." There was no way, he felt, but to force her into the open, though to do it he must be brutal.

Colour flamed into Mary's face. She drew her hands from beneath his and pressed them against her eyes. She seemed to press back her tears, because when she again looked at him, she had stopped crying.

"Mrs Whiteoak asked me," she said, almost indifferently, "if it wasn't so, and I was very angry and I said it was."

"You understood her? There was no mistake?"

"I understood perfectly. She accused me a second time and I said, yes, it was so."

"I see. And how did she take it?"

The triumph of that moment again lit Mary's face. She smiled her odd smile that had something of pain in it. She said —"Mrs Whiteoak was amazed. Even while she accused me she had not believed it herself. . . . I told her that horrible lie— just because I was furious. . . . You can see what a strange sort of person I am."

Philip went round the rustic seat and put his arms about her. He led her back and set her down and himself beside her.

"Mary," he said, "I can't pretend that I understand you but I love you more than ever and you're coming home with me and we're going to get married as soon as possible."

"And you don't hate me for what I said?"

"I adore you for it."

She relaxed her weary body against his strength. Her spirit, like a river that had found the sea, lost itself in his. She was cold, for she had not dressed herself for the wind from the lake. The warmth of his arm that pressed her to his side had a comfort in it that seemed to her godlike. His warm hands held her chilled ones. She looked out across the silver-and-green expanse of the lake and, in her fancy, compared herself to a sailing ship that had delivered its cargo, and now, lightened and buoyant, spread its sails to the breeze. She wished she were a poet. If she were she could, at this moment, she was sure, pour out her heart in a poem.

21

AT GRIPS

PHILIP TURNED in the saddle to look back at Mary, still waving to him from the gate. It was hard to tear himself away from her. He sat, turning in the saddle, to imprint her image on his memory. Yet a part of him strained towards Jalna and the announcement of his coming marriage. But first he would ride to the Rectory and acquaint Mr Pink with the change in Mary's prospects.

He had ridden over this road hundreds of times but never had it been so exhilarating, so beautiful, as on this blowy late September morning, with the waves, where the lake encroached on the sandy soil, breaking almost to the road. Something should be done about this road, but on this morning he would not have it different. The gulls circled above him, their wings flashing in the sun, their tucked-up feet yellow against their breasts, like useless appendages that they would never need again. One of them winged swiftly above the smartly trotting mare, as though in a race. The mare arched her neck and glanced in playful apprehension at the waves. Philip spoke lovingly to her and patted her neck. She was his, she was gentle, she was a female.

Inside the white picket fence of the Rectory Lily Pink was cutting flowers for the altar tomorrow. She stood frozen, with scissors poised, when Philip appeared at the gate.

"Oh, good morning, Lily," he said. "Cutting the last flowers before the frost gets them, eh?"

"Tomorrow is Sunday," she answered, not able to look at him, remembering how she had carried the tale of his doings to his mother.

Philip, at this moment, forgot all about that. He asked cheerfully—"Is your father at home?"

"Yes," she breathed, "writing his sermon."

"Oh——" Philip groaned his disappointment.

"Could I take a message?"

"No," he sighed, "I'll come again."

Mr Pink had seen him through the window. He hastened to the door and shouted—"Come along in. My sermon's done." He was like a boy let out of school. He noticed what a pretty picture Lily and Philip and the chestnut mare and the garden flowers made. He felt thankful for this beautiful and tranquil world. 'God's in His Heaven, all's right with the world.' He would bring that into his sermon tomorrow morning. He would say that, as long as men kept the thought of God in His Heaven watching over them, so long as they carried out the teaching of Christ in their lives, all would be well in the world. And no man living could deny that.

"Come in!" he shouted to Philip.

He was worried about Philip. He did not like the story that was going round, about him and Mary Wakefield. He hoped Philip had come to explain things. He led the way into his study and closed the door behind them.

An hour later Philip, having put the mare in her stall, entered his own door.

Renny flew down the stairs to meet him. "Daddy—Daddy —I'm glad to see you!"

Philip picked him up and hugged him. A wave of goodwill towards everyone in the house surged through his being. As it neared Adeline, however, it wavered and did not quite envelop her. A smile in which there was more than a hint of malice lighted his face when he thought of her.

Renny said—"I can turn a handspring. Come and watch me do it."

"It must be time for dinner," answered Philip. At Jalna that meal was in the middle of the day.

"Dinner!" echoed the little boy. "We had it long ago. But they're keeping some for you in the oven."

"I'm glad of that. I'm as hungry as a hunter."

"What were you hunting? Was it Miss Wakefield? Nettle says she's run away."

"That's nonsense. She is visiting Miss Craig."

"It's nice without her."

"Don't you like her?" Philip asked sharply.

"Well—she's like all the others. Always wanting you to learn things."

"And learn you'd better or you'll be at the bottom of the class when you go to school with Maurice."

"Granny says she'll teach me. She's having a nap in her room."

"Good. Don't disturb her."

Philip ate his meal in solitude but with the first zest he had felt since the morning of Mary's disappearance. Afterwards he did not want to meet anyone but escaped through the side door with his pipe, to find his dogs and take them for a walk in the woods. He must be alone, to think of Mary and of all the happiness that lay ahead of them. He knew she shrank from the difficulties of returning to Jalna as its mistress, but he would smooth away the difficulties. One object which must be smoothed away—obliterated—was Mrs Nettleship. Her sandy hair, her pale piercing eyes, her habit of gossip, had come to irritate him. What if she were a model of cleanliness and order, as Augusta was always reminding him? These qualities were, in truth, her most irritating. She must be got out of the way before Mary came.

He had hated to leave her at the Craigs', with that impossible Muriel. He would have liked to put her on his horse behind him, as they used in the old days, and enter the gates of Jalna at a gallop, in the first flush of his happiness. But his plan was to ask Mrs Lacey to take his dear girl into her house until the wedding. She could not refuse him that.

It ended by his going to see Mrs Lacey that very afternoon. But first he returned to the stable and left the dogs with young Hodge, and a message for his mother that he would not be home for tea. He knew well that Mrs Lacey would ask him to share the evening meal with them. He wanted to avoid his family till Sunday morning when he would of necessity meet them at church. After church he would tell the family what they might expect and also he would come to grips with his mother over the scene between her and Mary in Mary's bedroom. The air must be cleared before he brought Mary to Jalna.

He and Mrs Lacey were closeted together for a long while. Her romantic soul made her eager to forward his love affair. At the same time she shrank from incurring Adeline's anger. Ever since they had first met, many years ago, she had done her best to keep on the right side of Adeline and had admirably succeeded. She did not intend to risk words with her now. She told her fears to Philip and promised to talk over the matter with her husband and let Philip know the result on Monday. He had to content himself with this half promise.

He did not drive to church on the Sunday morning but took the winding path across the fields and, for the first time in months, arrived in time to put on his surplice without hurry and an urgent look from Mr Pink. The family always arrived in a body and their progress along the aisle was a spectacle of interest to the rest of the congregation which never palled. First came Adeline, her hand resting on the arm of her eldest son. They were followed by the Buckleys, Augusta's hand resting on Sir Edwin's elegantly crooked arm. Last came Ernest with a child on either side. The appearance of the group was that of the Old World rather than the New. Though they were so closely identified with the place where they lived they retained, in a remarkable degree, the atmosphere of the land from which they had sprung.

Adeline seldom sat herself in the pew without a moment's fresh shock at the realization that the husband she had so loved was no longer at her side. The years did not make it easier to understand or to bear. When she rested her head against the back of the pew in front, that moment was given to him. Then she would straighten herself and raise her eyes to the stained-glass window she had had erected to his memory. She would draw a deep sigh, look for the number of the opening hymn and find it in her book. She would glance down at Renny and hold the hymn book so that he might follow the words with her. Not that she needed the words. Every hymn sung in that church she knew by heart, unless, as on rare occasions, it happened that Mr Pink in an abandon of enterprise chose a strange one. Then her eyebrows would shoot up incredulously, she would sharply close the book, as though that were the end of it for her, and watch the singing choir, as though they were performing some strange gymnastics which she neither understood nor admired.

As the service progressed on this particular morning she watched her son Philip with concentrated interest. What was he up to, she wondered. Ernest had told her that he had gone to the Craigs', where Mary was. Obviously he was trying to reach some understanding with that queer girl, but, if it were marriage, why was he avoiding his family? And where was he last evening? Adeline could only conclude that he was afraid to meet her, for fear she could guess his plans and frustrate them. More likely still, Mary could not bring herself to marry him after what had happened, and small wonder!

But Philip did look comely this morning, with his fresh colouring, his clear blue eyes and clean surplice. He read the Lessons in a way that Adeline liked, though his brothers were very critical of his style. There was warmth in his voice and a ring of conviction that he believed in what he read. On the whole, Adeline thought, he would come safely through this affair. Ernest had not told her of Philip's stubborn attitude during their brief encounter, for he felt that, all too soon, the two must settle the affair between them. He quite dreaded the thought of it and yet, considering their mettle, felt a certain exhilaration in anticipating the climax.

But the climax was to be silent. Neither Philip nor Adeline was to utter a word when the moment came. A religious calm was to pervade the scene.

Philip had just read the Second Lesson. He returned to his seat at one side of the chancel. His surplice, to his mother's eyes, had a defiant swing. To Ernest it looked jaunty. Mr Pink rose and moved with dignity to take his place. Mr Pink's voice was resonant and the words which now came from his mouth might well in their volume have been uttered in a cathedral, instead of in this little country church.

"I publish the Banns of Marriage between Philip Piers Whiteoak of this Parish and Mary Wakefield of the same. If any of you know cause or just impediment why these two persons should not be joined together in holy Matrimony, ye are to declare it. This is the first time of asking."

Philip sat imperturbable, his hands clasped on his surpliced stomach, his eyes, looking unusually large and blue, fixed on some point above the heads of the congregation. A stir ran through the congregation and a whispering, as of a gust of wind over a little field of corn. The Vaughans, in their pew, cast sidelong glances across at Adeline. Admiral Lacey's face grew crimson. Mrs Lacey tried vainly to look innocent. Ethel caught Violet's hand in hers and they sat clutched. The remainder of the neighbourhood, the farmers from the surrounding country, the people from the village, young Chalk, the blacksmith, craned their necks to catch a glimpse of the Whiteoaks, or scanned Philip's face with curiosity. There were few who had not heard the story of what Noah Binns had seen in the orchard, at a time when everybody who knew anything knew the young lady was engaged to Clive Busby.

Nicholas's hand went to his moustache. He tugged it, as though he would tug away the smile that flickered on his lips. Ernest took out his white silk handkerchief and blew his nose. He felt it was a moment for action of some sort and that was all he could think of doing. The slight air of offence which was Augusta's natural expression, though it had nothing to do with her really amiable disposition, deepened. Sir Edwin nibbled at some mute declaration which a mind reader might have interpreted as—'I forbid the banns.'

But it was on Adeline that the scrutiny of the gathering was centred. From her black figure radiated the very essence of dissent. No envelopment of black stuff could hide its angry brightness. She rose majestically to her feet.

A thrill of fearful anticipation ran through the little church. Was Mrs Whiteoak going to forbid the banns? Every eye but those of Noah Binns in the last pew was fixed on her. Noah stared, hungrily inquisitive, at Philip. He saw Philip turn pale.

Lily Pink should by this time have been playing the opening chords of the *Jubilate Deo*. The congregation should be rising to sing. But Lily felt paralysed. She could not make her fingers press the keys but sat sideways on the organ seat watching the progress of that noble figure down the aisle. For noble Adeline looked, however lacking in nobility her impulse may have been, with her widow's weeds floating from her fine head, and her features composed in the very mould of displacency.

Looking neither to right nor to left she walked slowly and firmly to the door. As she reached it young Hodge, who had driven her to church, sprang forward and opened it. At the same moment Lily gained control of her fingers, the organ burst forth, the congregation rose, and Adeline departed to the sound of music.

Ernest, on seeing his mother leave the family pew, had made as though to escort her, but a look from Adeline had quelled his intention and he had resumed his seat crestfallen.

Now the service proceeded, with a kind of tremulous intensity, as though all present were determined to keep their heads. But, when it came to the sermon, Mr Pink found it difficult to introduce, with the spirit he had intended, those beautiful lines from Browning. It was not easy to assert that God was in His Heaven and all was right with the world when Mrs Whiteoak had vacated her pew.

At last the Recessional hymn was sung and the congregation poured out. They gathered in knots in the churchyard to discuss what had happened. The Vaughans and the Laceys hurried away, so that the Whiteoaks would not have the embarrassment of speaking to them. Hodge had taken Adeline home and now had returned with the carriage to convey the Buckleys and the children. Nicholas and Ernest had driven together in a trap.

Nicholas, untying the horse in the church carriage-shed, asked of his brother—"Shall we wait for him?"

"No," answered Ernest, almost violently. "I could not possibly drive with him. But, if you wish to wait, I'll walk home."

"Let him return as he came," Nicholas said tersely, and climbed into the trap.

As they drove out he greeted what acquaintances they met, touching his hat-brim with the whip, genially, as though nothing had happened.

But when they were bowling along the road, on which every vehicle was carrying people home from church, Nicholas exclaimed—"Philip deserves to be thrashed for what happened this morning. It was an insult to all of us and, of course, particularly to Mamma."

"You're sure Mr Pink wasn't aware that we knew nothing of the banns?"

"Pink aware! Nothing on earth would have tempted him to commit such an outrage."

Ernest declared solemnly—"It was enough to give Mamma a seizure."

"Gad, I'd hate to be in his shoes when they meet."

"Perhaps he won't show his face till after dinner. He may go to the Laceys'. I do hope he does. It's a peculiar thing but disturbances during a meal give me a dyspepsia."

Nicholas grunted, then exclaimed—"Lord, you could have knocked me down with a feather when those banns were read!"

"I thought Mamma was rising to forbid them."

"Small wonder if she had."

"Nothing can stop the marriage now. We shall just have to put up with it."

"Well, after all, she's a very attractive girl."

"Nick—would you willingly have Philip bring a girl of her loose character to Jalna, to be the mother of his children?"

"He swears she isn't loose."

"Do you believe him?"

"Philip's never been a liar."

"He might be to save the reputation of the woman he loves."

"Possibly. But I think that if Mary Wakefield had acknowledged it and it were so, Philip would not have denied it."

"Then what, in the name of heaven, possessed her to say such a dreadful thing?"

"In my opinion she wished it were so."

"Nick, you are a confirmed cynic."

They turned in at their own gate, scattering the fine gravel beneath the wheels. At the stable Hodge took charge of the horse. He looked downcast and even guilty, as though he had had a hand in the morning's doings. He was a sensitive young man and devoted to Adeline.

Her two sons found her seated in her own particular chair in the drawing-room. Augusta and Edwin were there also, the sympathetic audience, it appeared, to a monologue by Adeline describing her shock, her outrage, at the church.

Nicholas bent over her and kissed her.

"Well, old girl," he said, "that was a dramatic exit you made. I've never seen anything better—not on the stage."

She looked pleased with herself, though sombrely.

Ernest kissed her from the other side. He said—"I wanted to escort you out but I saw that you preferred to go alone."

"An escort would certainly have marred the effect," observed Sir Edwin.

"I showed the world," said Adeline, "what I thought of the announcement."

"The point is," smiled Nicholas, "that we can't do a thing about it."

"Oh, to think," cried Adeline, holding the hand of the son on either side of her, "that I should have brought my youngest child into the world to have him treat me like this! Eight years I waited after Ernest was born and then, when I was expecting another——"

Sir Edwin interrupted—"Philip's just at the door. If you care to repeat that, he will be in the hall in time to hear it."

Adeline gave him a withering look. Nevertheless she once more, and with even greater tragic emphasis, said:

"Oh, to think that I should have brought my youngest into the world to have him treat me like this! Eight years I waited after Ernest was born and then—when I was expecting another —I thought, this one will be like his father. He will have golden hair and blue eyes, and it's him will be the prop of me old age."

Midway through this speech Philip appeared in the doorway. He had had a lift in a farmer's buggy and had alighted at the gate soon after Nicholas and Ernest. He stood listening to Adeline without entering the room, his eyes steady on her face, his arms folded. There was something in the sunny warmth of his appearance that lightened the scale of disfavour weighting the room. Added to this, Adeline's affectation of speech, at such a moment, seemed to Augusta, Edwin, and Ernest most unfortunate. Try as they would they could not feel quite the same sympathy towards her. Nicholas thought—'The old girl's defeated and she knows it, hence the Irish.' He squeezed the hand she still held, and said sternly to Philip:

"Well, and what have you to say for yourself?"

"I had to do it," he answered. "I had to settle the thing at one blow."

"A blow! That's what it was!" exclaimed Adeline. "A blow, in front of all the world."

"It was not in front of all the world but just one little corner of it," he said, almost soothingly.

"It is *my* world," she answered sadly.

Looking at her it did seem a pity that she shone in only this remote community.

Sir Edwin said—"Dear Mrs Whiteoak, we all felt with you. Your distress was ours."

Augusta added—"I should have liked to leave the church with my mother, but thought better of it."

"After a look from her," supplemented Nicholas.

Philip came into the room. "If all of you," he said, "had kept cool, not a person in the church would have guessed you'd had a surprise."

Adeline sprang to her feet. "I like that!" she cried. "I like that, I do. I was expected to sit in my pew smirking while the Rector gave out the banns for my son's marriage and I knowing nothing of it. Is that what you expected me to do, Philip? Come, now, tell me!"

"I don't know what I expected," he answered sulkily.

Her nostrils widened as she said—"Or perhaps you expected me to take out a handkerchief and wipe me eye on the corner of it. Wipe me eye and bow me head and let out an Amen. . . . Is that what you expected? . . . Answer me, you good-for-nothing rascal!"

As these words vibrated on the air Sir Edwin put the thumb of his right hand on one ash-blond side-whisker and its fingers on the other, concealing his mouth, over which flickered an unseemly smile.

Philip's colour rose. He looked at her dumbly. He looked at the miniature of his father in the brooch at her throat.

"Or perhaps," she went on, "you even expected me to feel chastened that you'd insulted me. You maybe thought I'd rise in the pew and genuflect."

"Mamma," put in Augusta, "I don't think you realize how irreverent that sounds."

"Mind your business, Augusta."

Philip said—"I intended no insult."

"Well, maybe it was better than a poke in the eye with a stick. But was there a soul in the church, d'ye think, who didn't realize you'd insulted your poor old mother?"

Philip's eyes became prominent.

"You're not my *poor old mother*!" he said loudly. "You're my domineering mother who makes a scene, even in a church, when she is balked in having her own way. If anyone was insulted this morning it was I. Sitting there facing the congregation while you stalked from the church like a tragedy queen."

The last two words pleased her. She considered them and then asked on a milder note—"What was it like after I left? Did they go on with the service?"

"They did. You may be important, Mamma, but they couldn't stop the whole show because you left in a temper. And I had to sit there with every eye on me."

"In the olden times," she said, "a man might have been chastised with scorpions for no more than you've done."

"Those were the days for you," he retorted.

"Come, come, Philip," put in Nicholas.

"The point is," said Philip, "the banns have been read and will be read on the two succeeding Sundays and, a few days later, Mary and I shall be married."

Adeline ignored this statement and demanded:

"Did Mr Pink know I'd been told nothing of the banns?"

"He did not know."

"If I thought he had," she cried, "I'd bann *him*, and I'd not take three weeks doing it! I'd do it in as many minutes."

"Mamma," said Philip, "you are not an Archbishop or even a Bishop."

"Your father and I built that church."

"Is it yours now?"

"Philip," came from Ernest, "will you stop being rude to Mamma!"

"Will *you* stop defending me!" said Adeline. "I need no defence against an ungrateful young rogue like this."

"What have I to be grateful for?" Philip asked truculently.

Adeline threw up her hands in despair. She sank again into her chair and stretched out her long legs in an attitude of exhaustion. After a space she said:

"I have protected you against designing women who were after you in the past. And you were glad of it, weren't you? You have told me so with your own lips."

"Well—maybe. But I could well have protected myself."

She laughed scornfully. "The way you have protected yourself against this woman who took you as her lover in the room next the one where your innocent little daughter slept. No protestations, my man! She told me so herself."

"Now let us have this thing clear," said Philip. "It is clear between Mary and me. Mamma made Mary so angry by her

233

accusation that Mary wouldn't deny it. In her anger she accepted the slur on herself. That's what she says. What I think is that she was so intimidated she would have agreed to anything."

"You wouldn't say that if you'd seen her," said Adeline.

Augusta's contralto voice was now heard. "What Philip says reminds me of an occurrence when he was a little boy. Ernest and Nicholas were about thirteen and fifteen. They owned a beautiful collie, with an especially fine coat. One day the boys noticed that patches of it had apparently been cut off by scissors, right to the skin. Philip had got into trouble several times for mischief with scissors and knives. Naturally the boys thought he'd been up to his tricks. They accused him, roughly, the way boys will. I was there and I'm afraid I accused him too. He didn't say a word but just looked at us, as though he were pleased to have done such a bad thing. He was dragged before Papa, who thundered at him—'Did you do this, sir?' And Philip looked Papa straight in the eye and said yes. He was severely punished. Then, a few days later it was discovered that the dog had a peculiar form of eczema and that was the cause of the hair coming off in patches. I remember I was so upset over Philip's being wrongfully punished I cried. But when I asked him why he'd acknowledged a fault he'd never committed, he said he didn't know. I myself think it was because he was pleased that he should be considered capable of such an enormity.... Do you remember the occasion, Philip?"

"I can't say I do. I had so many lickings."

"A story to give one thought," observed Nicholas.

Sir Edwin looked admiringly at his wife. "Augusta," he said, "has an extraordinarily analytical mind."

Philip bit his knuckle, unable to decide whether the analogy of this anecdote tended to make his loved one appear better or worse.

The low rumble of the Indian gong that rose and fell again under the beating by Eliza told that the Sunday dinner was served. They were a family with excellent appetites and, when they had seated themselves about the table, and the four plump young ducks on the platter in front of Philip gave forth their good odour, not one present felt himself unable to eat his share. Philip was a good carver, having sat at the head of the table since his father's death. He carved slowly but with accurate

234

knowledge of the anatomy of the ducks, and every eye was on him.

The two children were more watchful of the faces of their elders than of the portions they were to get. Nicholas, Ernest, and Sir Edwin tried to draw the conversation into impersonal channels, but when the meal was no more than half over Adeline abruptly asked of Meg:

"Did you hear the banns read in church this morning?" Meg raised her face in egglike calm to Adeline's.

"Yes, Granny."

"Did you understand what it means?"

"Yes. It means that Daddy is going to marry Miss Wakefield."

"Did you understand at the time?"

"No. Nettle told me."

"Are you pleased?"

"No. I don't want him to."

"And what about you, Renny? Do you want your father to marry Miss Wakefield?"

The little boy's high clear voice came decisively. "If it will stop her giving us lessons I do."

Meg added—"Nettle says it's awful to have a stepmother."

"That woman," growled Philip, "will leave tomorrow."

"She's going anyway," said Meg smugly. "She doesn't want to stay—not with Miss Wakefield bossing her about."

"Not another word out of you," Philip said sternly.

Renny piped—"In the fairy tales stepmothers turn children into birds and animals. I hope Miss Wakefield will turn me into a horse."

A chuckle ran round the table. Philip forced a smile and exclaimed—"Then what should I do? I'd have no little boy."

"You could ride me!" Renny cried joyfully. "And I'd go faster than any other horse and you'd never need to touch me with the whip."

Philip covered his son's little hand with his. "If Miss Wakefield turns you into a horse," he said soberly, "I will mount you and the two of us shall ride away together and never come back."

Meg, since Philip's reprimand, had been on the verge of tears. Now she burst into them noisily and without restraint. Her father had shown preference for Renny.

Ordinarily she would have been told to leave the table, but

now Adeline called her to her side, embraced her, kissed her, and said—"Poor child—poor child."

"She's nothing of the sort," said Philip, "and she's behaving like a four-year-old."

"I quite agree," said Nicholas. "This howling for nothing is a nuisance."

"If she is behaving without restraint," said Adeline, "she is doing no worse than Philip."

"I think I have shown considerable self-restraint," he returned.

"I was taught," she went on, "by my dear father, that there is no better quality to guide you through life than self-restraint."

"That's the first good word I've ever heard you say for him," said Nicholas.

It was plain that Nicholas had gone over to the enemy.

"If you had been more like my dear father," Adeline retorted, "your wife might not have run off with another man."

"Mamma!" implored Augusta. "Remember the children."

"I do remember them and I wish there were more of them but Nicholas never got a chick. Neither have you and Edwin managed one. Now my father got eleven children and he taught them all self-restraint. My, but he was a fine man! If ever I have said a hard word about him I deserve to be punished for it. Indeed I never really appreciated him till he was gone."

She heaved a great sigh. "That is the way of it, with parents, and I suppose 'twill be the way with me. I'm not so young as I was."

"I never have seen you look better than you do at the present time, Mamma," said Ernest eagerly.

"Ah, I don't complain."

Eliza now brought in a peach shortcake, mounded with whipped cream, and set it in front of Adeline. Eliza's hand shook, as she set down the dish, for she had been greatly upset by Hodge's account of what had happened in the church.

Adeline was so impressed by Eliza's condition that, when she took up the heavy silver fork and spoon to serve the shortcake, her own hand trembled like a leaf.

"Eliza," she said, "will you please give the dish to Lady Buckley to serve? I don't feel able for it."

Eliza did as she was bid, with a look of deep commiseration.

"Why, Mamma," cried Ernest, "peach shortcake is one of your favourite dishes! Aren't you going to have any?"

"No today . . . not today," she answered, in a small voice. "I have no appetite for this meal. But don't worry about me. I shall just sit here quietly and enjoy the sight of your enjoyment. Meggie, go back to your chair, dear, and eat your shortcake. Renny, sit up straight and hold your fork properly. God knows I have done my best to train you in good manners, as I was trained. If I or my brothers behaved unmannerly my father would give us a clip on the ear that would send us flying."

For a space she watched, with a sad expression, the consuming of the shortcake, then she said:

"I think I shall go and lie down for a bit. I'm far from well. Boys, will one of you lend me an arm?"

Nicholas and Ernest at once sprang to her assistance. She left the room supported by their strong arms.

Augusta, with great good sense, talked cheerfully to the children, gave them second helpings and, when they had finished, gave them permission to leave the table. Nicholas and Ernest returned from their mother's room.

"How is she?" Sir Edwin asked anxiously.

"A little better," answered Ernest. "She wants you to go to her, Philip."

"Oh, surely she is not able to continue the discussion," said Augusta.

"I think," Ernest said judicially, "it will be best for Philip to go." He reseated himself, remarking—"This is going to give me indigestion." With a resigned air he again attacked the shortcake.

Philip said—"Excuse me, Augusta," and left the room, with a step that had more of stubbornness than conciliation in it.

"I do hope there is nothing serious wrong with your mother," said Sir Edwin.

Nicholas finished the last of his peach shortcake, leaned back in his chair and wiped his drooping moustache.

"There is nothing serious," he said, "beyond the fact that Mamma has the good sense to know when she's beaten."

In truth she did know and, as she lay on her bed waiting for Philip, she accepted the fact without bitterness.

Now he stood in the doorway, his head bright against the

237

dark curtains, just as his father had stood, in that same doorway, when he was a young man.

"Come closer," she said, "come to the bedside."

He came close and knelt down by the bed, putting his arms about her.

"Mamma," he said, "are you ill?"

"I'm better now." She put her long arms about him and drew him closer. He pressed his face against her breast.

"You're my favourite," she said. "My youngest. I can deny you nothing. If you want to marry this girl, you must." She gave a deep sigh of resignation and added—"Bring her home and I'll be nice to her."

Boney had been perching on Adeline's ankle. Now he walked the length of her body, picking his steps carefully. When he reached her head he sank to his breast and spread his wings as though to shield her. He uttered little clucking noises.

On the following day Philip was once more driving his chestnut mare along the road by the lake. On the seat by his side Mary sat, and behind the portmanteau was stored. It was a brilliant and chill morning, with coloured leaves flying through the air like small birds, and flocks of small birds, on their southward journey, blown through the air like leaves. A steady rhythm of drumming waves sounded on the beach, and the mare, as though taking pleasure in it, kept time with the beat of her hoofs. Each separate hair of her mane and tail seemed vibrant with life.

Mary sat clutching her hat with both hands to keep it on. The wind had whipped a lovely colour into her cheeks, a colour slightly deeper than that in her lips. The effect, Philip thought, was very pretty. He remarked:

"Your lips are less red than they were, Mary dear."

She caught the under one between her teeth and gave it a little bite.

"I have a confession to make," she said.

"Yes?" he smiled.

"I did formerly put a little paint on my lips." She scanned his face, anxious to discover the effect of her words, then added—"But I'll never do it again, if you like me better without it."

"I like you as you are," he said.

They were on their way to the Laceys', where it had been amicably arranged that Mary should stay till her marriage. It was necessary to pass Jalna on the way. At the gate Philip drew up. The whip slanted from his hand.

"Don't look startled, Mary," he said. "I'm not going to force you to anything you are against. But I think it would be well for you to come in now with me to meet my mother. You'll have to do it sooner or later and the sooner you have it over with the better. In fact I think it would please her to have you come straight to her before you go to the Laceys'."

"Oh, no—not yet! I don't think I can."

"Of course you can. . . . Come, now, be a sensible girl. Mamma will like you all the better for being forthright. And remember, you have me at your side."

Ah, she could do anything with him at her side! She could face a dozen Adeline Whiteoaks, having Philip to protect her. Yet her heart beat with painful swiftness as she nerved herself to consent.

"Very well," she said. "I suppose you're right. But, as for your mother liking me, I can't picture such a thing."

Philip himself felt a good deal of trepidation at the thought of the meeting. He felt very sorry for Mary, yet it was certain that the poor darling had made things much worse by her reckless lie. He put a hand over both hers that were tightly clasped in her lap and squeezed them.

"You'll feel the better for it afterwards," he said.

"I hope so, for I could scarcely feel worse than I do at this moment."

She wished the driveway had been ten times as long. She scarcely had time to collect herself when the trap stopped in front of the door, and Philip sprang out and turned to lift her down.

"I can't!" she cried, in sudden panic.

"You can't?"

"No."

"Then when will you?"

"Tomorrow."

"Very well." He prepared to mount again into his seat. Disappointment clouded his face. "But I thought you had better pluck."

"I will. I will." She could not bear him to be disappointed in her. Then again that moment, when she had faced Adeline in triumph, had got the best of her, flashed into her mind, hardening it to the ordeal. She almost flung herself into Philip's arms, for fear her resolution would again fail her. He set her on her feet.

"Straighten your hat," he said, with an appraising look. "It has too wide a brim for that wind."

She straightened it, took herself firmly in hand, and went up the steps and through the door.

Inside he kissed her. "Your house, Mary," he said. "Welcome to it, my darling."

She would have liked to cling to him, to obliterate herself in him, but he led her into the drawing-room and left her. She listened to his steps as he went down the hall in search of his mother. She heard Adeline Whiteoak's voice.

She heard her steps coming from the direction of her bedroom. Philip remained behind. Was he afraid of a scene, Mary wondered, or did he think it best for them to be alone together at the meeting? She did not know. She did not care. Just to have this terrible meeting over with was all that mattered.

But how could she speak to Adeline? Her mouth was dry as a bone. She stood straight, half-defiant, half-tremulous, facing the door.

Now Adeline stood there facing her. She looked a stately figure, almost as though she had dressed for the meeting, in a royal purple tea-gown of heavy silk, with a short train, and lace on the sleeves and at the throat. All day she had moved, eaten, and spoken, like a semi-invalid. But now her natural vitality took possession of her. Three swift steps brought her to Mary. As she came she opened her arms wide and Mary found herself enfolded against her strong breast, held there, inhaling the Eastern scent that always came from Adeline because of the boxes of sandalwood in which she kept her finery.

"My child." There was true warmth, as well as a melodramatic vibration, in Adeline's voice. "My child—all is forgiven!"

# 22

# HE WAS A LITTLE BOY

RENNY WHITEOAK was up at six o'clock that morning; though the month was October the day was warm as summer, yet with a finer, sweeter warmth. The bright blue of the sky was repeated in the little boy's jersey. In his insides he felt clean as a whistle. He was slim and agile as a minnow.

On his way to the stables he shouted, sang, and laughed, without in the least knowing why. Hodge was just unlocking the heavy padlock on the main door when he arrived.

"Hullo, Hodge," he yelled, as though Hodge were stone deaf. "I've come to help you with your work."

"Fine," said Hodge, throwing open the door with a grand gesture. "I'm in need of a helper. What wages do you ask?"

"A dollar a month."

"Whew. I can't pay all that."

"Twenty-five cents a month will do," Renny said quickly.

"All right. I'll hire you. We'll begin by watering the horses."

Hodge tramped in his heavy boots to where the buckets were kept, Renny stretching his legs to keep step with him. When Hodge picked up a bucket Renny took one also. The horses craned their necks out of their stalls to watch them. Low whinnies of approval marked their progress to the well beyond the farthest loosebox. Hodge lifted the heavy cover and the chill smell of water came from the dark below. He let down the bucket and brought it up brimming. Drops of water clung to the curly fair hairs on his arms. He filled Renny's bucket, Renny squatting beside him, their faces darkly glimpsed in the well below.

"Don't you ever come monkeying about here by yourself," warned Hodge. "You might fall in."

"Would you save me if I fell in?"

"How the dickens would I know? I'd be off working somewhere else."

"But if I screamed."

"The thing is," said Hodge, "to keep away from it. Here— don't try to lift that heavy bucket! You'll ruin yourself some day, the loads you try to lift."

Renny grasped the handle of the bucket and carried it with Hodge. He did his best to take a full share of its weight as it was lifted to old Laura's lips. She was in the largest of the looseboxes. She was thirty years old and had been Captain Whiteoak's favourite. As she dipped her small, intelligent head to the bucket she gave a kind glance at Renny out of her lustrous eyes.

"She likes me," he said. "Do you think she'll last till I'm big enough to ride her?"

"Shouldn't wonder. She's a great stayer. And look at her depth through the heart." Hodge ran a hand lovingly over her shoulder. "I've heard my father say that your grandfather valued her more than any horse he'd ever owned, and he'd had a good many, what with England and India and Canada."

"I value her too," Renny said stoutly. "I value everything at Jalna."

Joe, the older stableman, had brought oats and hay to the horses. Tom, a young boy, was cleaning the stalls, shovelling the manure into a barrow and wheeling it into the stable yard. Hodge was Renny's favourite and he stuck by him. Together they set about grooming the horses. Renny's hand was almost too small to grasp the currycomb but he worked hard, hissing through his teeth as Hodge did. His own lively Welsh pony was bright as a polished nut when he had finished with her and Hodge commended him. The pony turned her head and nuzzled Renny, slobbering lovingly over his ear.

Renny asked of Hodge—"Are you coming to the party this afternoon, Hodge?"

"Oh, I'll be around, if I'm needed."

Renny stood with his legs well apart, chewing a straw. "Do you know who the party's for?" he asked.

Hodge scratched his head on which grew a thatch of tow-coloured hair. "Well," he answered evasively, "I couldn't rightly say."

"It's for Miss Wakefield. She's going to be my stepmother."

"Oh. . . . That'll be fine—I guess."

"Hodge, would you like to have a stepmother?"

"Why—I guess so."

Renny uttered a hoot of derision. "What! And be turned into a snake or a toad by her?"

"You don't believe them lies, do you?"

"I don't know. Nettle said so."

"She's gone and a good thing too. . . . By jingo, it's time I went to my breakfast. And you'd better go to yours. You've got yourself dirty. Do you want me to help you wash at the pump?"

"Hurray! You bet I do." He was delighted at the prospect. He hopped along beside Hodge to the pump in the stable yard. Hodge produced a cake of carbolic soap.

"It'll be cold," he warned.

"I don't mind."

"Pull off your jersey then and bend over."

Off came the jersey and the undervest. The little white body was erect beneath the alert head.

"It's only my face and hands that are dirty," he said.

Hodge pumped enough water to wet the soap. He lathered Renny's hands and neck. "You do your face. I might get soap in your eyes."

Well soaped, Renny bent, with hands on his knees, beneath the icy stream Hodged pumped on him. His cheeks turned from red to pink, from pink to mauve. Hodge rubbed him hard with a rough stable towel. Then he stripped to his waist and Renny flung himself on the pump handle, pumping so hard that, at each upward swing, he was lifted off his feet. He laughed with joy to see the water sluicing over Hodge's square torso, drowning his tow head.

Now they could see the cows coming majestically from the cow stable after the milking. Tom was carrying two pails of milk towards the house. It was foaming over the top and Renny could smell its warm sweetness as it passed him.

"Have a drink?" asked Tom.

"Don't mind if I do," said Hodge. He took the tin mug from the pump and dipped it into the bucket. He handed it to Renny.

"You go first," said Renny politely.

"No. You're the boss," grinned Hodge.

Renny put the mug to his lips and did not take it away till it was drained. He was a little out of breath with the effort but the eyes of the two young men on him demanded a show of manly efficiency.

"Another?" asked Hodge.

"No, thanks."

Hodge emptied the mug twice and Tom did the same, then plodded on towards the house. Hodge went to the cottage, one of several on the estate occupied by the hired help, where he lived with his mother.

Renny ran swiftly up the stairs to wake Meg. He wondered why she always was so sleepy in the morning. He was scarcely ever sleepy and Nettle said that was the reason he was so thin and Meg plump. Nettle had been sent away because she hadn't been nice about Miss Wakefield. If you weren't nice about Miss Wakefield you went. Would he have to go, he wondered, if he weren't nice to her?

Meg was curled up in a delicious pink and white ball, with her golden-brown plait streaming across the pillow, like a handle to lift her by. He took it where the faded ribbon bow was and heaved it up and down, as he had the handle of the pump. She woke with a start, uncurled herself, and puckered her pretty face into a frown.

"Go 'way," she said, crossly. "Leave me alone. Ren—ny!" His cold fingers were tickling her neck.

"Wake up," he said, putting his face close to hers.

Meg's taste in smells was peculiar. She loved the smell of paint, of floor polish and the like. Now the smell of the carbolic soap that he had been washed with ravished her nostrils.

"Oo, what a lovely smell!" she breathed, and clasped his head close on the pillow.

He was delighted at having pleased her. He lay still a few moments, savouring the pleasure of being hugged by her, then his ravening stomach urged him to spring up. He pulled the bedclothes off her.

"Come on," he said. "Get up. They'll be bringing the tent soon."

"I don't care," she grumbled. "I'm not going to the party."

He was astonished. "Why, Meggie, there'll be ice cream and fruit punch and all sorts of things."

"I don't care."

But she did care and she wanted to see the marquee put up on the lawn. She rolled on to her behind and peered about for her stockings. They were under the bed and he got them for her. She snatched them and began, still crossly, to pull them on.

"I'm going," he called back over his shoulder, and clattered down the stairs.

The door of Ernest's bedroom opened. He appeared and caught Renny by the arm.

"You've been making a great noise," he said sternly, "racketing up and down the stairs. Don't you realize it's still early and some of your elders want to sleep?"

"I forgot."

"Forgetfulness of the comfort of others is an offence that cannot be allowed. You like us to think of your comfort, don't you?"

"Yes."

"Yes, what?"

"Yes, Uncle Ernest."

"Now, give me your hand and we'll go down quietly together. Your hand is cold. What makes your hand so cold?"

"I don't know."

"Have you been outdoors?"

"Yes. It's warm out."

"Good. We are to have fine weather for the garden party."

They seated themselves at table. Eliza set dishes of oatmeal porridge in front of them. Ernest thought how chipper Eliza looked since Mrs Nettleship's departure. He remarked to his nephew:

"This is an important day for you, Renny."

The little boy looked inquiringly into his face.

"There is a drop of milk on your chin. Wipe it off. Not with your hand. With your napkin. That's better. Now this day is important to you because today your father introduces to his friends the young lady who is to be your new mother. Everybody will have a chance to meet her and admire her. She's very pretty, you know. You should stand near her when she is receiving the guests and be very polite. If you undertake to pass a dish you must be careful not to tilt it. If a lady and gentleman are standing side by side, be sure to offer it to the lady first."

"Yes, Uncle Ernest. I thought it was Granny's party."

"She is giving it for Miss Wakefield."

"I thought she was giving it for herself."

"Really, Renny, you sometimes surprise me by your stupidity. Your mind is so much on your own affairs that you don't listen to what is going on about you."

"I listened to the banns being read."

"That has nothing to do with the party. . . . Well, yes, it has a good deal to do with the party, after all. Will you have an egg?"

"Yes, please."

Ernest chipped the top off a boiled egg for Renny and gave him a piece of buttered toast from a generous plateful, of which the slices were so well spread that butter oozed through them and formed little golden pools on the plate.

Ernest remarked abruptly—"I don't like your smell."

"It's soap," said Renny.

"It's nothing of the sort. It's stable. You *must not* come to the table after handling horses."

Renny hung his head. "I washed," he murmured.

"Did you change your clothes?"

"N—no."

"Well—hurry up with that egg. Then you may spread some marmalade on a piece of toast and leave the table. I cannot eat another bite while you are in the room."

He wiped his lips and leaned back in his chair, his forget-me-not blue eyes fixed disapprovingly on the little boy.

Renny finished his egg in two spoonfuls, took a piece of toast, and ran towards the door.

"Come back here," said Ernest, "and push your chair in—not roughly—gently. Now what do you say?"

"Please excuse me."

"Certainly."

He ran through the porch to the lawn. Men were there putting up the tent that had been brought from town. It was striped red and white, with a scalloped border. There were long tables supported by trestles. The men were jolly, laughing and sometimes swearing a little as they worked. The spaniels and the fox-terrier were there running in and out among the men's legs. But when they saw the toast in Renny's hand, they thought of nothing but that. He put bits into one white-toothed mouth after another. Then Jake, seeing his opportunity, took the remainder and ran with it into the shrubbery.

Dr Ramsay now drove up between the spruces and hemlocks. He alighted from his buggy and tied his horse. Renny ran to him.

"Hullo, grand-daddy," he shouted. "We're having a garden party."

"So I see," said the doctor, eyeing the gay tent without enthusiasm. "And what is the object of the party, may I ask?"

"Don't you know?" cried Renny, astonished.

246

"Aye, I know, but I'm wondering if you rightly understand."

"We're having it to show Miss Wakefield to all our friends. She's going to be my new mother."

"Aye. Can you remember your mother who died?"

"Oh, yes."

"She was my only child, you know."

"*Was* she?"

"Why, surely you knew that?"

Renny felt the sad reproach in Dr Ramsay's eyes. "Oh, yes, I knew," he hastened to say. Then he added quickly: "Will you bring Miss Wakefield some babies?"

"God knows. . . . Do you want me to bring babies?"

"Yes. I want a little brother. I'd take care of him. I'd teach him to ride."

"Well, well, we shall see."

"Grand-daddy, do you really bring them in your black bag?"

"Do you expect me to give away the secrets of my profession?"

"Calves," said Renny, "are too big to come in your bag, so the cows get them all by themselves. I saw one do it in a field."

"I hope Meggie wasn't there," said the doctor sharply.

"No. I was alone."

"Did you tell her?" Dr Ramsay's eyes were stern.

"No," lied Renny.

Adeline was sweeping across the grass to them.

"What a day!" she exclaimed. "We couldn't have chosen better. I always say this is the best time of the year."

"I'm glad you're so pleased," said Dr Ramsay dryly.

She took his arm and squeezed it. "Come now," she said. "Show your mettle and make the best of this, the way I do. To tell the truth I'm getting very fond of Mary. The way she's come out in the past ten days is amazing. She is a very complex character and it takes a character like my own to understand her. I've taken her right under my wing." Adeline curved a long supple arm as in illustration. "I'm giving her her trousseau out of my own pocket. When she was to marry Clive Busby I planned to give her a muskrat coat, suitable for the prairies, but now the coat is to be sealskin."

"That, of course," said the doctor, "will be more suitable for the mistress of Jalna."

Adeline drew back. "The mistress, did you say? The mistress! Ah, Dr Ramsay, I always shall continue to look on myself as mistress here, if I live to be a hundred—which heaven forbid!"

Dr Ramsay gave her an admiring look. "I know no other woman," he said, "so well fitted to carry off that weight of years as yourself."

"And may you be here to give me a dose of physic after the celebration!" she laughed.

He shook his head. "Not me." Then he asked—"Have you heard aught of young Busby?"

"Yes. Mrs Vaughan had a letter from his mother. He's well and working hard. There is a very nice girl out there whom he was paying attention to before he came East. Now they hope he'll settle down and marry her. I'm so glad, because Mary isn't fitted for life on the prairies. . . . Jalna is the place for her," she added complacently.

Dr Ramsay was a Presbyterian and had not been present at the first giving out of the banns but he had heard much of the scene in the church, and the look he now gave Adeline was not so much admiring as puzzled.

The other members of the family joined them and there was great activity in the arranging of tables, the laying of cloths, the placing of chairs for the small orchestra and those of the guests who preferred to eat their refreshments sitting. Children and dogs were here, there, and everywhere. Eliza, who had amazingly blossomed out since Mrs Nettleship's departure, was masterful in her handling of the situation. Young Hodge's mother ran hither and yon at her bidding. Philip seated himself on one of the long tables over which a white damask cloth had just been spread, and lighted his pipe. He puffed at it placidly till a concerted outcry brought him to his feet.

"By Jove," he exclaimed, "I didn't notice the tablecloth." He began to smooth it out but Eliza at once removed it and spread a fresh one in its stead.

Jake, seeing the discarded cloth in a basket on the grass, drew it out and dragged it into the shrubbery, unobserved by any but his parents, who disclaimed any connection with him.

By noon the scene was set for the garden party. After a light lunch everyone but Renny relaxed for a time. The Indian summer day was hot. He went to a field through which the stream ran in the open and was shallow with a chalky bed. He

248

set himself to work at a dam he and his friend Maurice Vaughan had been building in the holidays. He stood in the stream and heaved the flat stones from the bank into place. He plastered them with mud, stretching his small thin hands to their utmost, putting out all his strength in the heaving. He pictured the dam as a mighty construction, the stretch of water thus saved as spreading like a lake over the field. Three ducks swimming in the pool eyed his work with interest. Three farm horses came and drank.

Renny lost all sense of time; he forgot the garden party; he forgot the ice cream. He would have worked where he was till dark if Meg, all dressed in white, with a pale blue sash, had not appeared. She looked at him in dismay.

"Renny Whiteoak!" she cried. "You're going to catch it! Oo—look at you! People are coming. Granny's been looking for you everywhere. Hurry up! I've been dressed for hours."

He thought she looked pretty standing there.

"You look pretty," he said.

"You look awful. You may not be allowed to come to the party."

"I don't care." But he did. He hurried with her to the house and up to his room. He was turning a basin of water into a mud puddle when Adeline appeared. She gave him a look of disgust.

"Oh, you miserable boy," she said. "I've a mind to give you a good beating and lock you in a dark cupboard for the rest of the day. What would you say to that?"

Doggedly he lifted the heavy basin and emptied the mud puddle into the great slop-jar. Doggedly he heaved up the heavy ewer.

"Here!" she cried. "You'll spill it. Let me."

She filled the basin, snatched up the sponge, and began to wash him. She held him by one ear while she washed his neck, her elbow sleeves leaving her tapering forearms exposed.

"Ow! My ear!" he howled, but she kept her hold on it, both keeping him at arm's length and washing him.

"Now, strip," she ordered.

He scrambled out of his clothes and she, with a running commentary on his condition and on what her father would have done to any of her brothers had he been in the same, continued the cleaning process. When he stood, a white silver, with a russet top, before her, she relented and smiled. That was enough. He cast himself on her, hugging her, till she exclaimed:

"Come, come, you'll rumple my dress. . . . Now—here's your lovely white sailor suit. Let me put you into it and see how you'll look."

He stood admiring himself in the glass. The black silk tie, the lanyard, with the whistle tucked into his pocket, looked well.

When Adeline had brushed his hair she stood back to admire him. "You look the perfect Irish gentleman," she exclaimed.

"But the Whiteoaks are English, Granny," he said.

"I know that," she whispered, with her arch smile, "but we'll not tell anyone."

He could have shouted with joy when he heard the little orchestra playing, right on their own lawn. But he did wish there had been a drum. He liked the flautist best of all. He pressed close beside him admiring the nimble movements of his fingers on the flute.

Mary stood with Philip and Adeline receiving the guests. She had bought herself a turquoise-blue silk mull dress and a wide-brimmed leghorn hat with pink roses. Philip wore white flannels. Everyone agreed that you would have travelled far before you would have found a handsomer pair. And, if Adeline herself had travelled the world over to discover Mary, she could scarcely have looked more pleased.

Renny had never before seen so many people together except at a Fall Fair. He found time to tear to the stable yard and have a look at the dozens of horses and vehicles with Hodge. In his hand he had brought a large piece of cake for Hodge and, as he discussed the horses, he licked the sweet icing that had stuck to his fingers. He and Hodge agreed that there was not a horse in the yard which could compare to their own.

He returned to the garden party for more ice cream. He could see Meggie being helpful in her best dress. He could see Uncle Ernest with one of the prettiest of the young ladies and Uncle Nicholas with Violet Lacey. He ran and squeezed himself in between Philip and Mary. Philip took his hand.

Muriel Craig came, carrying a plate on which there was a generous helping of chicken salad and a well-buttered roll. She wore a dress of many-coloured Roman stripes with enormous sleeves. She had already been greeted by Mary but now she whispered to her:

"Could we possibly have a word together quietly? I have something I must tell you."

Mary led her to the shelter of the porch.

"What do you suppose has happened?" Muriel asked at once.

"I can't imagine."

"You will be horrified when I tell you. Two days ago my father and that horrible nurse of his went off together and got married! Isn't it appalling?" The irises of her eyes showed white all round them.

"Oh, I am sorry for you," Mary said warmly.

"It's heartbreaking. I shall never get over it." And she took a large forkful of chicken salad. "I cried all that night. I shall certainly have to leave home. I could not possibly live with that woman."

"There is one comfort," said Mary. "She will take good care of your father."

"He doesn't need her! He's getting better every day. But I must just resign myself. The first thing I shall do will be to visit my friend in New York. . . . I suppose if I'm to have ice cream and punch I'd better have them now. That charming Mr Biggs is getting some for me at this moment. . . . How nice you look, Mary! Really, it's surprising what clothes do for a girl."

"Thank you," said Mary.

"As for myself, clothes seem not to make any difference to me. As one of my admirers remarked the other day, I look every bit as pretty in a simple cotton dress as in silk mull."

As peach and pineapple yield their richest flavour just before decay, so this day showed the finest colouring, its breezes were most playful, and carried in them scents of ripeness, of distant wood smoke, of a sweetness to make one wonder. Magnificent threats of stormy weather to come showed in the west, but the garden party revelled in the very best of summer. The gaily striped tent, the pretty parasols, the hardworking little orchestra, would never grace a happier scene.

"But what are they all talking about?" wondered Renny. The snatches of conversation he overheard seemed to mean nothing. When he spoke he had something to say.

He said to Meg—"I've had three dishes of ice cream."

"I only had two," she returned, "but I had three pieces of cake. And I had a glass of punch."

"Why, we're not supposed to drink punch." He was both horrified and envious.

"I did."

"Did anyone see you? Who poured it for you?"

"Nobody. It was a glassful some lady set down and I just picked it up."

"Did you feel funny after it?"

"A little. The tent turned round."

"Isn't it turning now?"

"No. I'm all over it. I could drink another."

"Whew!" He looked at her admiringly.

At last came the time for the guests to leave. There were the handshakings, the renewed congratulations, the flurry and amiable crowding together of goodbyes. There were the rumbling of wheels and the glad clatter of hoofs. Last of all went Mary, with Philip to drive her back to the Laceys'.

Renny had run to the gate after the trap. They had waved back to him but still he felt rather lonely, standing in the sunlight by the gate.

The driveway was dark and the trees looked very tall. They shut out the light and Renny remembered ghosts and goblins and bad fairies as he trotted along the drive. On the lawn the men were folding up the tent, the musicians had vanished, without his having seen them go. The dogs, worn-out, were strewn on the porch. The grass looked trodden and lifeless. Beyond the ravine, through the trees, a crimson eye of sunset glowed. He ran round the house to where two farm labourers had loaded a wagon with barrels of apples from the brick-built apple house.

Renny clambered up into the wagon. He gripped the edge of a barrel to steady himself as the driver slapped the reins on the horses' backs. The spicy scent of the Northern Spies rose out of the barrels.

One of the men asked over his shoulder—"Did you have a good time at the party?"

"Oh, yes. Where are the apples going?"

"To Montreal. In the morning. The barrels have got to be headed in tonight."

"Why are you working late?"

"We didn't work all day. The boss gave us a holiday. But we thought we'd head in the barrels."

"Can I go with you to the station?"

"If you're up early enough."

"I'll be up."

He took an apple from the barrel he was clinging to. It lay, round as the world and cold as ice, in his hand. He sniffed it. It had a good smell. His mind flew back to another good smell —the smell of the Christmas tree. All his being tingled at the recollection of that scent. He remembered no farther back than last Christmas. That was far enough to remember. It filled him with a heady joy. For an instant he forgot where he was. Then the wagon stopped with a jolt. They were at the barn. The men jumped down. One held out his arms to Renny.

"Jump," he said.

Renny jumped into the man's arms and was set on the ground.

"What have you got there?" the man asked. "An apple? Don't you know you're not supposed to take one out of the barrels? You know where to get one, if you want it."

The man took the apple from Renny's hand, reached up, and put it back in the barrel. The other man was unhitching the horses.

"It's too dark to head in the barrels," he said. "We can do them in the morning." He led the horses clumping into the stable.

The first man brought sacking and covered the barrels. Renny ran into the stable. The smell of clean straw greeted him, out of the living dusk. Everywhere there were quiet movements and deep breathing.

"Here!" shouted both men. "Come out of there. Do you want to get locked in?"

Renny trotted out. It was almost dark. The crimson eye in the west had closed. The men were moving shadows.

"Goodbye," he called, over his shoulder, as he ran off.

"Goodbye," answered the men.

He looked in at the inky darkness of the apple house. He did so much want an apple. A figure stumped towards him from the direction of the kitchen. It was Noah Binns, who had been having a feed of leftovers from the garden party.

"Hi, Noah!" Renny called.

"Huh?" grunted Noah, stumping closer.

"Say, will you wait here while I go into the apple house?"

"Afeared, eh?" Noah's grin was just visible.

"No. But I thought someone might lock me in."

"Go ahead. But don't be long."

Renny ran down the moist stone steps into the darkness. In bunks, like sleepers, lay the apples, Spies, greenings, russets, Tolman sweets, snows, pippins, filling the air with their scent. He put his hand where he knew the snow apples were stored. He took one and hurried up the steps.

"A notorious big crop of apples this fall," said Noah. "Eat your fill. There won't be none next year."

"Why?"

"Tree bugs is at work under the bark, suckin' the good out of the trees. I seen 'em and heard 'em—suckin'."

"We spray the trees."

"A lot of good that will do. This bug is a new sort. He likes the spray. He's up from the States."

Renny stood a moment looking after Noah before he ran into the house. He was glad to get in and shut the door behind him. The red apple lay cold in his hand.

A sudden change had come in the atmosphere. The evening was chilly. A fire of birch logs was blazing in the drawing-room and everyone but Philip was sitting about it talking of the garden party.

"Well, young man," said Ernest, "it's about time you came in."

"Are you hungry?" asked Adeline.

"I just want this apple."

"I'm not hungry either," said Meg. She was sitting on a stool at Augusta's knee, holding magenta wool on her hands for winding. Her light brown hair shone in the firelight.

Renny went to Nicholas. "Uncle Nick," he said, "will you read out of the book to me?"

"Too late," growled Nicholas.

"But, if you don't read, we'll not finish the book before you go back to England."

"Very well. I'll read a few pages."

Renny brought the shabby leather bound book. He climbed to Nicholas's knee and stretched himself comfortably with his head on Nicholas's shoulder, who said:

"By George, you're a cold little codger. Where have you been?"

"Getting an apple. Have a bite?" He held the apple to Nicholas's mouth. He took a quarter of it in one bite with his strong white teeth. Renny looked at the pink-veined cavity in the apple, then set to nibbling round its edge.

Nicholas swallowed and read:

"As the evening approached, she placed on the stone fireplace a pot containing two of the salted bears' feet to stew for supper, and then we seated ourselves, to wait with anxiety and impatience for the return of our boy hunters. At last we heard the clatter of hoofs approaching at a sharp trot, and distant sounds of joyful cheering. I went to meet the riders.

"Like military hussars, they slackened rein when they saw me, and sprang from their chargers, took off the saddles, and left the animals free to enjoy the sweet grass and the fresh water from the brook at their own free will. Then they hastened to join their mother at the tent, who received them joyfully.

"Jack and Frank each carried a young kid slung across his shoulders, and the movement in Fritz's game-bag gave me the impression that it contained something alive.

" 'The chase for ever, papa!' cried Jack, in a loud voice; 'the chase for ever! And what splendid fellows Storm and Grumbler are to run over level ground! They so tired the little creature we followed for a long distance, that we were able at last to catch it with our hands.'

" 'Yes, papa!' exclaimed Frank; 'and Fritz has two such pretty rabbits in his bag. And we were very nearly bringing you some honey, mamma, only we stopped to hear the cuckoo.'

" 'Ah, but you forget the best!' cried Fritz. 'We met a troop of antelopes, and they were so tame, we might have brought one home easily had we wished.'

" 'Ah, stay, my boy,' I said; '*you* have forgotten the best: the goodness of God in bringing you all home safely to the arms of your parents, and preserving you from danger on the way. But presently you must give us a straightforward account of your journey, from the beginning, after you have rested.' "

On and on Nicholas read. A sense of wellbeing pervaded the room. His elders listened with an interest only second to that of the little boy. But it was he who was transported to the foreign land, to the company of the fantastical beasts and birds, the boy hunters. He was both there and in the safe cosy room, lolling on Uncle Nick, idly watching Meg turn her hands in the skein of wool.

A step interrupted the reading and Philip came in.

Nicholas shut the book. "Time for you to go to bed, young fellow." And he tilted Renny to the floor.

Adeline called him to her. "What did you do with the apple seeds?" she demanded.

"I swallowed them. I didn't want to interrupt the reading."

"Swallowed them! Ah, you must never do that again. Your grandfather tells me that seeds of all sorts are likely to get into the appendix and kill you. It's a new disease and you must be careful not to get it. Do you understand?"

"Yes, Granny."

"Now, thank your uncle for the reading and off to bed, both of you."

Meg objected. "It's not fair for me to go when Renny goes. I'm two years older."

"Well, you may stay up half an hour longer."

The wool was wound into a huge ball. It was for the knitting of a spencer. Meg rose and went to Sir Edwin. She stroked his silky whiskers.

"I love whiskers," she said.

"Thank you, my dear." He beamed at her.

"I hope," said Augusta approvingly, "that, when you grow up, you will have the good fortune to marry a gentleman with side-whiskers."

"Meggie is determined," said Nicholas, "to marry a man with a dark moustache like mine."

"Not a bit of it," smiled Ernest. "Meggie wants a smooth-shaven man like me."

"What sort do you want, Meg?" asked her father.

"One like you," she declared, and cast herself on him.

Renny said—"Thank you for the reading, Uncle Nick." He put his arms round the neck of each grown-up in the room and gave each a goodnight kiss.

Adeline said to Philip—"I hope Mary wasn't too tired after the party."

"Well, she was a little tired, but just pleasantly so."

"She looked as pretty as a picture," said Ernest.

"Granny," whispered Renny, in her ear, "will you come up and tuck me in?"

"I heard you," said Philip. "Your Granny has been on her feet all day. She doesn't want to climb two flights of stairs."

"Will you, then, Aunty?"

Adeline interrupted—"I will tuck the children in. Renny, don't forget your teeth and your prayers."

He mounted the long dim stairs. Eliza had lighted the oil

lamp in a bracket on the wall. The day stretched behind him, a medley of shapes, sounds, smells, which he did not try to disentangle or even think of. The real things were his bed, the lamp on the wall, and the great full moon just swimming above the treetops. The lamp was cosy but the moon made the drawing-room and the people in it seem a long way off and himself very small.

He hung over the footboard of the bed, dangling his legs. He pictured the apple seeds travelling through his body, getting ready to give trouble. Already, he thought, he felt a little pain. He stood up quickly as though listening. If he felt it again he would run straight downstairs. . . . But it did not come again.

He looked over at Meg's side of the room. There were the clothes she had taken off when she dressed for the garden party, lying in a little heap in a chair, her stubby shoes in the middle of the floor, toeing in. He walked about, looking at her belongings, handling the things on her dressing-table. He went to Miss Wakefield's room that was full of moonlight. He wondered if she would sleep there again or go down to one of the bigger, better bedrooms below. He hoped she would go to another room. He did not want to meet her the first thing in the morning and say 'Good morning, Mamma.' But he said it now, out loud—"Good morning, Mamma," several times. It sounded funny. . . .

He tried to remember his first mother, the one who had died. Though he tried hard he could remember only her arms, lifting him up. She was dead. In Heaven. Somewhere beyond the moon. He wondered if she liked it up there. Grand-daddy said she did. He looked out at the moon. Then suddenly he turned and ran back to his own room and began to take off his clothes.

He had just got into bed when he heard Meg coming up the stairs and, in a moment more, his grandmother. He was glad and shouted out—"I'm in! And covered up!"

"You'd better be," said Adeline.

She picked up the towel he had dropped on the floor and examined the smudges on it.

"I have a mind," she said, "to make you get up and wash all over again. Did you brush your teeth?"

"Yes, I brushed them hard. Look." He displayed them in a grin, one of the lower ones missing.

"Say your prayers?"

"Yes," he shouted. He leaped up on the bed and threw his arms round her neck.

She hugged him to her, making a cooing sound. "You've got high spirits," she said. "That's a good thing in this life. I wonder what life will do to you. I hope it will be kind."

"Granny!"

"Yes?"

"You promised me that you would come riding with me—one morning early! Will you do it tomorrow?"

"Ah, my riding days are over. I'm getting old."

"But you promised!"

"Well—we'll see."

"Tomorrow!"

"No. After the wedding. I've too much to do now for early riding."

"But you will, won't you!"

"Yes." She laid him flat and tucked the blanket round him. "Now, not another squeak out of you." She kissed him, turned down the wick, and walked over to Meg's bed. Soon he heard her descending the stairs.

"Meggie!" he called. "Come and kiss me goodnight!"

"No. It's too cold. I'm sleepy."

He sprang out of bed and padded to her bedside. His mouth found her cool round cheek. He knew she was smiling in the dark.

"Goodnight," she murmured, "sleep tight. Don't let the little bugs bite."

He ran back to his own bed and jumped in. His feet were icy. The moon was looking in at him, bigger than ever. It was too big. He pulled the blanket over his head to shut it out and was instantly asleep.

## 23

## THE WEDDING AND AFTER

THE WEDDING day dawned bright and chill. There was a new firmness to the soil. The first vehicles on the roads splintered the thin ice that gleamed in the ruts. The carriage in which

Admiral Lacey was to drive Mary to the church had been washed and polished till it shone. So had the Admiral, who was to give Mary away. There was great excitement at The Moorings as Mary and Ethel dressed for the ceremony. Ethel, in pale blue, carrying pink roses and violets, was to be bridesmaid. With her smiling face and high colour which later on would become florid, she looked very young for her age and quite suitable to attend Mary, who was unusually pale and grave. Standing on the verge of her new life she cast a feeling look backward at the months through which she had just passed. She would be glad, she thought, when tomorrow had come and she was truly Philip's. Never again would she look back.

"Girls, girls," cried Mrs Lacey, "you must hurry. There isn't a minute to spare, if you're to be on time. Ethel, you madcap, are you only now putting on your shoes? Violet, do help her. Mary, have you something old, something new, something borrowed, and something blue?"

"Of course she has, Mother!" cried Violet. "She is carrying her mother's white vellum prayer-book, which is old. Her dress and veil are new. Her garters are blue. And she has borrowed my best lace handkerchief."

"Speaking of handkerchiefs," said Mrs Lacey, "I must be sure to have one handy because I'm bound to cry at a wedding."

"For the love of God," cried her husband, from the next room, "somebody come and find my collar button!"

It seemed that they never would be ready in time but ready they were at last, when Nicholas drove up to the house in a phaeton to take Mrs Lacey and her daughters to the church.

"Upon my word," said Admiral Lacey, "I believe I've put on twenty pounds since I last wore this coat."

"You look fine," said Nicholas.

"It doesn't wrinkle across the back?"

"Not at all," lied Nicholas.

"That's good. Have your party left for the church yet?"

"My mother and the Buckleys and Renny have. Philip and Ernest and Meggie are to follow. Meg got mislaid somehow. Children are a great pest."

"What a blessing that your mother is reconciled to the match."

"Yes, and wants everyone to know it. She went early to the church so that she might be seen, smiling her blessing."

"She's a great character."

"She has her good points," smiled Nicholas.

Eliza, dressed in her best for the wedding, was searching frantically for Meg. She well knew how antagonistic to the marriage the child was. She feared that Meg would not turn up for the ceremony. A shame it was for her to spoil everything by her naughtiness.

Philip called out—"Eliza, don't search any more! Hodge and his mother are waiting for you. I must be off this minute."

He jumped into the trap beside Ernest, whose fair forehead was tied in a knot of worry.

"My God," he cried, "there goes the church bell!"

The bell sounded sweet on the sharp air.

Philip touched the horse with the whip. "We may comfort ourselves with this," he said, "they can't go on without us."

"Damned undignified for the groom to arrive at top speed."

"Better than with a lagging step. I expect there will be quite a crowd at the church."

"Your marriage to the children's mother was the last wedding from Jalna."

"Yes."

It was not a happy allusion at this moment. Both fell silent, remembering the day.

There were indeed many people in the church and about to enter the church. The carriage shed was full of vehicles. The bell was still ringing when Philip and Ernest, who was his groomsman, hurried to the side door that led into the vestry. By the time they were inside, it had stopped and the organ was sending forth a soothing strain.

But Philip was not soothed. His handsome face was flushed. He was excited and nervous. He had run his hand through his hair and stood it on end. Ernest now was calm.

Meg stuck her head in at the door.

"Were you looking for me, Daddy?" she asked.

"You have no right to come here," said Ernest. "You should be in the pew with your grandmother."

Her eyes grew large and mournful. "I was sad."

"Look at her hair!" exclaimed Ernest.

She had put on her new dress but her hair was still in the plait in which she wore it at night. Philip hastily pulled the faded ribbon from it and shook out the shining mass. He did not do it gently.

"You have no reason to feel sad," he said.

"Oh, you hurt me!" Her eyes filled with tears.

He bent and kissed her. "You must go round to the front door," he said, "and then walk quietly up the aisle to our pew. Where is your hat?"

"Here." She held it up.

He put it on her. She smiled up at him. "Your own hair needs tidying," she said, and ran off.

He ran his hand over it, smoothing it. Mr Pink appeared in his surplice.

"I think the moment has come," he said. "The bride is alighting from her carriage."

Philip stood at the chancel steps, Mary drawing ever nearer to him. At last she was by his side. He glanced at her quickly and saw her face, pale and beautiful beneath the veil. He saw the hand that held her mother's prayer-book tremble. Mr Pink began:

" 'Dearly beloved, we are gathered together here in the sight of God. . . .' "

The service proceeded. Each had answered "I will," Philip, in a full and confident tone, giving the promise with his whole heart; Mary, in a voice lower, but still firm. Then Mr Pink guided their two right hands to join, and so they gave their troth.

They loosed their hands. Then Mary again took Philip's right hand in hers and, her voice now stronger, made her promise. She could hear herself making it, as though she were an outsider, and to her, her voice seemed to ring through the church.

Again they loosed their hands. Then Philip laid the ring upon the Book, then Mr Pink delivered the ring again to Philip, and he put it on Mary's fourth finger, and holding it there said, in the same full and confident voice:

" 'With this ring I thee wed, with my body I thee honour, and with all my worldly goods I thee endow: In the Name of the Father and of the Son and of the Holy Ghost. Amen.' "

They knelt together.

'Well, well,' thought Adeline, 'it's done. He's had his own

way, and I hope good comes of it. No one can say that I didn't smile at this wedding. And no one will ever be able to say I'm not a good mother-in-law.'

When Philip and Mary had signed their names in the Register, when Lily Pink was tearing the Wedding March out of her soul, and family and friends were crowding about to congratulate the newly married pair, Adeline was the first to kiss the bride. She did it perhaps a little ostentatiously. In truth there were as many eyes on her as on the bride. As she walked down the aisle she was conscious of this, and moved as though her being were a pleasure to her. As friends and the farmers and their wives who had come to see the wedding, and whom she had known for many years, came up to speak with her, her smile became almost a grin. She would have liked to put on an Irish accent but thought better of it.

Because of the smallness of the Laceys' house only the relatives and a few friends were to be gathered there. Mary was glad. She longed for the moment when she and Philip would be on the train together, bound for their honeymoon in New York. Now, in the carriage, he took her hand, held it a moment in silence, then said:

"I'm the happiest man on earth."

"Oh," she said, "I hope we shall have long lives and be consciously happy every day of them."

"Of course we shall . . . You've had enough of unhappiness, my sweet. And I will see to it that you have no more."

As the last of the party left the churchyard Meg had again to be searched for. She had gone back to the vestry to find her hair-ribbon, which, faded and old as it was, had suddenly assumed the proportions of a treasure.

The wedding breakfast was delicious. The couple's health was drunk in champagne provided by Nicholas. The cake, a magnificent erection in ornate icing, with silver bells on the top, was Ernest's offering. Adeline expressed satisfaction with all the wedding presents, excepting that given by the Buckleys. She did not hide her dissatisfaction with it.

She said to Nicholas—"I admire the candelabra you gave them. Ernest's present was equally nice. But this"—she held, on her supple palm, a solid silver fernpot—"this is a penurious present. What do they want with a fernpot?"

"They might, at any time, decide to keep a fern," said Nicholas.

"What! Go to the woods and dig up a fern and bring it into the house?"

"Why not? They own a fernpot. They must have something to put in it."

"Oh, I do call it a miserable present. What did they give Philip on his first marriage?"

"I forget."

"Ask him."

"Mamma, this is no time for such reminiscences."

"Ernest, come here!"

He came, and she asked—"What did Edwin and Augusta give Philip and Margaret for a wedding present?"

"A fernpot," he answered, without hesitation.

"Where is it now?"

"In Nick's room. He keeps his pipes in it."

"Is that what it is?" said Nicholas. "I forgot."

Sir Edwin, seeing them gathered about the fernpot, strolled over to them.

"Edwin," said Adeline, "Ernest tells me that you and Augusta gave Philip a silver fernpot on his first marriage. Surely that is not possible?"

Her son-in-law wavered for an instant and then said—"We did indeed. We wanted Philip to know that our feelings were equally benevolent to both marriages."

Violet Lacey came running up. "They are ready to leave," she said. "And, oh, how lovely Mary looks in her going-away things!"

She did indeed. Adeline took her in her arms and held her close. "Goodbye, my dear," she said, "and I hope you will be very, very happy."

Their breasts together, they stood embraced, their eyes mysterious. Strangely, in that moment, Mary remembered the scene in her bedroom, her triumph over Adeline that had brought her so many tears. 'I had the best of her,' she thought, 'but never shall again.'

"Thank you, dear Mrs Whiteoak," she murmured.

Philip came, hat in hand, and was embraced.

The children pushed their way to his either side. He bent and kissed them.

"Shall you bring me something from New York?" asked Renny.

"I will indeed. Be a good boy while I'm away."

263

Mary kissed the cool cheek Meg turned half to her, then Renny's small pursed mouth.

"Goodbye, Miss Wakefield," he said, in his clear treble.

Everyone laughed. "Mrs Whiteoak," corrected his aunt.

"Not Mrs Whiteoak—but Mamma!" cried Violet.

He hung his head in embarrassment.

"Hurry," exclaimed Nicholas, "or you'll miss your train." He poked Philip in the ribs. "Like you did the last time. Remember?"

Philip would never forget. He caught Mary by the arm and they ran the short distance to the gate, in a shower of rice. They leaned from the carriage waving.

"Goodbye! Goodbye!" called everyone.

Renny ran to the road and stood there waving, listening to the beat of the hoofs growing fainter, watching the carriage till it was out of sight. Suddenly the world seemed larger, echoing to the sounds of departure, and he smaller.

He went back to the house where the others had returned. Dr Ramsay put out an arm and drew Renny to his side. "Poor wee laddie," he said.

The wedding was over, movements of a different nature stirred Jalna. Nicholas and Ernest, Edwin and Augusta, bent themselves to their preparations for travel. The Buckleys made theirs with the least fuss, confining their operations as much as possible to their own room. But Nicholas and Ernest were here, there, and everywhere. Their luggage strewed the hallways. Their strong voices shouted from room to room. Nicholas was happy at returning to his agreeable life in London. Ernest was exhilarated by the thought of new investments. The hearts of Edwin and Augusta yearned towards the peace of their home in Devon.

But Adeline was glad to be where she was. Canada was her country and at Jalna she had spent the happiest years of her life. She looked forward with complacency to the coming winter. Mary was an amenable girl, if something of an enigma. She herself could generally manage Philip. She would retain the reins. Opportunely a small school was being started by two capable women in the district and to it the children could be sent for a time. They had run wild long enough.

At last, after an upheaval greater than garden party and wedding combined, the travellers to England had departed.

Adeline was left alone with the children. There had been snow, the snow was gone and Indian summer warmed the November air, cleared the sky to a stainless blue, clouded the horizon with smoky grey. The light wind bore no heavier freight than the silver savings of the milkweed pod. The stream, broadened by rains, moved tranquilly past its banks.

"All it lacks are swans," Mary had said, on the day of the garden party.

"And swans it shall have," Philip had promised.

She had only to express a wish and he was eager to fulfil it. Now Renny had a wish and, after a good deal of persuasion, Adeline had yielded to it. Not that she did not want to humour him or did not herself enjoy the prospect of what he urged, but she had got a bit slack. To get up at sunrise had become something of an effort, especially to put on a riding habit and mount a horse and ride to the lake shore on an empty stomach, for who could eat a substantial breakfast at that hour? But the little boy begged so hard. It was nice to think how much he wanted her. She could not refuse.

It saddened her to think how she and her Philip had once, with light hearts and little effort, risen at sunrise, and ridden over the estate and galloped over the sandy country roads. Ah, the country had been grand in the fifties and sixties and even in the seventies! She wondered what it would be in another fifty years. She had heard that there were Chinese laundrymen in the cities and she herself had seen an Italian pushing a barrow of red and yellow bananas along a street. Well, Philip, her husband, wouldn't have liked it. He wanted to keep the province British. On her own part she rather liked mixtures.

As the mellow brick of the house was gilded by the early sunlight and the windows set ablaze, Hodge led Captain Whiteoak's old mare, saddled and bridled, to the door. Renny followed on his pony. Adeline came on to the porch wearing her riding habit, with its long skirt, and a bowler hat sitting jauntily on her head. The sun, touching her, brought out the red that still remained in her hair. She looked a fine figure. Hodge's eyes were full of admiration, but Renny saw only his grandmother coming to ride with him at last.

Hodge assisted her to the saddle. Laura was skittish and sent the gravel flying with her dancing.

"Laura, you ought to be ashamed of yourself," exclaimed

Adeline, "at your age!" She stroked the mare's shining neck. "But you're no more unseemly than I am. We just don't know how to get old, do we, pet?"

Under the evergreens, splashed with light and shade, jogged the mare and the pony, the elderly woman and the little boy. They passed through the gate on to the deserted road.

Adeline smiled down at Renny. "So you've routed me out early at last," she said.

He laughed up at her. "Yes. Aren't you glad?"

"I am that." She snuffed the air. "Why, I wouldn't have missed this for anything. It's glorious."

"We'll do it often, shan't we? Every day?"

"Well, perhaps not every day."

"Every other day then?"

"Take the pleasure of the moment and don't be looking ahead."

They cantered down the road. They did not speak again except to point out some small wild creature or comment on a new barn or admire an especially fine straw stack, till they reached the lake. Here they took the winding road by its shore. The air had changed. Now it smelt of the lake and had a coolness and a stir. Two gulls winged their way above its blueness, making haste as though to show their power. Adeline and Renny drew up to enjoy the view which, in truth, consisted of no more than the blue floor of the lake and the blue arch of the sky where no sail, no cloud, appeared. Nothing but blueness and a hazy horizon.

"It's a fine sight," said Adeline.

"Yes, it's a fine sight," he agreed.

"I've always admired this world," Adeline went on. "We're lucky to have such a splendid world to live in. When I was a girl in Ireland I used to look at the wild sea and the headlands and the grey mountains, and think how grand they were. When I married your grandfather in India, I thought how beautiful Kashmir was, with its flowers and its temples. When I go to Devon to visit your aunt and look out over the moors, with their heather and the rushing streams and the herds of moor ponies running wild, I think how splendid."

"But this is best," said Renny.

"Yes. It's best. And I hope there's a happy life ahead of you. Now your father will always tell you you're a Whiteoak and the Whiteoaks are English, but you must remember you're

266